THE FIRST EU
AN ALTERNATE HISTORY

A STORY THAT FOLLOWS A GROUP OF
YOUNG PEOPLE ON A WHIRLWIND JOURNEY
FROM RESISTANCE TO TOTAL COMPLIANCE
WITH THE UK GERMAN OCCUPATION

ALAN J CAULFIELD

authorHOUSE

AuthorHouse™ UK
1663 Liberty Drive
Bloomington, IN 47403 USA
www.authorhouse.co.uk
Phone: 0800.197.4150

© 2018 Alan J Caulfield. All rights reserved.

No part of this book may be reproduced, stored in a retrieval system, or transmitted by any means without the written permission of the author.

Published by AuthorHouse 06/08/2018

ISBN: 978-1-5462-9251-7 (sc)
ISBN: 978-1-5462-9252-4 (e)

Print information available on the last page.

Any people depicted in stock imagery provided by Getty Images are models, and such images are being used for illustrative purposes only.
Certain stock imagery © Getty Images.

This book is printed on acid-free paper.

Because of the dynamic nature of the Internet, any web addresses or links contained in this book may have changed since publication and may no longer be valid. The views expressed in this work are solely those of the author and do not necessarily reflect the views of the publisher, and the publisher hereby disclaims any responsibility for them.

Preface

I have something to relate in this book. It is what I think might have happened in the 1940s if different decisions had been made and world events had taken another path. To shape the fictional version, I've used facts and evidence from world events before and after this time.

The personal substance is loosely based on experiences of people I have known, working in many countries and traveling in even more. When living in South Africa, I worked for the German motor company Daimler Benz near Cape Town. It was their largest facility outside Germany, and most of my colleagues were German. I spent seven years there during the apartheid era.

In Cape Town there were many immigrant communities, the British and German being two of the largest. They were in friendly rivalry. It was well-known that good food and drink were always available at the German club.

I returned to the United Kingdom in the mid-nineties and was next sent to Germany by the Ford Motor Company, where I spent six years. I joined a fellowship in which the older members, both German and British, who had been trying to kill one another a generation before were now good friends. I never learned to speak German, apart from the essentials. In all the countries where I worked, English was always used for engineering.

On the reverse side, my grandparents were blown to bits by a direct hit on their house in East London during the war. My mother had moved out of that house a month before. When I had to attend Berlin on business, Mum asked me to ask Mr Hitler why he killed her mum and dad. Their gravestone reads, 'Killed by enemy action'. My sister wears the wedding ring her grandmother had on at the time, passed to her from our mother.

I was born towards the end of the war and have no personal recollections of it. But in discussions with friends, we often ponder how we would have handled the war years if we had been young men at that time. I have always had a great interest in the Second World War, having watched many documentaries and read many books, but I'm not an expert on the subject.

The scenes outlined in this book assume that Germany defeated and occupied Britain in the summer of 1942. Heydrich's brutal plan was taken from actual German documents of the time.

Acknowledgements

I'm grateful to many people who have assisted me with this book. Members of my local University of the Third Age (U3A) and others have given accounts of their wartime experiences. One member virtually completed the cover layout by herself, using photo editing. There are also people from around the world who have read the first drafts, giving me their useful comments and corrections. I owe them.

My good friend David died in November 2017. He was one of the last men still alive who was evacuated from Dunkirk in 1940. He was also one of the few who escaped out of Arnhem, a bridge too far, where he had a conversation with a German tank commander. I gained a lot of information from him and did a local radio broadcast with him in 2016.

I realised that the writing process has caused me to be rather antisocial at times. One of those times was in India in May 2017. So to all my Indian friends and my family in England, I'm thankful for their understanding.

Introduction

This book is rather topical, as Brexit is on everyone's mind. I therefore thought it may appeal to people who want to consider a fictional alternative. I think my version of events is feasible in its presentation of 'what if'—what if this world leader had been in power, or what if this completely plausible event had happened. Taking human nature into account, who is to say that the British, in similar circumstances, would not have acted like the German people who went along with and supported the Nazi regime? British colonial history is a case in point.

Since the book has been completed and put out to various people, some readers have expressed the view that this story couldn't have happened, because of the terrible way the Nazis acted, led by Hitler in the war. I've tried to justify all in my fictional account by showing how Hitler came under the influence of a well educated young women before the invasion of Britain which greatly softened his outlook.

What happened historically in Poland and other East European countries in 1939 and 1940 is definitely appalling. An older Polish friend of mine mentioned one of the first things he remembered from his childhood was seeing twenty-four coffins in the main street of his village. These contained the bodies of people executed by the Germans in reprisal for the murder of one of their soldiers. He spent his childhood to the age of nine in Nazi-occupied Poland and would never agree that my story could be credible.

I feel anything is possible under certain conditions, which I outline as the story unfolds. All occupied countries became less severely treated after the autumn of 1940, but the ruthless actions that took place up to that point had to be accepted in my story, especially the killing of many Jews.

Under the Nuremberg decrees and laws of 1935, Jews were deprived of German citizenship and were unable to hold government posts, teach, or even drive cars. They were also not allowed to marry or have sex with non-Jews. Existing mixed relationships and marriages had to be ended. These laws caused mass emigration of Jews from Germany and the rest of Europe. I don't know the exact numbers, but between 1936 and 1939, the recorded immigration of Jews into Palestine was more than one hundred thousand. These laws were pretty damning on the Nazi regime, and my story is not inclined to condone any of this.

I lived in South Africa after the fall of the white apartheid regime, under which many bad things happened. I observed a lot of formal reconciliation and forgiveness. One thing that happens in my story is the rescinding of all laws restricting the Jews under the new, moderate German regime of 1943.

The village where the main story unfolds is situated in a remote part of the English Midlands, hardly affected by the fighting taking place over the rest of the country. There were no spare men to round up for slave labour, as they were needed to work the farms. So there was no conflict in this regard. Also, there were no stately homes in the area to be commandeered by the German army. The German officers there were coincidentally moderate and readily adhered to the charm offensive ordered by their high command.

When I was an apprentice at the age of sixteen, for five years I mixed with many men who had been in the war. They told me stories about the relationships they had during wartime, and these stories are the basis for the erotic content of my story. Even if those men exaggerated their experiences, it nevertheless seems likely to me that there was more sexual activity than in normal times.

I spent time in Upper Galilee, Israel, in 1981, when there was a limited war going on with the Palestinians in southern Lebanon. I experienced the effect war had on the local population. Explosions echoed around the mountains all day and all night, and people were killed randomly by Russian Katyusha rocket attacks. These events definitely stimulated a 'live for the day' attitude.

Characters

British

Tim Handle, engineer
Florence, his wife
Ann, his sister
Molly Brooks, his mistress
Arthur, his Jewish school friend
Albert Black, farmer
May, his wife
Malcolm, their son
Fatima, his wife
Irene Butcher, farm girl
Sam, her boyfriend
Ray Cooper, village vicar
Sally, his wife
Sheila, their daughter 11 years old
Daisy, their daughter 9 years old
Dave, engineer
Constance, his wife
Andy, young farmer
Jean, his girlfriend
Sarah McDonald, his girlfriend
John, his brother

German

Reinhard Heydrich, SS Group Leader (UK & Ireland)
Tobias Schmitt, lieutenant
Dieter Vollmar, his platoon member
Gunter, his platoon member
Martin Vloch, captain, based in England
Hanna, his daughter 14 years old
Helga, his daughter 12 years old
Eva, his daughter 10 years old
Olaf Franscheld, chief of media based in London
Fritz, Theyse Molly's tutor
Jochen Klos, chief of media (farming) based in London
Karl Riesman, his deputy based locally
Horst Geissler, replacement for Olaf Franscheld based locally
Rolf, Molly's bodyguard

Susan, John's girlfriend
Auntie Joyce, their mother

Children on the Blacks' farm: Jamie, 15 years old; Jennifer, 12 years old; Wendy, 10 years old

Terry Bassett and Peter Ward, young naval officers

Tony, Coventry reporter
Katie, Horst Geissler's girlfriend

Ruth, Hanna's school friend
Roger Shawcroft, lieutenant with the German platoon

Hans Gerard, captain based in Scotland

Jean, his girlfriend
Young media girls from Germany
Angela Braun
Heidi
Myrtle

Klaus Staffle, soldier on Dale Farm

Ottomar Weiss, political trouble shooter from Berlin

Victor Gerber, supreme leader (UK & Ireland)

Volker Klass, head of Gestapo (UK & Ireland)

Chapter 1

HER BEST TIME

Tim stepped off the district line underground train and walked the half mile along tree-lined roads to the grand-looking, three-storey Edwardian house where he had spent the first year of his marriage. On his journey from Coventry, he'd noticed a lot of bomb damage, but this area seemed untouched. He was always worried about Florence living there, but she said that nowhere in the country was completely safe, including the research centre where he worked. The added problem in the East End of London and out into Essex and Kent was that German planes on their return journey from London would discharge any remaining bombs with no concern. Often civilian areas were hit.

He had a spring in his step as he bounded up the stairs. He knew what was in store for him. Knocking on the substantial door, he soon heard the sound of agile feet on soft carpet coming down the stairs. The door opened, he was pulled inside rather hastily.

Florence wanted a baby. They had been married for two years, and this time Tim's visit coincided with the mid-cycle of her period, the best time to conceive. At twenty-two, she was most fertile and yearning to see him on this visit. She had been furious when her manager at the munitions factory said she couldn't have time off, and threatened to walk out. In this wartime situation, they could have read the riot act to her. But Florence was in charge of her section and had a much-needed skill. They gave in and she got her four-day weekend.

There was another reason she wanted to fall pregnant and cement their marriage this Friday in mid-July.

'Oh my darling,' she amorously declared, meeting him in her most alluring outfit. She knew he liked her in this simple, sporty gymslip.

'Hi, Florence. You look great. What have I done to deserve such a beautiful wife?' This time Tim was looking forward to being with her. He hadn't made love to Molly for a few days, because of her heavy period. He dropped his travelling bag in the hallway.

'Come,' she said, putting her hand on his thigh as she pulled him up the two flights of stairs to their top-floor bedroom. They had been apart for two months, and Florence was missing him both emotionally and physically.

Those old feelings were coming back to him as he mounted the stairway in his stockinged feet. Shoes were always left by the entrance. It was a warm and cosy house, if rather large and grand. Once in their bedroom, the urgency of their desires took over.

There was a set pattern for their lovemaking. Tim had taught it to her, and she wasn't complaining. First they stripped naked, whether by taking one another's clothes off or by taking their own off. In this case, because of their passionate condition, it was a joint affair. They were naked in no time.

'Oh, you know I love that, darling,' she said as he kissed the side of her neck. He loved her lithe, slender body. She was fit, being an avid netball player—a young brunette with sparkling turquoise eyes, eagerly expecting to be well satisfied. He started by kissing her all over. This drove her mad with desire. He knew what Florence liked, and she soon reached her first climax. Soon enough they coupled in the normal way, their bodies moving together in an enchanting rhythm.

'I'm going to fix you hard this time. I can't wait any longer. You are so sexy.'

'Oh, fix me or whatever you call it. Do it fast. You don't have to be careful,' she urged. He thought she must have just finished her period.

'I love it; it's so great like that.' She was reaching her second climax. They were completely engaged, tongues exploring, oblivious to everything. They culminated together, then sank back onto the bed, keeping locked together in total bliss.

'You are so passionate this time,' he said. 'What has changed, my sweetheart?'

'Don't you like it then?' she asked. He grabbed her roughly. She cried, 'I love it rough—you know that.'

'Yeah. Let's have a bath together. Have you got something to eat? I've got a bottle of red wine in my bag.'

'Oh my word, I've got two bottles of sherry as well,' she said.

'So we can get well sozzled. I'll open mine right now.' He hurried downstairs to open his bag, which he'd left in the ground-floor entrance hall. 'Where's the bottle opener?'

She ran down and on into the ground-floor kitchen. They were both still stark naked. She soon had the opener and two glass tumblers. It was straight to the bathroom on the first floor for them.

They each had good jobs and plenty of money to buy wine and sherry, which were becoming scarce and expensive. Imports had to run the gauntlet of the U-boat blockade, and the local stocks were running low. Florence had been saving for the snacks and food for this weekend with her parents' help. Luxuries were not the norm in these days of rationing, but if wise and flush with money, one could get around this.

'Come on, I want to get drunk.' He opened the bottle and filled the tumblers. They finished the bottle while running the bath. Florence went back down to the kitchen to get some biscuits and snacks, already prepared. Both feeling quite tipsy, they almost fell into the warm water. They ate as they fondled one another under the soapy water. It was quite a messy business, but, being slender, at least they easily fitted in the large enamel bath.

'I want it again,' she said, whipping a towel from the rack as she jumped out of the bath. 'You may like what you see.' She got down on all fours, presenting her bottom.

Tim couldn't resist. He took her on the bathroom carpet, with a large towel rolled up under her head as a pillow. She knew he loved it like that. Pushing against one another in slow, pulsing movements, they took their time.

'Ooh, that's so lovely. Do it hard!' she cried.

He pulled her against him.

The First EU

'I'm coming again,' she said breathlessly.

'So am I.'

'I can feel it in me. It's too beautiful.'

When they finally disengaged, they slipped back into the bath, relaxing in one another's arms for a while. Afterwards, they had to clean the mess up, but at least they were both washed and satisfied, being a little drunk, of course.

Tim knew that Florence's mother was a bit prim and proper. 'I wonder what your mom would say if she knew what we were doing to mess her bathroom up like this.'

'My mom is not always so prim and proper, and if a baby resulted, she would be more than happy.'

'Oh. I thought you said I didn't have to be careful.'

'Yes, because I want to have your baby, you silly thing. It's only Friday midday, and my parents won't be back until Sunday late in the evening. They are staying with some friends for the weekend in Essex. They took the train early this morning. So what are we going to do by ourselves, I wonder?'

'Well, my darling, more of the same. I want to enjoy you this long weekend.'

'You are welcome.'

Tim didn't want Florence to fall pregnant but it was too late to worry now. He just continued to enjoy her for the rest of their time. By the time their amorous break came to an end on the Tuesday morning, when Tim had to get the train back to Coventry, they were both rather spent. He was feeling that old love for her, which, in his absence, had been waning a bit. 'You may fall pregnant this time.'

'Oh, Tim, I told you I want your baby. I want us to be a family, especially in these uncertain times,' she said with some pleading in her voice.

'We will just have to take it as it comes,' he said, knowing full well the implications a pregnancy would have for his complicated love life.

This was on Tuesday. The armistice was signed the following Thursday, and early the next morning, the Germans made their pre-emptive surprise attack.

CHAPTER 2

WORK IN COVENTRY

Tim Handle was a young designer of advanced weaponry, working for the secret jet propulsion laboratory at Whitley near Coventry. This was a hundred miles northwest of where he had been living until a year before with his young wife, Florence, at her parents' home close to Dagenham, near London, where he had just spent a long weekend. At work, his dress was always immaculate, with white shirt and tie. He had the gait and movements of an athlete, bounding up the stairs and quickly reacting to catch the odd item that may fall off a desk. He never took up smoking like so many of his friends and colleagues.

By the summer of 1942, events had taken their toll on the United Kingdom population. There was much anxiety about full-scale war, and people were finding all sorts of ways to take their minds off the worrying events of the last few years. Tim was a twenty-four-year-old, good-looking young man with a carefree personality. Without even realising it, he had influenced young Molly Brooks, a teenager in the typing pool where he had his reports typed. Being away from home and familiar with the ways of the ladies, it was easy for him to start a relationship with Molly, who doted on him. She was a vivacious young lady whom one could imagine becoming a little overweight later on in life. Nevertheless she could be agile when flaunting her body in a flirty sort of way.

Their affair was rather intense. Everyone was living without a care for tomorrow because of the grave situation. Instead of taking to drink as many did, these two drowned their worries in one another. In actual fact, they had been living together for six months. Although they had tried to keep it secret, their relationship had finally been found out by their work colleagues. In normal times, the situation wouldn't have been tolerated.

With the landing of the German troops and then the surrender four weeks later on 20 August 1942, everyone was told to keep calm, carry on as usual, and follow the thorough German surrender instructions. But it soon became apparent that nothing could carry on as usual. Some people, mainly the young, made plans to join the resistance, as in Tim's case. His plan was to leave his employ, being much sought after for his knowledge, which he didn't want to share with the Germans.

His young wife in Dagenham had recently fallen pregnant. Long trips were never authorised for young engineers, and Tim could only get a long weekend about every two months. Florence had a skilled job in a munitions factory. This was considered protected work, and therefore she was not allowed to join him in Coventry. For his part, no one working on his secret project was called up to fight.

Even if they had wanted to, permission would have been refused. The security at the centre was high, and Tim's affair with Molly had been noted by the security people right from its beginning.

The situation for Tim was quite an emotional dilemma. One might say he had two young wives to consider. Although Molly knew about Florence, Florence had no knowledge of Molly—or so Tim thought, anyway. Tim wanted Florence to move in with relatives living in Scotland, because of the ever-increasing bombing around Dagenham before the surrender. An arrangement had already been well planned, although permission had not been granted because of her work. They hoped the pregnancy would change this.

Now that the surrender had been signed and the bombing terminated, Tim hoped to activate the same arrangements he had made previously with her relatives in Scotland. Florence would be able to rest there, away from the chaos of London. Tim hoped it would be easier to travel to where her relatives lived, in Glasgow and a remote part of southern Scotland. Perhaps this remote area wouldn't be affected by the occupation too much.

Tim had attended a mixed grammar school in West Ham, East London, getting excellent marks in all his subjects for his Higher School Certificate at the age of eighteen. His parents had sacrificed everything to pay for his education, which helped him acquire a student apprenticeship at a local company making and repairing small, specialised steam turbines. He had spent the first year of the apprenticeship in all the different workshops, where he acquired practical proficiency. After this, he spent a year in the drawing office and then on to project management. In this time he gained a degree in engineering at the local college of technology, studying part-time with one year full-time.

At the end of his training, he was readily taken on as a project manager in the turbine refurbishment unit, but soon after was snapped up on good pay by the Jet Engine Research Centre in Coventry, a quasi-governmental establishment.

Right from school age, Tim had received good advice and encouragement from his parents. His father was a specialist toolmaker and his mother a shorthand typist. He had a younger sister, Ann, at home in West Ham.

One interesting stipulation of his schooling had been that all grammar school pupils had to study a foreign language, but this could not be Hebrew. A large contingent of Jews attended the school, and their extracurricular study of Hebrew would have given them an unfair advantage. Tim took French as his compulsory language, which was the norm at his school.

Tim was good friends with Arthur, a Jewish boy, who attended the same school and lived close by. Until age thirteen, they could hardly be separated. But Arthur's parents didn't encourage the friendship, and they drifted apart eventually. Arthur became a top London surgeon later in life, after surviving some horrendous conditions following the German invasion.

Tim had been quite a sportsman in his time, being a school champion sprinter and long jumper. He also enjoyed playing football and rugby. He belonged to small clubs until the age of twenty-three, at which time he was drafted to the research and development centre in Coventry. He was a skinny five foot eleven inches. When he stood with Molly, a vivacious, blue-eyed, natural blonde four inches shorter, they made a good-looking couple.

They had met more than a year ago. Since starting their affair, he hadn't needed another exercise. Molly kept him fit, especially after they moved in together. Molly, who had just turned nineteen, was what some might call a nymphomaniac—for Tim anyway. At the beginning of their relationship, this had affected Tim's work, which did require much concentration at specific times. In fact, he was reprimanded by his supervisor for not pulling his weight. He didn't know about Tim's nocturnal activities at the time. This was a wake-up call, and Tim made sure it didn't happen again.

Of course with their intense affair, Molly was attached to Tim, the more so as she was young and he was her first lover. He was careful not to make her pregnant. She took no heed of it. In fact, they never spoke about babies. As Molly approached sex with such gay abandon, he wondered if she knew of the connection.

Molly Brooks came from a close family who complained about her going out with Tim. The complaints faded after her eighteenth birthday. Mind you, they didn't find out he was married until later. Tim wasn't absolutely sure Molly had been a virgin when they met, although she didn't seem to know much about sex. He had seen her kissing and cuddling her father, whom she was fond of, but he didn't want to go there. He was happy she was sexy and just left it at that.

Luckily Tim had no problem with money, saving quite a lot over the year he had spent in Coventry. One reason was his generous living-away allowance. Because he had been living with Molly this money had accrued. They enjoyed staying in, listening to music, cooking, doing the housework, and making love.

Florence had her own money and help from her parents. Now she would be going to Scotland, where Tim hoped to join her at some stage. He could forget about her for the time being and concentrate on his own plans, which included Molly. He knew this was wrong and that he shouldn't be forsaking his beautiful young wife, who had just fallen pregnant. It was the times, he kidded himself.

His idea was to hide on remote farms with cooperating farmers until the dust had settled after the surrender, and then see if he could find and join the resistance. Many young men were thinking like this. He had always been interested in the military. When he was fourteen, he had joined the army commandos. They had given him basic weapons training and survival training. He had left that when he was eighteen, but still volunteered for weekend groups. One weekend they had trained in unarmed combat and street fighting; he had sustained three broken ribs. The doctor signed him off of that activity for three months, although he went back in two to complete the course.

Chapter 3

THE SECOND PHONEY

In the time Tim was establishing himself at the jet propulsion laboratory, the war was carrying on. After the failed attempt to invade the United Kingdom in 1940, Hitler composed himself and started listening to his generals. He dismissed Goering as the head of the Luftwaffe and assigned a proven military strategist, who started targeted bombing of British aircraft and munitions factories plus military bases, using good intelligence. Number one on their bombing list was the British radar facilities. Many of these raids were sneaked in at night. They found ways to nullify the British radar cover and developed their own radar and guidance systems. Even though provoked by the British bombing of civilian areas in Germany, the Luftwaffe continued to concentrate on military targets in Britain and did not specifically bomb civilian areas. Initially, the British had the advantage of heavy bombers. But these were very vulnerable, and the United Kingdom was running out of strategic resources to sustain them.

The war continued between Germany and the United Kingdom, but not on land. This lasted for nearly two years. In this time, Churchill was desperately trying to get the US involved. He visited on three occasions, but after the death of President Roosevelt in 1941, he came up against a brick wall. The US, with its large German and Central European populations, was not interested in helping a declining imperial power led by a warmonger. The demise of the Jews was not fully understood at this time.

There were many sea battles. In the surface engagements, the United Kingdom normally came out on top, but German submarines were sinking vast numbers of British merchant ships. The Germans had developed homing torpedoes and a new class of submarine with an underwater speed and range that could almost overhaul the average merchant convoy. These were built in their hundreds. Germany didn't need so much steel and manpower for tanks and heavy artillery, as they had decided not to attack Russia.

The US didn't send any of their ships in the convoys. Therefore no US vessels were sunk. There was an unofficial limit of one hundred and fifty miles off the coast of the US and Canada where the Germans did not operate. Beyond this limit, any ship steaming in the direction of the United Kingdom was fair game. At this stage, it seemed the US was happy to stay out of the war, supplying goods and equipment to the United Kingdom in exchange for gold or strategic places that were part of the far-flung British Empire. They were also selling specialised equipment to Germany via neutral Sweden.

The situation in the United Kingdom was becoming more and more desperate. Some draconian measures had

The First EU

to be introduced. Martial law was enacted. All men who were of fighting age and not in protected work were called up. Women and children were employed, with payment in meals only, for food production and clearing bomb damage. Nearly all industrial work was now for the war effort.

On the political front, in the two years from mid-1940 to mid-1942, Germany concentrated on building better relations with the European countries they occupied, diverting their joint will against Britain. This wasn't difficult as far as France was concerned, especially after the British sinking of a number of their warships in North Africa, killing twelve hundred. In Poland and Czechoslovakia, it was not so easy to gain support, but offers were made and in the end, Germany had the whole of occupied Europe on its side.

The Germans ceased killing Jews as part of this strategy, although the Jews were still restricted. This didn't seem to bother the average European. Many had benefited from the demise of their Jewish countrymen. Where possible, however, assets were returned to their original Jewish owners. Of course, there were many who objected to the treatment of the Jews, but they were in the minority.

The story put around about the United Kingdom was that the English and their empire were a spent force, the same as the Ottoman Empire had been twenty-five years before. The United Kingdom was now the only country left at war with the whole of Europe.

In the summer of 1941, Germany secretly negotiated with Turkey for several months, obtaining an agreement for their expeditionary army to traverse the eastern part of Turkey from its ports on the Black Sea into Iran. From there, they would sprint south to the Persian Gulf and battle the British for control of the oil fields and refining facilities. The German army of three hundred thousand, with tanks and other heavy equipment, was commanded by Field Marshal Rommel.

Although Hitler had a non-aggression pact with Stalin, he didn't trust his fellow dictator and only let him know about the plan two days before the embarkation of the German army from Romania. Germany was occupying Romania. The Turks remembered Churchill's involvement in actions against them in the previous world war, so there was no love lost for the British from that quarter.

Turkey was always worrying about Russia and was happy to get a powerful friend in Germany on side. Germany also gave the Turks pledges about future help for their economy.

By now it was becoming clear to all that unless the US came to their aid, Britain would lose the war—and the US didn't seem inclined to. In turn Hitler was happy to keep away from Russian territory.

As the German army was being transported across the Black Sea, it was imperative to keep the British Navy out of that area. This was achieved by Turkey, who controlled the entry from the Mediterranean via the Bosporus. The joint navies of Germany, France, and Turkey were also deployed in the Aegean Sea and the Black Sea. The reason that Hitler went this route was to avoid the British navy. He realised the British still had the edge when it came to sea power and controlled the Mediterranean. Except for the U-boat war in the Atlantic, Germany's plans to wreak surface havoc in British sea lanes throughout the world had come to nothing. All long-range battleships deployed from Germany had been neutralised.

The First EU

Germany didn't ever come to the aid of the Italians, but indirectly helped them in Greece and North Africa, as all the British troops in the Mediterranean withdrew to fight Rommel around the Persian Gulf.

Hitler had control of the French navy. It was the fourth largest in the world at that time. He sent a fleet around the Cape of Africa to the Middle East, calling in at Lüderitz in South-West Africa (Namibia) for supplies halfway. This force was decimated by the British navy in the southern ocean off Cape Town and chased up the east coast of Africa. Only eighteen out of the original fleet of thirty vessels made it through to the Persian Gulf. It was the faster ships that made it. There was only one battleship among them, the other two having been sunk.

Once near the Persian Gulf, the remaining ships gained air cover, as Rommel had control of that area and aircraft had been deployed to the captured British air bases. A few months later, Germany had control of the Suez Canal. It ousted the British using part of Rommel's force with the help of the Egyptians, and the German, French, and Turkish navies. There were one hundred and fifty thousand British prisoners from the fighting in the Persian Gulf. Later, a further fifty thousand were added from the Suez Canal. These were put to good use on infrastructure work in those areas.

Germany could now concentrate on the isolation and then the invasion of this small, aggressive island country off the Atlantic coast of Europe. After all, the UK had declared war on Germany. Stalin had no need to be friendly with the British; German Europe was his biggest trading partner. So Hitler had the Russians on his side when the invasion of Ireland and then the United Kingdom was being considered.

Chapter 4

THE INVASION

In the time since Germany's invasion of France, they had been covertly building up and practising for an invasion of Ireland and then the whole of the United Kingdom. One key part of this strategy was the development of heavy transport aircraft. Two German companies were commissioned to develop these aircraft: Messerschmitt and Heinkel. One hundred of each make was ordered. The Messerschmitt was thought the better.

In the event, there wasn't too much fighting to be undertaken in Ireland. After its fall, the Americans withdrew their support from the United Kingdom completely, saying the British should negotiate surrender as there wasn't any chance they could survive against the whole of Europe. The Americans thought the United Kingdom and its extended empire were on their last legs.

In June of 1942, after using a diversionary ploy to evade the British navy and air force, Germany landed a joint European force of fifty thousand crack fighting troops and

The First EU

engineers with equipment on the southern side of Ireland. Many of these troops were transported in submarines, the balance being flown in. This transportation occurred at night. They had practised many times. The task of the first to land, the elite, was to secure landing strips and places where submarines could quickly discharge further transported troops. There was limited local opposition, as there had already been collusion in Ireland against Britain. A presence was rapidly established, and many more troops and equipment were flown in. Although there was desperate opposition from the RAF and Royal Navy, and some German losses, within three weeks the whole of Ireland was overrun—including Northern Ireland, where many thousands of British troops were captured. The remaining part of the United Kingdom—England, Wales, and Scotland—was completely surrounded.

The Germans were using a wonder weapon: a recently developed guided missile, which could be launched from a medium bomber and guided to its target. This wreaked havoc with the Royal Navy, keeping them away from the larger merchant ships transporting the tanks and field guns to Ireland. This wonder weapon also had a smaller version for use in the field against tanks and lorries.

Soon after the invasion of Ireland, the British stepped up their bombing of German cities, using new long-range fighters to protect the bombers. Hitler started to suggest an armistice would be feasible under certain conditions; in this way, further bloodshed would be avoided. Two weeks after the invasion of Ireland, Winston Churchill mysteriously died. Some said he had been poisoned.

The British appeasers who headed up the armistice negotiations were completely out of their depth. They shouldn't have been so naive as to think this agreement was going to be honoured when no other similar agreement had been. The agreement negotiated gave the mainland United Kingdom control over its own affairs. Its empire was to be run in partnership with the Germans. There would be no further armed action between the two countries as long as the ceasefire and surrender agreement was implemented in full.

Upon the signing of the armistice, hostilities ceased at midnight on 23 July 1942. The following morning, at first light, the Luftwaffe attacked the RAF and other strategic facilities with more than two thousand aircraft, destroying or neutralising more than half of the RAF planes, most still on the ground. At the same time, crack fighting troops were flown to strategic locations in Scotland by heavy transport planes. These heavy transports had been designed for short take-off and landing on rough terrain. After three days, there were sixty thousand German troops on the ground. Over the same period, a further forty thousand troops were landed by submarines at remote locations around the coast. A further, similar invasion of Wales was successfully achieved around Cardigan Bay.

Both in Scotland and Wales, the main task of these forward troops was to secure ports for the landing of equipment like heavy guns and tanks. Of course, these ports were still within range of the Royal Navy, but the British ships were coming under constant attack. There were German losses, but a lot of activity took place at night. The heavy equipment, once landed, was moved inland as soon as possible.

Within a few days, the German army commanded by Rommel had fought over the rolling hills of central Wales into the Midlands of England and onwards. This was the main thrust of three hundred thousand men, which had to neutralise the south-east and the seat of government. Ronstadt with his army, landing in the lowlands of Scotland, had to neutralise that area and then fight down through northern England. Ronstadt had two hundred thousand troops.

When the armistice was signed, a lot of Britons hadn't thought it would last, but they hadn't expected it to be broken so soon and so comprehensively. The reason given by the Germans for the invasion was that they were not happy with the terms. The British had been asking for too much, were stubborn, and were not negotiating in good faith.

It took the British a little time before their forces were completely up and running. The British navy didn't have time to invent a counter to the new German guided missiles, but its ships still did inflict some damage. They could do nothing to help the land forces once the invaders moved inland. The air transports purposely landed where the naval guns couldn't reach.

One of the major factors from the invasion of Ireland onwards was the deployment of the new guided missile systems en masse against the Royal Navy, and the deployment of a smaller version against the British land forces. This definitely tipped the balance. The British had just developed a new anti-aircraft gun, which was successful—but not enough of them had been manufactured. There was a shortage of components owing to the Atlantic blockade.

The south of England came under relentless bombing by the Luftwaffe from France, Belgium, and Holland. A gallant rearguard action was fought, but the British were outmanoeuvred, outgunned, and out of practise compared to their German opponents. Towards the end, they were outnumbered also. Hundreds of thousands of extra troops were shipped in by the Germans and met little resistance. Four weeks later, there were eight hundred thousand German and European troops in the country.

The final surrender was unconditional and signed by the head of the armed forces of the United Kingdom on 20 August 1942. The country was in shock. The British head of state, King George VI, broadcast to the nation that they should cease all resistance and follow the reasonable instructions of the German authorities as laid out in the final surrender agreement. This broadcast was made from the battleship the *Prince of Wales* in the Atlantic 200 miles north of Puerto Rico. It was transporting the king and the extended royal family into exile in Canada.

With this number of German and European troops in the United Kingdom, the harvests that needed to be gathered in Europe were endangered. It was imperative to stabilise the situation and get as many men back home as soon as possible. Half of the invasion force was back home by the beginning of September, accompanied by hundreds of thousands of prisoner slave labourers.

The leaders of the USA were isolationists and didn't want to get involved. There was no help from that quarter. Japan had decided to cooperate with the USA rather than oppose them. This helped the Japanese gain control of the oil and raw materials they required without going to war. They staged a mock withdrawal from China to show their goodwill.

The First EU

The balance of power in Europe was much in Germany's favour. They either occupied or had cooperation from all of Europe to the border of the Soviet Union. They had control of the whole of the Middle East, including the Suez Canal and the oil fields. Now the only part of Europe that had been in opposition, the United Kingdom, was under their control. A time was dawning for the rule of Germany in Europe.

Chapter 5

THE KING

On the evening of the eighth day of fighting under cover of darkness, the battleship HMS *Prince of Wales*, with three destroyer escorts, all fully fuelled up, left Falmouth for Canada. They were carrying the king and extended royal family into exile. Their complement excluded the Duke of Windsor.

Taking a southerly route to avoid U-boats, they met up with two fuel supply ships waiting in a prearranged position north-west of the British Virgin Islands. They took on fuel and other supplies and approached the USA. They opened communication, knowing their position would be conceded. First they asked for permission to enter the non-aggression zone off the coast, which was granted. Then they made contact with the United Kingdom. This was on an intermittent line from a mobile communications unit in the Forest of Dean near southern Wales, one of the last still operating.

It was nearly three weeks into the fighting and a day after opening radio contact that the king gave his address to the nation. It was recorded through the same mobile unit and then broadcast every hour on the hour through the BBC, which still had three local stations operating in Wales and England. He was introduced: 'This is a broadcast to the peoples of the United Kingdom by your king, His Majesty King George VI.'

Then the king's voice was heard. 'Fellow British citizens, I must give you this grave message. The fighting has not gone well for us. German forces are in complete control of the majority of the country, with 90 per cent of our armed forces already neutralised. The instruction has been sent out that it is pointless to continue the fight, although some are fighting on. I would say to them that they must stop. To carry on will be a futile loss of life. The occupiers are pouring more troops and equipment into our land as I speak, with little or no opposition. The Germans have shown us their instructions. These will go out to the people on leaflets by air drops and other means within a day or so. I can tell you that, under the circumstances, they are generous and also thorough. We must keep calm and live as usual. One day something good will come out of this grave situation, as it must. I wish you all God's blessing and look forward to the day I can return as your king after this hour of darkness.'

The Germans knew a speech was imminent because there had been contact with the battleship *Prince of Wales* straight after they opened radio communication. The Germans had discovered soon after his departure that the king had left the country. The fighting was going well for them, and they wanted to send instructions that, they hoped, he would include in his address. When the Germans found the speech had been transmitted and that it asked the British people to stop fighting and cooperate, they made it easy for the broadcast to continue. Thus, most people soon heard it through the BBC, whose studios were not destroyed.

After the *Prince of Wales* gave its position away, a race began between America and Germany to capture the king before he entered Canadian waters. The Germans had little chance, though, with only U-boats in the area.

This turned into an unfortunate incident in the war. After the small British force received permission to enter the one hundred and fifty mile non-aggression zone off the East Coast, the Americans insisted that the king be turned over to them. Maybe they wanted him as a bargaining chip in this time of turmoil. Although most German U-boats had been called back for the invasion of Britain, a few were left out in the far Atlantic and two intercepted the small British fleet at this time. The Americans did manage to capture the king, but only after a fight with great loss of life.

The admiral of the British fleet stated that his orders were to hand the king and his entourage over to the Canadian Prime Minister. The Americans already had warships close by. When repeated American requests to turn over the king were refused, the Americans fired warning shots. The British admiral took this as an act of war. Unable to get a clear response from the United Kingdom's government, which hardly existed by this time, he decided to engage any US warship within range.

Torpedoes from the British destroyers—and, possibly, one of the U-boats—sank the American battleship that had fired the warning shots. Two American cruisers were completely mangled by the *Prince of Wales*'s fifteen-inch guns. One sank after a hit to its magazine; the other was finished off with torpedoes. Two American destroyers were likewise sunk by torpedoes, and two others were also mangled by the *Prince of Wales*.

From then on, the Americans kept their distance. There was little damage to the small British fleet, which sailed on at full speed beyond the non-aggression zone. The admiral knew there would be American planes coming soon enough from the mainland. The fact that they had inflicted so much carnage on the Americans was probably due to the fact that the US was not expecting a confrontation. Its navy was also completely out of practise, not having engaged in any modern-day sea war.

From the Caribbean, the little British fleet had the whole of the East Coast to cover before entering Canadian waters. Although they kept as far from the coast as they could, in the days that followed, American warplanes from land bases relentlessly attacked, concentrating on one side of the *Prince of Wales* in the hopes of causing a capsize.

On the first day, there was a great loss among American planes due to protection from the British destroyers. The *Prince of Wales* was damaged but still steamed on. The destroyers and the *Prince of Wales* had the latest high-powered, long-range anti-aircraft guns mounted—the same ones that were placed on five heavy armoured cars in Scotland to great effect.

The second day of attacks caused the *Prince of Wales* to slow greatly. On the third day, it turned turtle, sinking within a few minutes with most still trapped on board. The king, the queen, and their children, along with the admiral, had been transferred to the least damaged destroyer the previous night.

Finally, after sustaining critical damage off the coast of Nova Scotia, this destroyer was slowed to a crawl. When the next wave of American planes approached, the white flags were flown. The king and all on board were now in American hands. The two other destroyers were attacked with airborne torpedoes, sinking with most hands aboard. Few were rescued. The US had lost many, and there was great bitterness.

The total loss on both sides was nearly six thousand. Two-thirds were American personnel. The Americans took control of Canada a few months later and would have gained custody of the king anyway. The admiral could have ignored the warning shots, but his own country had been decimated by that time. Who knew what was going through his mind? Besides which, the next shots could have been for real. The Americans didn't need the king at the time; they could have been less hostile. The Germans, although they were trying to shadow the British and did get close, had no chance of matching the British fleet's speed with their U-boats.

The admiral was interned for war crimes, and the king and his family were put under house arrest in a mansion on the outskirts of Washington, DC. The rest of the surviving crew were put on the last destroyer, which was limping home with a German U-boat escort. The Germans were more than pleased to receive them, even the injured. They wanted to make heroes out of them and use them for the new British/German navy. The Americans missed a trick here, as they needed good men in their own navy. But because of the loss of life, there was much anger towards the British.

By this time, nearly all fighting in the United Kingdom had ceased. A few days before the British surrender, a flotilla of seven warships from the Royal Canadian Navy sailed out to meet the strange convoy of one damaged British destroyer and two German U-boats. They had not come in anger, knowing the surrender in their homeland was near. They negotiated with the Germans to return with them to the United Kingdom. Most had families there and, following the recent naval battle between the US and the United Kingdom, had decided they would be better off back in Britain, even under German rule. It was fortunate for the hundreds of British injured on the crippled destroyer, who were transferred to the two Canadian cruisers, which had much better medical facilities.

Not many people knew that the *Prince of Wales* sank with sixty tons of gold bullion on board.

Chapter 6

THE SS ENGINEERS ARRIVE

A team of smartly uniformed, rather menacing Germans arrived at the Jet Engine Research Centre in Coventry. They had been expected and were the senior members of a special engineering team.

Before anything else, they marched into the personnel department and asked for all records, initially checking for Jewish-sounding names. There was only one. He was a wages clerk and nobody knew what had happened to him.

Then the Germans went after the people employed on the top-secret work. After it became evident there were a number of key workers missing, a list of names was sent to the Gestapo—including Tim's. The British police were already working under the Gestapo, and all stations received this list for urgent attention.

Along with Tim, there were another four members of his research team of eight missing. If they weren't found, the programme would be in big trouble. All these key workers had had the idea of hiding, but most of them did not plan their escape as well as Tim did.

The only person who had an idea where Tim was—besides Molly—did not work for the centre. He was a friend through the street-fighting group Tim attended every Wednesday. Fred was a devout Christian and knew the farmer at Dale Farm. After Fred spoke with him at Sunday service, the farmer gave consent for Tim and Molly to stay on his farm. On the final Sunday before the Wednesday pick-up, the details were given to the farmer.

Irene the farm girl was dispatched on the day. Fred told the farmer that Tim would be willing to pay well for the service, but the farmer said he only wanted out-of-pocket expenses. He was more than willing to help, having lost his two sons in the war. Tim was happy with this arrangement. He did pay a nice bonus to Irene for the risk she took in driving them; he didn't tell the farmer about this.

Three of the other four research workers went up north where they had relatives. With money for bribes, it was easy to get either bus or rail transport in the chaos of the invasion. The last team member went to London, where he had friends and hoped to disappear in the throngs of the bombed-out city. Two who went to relatives in the north were soon apprehended by the police. The one who went to London did disappear for a while, by moving from one group to another, but was finally caught in a roundup where his identity came out. The final one who went up north, Dave, escaped because the police were still not fully compliant with their German masters where his relatives lived. They helped him, and he escaped into the country and then over the border into a remote part of southern Scotland.

So, two weeks after the SS take-over at the centre, there were only two key workers missing. The three who had been caught knew they would be in big trouble if they didn't fully cooperate. As the Germans were on a charm offensive regarding the centre, they treated the absconders well, considering other things that were going on in the country at the time.

The SS engineering group were very systematic and got the jet engine research programme up and running sooner than a lot of people had thought possible. They missed the two key people still in hiding, and extra pressure was put on the police for results, but to no avail. All family members were kept under surveillance, and phones (when people had them) were tapped.

As time went by and the centre progressed with its work without the two fugitives, their absence became less important. As far as the Gestapo was concerned, these two were merely criminals now. They may have joined the resistance, so had to be found. They wouldn't get the good treatment their colleagues had received after capture.

CHAPTER 7

FLEEING TO DALE FARM

'Wow, that was so beautiful,' sighed Molly after a half-hour session with Tim. In their preparations, the pair had been away from one another for nearly a week, which was unusual for them. They had their reunion in the small back room which had been Molly's bedroom before she moved in with Tim, while Molly's parents were at a local community meeting, called to discuss the occupation instructions.

'Right,' said Tim, after getting cleaned up and dressed. They liked to make love naked; a race to strip off was a normal part of their pre-sex games. 'We'll be leaving by farm truck at nine. Are you ready?'

'I've got these two bags full, should have everything,' said Molly, also getting cleaned up and dressed. Her voice was higher pitched than usual and rather excited. This was going to be an adventure more serious than she had ever imagined. They'd heard of the Gestapo, but had no experience of them, like most people in the United Kingdom.

Tim had taken off sick just over a week after the final surrender. Since then, he had been making plans and vacating his apartment. Molly had moved back in with her parents, not telling them of her pending elopement. They had recently found out that Tim was married. They didn't make much fuss about it—because of the times, probably—but were happy to see her return home. He couldn't leave Molly behind, although she could be a liability. She was insisting on standing with him and joining the resistance when he did. She thought the Germans were creepy with their racial purity doctrines. Tim had moved in with Fred and his girlfriend, who knew about his plans also.

Nothing had happened at the research centre in the week after the occupation began, but word had got around that a special SS engineering team would be visiting within a day or so. Tim decided never to return. Molly had kept at work until the day before their departure into hiding.

As Molly and Tim prepared to leave, she left a note for her parents, saying she would contact them in a week or so, and not to worry. She was worried though, because she had been interviewed by the SS team at the centre two days before. They had asked her if she knew where Tim was. This frightened her, and she was glad to be leaving. Her colleagues told her she was lucky it wasn't the Gestapo who had interrogated her.

Just before nine, they were waiting at a prearranged place on a secluded lane in the small village outside Coventry, Molly's home since birth.

'This is the lorry,' said Tim.

The driver—Irene, a farm girl from where they would be hiding—looked rather agitated. 'Get in quickly. We can't drive tonight. I saw a roadblock being readied on the outskirts of the village. They will be suspicious of me travelling late at night, and if they search the lorry, the game's up. I shouldn't have agreed to drive you so late. It's ridiculous. You know the police are already working under instructions from the Gestapo.'

Tim thought if it became known that he was absconding from the research centre, he would be turned over to the SS straight away. This was a daunting possibility, especially as Molly was with him as well.

'We must find a place to park up until sunrise,' Irene insisted. 'In the morning it will not be suspicious. The police will just think I'm on my way to work. I know a place by an abandoned stable just up the road.'

'Let's go,' said Tim. 'Oh, sorry—Irene, pleased to meet you.' He already knew her name from the phone calls,

'Hi.'

'This is Molly.'

'Hi.'

'Hi,' Molly responded.

Irene put the old lorry into gear, and they were off to the abandoned stable. Tim didn't want to offend Irene and whispered to Molly, 'Be a good girl tonight. We'll have plenty of time at our new home to catch up.'

Tim was startled in the early hours by the attention of Irene, who must have been feeling a bit that way inclined. As Molly was still fast asleep, he was able to extricate himself from his amorous collaborator without creating much fuss. *Maybe she has been without a man for too long*, he thought. He couldn't help but observe that Irene had a well-proportioned, firm body, probably caused by her daily work routine. She had a smooth skin, but there was some hardness in her face. Even so, she had a good, healthy look that would turn heads if she dressed up.

He didn't say anything, hoping his polite rejection would do the trick and she wouldn't come on to him again. He had enough to do satisfying Molly and didn't want more complications in his life.

In the morning they didn't see any roadblocks and had a straight run to the farm. The fugitives hid under a canvas sheet, covering what was made to look like hay. The smell of hay mixed with petrol in the back of the lorry was quite intoxicating for the occupants over the two-hour journey. They knew they had reached their destination when a strong farmyard smell permeated the air. Even so, they kept under the cover until told it was safe.

Irene was a single woman of twenty-six. She had cycled the forty miles to the farm in one day two years before with her few possessions, fleeing an abusive relationship. She had lived in the Birmingham area. Irene was happy working on the farm; she had found peace of mind after arriving in rather a bad emotional and physical state. She'd had previous knowledge of this farm couple and had an idea they would not turn her away. This proved right. They asked few questions before opening their home to her. The farmer and his wife were devout Anglicans, who found in Irene a good, honest, hard-working girl to help on their farm and with their evacuee family group. Irene was also a Christian in her beliefs, if not so devout.

When Irene arrived at the farm after her long bike ride, she had two black eyes and a swollen lip—some proof that she was being abused. In the two years since, nobody had come to the farm looking for her, although she had correct documents and registered at the local police station. The farm couple assumed her family and abuser didn't know where she was, and that this must be what she wanted. She sent her mother a letter after a week, saying she was well.

Two weeks after the final surrender, and three days after the SS engineering team arrived at the centre, Tim and Molly arrived at the farm. It was located three miles along a winding country lane, with other farms and a little church along the way. The farmhouse was a large, solid, traditional, thatched-roof building about one hundred and fifty years old. Oak and elm trees surrounded it in what seemed like a disorderly manner. A barn and other farm buildings were close at hand.

The farmer and his wife welcomed Tim and Molly. 'Hello. My name is Albert Black. You can call me Uncle Albert. This is my wife.'

'You can call me Auntie May. Pleased to meet you.'

'Hello,' said Molly and Tim.

'Now,' said Uncle Albert, 'this is a God-fearing household. Here are your hiding places in these attic rooms. This is where you will sleep and store all your things. There are a number of other places you can use in case of danger. Irene will show you these places in the barn lofts and outbuildings later. The ladder will always be pulled up when you are sleeping.'

Uncle Albert, realising that Molly and Tim were not married, added, 'You will sleep in separate rooms, please. As mentioned, we are a godly home.'

When the ladders were pulled up, there was no way of getting between the rooms in the attic. Irene slept under one part of the attic and the couple under the other, so it was almost impossible to redeploy the ladders without waking someone. Molly looked a bit unhappy about this prospect, but that was it. They couldn't upset their hosts, who were taking a great risk in putting them up.

A week before Tim and Molly arrived on the farm, three children had left it. The children, all from one family, had been evacuated to the farm at the beginning of the war, and were sent back to their parents. This was one of the instructions circulated by the occupying forces. The day of the final surrender, twenty million leaflets were dropped by air, covering the whole country. The same instructions had been put in the local and national newspapers and pinned up in post offices and town halls. The king had referred to them in his speech to the nation.

CHAPTER 8

HEYDRICH'S BRUTAL PLAN

Now that Hitler had complete control of Europe, including the United Kingdom, there was no reason for him to continue to go lightly in the occupied countries. He reintroduced his controversial policies involving the Jews. He was determined to punish Britain for opposing him for so long and for bombing Germany indiscriminately.

Heydrich, Hitler's protégé, who was currently the SS leader in Czechoslovakia, was sent to be the SS leader in the United Kingdom. He arrived in the second week after the surrender, just before Tim and Molly were installed in their new home. This was seen as a bad omen. Heydrich had narrowly escaped death in an assassination attempt two months earlier. It came out later that the British had supplied the would-be assassins with weapons and training. Heydrich still had a limp from that gunfight. One could imagine that the British would suffer greatly unless they completely complied with everything the Germans requested.

As the Germans expected Britain to resist, Heydrich had a plan—a simple but brutal plan—which he put into effect immediately. Part of the plan was to round up two million men who were not involved in essential work and send them to Europe as slave labour. Using these men as hostages, the Germans would be able to stop any resistance in the United Kingdom itself and gain control of the far-flung British navy and then the British colonies.

When the latter two goals did not progress quickly enough, two hundred of these men were executed before they even got to their slave camps in Europe. Over a million men had already been rounded up by the second week of Heydrich's reign of terror. But the round-up was slowing down. Many men evaded capture and went into hiding—and of course, many men were still needed in essential jobs. Most of the army rank and file were put into the slave labour group. These men were also gathered from southern Ireland.

After Heydrich had been in the country for just three weeks, he realised that the two million target may have been a bit optimistic. After one and a half million had been achieved, the push to round up more men slackened. Only people who didn't have work were sent for slave labour after that. Those found in hiding were brutally treated before being sent to the camps.

Another part of Heydrich's plan was to liquidate nearly five thousand academics and prominent members of society, especially any who had ever criticised Hitler's regime. Included in the list were Winston Churchill and the philosopher Bertrand Russell. The Duke of Windsor, who had abdicated as king in 1936, was to be reinstalled as king. Winston Churchill had mysteriously died already, and nearly half the people on the list were executed in the first week.

There was panic. No one knew who was on the list. Many tried to go into hiding, but the Germans had the police forcibly on their side. An English-speaking Gestapo member had been placed in every police station in the country. These men had been in training for this day and were already familiar with United Kingdom police procedures. Their assignment was to change things to the German way.

Five hundred thousand German and European troops were still in the country. They were also utilised to scour the country for people on the liquidation list and men slated for slave labour.

Because of these terrible actions, the Duke of Windsor was not keen to cooperate with the occupiers. The idea of bringing him back as king was left by the wayside for the time being.

Chapter 9

ARTHUR'S FAMILY

Hitler had been soft-pedalling regarding the Jews for two years, compared to their previous harsh treatment—especially in the first year of the war, after the invasion of Poland in 1939. The hundreds of ghettos that had been set up in Germany and German-controlled Europe were now dismantled and all occupants, mainly Jewish, were sent home. This was problematic, as often their homes had been taken over. But in the end, with this new policy, these things were mostly sorted out.

After the occupation of Britain, the harsh Jewish policy was reintroduced. Discriminatory laws were enforced again, and hundreds of ghettos were re-established throughout Europe, the United Kingdom, and Ireland. Hitler had come under the influence of a young women for two years which helped soften his anti-Jewish policies by 1942 but this women mysteriously disappeared around the time of the invasion of Ireland.

The First EU

There were virtually no Jews in the German armed forces. They were not allowed to enlist owing to the 1935 laws; also they were not considered aggressive enough to be good fighters. Hitler had an idea of giving Jewish possessions to returning soldiers who had fought well.

Even before the recent fighting, Hitler and his top people had been looking at reintroducing the ghettos in mainland Europe. A week or so before the ceasefire, ghettos were being considered in a number of main centres where Jews resided in Britain. Jews in obvious view, like Arthur's family, were in line for being sent to these ghettos straight away. All Jews in the United Kingdom were in great danger.

Although Heydrich as the United Kingdom's Gruppenfuhrer was not in place immediately after the ceasefire, his instructions were being carried out. There was no need to keep the rest of Europe on side, and there was no threat from the USA. Hitler didn't have to worry; he could do whatever he wanted.

The first to see this change was the invaded United Kingdom. Many of the prominent British people on the liquidation list were Jewish. As a shoemaker, Arthur's father was not on this list, but his business was shut down. All Jews—men, women, and children—were rounded up and placed into hastily organised ghettos. Arthur's father thought of immigrating to Palestine, as many Jews in Europe had done when Germany brought in highly discriminatory laws against them. Unfortunately for him, he thought he would be safer in London.

Arthur was serving as a junior surgeon at a military hospital just outside London when the German SS called on his father. The family knew this was coming, so they had cases packed and didn't resist at all. Even so, they were roughly treated. Arthur's father was thrown to the ground, and his eighteen-year-old daughter had her clothes torn by the rough pawing of a couple of soldiers.

The first ghetto was in an old, dilapidated part of Whitechapel from which the existing residents had been expelled. It was only a small block surrounding a burial ground, but already had fifteen hundred people crammed in during the first week. Within a couple of months, this ghetto would expand to hold more than a hundred thousand over a much larger area.

Arthur's father, who had lived just a few doors from Tim's family, took money with him to the ghetto. After the sale of his business stock and other things, he had quite an amount. He could pay for the food being supplied by the German authorities—but many others couldn't.

After a couple of months, the ghetto turned into an absolute nightmare. Dead people, including children had to be cleared from the streets on a daily basis. The smell was terrible. Arthur's people were fine for the moment and shared their food, but they couldn't feed everyone.

There was a great shortage of surgeons, and Arthur with his good record, was in great demand. Where he worked in London there were both British and German casualties being treated. Although it was known he was Jewish, nothing happened to him. He managed to contact his family in the Whitechapel ghetto. He asked that his family be treated well, and this did happen. It couldn't be made too obvious, but at least they weren't hounded and his sister wasn't molested.

Chapter 10

LOVE ON DALE FARM

On the farm, Tim and Molly offered to do any work the farmer could find for them. Tim didn't know much about farming, but by observation he could see that the farm could be run more efficiently and an increase in output easily achieved. There was a small tractor that hadn't been working for a year, and Tim got to work on it. Luckily it hadn't seized up completely. He freed the pistons and cleaned out the carburettor, fuel tank, and lines. Then he got it started with clean petrol. The farm enjoyed extra rations of fuel for their lorry and tractor.

The farmer was delighted with Tim's efforts. These seemed to put new life into him. He had reached the depths after the death of one son and then, a year later, the report of the other missing in action. With the arrival of these new young people, he started to plan things. The first was to plant the latest table variety of apple trees in the field behind the farmhouse.

With the tractor working, it was much easier to clear the field. This included removing a number of small trees. The trees were cut down and their roots pulled out with the tractor. When the field was cleared of trees, it was ploughed to get rid of the smaller shrubs and plants.

The farmer had all sorts of attachments for the tractor, including a special auger for making holes, which ran from the power take-off at the rear. Tim became expert in making these holes. The farmer and girls followed up with the apple saplings, compost, and topsoil. On the first day after the field was cleared and ploughed, they planted seventy new trees.

The farmer, who could see that the young couple were rather amorous, turned a blind eye when they disappeared together every afternoon with their lunch bag and blanket. This frustrated Irene, who wished she could have Tim's attention instead.

It so happened that when Irene picked up the young apple trees from the local nursery, all hands were needed to plant them as soon as possible. While this was happening, there were no disappearing acts for Tim and Molly.

Irene had fallen for Tim the first time they met. It wasn't due to lust alone that she had made a pass at him in the back of the truck. She had fallen in love with his voice while they were making arrangements on the phone. He never learned of this. She realised Tim and Molly were an item, and upon Tim's polite rejection, she decided she must forget about him and look for another man. The problem was she still had mental scars from her experiences with an abusive partner.

Irene bathed at the bathhouse in the village when visiting there. Also every Thursday after work, she was allowed to have a hot bath in the large galvanised bathtub in the farmhouse. In the winter, she bathed in front of the fire. Now that Molly had arrived, she also bathed on the same evening. The farmer's wife bathed on Wednesday night, and the farmer and Tim made do with a cold shower using a hosepipe. For Tim that was every night, for Uncle Albert not so often. The girls washed off the farm dirt on a daily basis using water from a water butt and a bucket put there for the purpose.

It was after the girl's hot bath on the third Thursday, exactly two weeks after Tim and Molly arrived, that Irene quietly made it into Tim's attic hideaway by climbing onto the kitchen roof and lifting some of the thatch. Being of average height and quite slim, she could easily squeeze through. Irene had entered the attic just above her own room in this way a couple of times to check it out. It was easier than deploying the ladder. Molly's room was not easy to enter as there was no adjoining roof.

A few months after arriving on the farm, Irene had taken up with one of the local farmhands, Sam. They'd had an on-off relationship for nearly a year, but he didn't fire Irene up much. His attitude to sex was 'wham bam thank you ma'am'. It was the last thing she wanted. Also, Sam, with his village upbringing, had limited conversational scope. So theirs was a relationship of convenience encouraged by the farmer, who sometimes needed a strong pair of hands on the farm. Their lovemaking was minimal because Auntie May wouldn't let them use Irene's bedroom. In the back of the farm lorry was their usual place.

Sam had finally received his call-up to the army six months before, when it became certain Hitler was preparing an invasion. Irene hadn't encouraged anyone else, as there was only more of the same in the area.

Tim was fast asleep when Irene crept through the thatch. Before he knew it, Irene was beside him, all fresh and clean and smelling of bath soap. What to do? He didn't want this situation at all. He could have insisted that she go, but he was a man and hadn't enjoyed Molly for a week. He had been spending time working with and getting to know Irene over the last two weeks. She had a slim, athletic body, very different to Molly. He knew he shouldn't, but Irene looked very appealing.

She whispered, 'Don't reject me again.' This time it was unlikely. Tim felt sorry for her, having heard her sad story from Uncle Albert.

He whispered back, 'You look and smell great. Just once. We must be quiet. I hope you enjoy it.' He thought he would make her mad with desire the way he always did to his lovers.

'Oh Tim, I will, I will.'

Tim only had his underpants on. These came off straight away. He gently removed Irene's clothing, making as little noise as possible. He became more aroused than he had ever been with Molly or Florence. He couldn't understand why,

Irene was an inch or so shorter than Molly and had a lovely, slim body. Fair enough. But her breasts were rather small. She had a slender neck. Because of her passionate outlook, her face had become beautiful and at peace. This was magic for Tim and probably the reason for his heightened enthusiasm. He decided that tonight would be Irene's.

'Do you want me to kiss you all over?'

'Please do. I'd love that,' she said, knowing full well what his words meant. She rolled her eyes back in anticipation.

Tim removed her panties by easing her buttocks up and giving a gentle tug. With long, passionate kisses, Tim started on the side of her slender neck. This greatly aroused them both. He spent time on her most sensitive places. Giving her pleasure aroused him.

'It's so beautiful. Please don't stop. Oh, never stop.'

Tim raised his head. 'Quietly Irene.' He gave her the same treatment again. Feeling the quivering throughout her whole body and hearing her quiet gasps, he knew she was climaxing. He wanted to take it slow, but he couldn't wait.

'I'm going to do you now—all right, Irene?'

Her look said, *Yes, please, Tim.*

He entered in an instant as they French kissed. She pushed against him with that slow, gentle rhythm of experienced lovers. Tim knew she was reaching her climax again because her French kissing became wild. His body reached that euphoria as well.

When they were done, they relaxed back in each other's arms, talking in whispers. 'I knew it would be good, but I didn't know it would be this good,' she said.

'I like to please. What am I going to do with you now, my oh-so-sexy friend?'

'I know you're clever enough to sort something out, my lover.'

They were both well satisfied and fell into a peaceful sleep, slightly intoxicated by the smell of the wet thatch. Luckily they woke up at the crowing of the rooster just as the night was ending.

Irene felt she couldn't be any happier or more fulfilled. For Tim, it was another story.

The war and uncertainty made everyone more amorous; it wasn't only Irene and Tim. Such liaisons were happening all over the country. Maybe it was nature's way of replenishing the human race after great loss.

Chapter 11

TIM'S PAST

Irene was dressed in no time. Giving him a long, tender kiss, she whispered, 'I love you.' He didn't reply, and she understood. With a brief, loving look, she was gone. Nothing more was said. They knew the farmer and his wife might be waking up—not to mention Molly.

Before Tim went to sleep again, he thought, *What have I done?* and *What a fantastic night.* He didn't quite understand why the lovemaking had been so good. In a beauty competition, Molly and his wife Florence would always come out ahead. But Irene was beautiful to him, and beauty is in the eye of the beholder, they say. Tim was just too popular with the ladies. He couldn't help it but did enjoy it. Though she may have been abused in the past, Irene was still a healthy woman, he thought.

Tim had had sex with girls from the age of seventeen. In the early days, he had a regular girlfriend of fifteen. She was his first girlfriend and very sexy. Tim's parents were easy-going. Well, his mother was. His father objected but didn't have much say. Tim would take Lesley into his bedroom and lock the door nearly every night. Lesley lived a few houses down the road. Their relationship was too immature and destined to end, which it did after two years.

One thing Tim learned from her was that she loved French kissing when she was climaxing. After a while, he just took this as a normal part of lovemaking and introduced it to all his future partners. Another thing almost unique to Lesley was that she was double-jointed which did make things interesting to say the least.

After Lesley, Tim found it difficult to find a regular girlfriend. Maybe one reason was that he was studying hard for his engineering degree. He'd had continuous sex for two years and then nothing. Exams passed, he decided to find ways he could easily get and keep another girlfriend. He studied a few books, including some by women authors. He also read French books, discovering their way of making love.

He started to practise being relaxed and joking with all the girls he fancied, making them laugh as much as possible. When some of them showed interest, he asked them out. If they showed more interest, he would jokingly suggest things to them. In the end, they were normally the ones chasing him and making the first move, even though one of them was a virgin.

In his lovemaking, he always concentrated on making sure his partner had all the pleasure first. He kissed them all over in the French way without expecting anything back. This was new to most of them, but they loved it. He found it most gratifying, much more than his 'wham bam thank you ma'am' relationship with his first girlfriend. They all wanted him in them after this treatment, and he was very popular with the ladies. He was nothing special but was expert in technique.

He realized that, without knowing it, he had been giving Irene the messages he had learned. But that couldn't explain her coming on to him in the lorry the first time they met. He still wondered about that.

Tim lay in bed for an extra hour, thinking about what was going to happen now. He couldn't face the two girls together at the breakfast table. He was sure Molly would be suspicious. Maybe she suspected something already.

He told Molly he had been reading all night by candlelight and was tired. He thought he shouldn't have been so friendly with Irene, but it was just his way. All was soon forgotten because Lieutenant Tobias Schmitt arrived at noon. This day changed things forever.

Chapter 12

THE FIRST VISIT

Irene was still looking radiant from the previous night's activities. Though she did not realise it, this drew the attention of the German second in command—Dieter, the other English speaker in Lieutenant Schmitt's unit.

A small group of German soldiers in an armoured car finally got to this remote farm in the Midlands. These soldiers had landed and fought their way through Wales with Rommel's army group as mechanised infantry. Anyone approaching the farm could be seen for at least half a mile. If they were in a vehicle, they could be heard from much further away. In this case, they were heard before they were seen, the engine being different in sound to anything local. The alarm went out straight away.

At about noon, Irene came running to where Molly and Tim were working in the field at the back, planting apple trees. 'You must hide! The Germans are coming. Get into Molly's attic.' That room was away from the kitchen and main room; they had agreed to use it in case of this situation.

The First EU

'Quickly!' shouted Tim.

Uncle Albert and Irene pushed the wardrobe under the small loft hatch. This attic hatch was small. Molly had got used to entering by breathing in momentarily as she squeezed through.

Although terrible things were happening elsewhere in the United Kingdom, the occupational forces were under instructions to be friendly and polite to the local population, as well as being vigilant. This wasn't difficult. Most Germans were naturally polite, and the vigilance went without saying.

Every unit had at least one good English speaker. This unit, it turned out, had two, plus another two who had some English language skills. There were seven soldiers in all. When they arrived at the farm a few minutes after being heard, the leader—immaculately dressed with the swastika prominent—introduced himself. 'Good afternoon. My name is Lieutenant Tobias Schmitt. Could I have your papers, please.'

The farming couple looked very worried. They didn't have proper identity documents, apart from the farm deeds and birth and marriage certificates. Uncle Albert should have requested documents through the local registrar in Lichfield, but hadn't got around to it. The local police, as required from the beginning of the war, should have insisted all people in the area acquire their documents. But in this case, they hadn't bothered, as this farmer was well known to them and never left the area. He was also a devout Christian and churchgoer.

'Well, sir,' said Tobias Schmitt, 'as you haven't got your proper identity documents, can I please look at your birth certificates?'

Luckily they had these. He wasn't too hard on them, seeing they were upset. He checked for Jewish-sounding names and found no problems.

'Please make sure you get this sorted out as soon as possible. The village police will have to explain why they haven't confirmed your identification. They may be in more trouble than you for their lapse. You must get these papers, as I will be visiting again soon.'

'Here are my papers,' Irene said, handing them to the lieutenant.

'Thank you.' He examined the papers quickly. He had been doing this for a few weeks already and knew what to look for—gun licenses and driving licenses, for example.

'I see you have a heavy lorry driving license. Interesting,' he said. Coming closer to Irene, he could see she was a fine-looking woman, although her clothes were a bit dirty. 'Is there anyone else on the farm or that you know of in the area?'

'We had a few people traveling through a week or so ago, but haven't seen anyone lately,' the farmer said.

'Who were they?'

The farmer didn't want to answer.

The lieutenant said, 'It will be very hard for you if you don't cooperate.'

Eventually, the farmer said in a faltering voice, 'The men asked for help because they did not want to be rounded up for the labour camps.'

'Did you give them help?'

'I gave them something to eat and said I couldn't give them any help, as I would get into trouble.'

'How many were there?'

The First EU

'Four. They left on bicycles along the road you came in from.'

'Did you report this to the police?'

'No. I haven't a telephone, and the station is three miles away.'

'That's no excuse. You have a lorry and could have driven there.' But the lieutenant was becoming calmer. He realised there was nothing he could do if the incident happened a week ago. Plenty of men were trying to escape the round-ups; his unit had already found dozens of them. He instructed his men to have a quick check around the farm.

Addressing the farmer's wife, Schmitt asked, 'Could you please prepare a meal for my men?'

'Right away. It will take about twenty minutes. Irene, please bring two dozen eggs from the chicken shed and some potatoes and onions from the outbuilding. I will get the bread and cheese from the pantry.'

In no time at all, the smell of frying onions brought the rest of the group back to the house with nothing to report. Seven plates were filled, with a mug of farm-made cider at each. The men were most appreciative of this wholesome feast, as they had been living on army rations for nearly four months since their deployment in southern Ireland.

With no more problems to discuss, the talk around the dinner table became more relaxed. The other English speaker started to chat. Dieter was a young, fair-haired, sharp-featured man. He had an obvious interest in Irene, who had just had a quick wash and brush-up.

'Are there any social activities around here?' Dieter asked her. 'Is there a local dance?'

'There used to be a dance in the church hall,' Irene said, 'but that has stopped since the surrender.'

'Can it be started up again?'

'There aren't enough men. The ones who went to the army won't be coming back. They've gone straight to the labour camps.'

'Well, that's unfortunate, but there are seven men here. And we could get more. Do you think you could organise something?'

'I'll ask the vicar's wife. It's not something I could organise myself. These are difficult times.'

'Yes, I understand.'

'Look, men, we have other places to visit and time is running,' the lieutenant intervened. 'Finish your food. We must be going.'

Turning to the farmer, Schmitt added, 'Thank you for the meal. It was much appreciated. Please sort out your identity documents. I will be speaking with the local police, and I expect you to have all in order when I call again in two weeks.'

Dieter whispered to Irene, 'Could you please leave a message at the local police station about the dance?'

'Yes, I'll try.' Irene said.

He walked to the armoured car with the rest of his unit. The lieutenant was writing in his notebook as they disappeared down the road.

Getting involved with the dance was the last thing Irene wanted to do, but maybe the vicar's wife would take the lead. The vicar's wife was an educated, good-looking lady with two school-age children.

The German patrol had been on the farm for only an hour and a half, but for Molly and Tim, it seemed like a

The First EU

lifetime. Luckily, they hadn't suffered any coughs or sneezes. They had heard some of what was said downstairs.

There was a lack of food due to the Atlantic blockade, and most farms had been commandeered by the government. But Dale Farm hadn't been bothered because of its remoteness and size. A variety farm of ninety acres, it was just large enough to support its occupant's family. Uncle Albert sold some crops and eggs for cash at the local market, and he raised a few animals for their own needs: three plough horses, a bull, a few cows, and some pigs and goats. Of their two sons, one had been killed in the evacuation of the British Army from Dunkirk, and the other who was deployed in the Persian Gulf hadn't been heard from since the fighting there with Rommel's Army the year before. This was very sad for them, but having strong faith, they took it all in their stride.

Irene had been a blessing for Albert and May after the loss of their sons. She was honest and hard-working, and had some prior farming knowledge from her childhood summer holidays with her auntie and uncle on their farm in Kent. She was particularly good with the plough horses. Irene had also been a big help with the three evacuated children who had been on the farm at the beginning of the war.

Since the occupation, things were changing. The Germans had known of the food shortages in the United Kingdom. They should have, as they had been responsible for them. They had drawn up plans before the invasion to improve efficiency on all farms in the United Kingdom, no matter what size. It was this that Lieutenant Schmitt had been making notes on. Dale Farm, he thought, was inefficiently run, although he could see they were making an effort with the planting of the apple trees at the back.

Chapter 13

FLORENCE SPOTS DAVE

Tim and Molly were still safe, although a bit shaken by the visit of the German armoured car patrol. Tim's former co-worker, Dave, was in a more precarious situation. The police had apprehended him at a relative's home near Newcastle—and then encouraged him to flee.

He made his way into southern Scotland, sleeping in a barn on the outskirts of a village. It was late summer and still not too cold. The terrain was far sparser than in the Midlands, where Dave had lived and never been outside of. The rolling hills were devoid of trees.

He'd noted there was a small pub in the village. Making sure he was not observed, he made his way to the road and then on to the pub. The door to the saloon was open. There was no one in this cosy, carpeted room with plush chairs scattered around. He was feeling rather hungry, so he called out, 'Hi, barman, could I get something to eat and drink?'

The First EU

Someone appeared from the back. 'We don't open until ten o'clock. But you can sit here until then. I'll tell you what we have.'

Before he could start, Dave waved his words off. 'I'll have a ploughman's and a pint of beer.'

'It will be ready at ten.'

While he waited, Dave thought about the story he would be asked for. He was on his way to Glasgow, where he had been offered a job in a shipyard as a draughtsman. As he didn't have much money, he was travelling by road and hitching lifts from place to place. He stayed away from the main routes, where the Germans were checking everyone and rounding up men for the slave labour camps.

There were no round-ups by the occupiers in these remote areas. There were only a few farmhands around, and they were needed on the farms. In this village, they had only seen three German patrols in the month since the surrender. The patrols were just checking papers and looking for Jewish surnames, with no success.

Unbeknown to Dave, another occupant recognised him. Florence slipped him a note, making sure no one saw. It said, *Don't say anything, Dave. This is Florence Handle. Come to the bar when you have finished. Make out you are chatting me up. I need to know about Tim. You don't know me, remember.*

Dave was so surprised, he couldn't wait to finish his food and get to the bar. Florence was a slim brunette of an age when everyone looks good, but she was particularly radiant lately because of her early pregnancy. Dave was twenty-six, fit, and slightly taller than Tim. They had both been in the same street-fighting club back in Coventry.

When Dave appeared at the bar, Florence was sitting with two young men. 'Could I have another beer, please, barman?' Dave asked.

'Coming up,' said the barman. 'You're not from around here, then.'

'No. I'm on my way to Glasgow to take up a new job. Because I've got no money, I'm travelling by road and thumb.'

Florence, listening, knew this wasn't true.

'You have to be careful now on the main routes,' the barman warned. 'The Germans have got those all staked out. I hope your papers are in order.'

'Oh, of course.'

Florence interrupted, 'You from down south, then? It sounds like you are.'

'Yes. I was working in Coventry. Before the surrender, I organised this job, because it was a strategic position and they said I would still be needed.'

'I used to know someone in Coventry called Tim Handle,' said Florence.

'It's a big city.'

There was a short silence. Then Dave said, 'What brings you to these parts? Your accent doesn't fit in here either.'

The two men with her looked up. She excused herself to the ladies' toilet without saying anything. On her return, she passed Dave another note. It read, *I know you must be in trouble. Meet me in the bar at six tonight. Don't ask me any more questions now.*

Tim and Molly had arrived at Dale Farm two weeks after the surrender. Before he went into hiding, Tim had told Florence she must go to live in Scotland as soon as possible. Doing so would be less stress for her pregnancy than living in London. Because of the surrender, British munitions were not required. There had been no problem with Florence leaving her job and travelling to her relatives in Scotland.

Tim and Florence had a secure telephone link through friends. They had set the same time every night for discussions if required. They kept their calls to a minimum, but all was sorted out in those calls. She knew Tim was going to be out of more regular contact for a while.

Chapter 14

FLORENCE IN SCOTLAND

On the same day as Lieutenant Schmitt's visit to Dale Farm, Dave was waiting at six o'clock, as requested by Florence, in the saloon bar of the small village pub.

Florence had arrived by train two weeks before, and the two young farmer relatives of hers had welcomed her. They had fought with the British army briefly in Scotland after the German invasion. They were savvy enough not to fight to the end, but had escaped to their farm just before the final surrender. They were not average farmer's sons; they had been educated at private schools and then university until interrupted by the war.

They were determined to keep up resistance after the occupation and knew many people who were like-minded. They understood exactly what the situation was regarding Tim and Florence. The first thing they did for Florence was change her identity documents. Having contacts in the council offices at Dumfries, they got different details and local stamps on her new identity documents as Mrs Florence Randall.

They had also helped her to concoct a plausible personal history. Her new story was that she had lived with her husband near London, but he had been drafted into the army six months previously. She fell pregnant while he was on weekend leave two months before. They decided to get her away from the chaos of London, to friends on this remote farm. As she had been born in the area, her documents had the local stamps on. The 'friends' on the farm were actually her cousins, their mother being Florence's Auntie Joyce.

From there she had no need to lie; her actual experience could be used. Things had taken a dramatic turn with the final surrender, meaning travel was difficult. She had just managed to get on one of the final trains to Scotland not controlled by the SS. She used her good looks, charm, and some extra cash to get a ticket. She hadn't heard from her husband since the final surrender.

Florence explained to her cousins about Dave, whom she knew as a good friend and colleague of Tim's from her visits to Coventry. She hadn't seen Dave for a while as Tim had usually gone south to visit her. Of course, this was because he had taken up with Molly.

'Dave and Tim were key workers at the development centre,' she said to Andy, the oldest of the two farm brothers. 'A few of them wanted to join the resistance, Tim and Dave among them.'

'We will help anyone who wants to join the resistance. The main thing is trust. It's a matter of life and death. The problem is he has been seen in the village now, and his story was that he was on his way to take up a new job. So if we take him in, he must stay out of the village for a while. After that we could say that the job in Glasgow didn't materialise, or he nearly got rounded up and decided to return here.'

'All right. I will slip him a note in the bar tonight.'

'He must make his own way to the Dumfries train station. We will clandestinely pick him up and take him back to the farm. He must sleep in one of the outbuildings and lie low until we decide how we can use him in the resistance. I will go to the bar with you tonight, and we will talk freely with him about his plans to move on to Glasgow You will hand him your note. The note will instruct him to stay in the village tonight, as it's getting late. Tomorrow afternoon we will pick him up under the oak tree in River Street, three hundred yards from the train station, at two o'clock.'

'That seems well thought out,' said Florence.

'With Dave's education and combat training, he could be useful to us—as could your husband.'

Dave was in the bar as arranged and everything went to plan. He stayed in the inn that night and was picked up at the agreed place the following day. The pickup point was secluded, but the drive back to the farm was a nerve-wracking business. Andy was relieved when he and Dave reached the farm. Dave stayed out of view in the rear of the lorry under various bits of farm rubbish for the whole journey.

On the farm, with open fields and hills around, they could see and hear any approaching vehicles for miles. There was only the family living at the farm just then—Andy, his younger brother John, their mother Joyce, and Florence. Sometimes there were other workers on site at harvest time, but this had just passed. Andy was glad of this; he didn't want to broadcast to the world that he had a new lodger.

Florence's mother had come from a large family in the slums of Glasgow: six sisters and four brothers. She had run away to London at the end of the First World War and luckily had got work and met a young engineering draughtsman. They were married, and their first and only child had been Florence.

All the Glasgow sisters had been good-looking. Joyce had met a lucky farmer who survived the First World War completely unscathed. Their two sons, Andy and John, were now aged twenty-three and twenty-one respectively.

The brothers didn't have girlfriends at this time and didn't seem that worried about it. Unfortunately, their father had been killed in a farming accident. He was run over by his own tractor and pinned to the ground while it was still driving. There had been no one around to intervene right away. He was later found barely alive and survived for three days in hospital.

His sons had received special dispensation from the army to work on the farm over the harvest time. The farm had over nine hundred acres of common oats under cultivation. This made it a target under martial law, but with the two sons doing so well, it was left alone. The only stipulation was the harvest had to be sold to the government at a price determined by them. The harvest had been sold before the armistice in July, and the two young owners were drafted back to their company.

Chapter 15

OFFICER BROTHERS

After the invasion on 24 July, the fighting had been fierce. It was Andy and John's responsibility to make the roads clear for the British army's heavy armour, including tanks, to get to where it was needed.

The Germans were establishing landing areas far inland on flat land, though not necessarily proper runways, where their new heavy-lift planes could touch down. These planes had been fitted with special landing equipment for rough terrain and had short landing and take-off capabilities. One such area was quickly identified in western Scotland.

The Germans had a head start because of their immediate betrayal of the cease-fire and surrender agreement. The first task for the Germans was to knock out the RAF. In this, there was initial success, with fifty per cent of the planes destroyed on the ground. The ones that managed to take off put up a courageous fight, but further losses were incurred. The RAF shot down as many as they lost, but the destruction of their airbases was a major factor, hindering their turn-around time for getting the fighters back up into combat again. The fighting was relentless. Planes flew from all parts of Britain to the combat areas. The airbases in the east of the country were the least affected by the initial attacks. But fighting planes from those bases had a long way to fly.

The brothers' division was attacked relentlessly by the Luftwaffe. By the third day, there wasn't much help from the RAF. Many of their comrades were killed in the fighting. They were lucky and had new, long-range, anti-aircraft guns fitted to five heavy armoured cars. The brothers both commanded one of these vehicles. The division had been practising with the guns over the previous weeks. The five guns accounted for twenty-nine Luftwaffe planes, including two heavy transport aircraft. The Germans quickly got the message and kept away from these vehicles. That was probably why the brothers had survived the fighting.

At night they did engineering work, making roads for the heavy armour, filling in bomb craters, erecting makeshift bridges, knocking down stone walls, and so on.

The Germans landed a few dozen tanks within the first week. These were the latest development in tank design, and they completely outgunned and outmanoeuvred the British tanks. It was no exaggeration to say that each of these newly designed German machines could account for many of their enemy's tanks. By the end of the first week, things were going badly for the British, with great losses in men and equipment. This is when an unconditional surrender came under consideration.

SS units spearheaded the invasion. Regular German troops and other European nations' troops came in later and didn't have much fighting to do. The farming brother officers, realising what was going on, stopped fighting. Well before the final surrender announcement, they made their way back to the farm, using various diversions to avoid German and British army patrols.

Some British fought on, but it was a lost cause. Many were needlessly sacrificed. The major fighting was all over in seven days—in Scotland, anyway—and the brothers were back on the farm in ten days.

By the time Florence arrived at Dumfries train station, Andy and John had been back from the fighting for six weeks. By the time the chance meeting with Dave took place, Florence had been with the brothers for two weeks. She was well established with a story and ID documents. That was good enough for the Germans. Only if there was some suspicion would a detailed investigation be made.

Chapter 16

DAVE ON THE OAT FARM

The lorry, with Dave covered up in the back, came to a noisy halt in front of the main farmhouse on the Oat Farm.

'Hello, Andy!' shouted his relieved mother, Auntie Joyce. 'Were there any problems on the road?'

'There were roadblocks around Dumfries. I was very worried with Dave in the back. I managed to drive around them, and there wasn't any on the road here. If there had been, it would have been difficult. In fact, I will not make a pickup like this again. I will do it some other way.'

Turning to his passenger, Andy said, 'Well now, Dave, there is no one on the farm who doesn't know what we are about, so we must have a long chat regarding where to go from here. If anyone comes round—even locals, and of course German patrols—we must keep you completely hidden. There have been reports of farms being checked for papers and the like. I expect a visit soon.'

'OK. The first thing I need to know is where I can hide if they do visit.'

'You are right. We have a well at the back of the house which is not used now. It still has water in. Eight feet down, there is a recess in the side wall, with a concrete cover that hooks in place. There is plenty of room in there to stay for a day or so, but you won't be able to stand up. Since I've been on the farm, this recess has never been covered by the well water. We'll show you now. You must be able to get in there in a few seconds, so you had better get some practise.'

Dave was shown the rope and how to get down to the recess and close the cover. It wasn't a problem for a fit, slim young man like him, but he did practise it a few times. He made up a little sack of food and other things, ready for a few days' stay at all times.

Life on the Oat Farm was quiet. No German patrols were reported in the area. There was time to talk. Dave knew that Tim had taken up with Molly and that she had gone into hiding with him. Of course, Florence knew nothing and was forever asking about Tim.

Soon after he arrived, the brothers approached Dave. 'We need to get a foolproof identity document for you to stay on the farm,' Andy said. 'It's a pity Florence is married to Tim, as the easiest way to get a good identity for you is to make you Florence's husband who has come up to join her and help on the farm.'

'Look, guys, I must tell you Tim has been having an affair with a beautiful young girl called Molly. He has actually gone into hiding with her. I'm sick of listening to Florence harping on about Tim as though he were some kind of saint, asking all sorts of questions which I have to mislead her about. I would love to become Florence's husband on paper—and in reality. I'm falling for her, to be quite frank.'

The First EU

Florence had been radiant lately, which made Dave mad with desire for her. He didn't mind that she was pregnant. Dave hadn't been with many girls in his life. As a bit of a workaholic, he normally put his work before social life and girlfriends. His easy conversations with Florence were affecting him. Florence was besotted with her husband and talked about him all the time, looking for any snippet of news. None was forthcoming.

The brothers were getting a bit worried about Dave. Either he could stay on the farm and join their resistance group, or he must go. They could not take any risks. To stay on the farm, he must have his identity documents.

Tim was not their blood relation, and they had no particular affection for him. They thought he was a bit of a ladies' man and were not happy about him having done no fighting in the war, even though they knew he had been working on the same secret project as Dave.

'Look, Dave, you must approach Florence about our suggestion,' said Andy the following morning. 'We will tell her also. Whether you want to have a normal marital relationship, we are not interested. That is your business. If she agrees to the public side of the matter, it will be more security for her. If not, you will have to go.'

After the brothers put their ultimatum, Dave had a word with Florence. 'I've been speaking to Andy and John, and they suggest my documents say that I'm your husband, Mr Randall. What do you say?'

'How could I agree to that when I'm married to Tim?'

'The problem is we don't know where Tim is, and unless I can get a good cover story for being here, Andy and John say it will be too risky for them. I'll have to leave and find somewhere else to stay.'

'Well, what happens when Tim gets here?'

'I understand, but these are difficult and dangerous times. It's been three weeks already and Tim hasn't made contact.'

'I was hoping Tim would leave Molly and come back to me for the baby.'

'You know about Molly then?'

'I've known for ages. Why shouldn't I? Everyone else knows,' she lamented.

'Yeah, I knew. I told Andy and John. They were not at all happy.'

'Tim is in hiding and is wanted by the Gestapo!' she wailed. 'And we have a baby coming along.'

'I will take care of you and the baby.'

'Thank you, but I want my Tim back. I appreciate your concern. I know Tim will try and join me on the farm; he said so in our last phone conversation. Why do you look at me like that, Dave?'

'Tim went into hiding with Molly.'

'I don't believe you!' Florence rushed, crying, to her room.

This tearful evening put paid to any further talk of Dave being the paper husband of Florence. They heard nothing from Tim. Then, two days later, Auntie Joyce had a word. That evening, Florence said to Dave, 'All right. You can be my paper husband.'

Andy and John were delighted. They didn't want to lose Dave after getting to know him, and had been working on the documents already with their contact in the council offices. Within two days, Dave had the documents and had registered at the local police station. Now Dave and Florence were Mr and Mrs Randall. Their story was the normal one of a husband travelling to be with his wife, especially as she was expecting their first baby.

Two days later, a patrol came to the farm. The German in charge could see everything was well run and that the operation needed all the men it had. There was no problem with their stories either. Dave was sleeping in the hall, but his bedding was cleared away in the daytime. Florence was sleeping in a double bed.

John had started going with a young girl from the village whose boyfriend had been rounded up a couple of weeks before. Andy was visited by a girl he'd known at university. She seemed to stay over, and no one worried—it was the times.

Although the farmhouse was a large building by Scottish standards, now there were three couples there plus Auntie Joyce. There were only four large bedrooms, which was why Dave slept in the hallway. This was quite inconvenient. His housemates gently suggested that he and Florence share one room. This was not what Florence wanted, but she agreed, with the condition that there be no bodily contact or nakedness.

This was an impossible situation for Dave. He desired Florence too much. He could not share the room with her under those conditions. He decided to sleep in one of the outbuildings. That would be all right for another couple of weeks, though not so good when the cold weather started.

Florence knew Dave desired her very much. She didn't encourage it, though she was grateful for his company, still not knowing what was going on with Tim. Tim was much better looking she thought. But through their friendly conversations, she started to warm to Dave. She knew they would not be able to share a bedroom without becoming intimate.

The day came when she said, 'Dave, why don't you sleep inside tonight? it's getting cold outside.'

It was indeed getting colder, so he came in. 'I'll make a bed on the couch for you,' Florence offered. She didn't mention anything about bodily contact or nakedness this time.

'Thank you,' Dave said, not looking at her directly.

'Look at me. Just give me the time. I'm still in love with Tim.'

'Good night, Florence.'

Chapter 17

PROMISE OF A DANCE

Down south on Dale Farm, everything changed after the patrol made their visit. The farm household was on tenterhooks as to when the patrol would return. And after the night of passion between Tim and Irene, things changed for the younger occupants even more.

Molly had an idea that something had happened. Irene was really in love with Tim, although she tried to hide it. It was pretty obvious when they were working together or just in the vicinity of one another. Molly was also in love with him, but Irene's love was more mature love. Molly didn't know what to do about her dilemma. She was also quietly panic-stricken about the Germans and their possible return.

Irene had promised the German second in command, Dieter, that she would inquire about holding a dance. She had to drive to the village to pick up identity applications for the farmer and his wife. These had to be completed, signed, and returned to the police station to be sent away. Tim had asked her to phone his wife's cousins in Scotland, and of course she had to contact the vicar's wife about organising the dance.

Molly had heard about the dance and was interested. Although she hadn't seen the Germans, hearing their conversation, thought the second in command might be nice. She was unhappy at the farm not being able to be with Tim so often. He was still talking about his wife and now there was this new suspicion with Irene which made her very unsure of things. The idea of becoming a resistance fighter was wearing a bit thin.

She thought of going to the dance, her story would be, she had run away from work being worried about the SS taking over. This would be alright with her current ID and home address at her parents. Tim was in a different position; he was definitely high on the Gestapo wanted list.

Irene went to the post office to make the long-distance call and was pulled aside by the clerk. The clerk told her calls were being intercepted and listened to. So she thought she had better talk to Tim before doing any more.

She went on to see the vicar's wife, whom she knew from attending church with the farmhand Sam. Sally was a flirty thirty-year-old, much younger than her vicar husband.

'Hi, Sally. I've been approached by a member of the patrol that attended the farm a few days ago. He wants to know if a dance can be organised that the German young men can attend.'

'My, that's not going to be easy, Irene, I've seen these Germans around. Some of them are quite dishy. But with all that's going on at the moment, I can't see how we can mix the German and English men. It would be unfair. There are so few British men here now, what with the call-up and the labour camps. We only have farm workers. On the other hand, there are plenty of women.'

'I must leave a message at the police station for Dieter.'

'Oh, on first-name terms, then, are we?'

'Well, I don't know his surname. We gave his patrol a meal at the farm. There were seven of them. Dieter is tall and has pointy features, but the lieutenant, Tobias Schmitt, is quite dishy, well-proportioned, and good-looking.' Irene thought that description may interest Sally.

'That's it, then. Leave a message at the police station. I will deal with the lieutenant, on behalf of his men and Dieter. We can't be too hard on them. They are only doing their job and have been on a charm offensive around here. I will speak with my husband Ray. We should be able to arrange something in the church hall.'

Chapter 18

SALLY AND THE LIEUTENANT

Sally wondered if she had bitten off more than she could chew by offering to hold a dance for the German occupiers and the local women. The national news was terrible. But the Germans in the local area had been very polite and helpful, and in the long term, after this terrible time, better things must come along one day. People would have to get along.

She had always been the master in her relationship with her husband, but she thought this may be a bit too much for him to stomach. Still, it was done now. She would tell him and looked forward with curiosity to her meeting with the German lieutenant.

Sally was a vivacious woman with an average build and a cheeky personality. There was speculation that she indulged in the odd affair, but no proof. Her husband was nineteen years older than her and rather overweight.

It didn't take long for the lieutenant to receive her message and attend the vicarage. Just after school, there was a knock on the door. Lieutenant Schmitt was standing there.

'Hello, Mrs Sally. I'm sorry I don't know your surname. My name is Lieutenant Schmitt, and I have a message to speak with you about the possibility of a dance being arranged for my men in the village.'

'Yes, please come in. My husband is on his rounds at the moment, but we can talk in the lounge. My name is Sally Cooper.'

Her two daughters, aged ten and twelve, were mesmerised by this handsome soldier in his smart uniform.

'So my second in the troop, Dieter Vollmar spoke with Miss Irene. She said she would inquire, and here I am. Mrs Cooper, I hope you can organise something.'

'Well, you must realise these are difficult times for our country. The news is always very grave. It's difficult to get some cheer into people. But I must say the German soldiers in this area have been most polite and helpful. To continue the good relations, we—my husband and I—have decided to give you a dance in the church hall this Saturday night. Just your troop of seven, I was told. There may be some farm lads too, and of course the local girls. You know Irene already. She should be attending, and I will be there. Because of the war, there are more young ladies than men in the village at the moment, so I expect several of them to turn up. You should have a good time. I'm not going to say that many will attend; people must make their own minds up.

'So it's Monday today. We will see you on Saturday with your patrol. The start time will be seven o'clock. There will be no alcohol sold or allowed, and it will end at midnight. The music will be by a record player with an amplifier and loudspeakers. If your men have any records, please bring them along.'

'That sounds great,' said the lieutenant. 'Thank you, Mrs Cooper. I anticipate an enjoyable evening. I trust we can persuade some local people to attend.'

'I'll do my best, Lieutenant. I will certainly be there.' She gave him a coy, intimate look, which he recognised but didn't respond to.

'Thank you again. I look forward to seeing you Saturday. I must get on.' Standing up to go, he bent over and kissed her hand.

'How do I contact you?' asked Sally.

'Leave a message at the police station; I will have it checked twice a day.'

The two young girls were still mesmerised as he walked out the door—as was Sally, in a different way.

After the handsome German left, Sally was determined to make this dance a success. It was possibly the first time in the country that the despised occupiers would be welcomed as friends to a social event. Considering the desperate situation the country was in, what else could the local population do? There was no point in fighting any more. To show some warmth and friendship to them must be worthy. This would take a lot of courage, but she knew it was right.

Chapter 19

PROBLEMS WITH THE MUSIC

She quickly called a meeting of the church committee and told them what she had done. They were horrified and asked her why she had gone ahead without asking them. She said that the vicar had agreed. They just looked at one another; they all knew the vicar did anything his wife wanted.

Duncan, the man who operated the record player and speakers, said, 'I'm not interested in helping with this ridiculous venture. I'm going home. Good night to you all.' Then he walked out of the meeting.

So this was the first problem. The other person who knew how to operate the sound equipment had been drafted to the army, and nothing had been heard of him since.

Sally got a better response from the other members of the committee, who agreed that in these terrible times, it would be better to be friendly with the Germans than hostile.

Word was put around and notices put up. The committee met again the following day. There was an excited sense they were doing something really good and special. Sally was surprised when the members reported there had been a lot of interest, especially from the ladies of the village. The village was quite large, with over two thousand inhabitants. Dozens of people were interested in attending, but still there was no one who could operate the record player. It was a bit temperamental, and no one wanted to interfere with Duncan's wires and settings.

Duncan was adamant that he was not going to help. Sally had a brainwave and left a message for the lieutenant that they needed someone to operate the record player. He called at the vicarage within a few hours. She opened the door.

'Hello, Mrs Cooper. I have a man who should be able to operate the record player. He can attend tonight with Dieter Vollmar, my second in command. The music man doesn't speak much English.'

'Fine, that sounds great.'

'Who do they have to report to?'

'That sounds very official,' said Sally, smiling at him.

He looked slightly embarrassed. 'Sorry for sounding too official.'

'I'm only joking,' she reassured him. 'They can call at the vicarage. What time will they be here?'

'At seven o'clock, after we have finished our work for the day.'

'Great.' They concluded, the lieutenant still looking a bit sheepish.

The two soldiers duly called at the house and were taken to the church hall close by. Dieter and the technician soon got the sound system working—they didn't worry about upsetting Duncan as the village people would have. The wires and settings were a bit mixed up, they found. After sorting the connections out, they tested the system with a few of the latest jazz recordings, played quite loudly. Some in the village heard this, including Duncan. He rushed over and was completely surprised when he saw the Germans. He said nothing, walking out with a frown on his face.

'Mrs Sally, why does that man look so annoyed?' asked Dieter.

'Don't worry. You are working for me.'

'All right, then.' Dieter knew that some people would be against the dance, but he hoped it would go ahead.

'Thank you, Dieter. I'm so happy now that you have fixed the music system. Will you boys be able to play the music on Saturday?'

'Of course, Mrs Sally. We will be here half an hour before the start.'

'Great.'

Now just for the people, thought Sally.

The lieutenant asked Dieter and the music man to check everything was all right at midday on Saturday, just to make sure nothing had been sabotaged.

Chapter 20

MOLLY'S GETAWAY

Molly wasn't happy about the fact that she hadn't been able to engage in her regular erotic coupling with Tim since the planting began. After the visit of the German army patrol, she realised just how precarious their situation was. A few days before the dance, Molly decided she wanted to go back to her parents. She said, 'Irene, I'm so worried about everything, what with the Germans calling here last week. Although I love Tim and will miss him so much, I want to return home to my parents. Can you help me?'

'I can help you, but it's not going to be easy. We must plan it. I can't run you back until next week at the earliest because of the dance. Then I must get an extra ration of petrol and will have to ask the farmer about that. I will ask the vicar's wife if she can help. The main thing is we mustn't put Tim in danger.'

'You love him, don't you, Irene?'

Irene said nothing, and that said it all.

A tear came to Molly's eye, and she said, 'I will do anything for Tim.'

Irene thought that if she could get Molly, who was very attractive, off with one of the Germans, it would protect Molly in case she had some difficult questions to answer on her return home. The Gestapo probably knew Tim and Molly had run away together and would interrogate her about Tim's whereabouts. The first German she thought of for Molly was Dieter, whom she wanted to deflect away from herself.

'I think it would be a good idea if you went to the dance on Saturday,' Irene said. 'We can find you a place to stay in the village, maybe even with the vicar and his wife, until we can get you back home.'

'All right,' said Molly. 'I don't have much choice, do I?'

'Not really. You can come with me to the dance.'

'Fine, Saturday,' Molly said with tears in her eyes. 'I don't know how I'm going to live without Tim.'

Tim was a bystander in all this. Molly had made the decision. Tim was sad, but he understood. He knew his hiding place on the farm would only last until Molly was questioned. He had completed his first mission of withdrawing himself from his critical work at the research centre. Now he wanted to get moving, join his wife, and find some resistance fighters. It was better that he travelled on his own from now.

Molly joined Tim in his attic room for the last two nights, and the farmer and his wife said nothing. Irene wasn't happy about this, but what could she do? Molly and Tim had been together for over a year.

Alan J Caulfield

Irene and Tim made sure Molly didn't know where Dale Farm was. The less she knew, the better. She knew the name of course.

On Saturday before noon, after thanking Albert Black and his wife, Molly said her tearful farewell to Tim. 'I will always love you, Tim. Come for me. I will wait.' Then she climbed in the back of the lorry with all her possessions, covered herself with a blanket, and was gone.

Irene drove the lorry straight to the back of the vicarage. Irene had talked to Sally a few days before and knew they were desperate for young ladies to attend the dance.

'Sally, I have a young lady here who was on her way to Uttoxeter and got on the wrong bus. I picked her up at the western junction. I told her about the dance, and she is interested in attending. Is it possible she can stay here? She said she has plenty of money.'

'The only spare room we have is the one reserved for you. It has two beds, if that's fine by you. I will have to have a look at her first; do you know anything about her?'

'Not really, but she showed me her papers. They look all right. Her name is Molly. She's good-looking although a bit dirty.'

'It should be all right. Bring her in.'

Irene led Molly into the vicarage. Sally looked her over. 'Hello, Molly. My name is Sally. I hear you're interested in the dance tonight. Have you got good clothes?'

'Yes, they're in my travelling bag.'

'Good. You will have to share a room with Irene. The cost includes a meal, which will be served at six thirty. I'll show you up.' Molly, still a little upset, followed Sally up the stairs. 'You can pay tonight at mealtime.'

'Thank you, Miss Sally. Thank you, Irene, for giving me a lift.'

'No problem. I'll see you in the room later. See you later, Sally.'

'See you, Irene.'

Molly knew she had to attend the dance. She was slightly interested in Dieter, whom she had overheard from her attic hideaway. The bedroom she was given had a bath and toilet. The vicarage had three guest rooms like this.

It was only midday, and Irene had some things to do for the farmer and his wife: deliver their identity document applications to the police station, get some petrol coupons, and deliver twelve dozen eggs to the egg board. She was finished with the errands before two, and then Irene went back to the vicarage. She wanted to get cleaned up and rested before the dance.

Although Irene wanted to get back to Tim as soon as she could, she had booked a stay in the vicarage for Saturday night. It ensured Molly had somewhere to stay, as the rooms were large enough to take two. And it would save Irene driving back along the dark, winding road in the early hours of the morning. The lorry's lights were not the best. Irene also wanted to make sure Molly didn't do anything to harm Tim.

Irene knocked on the room door and entered. She could see Molly wasn't happy to share the room, especially in her sadness after leaving Tim, but she had no choice. There was no other accommodation.

'Hi, Molly. If you've had a bath, I will have one now and then a little rest before the dance. Luckily there are two separate beds. I think the other rooms only have one large bed.'

Molly rested while Irene had her bath. They were two women who loved the same man. One was built for comfort and the other for speed, you might say. Irene could see Molly was a most beautiful woman with a full body, large bosom, and a shapely bottom and legs. She had a pretty face with blue eyes and natural blonde hair. She was slightly taller than Irene and would definitely turn heads at the dance.

After half an hour, Irene finished her bath and went into the room, where she was assessed in turn by Molly. Irene had a slightly hard but pretty face with an old scar on her left cheek. Although slim, she had shapely legs and firm, small breasts. Her hair was reddish brown. At twenty-six, she was seven years older than Molly.

They didn't talk much, preoccupied with their own worries and thoughts. They made themselves look as good as they could with a wartime ration of makeup. Each wondered what the dance would bring.

Irene wanted to get back to Tim, but she knew this could only happen tomorrow. The main thing was to stop Molly doing anything that would give his hiding place away. Irene knew Tim would be leaving soon and wondered what she would do then. She loved him.

Chapter 21

THE MIXED DANCE

When Sally became aware of the interest from the local ladies regarding the dance, she contacted the lieutenant again and said he could bring more men as long as there were some English speakers. The hall could hold two hundred, with space for tables for tea and cakes around the sides and a stage where the music would be played from. In a large alcove near the door, the music wasn't so loud.

Dieter and the music man contacted Sally at midday on Saturday, as instructed by the lieutenant, to check the equipment. They returned at six thirty and quickly tested the system for a final time with their own records. There was a large collection of records already in the hall, but a lot of them were rather dated. Sally had advised the Germans and the locals to bring their own records and mark them with their names, to avoid any mix-ups.

There was no entry fee for this first mixed dance. It was seen as an experimental goodwill affair. If it became a regular event, as Sally hoped it would, then charges would be made so the church didn't have to cover the costs.

Right on time at seven o'clock, the Germans arrived: eighteen in all, the lieutenant's platoon plus a selection of other men, most of whom could speak a bit of English. The lieutenant had deliberately kept the event quiet as he didn't want any SS or Gestapo men attending. He had also told all his men that this was a privilege. They should be on their best behaviour and not be provoked whatsoever by the local men or women. He would not allow any drinking beforehand or in the hall. Even so, some soldiers brought concealed hip flasks, and some had a drink prior. Sally had also put it out that to the locals that they should not drink beforehand or take drink into the hall. One or two were seen in the local bar, but in general, her warning was adhered to.

Both Sally and the lieutenant knew this was something special they were organising: perhaps the first time cross-cultural social event since the invasion. It was intended to promote goodwill, and it gave them a sense of excitement.

The previous day, they had discussed various scenarios and knew things could be difficult. Sally had suggested that they employ four local men as bouncers to counter any drunkenness and unruly behaviour on both sides. These bouncers would have the last say. All big local lads, they had often been bouncers at similar events. The lieutenant agreed and told his men the story. No weapons were allowed in the hall, which went without saying, but Sally did remind the lieutenant.

The two armoured cars that transported the German soldiers parked at the back of the vicarage, out of sight, and two men were left on guard duty there. The rest, leaving their rifles and revolvers behind in the vehicles, proceeded to the church hall. They had pulled lots to establish the rota of guard duty, covering one-hour shifts for this purpose over their five-hour stay. One of the two on guard duty always had to be an English speaker.

Alongside the four bouncers, the Germans were the first to arrive. As was normal, the locals drifted in from about seven thirty. The lieutenant had begun to worry that the dance would be boycotted by the time Sally, Irene, Molly, and two sisters and a friend who were in the church choir arrived. No local people had arrived before them. Sally was accompanied by her husband the vicar, whom Sally introduced.

'Good evening,' the lieutenant said.

'Good evening to you, Lieutenant. I want you to enjoy the evening. This is a momentous occasion. I hope as fellow Christians, we can make it a success,' said the vicar, who couldn't have been more different from this fit, efficient, young fighting man.

Chapter 22

MOLLY HEARS THE VOICE

Molly was listening for the voice of the man who had asked Irene to arrange the dance—and then she heard it near the record player. She was stunning, although still looking a bit sad, which seemed to enhance her looks tonight. Molly made heads turn. She knew but ignored it, going straight to Dieter. 'Excuse me, have you got some good English music? I want to dance tonight.'

Dieter wasn't used to receiving direct attention from women, let alone a beauty like this, and now the attention of his comrades and the few women who had just arrived was on him. He couldn't even open his mouth to reply. Molly saw the effect she had and pulled back, but she did want to have a conversation with him. She knew his English was quite good.

Dieter was tall and lean, and had a sort of pointy-looking face. He was not that popular with the ladies and had no girlfriend at the present time. He had only been with one girl, and she had been a part-time prostitute, they said.

The First EU

Molly wanted to concentrate on him this evening because she saw no threat from him. Of course, she had seen no threat from Tim at the beginning either.

She sat down near the record player and started again. 'My name is Molly. Pleased to meet you.'

Dieter was still a bit perplexed, but finally got out, 'Oh! Hello, Molly. My name is Dieter Vollmar. I'm in Lieutenant Schmitt's platoon.'

'Do you dance, then, Dieter? I like to dance.'

If nothing else, Dieter could dance a bit, although he had only practised with the people at the dance school in Cologne. He had learned the basics to help his chances with the ladies, although it hadn't improved his quest so far. 'I can dance a bit, but I'm not very good.'

'Oh! We must have a dance later,' she said.

All eyes were on them again, and although Molly loved the attention, she could see it was making Dieter a bit hot and bothered. He couldn't understand why she was talking to him when there were many other better-looking Germans around. The attention came because Molly was so good-looking, and his platoon chums were waiting to see how he was going to handle the situation. They knew he was not that good with the ladies and a bit shy.

Molly guessed this. 'Can we just ignore the rest of the people here? I'd like to talk away from this noise.'

'Yes, that would be a good idea. But I don't know this place.'

'I don't know this hall either, but I see there is a place at the back near the entrance. Maybe we can get a drink of something there. At least we will be able to hear one another.'

So the attention went away from them for a while as they disappeared into the alcove. There were other people there, committee-member friends of Sally's, so it wasn't embarrassingly intimate, which neither Molly nor Dieter wanted. He relaxed a bit, although he still couldn't fathom why this beautiful young woman was spending time with him.

He offered, 'I'm from Cologne, in western Germany. I was drafted into the army six months ago.' He knew he mustn't talk too much about the army. 'I have no brothers, but two much older sisters. I lived with my parents until joining the army. I went to university and did a degree in English. When I left, there were no jobs for English speakers, so I trained as a mechanic and worked at that. I kept my English going by joining an English conversational group that met near the cathedral.'

'How old are you, Dieter?'

'Twenty-four.'

'Sorry. I shouldn't be so nosy.'

'Nosy? What is nosy?'

'It means I'm asking too many questions and being too inquisitive.'

'Oh, that doesn't matter.' Dieter was beginning to relax and enjoy his conversation with Molly.

'I will tell you about myself after we have a dance, but I can tell you I'm not from around here,' Molly said. They talked for a few more minutes and then moved to the edge of the dance floor.

'You are very beautiful,' Dieter said. 'My German buddies are going to be most envious when they see us dancing together.'

'Oh!' said Molly, trying to play it down. 'I'm not that good-looking.'

A good number came on. Hardly anyone had yet started dancing; the dances didn't normally come alive until nine o'clock. It was good that Dieter had practised to this number at the dancing school. It just so happened that Tim was a good dancer, and he and Molly had danced to this number also. Molly herself had had dance training before she met Tim.

'I love this number. It's a jive. Let's go!' she exclaimed.

They were a striking couple on the floor, as Dieter was an athletic six-footer. They were the first mixed couple to dance, and every eye focused on them. Dieter wasn't as good a dancer as Tim, but Molly was skilful enough to guide him, and their dance jive looked quite presentable.

Then a slow number came on. Dieter went to sit down, but Molly pulled him back. 'Don't you want to dance with me anymore?' she said, coyly smiling at him.

'Of course I do.' He was in a state of near-shock by now.

Others got up for this slow, easy dance, including some other mixed couples. So Molly and Dieter weren't the only focus of attention anymore. Their jive seemed to have got those who were holding back motivated. The lieutenant was actually dancing with Irene, and all the three choir girls had German dance partners.

Dieter and Molly had been dancing for nearly half an hour by the time they decided to take a rest. During the slow dances, Molly had been pressing herself against him when others couldn't see. She knew this would arouse him, and it did. By now Dieter had got over his embarrassment and confusion. He still couldn't believe Molly was real and not a dream.

Unfortunately, just as they sat down and started to talk again, one of his chums came up and reminded him it was his time for guard duty. 'Oh well, I will wait for you,' Molly promised.

Molly had already decided she couldn't wait for Tim. She loved him very much, but the cards were stacked against them. He was married, though he'd said he would leave his wife. Then there was Molly's suspicion that something had happened between him and Irene, who obviously loved him. Last but not least, there was the German patrol that had attended the farm. This had been the final straw. Molly had been petrified in the attic room, where she had to stay so still for what seemed like a lifetime. She had strong feelings for Tim that she knew would last forever, and she wouldn't do anything to endanger him. But now she just wanted to go back to her old life as much as possible. Maybe she would get together with him sometime in the future. In these uncertain times, that was all she could hope for.

Chapter 23

MOLLY AND DIETER

Molly had decided she needed to have someone to help her, and Dieter was an ideal candidate: an English-speaking, low-ranking soldier in the German army, stationed locally, who was rather sweet and inept with the ladies. That last point in particular could be an advantage. She had heard about some of the bad things that had been going on in the rest of the country. The people in this area had been treated well and benefited from the German charm offensive that was in general effect.

While Dieter was on duty, Molly was constantly bothered by his buddies trying their luck. They didn't think Dieter had a chance with such a beauty. She politely rejected them all, while maintaining a conversation with Sally about the local area.

The lieutenant, seeing that Molly was being bothered, came over. 'Would you like to dance? I'm Lieutenant Schmitt. You've caused quite a stir here tonight.'

'I would be pleased to,' Molly replied, and introduced herself in return.

The lieutenant, who was a confident dancer, took the lead, and they danced well to a few popular numbers. Turning heads, of course.

'I'm Dieter's senior officer,' he said. 'Are you waiting for him?'

'Yes, I am, Lieutenant.'

'Well, he should be finished with guard duty in about ten minutes. I'm sure he will be pleased to join you again. Meanwhile, I will tell my men to leave you alone if you want.'

'Well, I don't want to be rude. I don't mind dancing with one of them until Dieter returns.'

The lieutenant called over a good-looking young man and asked him if he would dance with Molly. Of course, the young man was there in an instant. 'Would you like to dance, miss?'

'Yes.'

'My name is Thomas.'

'Let's go then, Thomas.'

He was a good dancer, twenty-two and slim. They flew around the floor to some fast numbers.

Then Dieter appeared, looking rather glum when he saw Molly being propelled by Thomas. He didn't have to worry. Molly quickly returned when the next piece of music came up. She rather fancied Thomas, but was beginning to like Dieter with his awkward ways. She thought he was rather sweet. Unfortunately, Thomas didn't speak much English, and Molly had to keep her plan in focus.

She told Dieter that she had run away from Coventry three weeks before because she was afraid of the Gestapo coming to the research centre where she worked. She had been staying in the local area, but now wanted to go back to her parents. Smiling, she told him she would stay longer in the village if he wanted her to.

The dance went well, with ninety-eight locals turning up, over sixty of them ladies. After Molly and Dieter broke the ice, all the German soldiers had plenty of ladies to dance with.

The evening ended shortly after midnight. The lieutenant made sure his men got into their two armoured cars and were transported to their makeshift barracks on the outskirts of the village. Some of the local girls, especially the three choir girls who'd attended with Sally, had found soldiers that they wanted to keep in contact with.

The lieutenant was interested in Sally but also made a bit of a play for Irene, whom he found pleasant to talk to, if rather standoffish. Regarding Sally, he could read all the signs she was putting out. He knew that giving in to them would cause quite a stir, as she was not only married but married to the vicar. He liked Irene but didn't know her story. He really liked Sally and knew her story. From that point forward, he decided, he would just play it by ear.

Of course, the talk of the dance were Molly and Dieter. What made it more interesting was that none of the locals had seen Molly before. Surely such a young lady would have been noticed?

When Molly and Irene came down for breakfast the next morning, Irene asked Sally, 'Is it all right if Molly stays in the vicarage for a few days? You'll be paid well. Molly comes from Coventry and ran away from her job at the Jet Engine Research Centre when the SS arrived.'

'You know I must inform the local police about anyone who stays here.'

'Molly has her identity documents on her. That shouldn't be a problem.'

'But they may find out she has run away from her job.'

'Well, just leave it a couple of days before you go to the police then, if you don't mind.'

'All right, but no longer.'

Chapter 24

AN ANSWER FOR MOLLY

Having spoken at length with Molly, Dieter believed he understood her dilemma. He decided he would ask the lieutenant what to do. The main thing was to keep her out of the hands of the Gestapo. Throughout the country, the police were now under their control. As Molly had gone absent without leave from the top-secret Jet Engine Research Centre, she would be on the Gestapo wanted list, and her information would have been circulated to all police stations.

The lieutenant was pleased with the outcome of the dance. Most of the young German soldiers had made contact with local women to a greater or lesser degree. In the end, there had been twenty-six soldiers at the dance. Eight newcomers had asked for permission at about nine o'clock, which had been agreed to by Sally and the lieutenant. Dieter and Molly were the best of the German/English liaisons. The three choir girls planned to meet their soldiers at the vicarage and church. Irene and Sally were the focus of the lieutenant, whether they wanted this or not. Others had exchanged details or planned to meet again. All the German soldiers were now trying to learn as much English conversation as they could to help their romantic prospects.

When Dieter told his superior about Molly the following morning, the lieutenant decided, 'I will ask Mrs Cooper, just to help the situation and acquire more time to find Molly's exact story.' Dieter looked puzzled. 'The vicar's wife, Dieter. I will ask her this morning not to take Molly's documents to the police station just yet. If the police ask anything, she can refer them to me.'

So Molly was safe for now, and therefore Tim was safe also.

Irene stayed for the morning service and saw the lieutenant speaking with Sally. He attended the service with Dieter and some of the other soldiers. Molly was also there and spoke with Dieter.

Irene and Molly's story was that Irene had picked Molly up on the road when Molly waved from a country bus stop. Irene had been coming into town to do business and attend the dance. Molly had been staying at a bed and breakfast in Nuneaton, and the proprietors had asked her to leave. They knew Molly had absconded from work at the research centre and had wanted to help her to begin with, but they became concerned when they heard about the terrible things the Gestapo were doing to people who were helping fugitives.

Molly had taken a bus through to Lichfield, wanting to get as far away from the research centre in Coventry as possible. She had taken another bus and realised she had boarded the wrong one if she wanted to get to Uttoxeter. She got off on the outskirts of the village. That was when Irene's lorry came along.

The First EU

Molly had known a beautiful young woman would attract attention, so she had dressed scruffily with a dirty face and dishevelled hair. She had been in a real state when Irene picked her up, but she was much happier now, especially after meeting Dieter.

Irene found out that the lieutenant had asked Sally not to inform the local police about Molly right away. Tim had another week or so at least.

'Hi Tim,' Irene said cheerfully as she got out of the lorry at the farm.

Tim had been making plans to leave and looked rather glum.

'You don't have to leave just yet,' Irene advised him. 'Molly was a real hit with the Germans last night and will not be properly identified for a week or so. The lieutenant and Dieter are protecting her from the Gestapo.'

Tim looked a little more relaxed. 'Well, I'm a little perplexed about Molly, but I can understand her position. I'm sure you were also a hit with the Germans. I can't believe at least one or two of them didn't make a pass at you last night.'

'I did think Dieter would, but Molly took care of him. I'll explain that later. I kept myself to myself. The only one who made a bit of a pass at me was the lieutenant, although I was rather standoffish with him. I couldn't refuse his request for a dance. Anyway, I think he is rather struck with the vicar's wife. They have been working together all week, organising the dance, and she is vivacious and rather flirty. I think she is struck with him as well. We will have to see what happens there.'

Chapter 25

TIM GETS A FAKE ID

'What now, Tim?' Irene asked.

'I'll have to leave sometime. I want to make my way to Scotland to be with my wife.'

Although she had expected something like this, it was still a hammer blow to Irene's emotions.

Albert Black and his wife suspected Irene had feelings for Tim. They were interested in anything that affected Irene's happiness. They had become very fond of her. As they had lost their two sons, she became their daughter, their family. They knew she had come from an abusive relationship. That hurt had been very evident when she first arrived.

In this case, they wanted Tim to stay if it would make Irene happy. The farmer spoke to Tim about getting him a new identity so he could stay on the farm. 'I have contacts through my church people in Lichfield.'

'I would be grateful if you could arrange a new identity. It would help me no end, especially if I have to travel,'

'Well,' said Uncle Albert, 'I would be very happy if you could stay on the farm. You have been so much help. But if you want to leave, I will bid you Godspeed.'

'Thank you, Uncle. I appreciate your offer.'

Even after Tim said he wanted to join his wife, Irene was so keen to join him in his attic bedroom that she entered through the thatch before the farmer and his wife had gone to bed. This time she took the lead, guiding Tim to the stars and back. He came within a couple of minutes and then again a couple of hours later. They talked softly all the time. They coupled with love, not worrying about the noise.

Within a few days, Tim had the identity of a fallen soldier who had been the same age. Tim also had a story: he'd come from the East End of London, a technician and manager at a tin manufacturing factory, unmarried. He'd heard that Albert Black wanted help on the farm through his local church, and he wanted to get away from the chaos of London.

Tim's new identity really cheered Irene up. They were openly amorous now, with no comment from the farmer and his wife. Indeed, Auntie May suggested Tim move into Irene's room. The farming couple were devout Christians, but they turned a blind eye to what made Irene happy.

She almost glowed during this time. Tim applied his loving treatment, which he used on his ladies without even thinking. He had learned to please women, especially from French books. Irene was the oldest of the lovers he'd had. She was experienced in lovemaking and made sensible, intelligent conversation. Tim found it easy to be relaxed with her. He was falling for her more and more every day.

He assumed his new fake name: Tom Clark.

Chapter 26

THE PHOTOGRAPHER

It happened that there had been a photographer at the dance. With the permission of Sally and the lieutenant, he was allowed to take some photos for the local newspaper. This man had the latest equipment and took a lot of good photos. It seemed he couldn't keep his lens away from Molly, who had been dressed in her latest skimpy dancing dress.

So this photographer went to the *Lichfield Echo* with photographs and a story. And it happened that someone from the German media and propaganda department was there from London and saw the photos of Molly dancing with German soldiers. He was immediately interested and asked to see all the photos that had been taken at the dance. The German telexed these to the head office in London.

The chief was impressed. He decided a good story could be made from this material, promoting good relations between the German occupiers and the British population. This relationship had been going through a bad patch recently. Two hundred slave labourers had been executed

The First EU

because of German difficulties with the British navy and British colonies plus many other people had been liquidated.

The chief drove with four others to Lichfield, where they were taken on to the village. There they saw Lieutenant Schmitt, who took them on to the vicarage, where all involved had been briefed.

It was the Thursday after the dance. There was to be another mixed dance that coming Saturday. Molly was fully installed at the vicarage, and with recent events, it looked like she would be there for some time. She was sitting with Dieter, dressed simply but looked stunning as usual. Some of the dance committee, plus the vicar, Sally, and Irene, were there. They were all waiting for the high officials from the German media organisation. The officials duly arrived with the lieutenant.

Lieutenant Schmitt introduced the chief and his men to the vicar and the rest. The vicar said, 'What do you want us to do?'

'It is good that we can sit down and talk,' said the chief. 'Ladies and gentlemen, as the lieutenant said, my name is Olaf Franscheld and I'm the chief of media for the public outreach effort sponsored by the German authorities. I'm based in London. We want to make an example of your dance to show that the German and British people can get along on a personal level. We want to make the beautiful Molly here the heroine of our story.'

Molly looked nervously at Dieter, who was holding her hand.

'Don't worry, Molly,' Franscheld reassured her. 'You won't have to do anything special. Just continue to stay here and be friends with Dieter, as you are already. We would like to take photos of you from time to time. Sometimes with Dieter, and sometimes not.'

Molly's courage started to come back. 'Well, that's OK, sir, but remember that although I do like Dieter, we have only known one another for a few days.' Molly was still thinking of Tim.

'I remember. We are not going to ask you to marry Dieter. But you have caused quite a stir by spending most of your time at the dance with him last Saturday.'

'Yes, I do like Dieter. I will do as you say, Mr Franscheld. I would also like to see my parents within a week or so. Lieutenant Schmitt will explain the issues involved.'

The chief was a bit taken aback by this young girl's regained confidence. He gave a quick look at the lieutenant, who nodded.

'Very well, Molly. Do we have an agreement then?'

'Yes, Mr Franscheld. But just one more thing? Since the dance, I have spent time in the company of Dieter and his soldier friends, and I often hear my name mentioned in German conversation. So I would like to learn to speak, read, and write the language as soon as possible. If I'm going to be your poster girl, I hope you can help with this.'

'Of course. What would you like?'

'A tutor and some books of instruction.'

Franscheld looked at one of his colleagues standing next to him. 'Is this possible?'

The man nodded.

'There you have it, Molly. This will happen straight away. You are an interesting young lady, and I look forward to working with you.'

'Thank you,' said Molly finally.

Later, after the meeting and getting Molly's story from the lieutenant, Franscheld said, 'Whatever Molly has done in the past—like running away from her job because the SS team came to the research centre—we will forget about, because she can be such an asset to us. You saw how she spoke to me. She is beautiful, intelligent, and confident. If we can put her to good use, it can help our regime no end. Lieutenant, I know I don't have to say this to you, but I will, Molly must be protected from her own people.'

'I do realise this, Mr Franscheld. I will be assigning men in shifts. There will always be two armed soldiers guarding her. She has told me she will be spending all her time learning German. I also know she will exercise by practising her unarmed combat moves, and will organise ongoing dances in the church hall. She told me she has cleared the use of the church hall with the vicar and his wife, with times to be confirmed.'

'What a girl,' said Franscheld.

Molly's new situation obviously affected Tim's situation, which became much easier. He had his new identity documents by the Wednesday after the dance. Irene, who was very much in love with Tim by this time, kept abreast of events by regular visits to the village. Irene didn't show too much familiarity with Molly. They were supposed to be strangers who met hardly a week ago.

All that had happened with Dieter and Molly and the dance was now taking a lot of time and effort. It meant that the lieutenant and Dieter were not following up with their work with the farms they had earmarked for improvements.

Over two weeks passed before Dale Farm was visited again by a German patrol, and this one wasn't the lieutenant's platoon. It was another, working from comments written by the lieutenant on the farm efficiency sheets. Through Irene's visits to the village, the farm's inhabitants knew (plus or minus a day or so) when the visit would be. This time Tim was not in hiding, but openly living on the farm.

Chapter 27

TOM AND THE CAPTAIN

It was nine thirty on a Monday morning when the German patrol drove up the farm drive. All the farm's occupants gathered to welcome them. Some of the soldiers recognised Irene from the dances. The leader of the group, Captain Martin Vloch, checked Tim's papers. Tim was answering to the name Tom now.

'There is no record of you being here when Lieutenant Schmitt visited last,' the captain said sternly.

'That's right. I arrived a few days after the lieutenant called. I came from London through church contacts, and I presented my documents at the local police station the following day.'

'I see. I will have to check up with the police. We will take you back with us.'

The farmer intervened, saying, 'I need Tom. My two sons have been lost in the war.'

'Don't worry. If all is in order, as I'm sure it will be, we will not keep him. He will be free to return.'

The captain went through all the deficiencies the lieutenant had noted in his report with Tom, as he could see Albert Black wasn't well organised or good at paperwork. The captain said, ignoring the farmer, 'Tom, I can see you understand what is in this report. You will be able to implement the recommendations. I'm sure all will be OK at the police station, and then we will be able to get down to the work needed here. As you know, your country is not producing enough food to feed itself at the moment. All farmland must be efficiently utilised for maximum yield. This farm, growing the correct crops and raising the animals suited to it, will be able to quadruple its output. Quite frankly, it will not be allowed to carry on as it is.'

'Yes, all right. Could I ask you one thing, Captain?'

'And what is that?' The captain thought Tom wanted payment and was on his guard.

'I would like to learn to speak German.'

The captain was pleasantly surprised. 'Excellent, Tom. Firstly, you will need some books. Then I will see if I can allocate someone to help you. Maybe one of the men who will supervise the implementation of the efficiencies we will be putting in place. Yes, good,' said the captain again.

There were seven men including the captain. One of these spoke English as well as the captain did. All the others were learning English, especially now that there was an opportunity to meet local girls after a dance. Their abilities varied. Some could just about hold a conversation in English, others not.

Auntie May treated the whole platoon to a farm-fresh meal, as she had Lieutenant Schmitt's platoon before. They too thoroughly enjoyed it.

As Tom had already submitted his documents with no problems, he didn't expect a problem this time. But when he got to the police station, there was a Gestapo man waiting who had a list of all the people they were looking for. None of the names on the list corresponded to Tom's, but one photo did look similar—the photo of Tim Handle. Still, Tom's hair was much longer than Tim Handle's, and he was wearing farm clothes. Anyway, Tom's story seemed quite credible, and the Gestapo man was under pressure from the captain not to look at Tom too closely.

'Come, Tom, I will run you back to the farm,' the captain offered once Tom was cleared. 'Then I want you to attend the village tonight, cleaned up and wearing smart clothes. I will introduce you to some of the other German and English people working with us around here. We are using this village as an example of good relations and have the German media people from London involved. They are pushing this now; it's their top priority. You seem intelligent and cheerful, and as you want to learn German, we can help one another. I'm sure you would like to join our team.'

'Well,' said Tom, looking slightly surprised. 'I'm honoured, Captain.'

The captain ran him back to the farm as promised. Along the way, he was able to find out a bit more about him. 'I will see you at the vicarage at six o'clock,' the captain said as Tom got out of the car.

'Yes, Captain. Irene will run me to the village.'

'Good. I will see you at six.'

'Certainly,' said Tom, and off the captain drove.

Irene was ecstatically happy to see Tom, but controlled herself because the captain was there. Unlike Tom, she had been worried, even terrified of him having to go off with the Germans. 'What happened?' she asked.

'Well, the captain seems to have taken a liking to me. He wants me to get involved with the good-relations media people. I don't know more than that. I mentioned I wanted to learn German, and I think that had something to do with it. Although I don't really want to learn German that much. I asked him deliberately to get in his good books.'

Tom had just over an hour to compose himself, have a snack, a wash and a brush-up, and put his best clothes on.

Irene did the same. As neither of them knew what was going to happen, she thought she might as well be ready. She took a quick, cold shower outside and wrapped a towel loosely around her to go back to their room.

Tom couldn't help himself. Seeing those familiar, lovely legs gliding by, he grabbed her. She gave a startled squeal, but within seconds her tongue was returning his kisses. They fell back onto the bed, pulling off his only item of clothing, his underpants. Naked, they joined in a delightful, brief time of intense passion. All their recent anxieties dissipated in this one act. It was even sweeter because they hadn't been sleeping together for a few days while waiting for the second visit of the Germans.

Their dalliance didn't put them back much, though they would have preferred longer to wind down and relax. Tom was beginning to return Irene's intense love. Today was special. It seemed their problems with the Germans were finally coming to an end.

'Come on, Tom,' Irene said at last. 'We must leave now. I don't want to have to drive like a maniac to get there on time. You know the Germans like everything punctual and efficient.'

Tom dressed in a rush, jumping into the passenger's seat while still combing his hair.

'Goodbye, Auntie May! Goodbye, Uncle Albert!' Irene and Tom shouted as Irene engaged the clutch. Tom's new ID had a lorry-driving license on it, but Irene was used to the old lorry and its quirky ways, and Tom hadn't driven it before. He left it to her.

Off they went, arriving at five minutes before six. Both dressed in their Sunday best, they walked up to the door.

CHAPTER 28

SURPRISES AT THE MEETING

'Hello, Irene,' said Sally as she opened the vicarage door.

'Hi, Sally. I have run Tom in for a meeting with the captain. Tom, this is Sally, the vicar's wife.'

'Pleased to meet you, Tom.'

'A pleasure, Sally.'

'Please come through. The captain, lieutenant, and some other people are here.'

As Tom walked into the main room, he suddenly had to catch himself. Molly was sitting there quite calmly, talking to one of the Germans in the middle of the room. She also gave an involuntary start on seeing him. This wasn't noticed by most in the room, though Irene of course noticed.

She asked Sally if she should stay or not. After a brief conference with the lieutenant, he said to Irene, 'Please stay. We will not be discussing anything top secret, and you may be involved as well.'

So they went around the room and introduced themselves. There were nineteen in the room, including Ray the vicar, and Sally. Tea, coffee, and cakes were served. After about twenty minutes of speaking among themselves and getting to know one another, the farming project manager got up.

'As I said a little while ago, my name is Jochen Klos. I am the chief for the farm efficiency programme the German authorities are launching in the United Kingdom. I'm based in London. A fortunate set of circumstances has combined to make this village the setting for our media campaign to promote good relations between English and German peoples. The story, I think, goes like this. When Lieutenant Schmitt here visited Dale Farm, Dieter asked Irene if she could arrange a dance. The vicar agreed to the use of the church hall, and a dance under strict conditions was arranged by Sally and Lieutenant Schmitt. The dance went off well, and our beautiful heroine Molly became friends with Dieter.

'We have taken many photos and movies of Molly, sometimes with Dieter. They are in newspapers and cinemas around the country. Molly is learning German and has made remarkable progress.

'Now we want to take this a stage further and draw a line under the fighting and resistance. We want to see how successful we can be when our two great nations decide to cooperate. I will hand you over to my deputy, who is running this media campaign locally. He will fill you in on what we are planning, or what we would like to do with your approval and help. Thank you.'

Chapter 29

THE EFFICIENCY DRIVE

'Good evening, ladies and gentlemen. My name is Karl Riesman. We want to promote two stories. The first story has already been launched, regarding the beautiful Molly here as our heroine and Dieter as her German friend. We are charting their progress in photos and short movies for national consumption.

'In the second story, we hope to show a young man working with our German efficiency teams to improve the productivity of local farms. We think Dale Farm is an ideal candidate for our efficiency improvements, and with Tom on board, we think this could successfully be undertaken. Tom has a good grasp of the methods and procedures necessary—not only farm specific, but problem-solving in general. We would like to make you the star, Tom.' Riesman looked at him. 'So what do you say? Go ahead, stand up!'

Tom readily took the spotlight. 'Well, ladies and gentlemen, this has come as a bit of a surprise. I would be game for it. With my technical training, I should be able to work with the German experts without any difficulties. The main thing is to get all the farmers to agree and cooperate. For instance, the owner of Dale Farm lost both his sons in the war and therefore is not happy with the occupying forces. My advice to him is to cooperate, because the alternative is so terrible. But he and his wife may not care about this. Irene and I, although I have only been on the farm a short time, get on well with the farm couple. I hope we are able to persuade them. If we can, all should be well.'

Riesman interjected, 'Tell us a bit about yourself, then, Tom. What are your hobbies? Have you got a girlfriend?'

'Hm. I like unarmed combat—we sometimes call it street fighting—and weapons training, but haven't done much of either lately. I also like dancing. As for girlfriends, I don't really have one. But I do get on quite well with Irene.'

She couldn't disguise the fact that she was pleased with this statement.

'Good, Tom,' Riesman said. 'You go and persuade the farming couple. It will be difficult if they don't cooperate. I mean very difficult.' He looked gravely at Tom.

'All right, Mr Riesman, but threats will get us nowhere. I will do my best.'

The captain exchanged glances with the lieutenant, as much to say that Tom was getting a bit too bold.

Karl Riesman didn't comment on that, however. 'Molly has already started a combat class in the church hall, I believe. Maybe you would like to attend.'

'Yes, I would. What nights do they have these sessions?'

'I think it is every night from Monday through Thursday. Is that right, Molly?'

Molly nodded brightly.

'Thank you, sir,' said Tom. 'I will go along to observe tonight, as it's Monday. But I may not take part. I have my best clothes on.'

The meeting came to an end with Jochen Klos saying, 'I'm glad you have all agreed with our media campaign. I'm flying back to London tonight but will be kept informed on progress. Karl Riesman will be stationed locally.'

The captain drew Tom aside as the meeting broke up, and handed him two folders of A4 paper. 'I want you to study these files. One folder contains our procedures for improving farm yields, and the other is a joint report compiled by Lieutenant Schmitt and myself. We will be visiting the farm on Wednesday. I want to start on the changes straight away. As we get underway, a film and photography team will be in attendance some days.'

'But I haven't asked the farmer yet!'

'I leave that up to you.'

'All right.'

Molly, meanwhile, was off to one side. As Tom turned away from the captain, folders in hand, she called, 'Tom, I will be going over to the hall in about ten minutes, after I get changed. If you want to see how we train, you are welcome to look in.'

Chapter 30

STREET FIGHTING

Not long after, Tom and Irene walked over to the church hall, about fifty yards away. There were a number of people there already, some locals and some soldiers. Molly hadn't arrived yet. Tom and Irene could see that her students were quite proficient, especially the German soldiers. It also seemed that this evening event was becoming quite popular. A couple of the soldiers had even started a class for the under-elevens. Although hesitant at first, parents were now sending their children in such numbers that there was talk of extra sessions to accommodate them all. Whatever way one looked at it, this was good news for the good-relations campaign. Molly was fast becoming a star.

After they had been at the hall for about twenty minutes, Molly turned up with Dieter. Tom had only met Dieter this evening but recognised the voice from the first visit of Lieutenant Schmitt's patrol. It seemed a distant memory in light of all that had happened since.

'Hi, Molly. Hi, Dieter,' said Irene. 'You know Tom here from the meeting.'

'Hi,' said Tom. Molly and Dieter acknowledged him. Molly looked fitter and leaner. Tom thought she must have lost a few pounds since her tearful departure from Dale Farm three weeks before. She looked radiant, and Tom wondered if she had just been with Dieter. She was giving nothing away, treating Tom as she should—as a complete stranger.

'Tom, are you going to show us anything from your unarmed combat days?' asked Dieter.

'I would love to, but I haven't got the correct dress. I don't want to ruin these good clothes.'

'I'm sure we can find some gym clothing for you. Kurt, you're about the same size. Have you got a change of clothing Tom can wear?'

'Yes, but they are back at the barracks.'

The captain, overhearing this exchange, said, 'Kurt, please get them. You can use the patrol vehicle.'

'Yes, Captain.' Kurt left straight away.

In the fifteen minutes it took Kurt to return, Tom studied all the people in the hall. There were a lot of young ladies attending, and a few local lads, including some of the farmhand bouncers who had worked at Saturday's dance. They were ponderous in their warm-ups.

The Germans looked quite polished and were obviously using a known format, probably developed for the German armed forces. Two soldiers were running the warm-up session going on when Tom and Irene arrived. People practised kicks and punches. This was the same format as Tom's old warm-up back in Coventry, but with different moves.

The First EU

Molly was quite good when it came to unarmed combat. Tom knew this because she had trained alongside him for over a year in Coventry, using the British police and marine training format which he was also competent in.

After sustaining three broken ribs, dealt out by his work colleague Dave while practising, Tom had made a special effort to improve so that would not happen again. He ended up one of the best in his training group and was practising right up until he absconded.

Some moves could end in injury. Obviously these were not practised to their fullest extent, but were taught to be used in dire circumstances. They were also taught that one should always avoid a fight if at all possible. The hundred-yard dash was the best form of defence.

Tom could see that Dieter was awkward when he was warming up with practise moves, and also when he started practising with his fellow soldiers. Tom could only assume that he kept going to try and impress Molly. He was pretty hopeless now, but could improve if he kept at it. Some of the other soldiers were quite good, but Tom reckoned he could take any of them on.

Kurt returned with gym clothing. Tom thanked him and, once changed, started to warm up with kicks and punches. He was quite skinny and not so tall, and one wouldn't think he could be that good. But Tom was confident.

He went over to the bouncers and said, 'Hi, guys. Do you mind if I practise with you? I don't know anyone here. My name is Tom.'

'Sure,' said Sam, the largest of them.

Irene was sitting near the stage, talking to Sally. She saw that her old 'wham bam thank you ma'am' lover was talking to Tom. This is the first time she had seen Sam since he left for the army.

'I can show you a few tricks,' Sam said.

'Yes, sure,' Tom replied.

They started slowly. Then Sam made a lunge for Tom, which he deftly avoided. Sam went sprawling. 'Oh, sorry about that, Sam.'

'You're pretty quick.'

'I suppose it's because I'm small.'

Sam tried another couple of times to floor Tom. Tom avoided the attempts with ease.

'I should be able to take you down, Sam.'

'I don't think so.'

Sam made another lunge, and this time Tom moved to engage him. Before Sam knew anything, he was on the floor with Tom on top of him, holding his arm so he couldn't move.

'Wow, how did you do that?'

'It's something I learned in the army cadets.'

One of the other bouncers tried his luck with the same result.

The captain was looking on and was quite impressed, but he didn't think this skinny guy would be a match for the best of his men. He called over, 'Hi, Tom, why don't you come here and show us some of your moves?'

Tom excused himself from the rather bewildered farmhands and went over to the captain.

'I see that you floored those two big guys over there. You must be trained in unarmed combat.'

'Yes, it was part of my army cadet training. After I came by three broken ribs from a buddy, I didn't want it to happen to me again, so I took extra lessons.'

'Let's see what you can do with my men. We also train in unarmed combat in the German army. Have a go with Heinz here.'

Heinz looked quite a bit heavier than Tom, but not that much taller—broad and muscular. With the farmhands, Tom's task hadn't been difficult, but with this guy, he would have to fight like he used to fight the instructors back in Coventry. After a year of training sometimes he was beating them.

In the event, he beat Heinz as easily as he had beaten the farmhands.

The captain said, 'I'm impressed. We obviously need more practise. At the moment, you are number one here. Remember that you have the German procedures and the report to take in. We will be coming to the farm on Wednesday, so you've only got tomorrow for studying.'

'Yes, Captain.'

'I've been talking with the media crew, and they will also be out on Wednesday to take footage of the farm before the implementation of the efficiencies.'

'All right. I'll see you Wednesday, Captain.'

Molly and Dieter were practising kicks and punches in a small group that included the choir girls. After Tom dispatched the two farmhands, they and most of the other people in the hall showed up to watch Tom and Heinz, which didn't last long. After this, and thinking about the work coming up, Tom asked Irene to drive back. It had been quite an evening.

Molly was protective of Dieter, who wanted to have a contest with Tom. She knew he would be humiliated, so she persuaded him against it in a nice way. Molly wanted to know if Irene and Tom were an item, but unfortunately she could not be seen to be talking to Tom freely, as they were supposed to be complete strangers.

The reverse was likewise true: Tom wanted to know if Molly and Dieter were an item. Neither of them would find out about the other's personal situation for a while, however.

Tom was starting to reciprocate Irene's love. Molly was keeping Dieter at arm's length. Although she did like him and appreciated the help he had given her, she wasn't attracted to him sexually. There were other young Germans she fancied more than Dieter. She didn't know how things were going to turn out.

Chapter 31

IRENE'S STORY

Molly was enjoying the limelight and was allowed to see her mum and dad, as she had requested. The Gestapo and the German media people sorted out her absent-without-leave problem, not asking too many questions about how she ended up in the village or, surprisingly, about Tim Handle either.

Her German was coming along well. She seemed to have the talent to learn the language. Her IQ was high although she hadn't attended university. The job at the research centre had been easy for her, and she had been bored a lot of the time. She was enjoying this new job with the Germans. It was exciting and kept her busy. She had a nice young German tutor who had been flown in from Germany. She had been taught by Dieter for the first week, but the new man was a professional teacher and brought along all the latest books for the purpose.

Tom and Irene couldn't keep their hands off of one another on their drive home, which almost caused the lorry to crash. They got back to the farm quite early, about ten o'clock. The old couple were just getting ready for bed. Seeing their amorous state, Uncle Albert gave them each a pint bottle of home-made cider. They certainly didn't need the extra motivation; it was quite strong.

They were looking forward to being alone and talking sweet nothings while making love in different positions. Irene let Tom take the lead. After they were finished, they weren't too tired, and they talked well into the night.

Irene knew the truth about Tom's past and situation. She didn't want to think too deeply about how it would all be resolved. Tom didn't know about Irene's past much. In her case, the cider brought out much more.

Lying in one another's arms, enjoying that peaceful after-lovemaking feeling, Irene said softly, 'You know I've been abused, don't you?'

'Yes.'

'I have been frightened to tell you the story until now, not knowing how you would take it.'

'Don't worry about that. The past doesn't matter to me.'

'I come from a poor family. My father died when I was twelve, but I had a rich uncle who gave money for my education, which was in a private boarding school for girls. He also gave me generous spending money, so no one knew I was from a very poor home. I went to this school until I was eighteen.

'Then my uncle died and there was no more money. He left me nothing in his will, and his wife resented the money he'd spent on me.

'At this school, I lost my virginity at the back of the church one Sunday after the morning service. We used

The First EU

to meet boys there from another private school, and flirt and mess around like teenagers do. Many girls lost their virginity after Sunday service. I liked this good-looking boy; he was one year older than me. But with him finishing his schooling and moving away, nothing more happened. The following year I was too busy studying for my exams to get involved in that sort of thing again.

'With the education my uncle Joe had given me, I got a good job at a law firm in Birmingham. I lived at home and helped my mother with the housekeeping. We were doing quite well. I had an affair with my boss from the age of nineteen or twenty, and it lasted for over a year. We used to meet twice a week in an apartment that belonged to one of our clients. He was married, of course. After being headhunted by another firm, he moved on and that affair came to an end.

'Then, at twenty-two, I fell madly in love with an older local man. I met him on the bus to Birmingham every morning and attended the local pub with him. By the time I found out that he had a wife and two children plus another girlfriend with one child, it was too late. I was head over heels in love by then and thought it would all sort itself out.

'Coming up to twenty-three, I fell pregnant. Unfortunately, because of my stressful situation, the baby miscarried, I was in a terrible state and lost my job in the law firm.

'My boyfriend had always been a bit violent towards me, and I thought nothing of it. The violence increased after the miscarriage. I had moved back with my mother after some time on my own, because with no job I couldn't afford the upkeep of my own place. My boyfriend started coming to my mother's house. So I moved in with a friend to protect my mother. The beatings got worse. A few times, the police were involved. Because of this, my friend said I must leave. When I finally ran away and ended up at Dale Farm, I was on my last legs.

'The police at the village contacted the police where I had come from as a matter of routine, and found out about my unfortunate circumstances. They decided not to tell my family where I was. The police at the village told me to send a letter to my mother. I did this and then corresponded regularly after, but we haven't met for two years.

'Darling, I must say that Uncle Albert and Auntie May have been fantastic to me, even though they didn't know me before. This is why I want to protect them against the Germans. The police told them about my problems, and they didn't say anything.'

'Darling,' said Tom, 'your story makes me want to love you even more.'

He made sure from then on to be even nicer to Irene, using his cheerful softly-softly approach and his French way of lovemaking, which all women enjoyed. He won Irene's heart over and over again, and promised, 'I will also safeguard Uncle Albert and Auntie May.'

Chapter 32

HAPPINESS FOR IRENE

'Darling, what do you feel about Molly now?' Irene asked.

'I still feel for Molly, and she is looking well. But we have made our decisions, and because of the terrible consequences of the truth coming out, we have no way of ever getting together again.'

'What about your wife?' she continued.

'Given my relationships with Molly and now you, plus all that has happened, my feelings for my wife have become confused. I worry about her and want to make contact, wondering if she is well. We have a baby coming along, after all.'

This wasn't comforting to Irene, but she hadn't expected anything else. She knew what type of person Tom was by now.

'You know darling, I'm doing the exact opposite to what I set out to,' Tom mused. 'I wanted to become a resistance fighter. All the team members who went absent from the research centre were like-minded. I wonder where they are now. There were five of us in all, and the research programme couldn't run without us.

'Look where I am now, a total collaborator. My photo will be splashed over the whole country soon. It's almost certain that my original identity will be uncovered. I think when I get friendlier with the captain, I'm going to square with him. I'll need to be protected from the Gestapo.

'We hear about the terrible things that are going on, but in this area, the Germans seem good. I can't believe these men would agree with those atrocities. Rumour has it the Germans are rounding all the Jews up and putting them in ghettos. They executed two hundred men from the slave labourers, and a lot of important people are going missing. If we resist, we will only end up dead. And these farms need to be brought into an efficient system.

'There is nothing bad that has affected me yet. Molly told me she has a twenty-four-hour armed guard. Maybe I should speak to the captain about us. I think they would leave a couple of soldiers here.'

'I would prefer they didn't do that,' Irene said, valuing her private time with Tom. 'You can protect me.'

'Oh, darling, with my life. I'll do my best. A time may come when I can help the resistance, but not yet. Let's just enjoy one another and be happy. Goodnight, Irene darling.'

'Goodnight, Tom, my lovely.'

In the morning, Tom woke Irene and they made slow, gentle love. He wanted to be nice to her now to make up for her sad past and the story he had heard the previous night.

The worry had gone from Irene's face. Tom and the farm couple had noticed. It was a happy time for Irene.

The First EU

They weren't called this morning, but Tom and Irene couldn't stay in bed too long. They had a lot to do and a lot to explain to Uncle Albert and Auntie May, so they all could keep out of danger.

After Irene and Tom explained about all the changes that would be required to make the farm efficient, the Blacks agreed to cooperate. With one proviso: Tom must remain on the farm. Uncle Albert said, 'I don't know about all these procedures and reports. You young and well-educated people must help me.'

'Of course we will, Uncle Albert.'

So Tom read the report and went through the procedures the Germans would be using, making notes. He condensed his scrawled thoughts and wrote them out in clear, simple form. That evening, Tom went through it with Uncle Albert, who seemed a bit bewildered as to the far-reaching changes coming to his little subsistence farm.

CHAPTER 33

WHERE'S TIM'S WIFE

Tom decided he had to try and contact his wife and her cousins in Scotland. It wouldn't be easy, because trunk calls could be listened to. Before the invasion, this hadn't been such a problem, but now one just didn't know who the collaborators were.

In the end, although she didn't know if the outcome would be good or bad for her, Irene offered to. She had a friend who was an operator at the local telephone exchange. Irene made sure that she was the one who put the call through.

Tom put on his Tim hat again and got through to Florence. Andy, the elder brother on the Scottish farm, answered the phone.

'Hi, it's Tim. Could I speak to Florence, please?'

Immediately a danger sign came up for Andy. 'Mrs Randall isn't here at the moment, but I will tell her you called. Is there any message?'

Tim played it cool. 'Her friend Irene wanted to know how she was getting on.'

'Tell Irene she is well and healthy.'

'Fine, I will. She may call herself in a day or so.'

'Florence is living here with her husband. He joined her recently from London after being demobbed.'

'All right,' said Tim, hardly containing his surprise. 'I'll let Irene know. Goodbye.'

Andy also bid his farewell and put the phone down. He decided he wouldn't tell Florence about the call. When his brother John asked who had called, Andy told him not to say anything.

Florence was in the village, shopping with Auntie Joyce. Florence wouldn't normally ask about a phone call, as it wasn't her house and there were a lot of calls coming through for both business and family.

Dave, who was in the house when the call came through, heard 'Mrs Randall' mentioned. He asked, 'Who was that on the phone for Florence?'

'It was Tim Handle, saying he was phoning on behalf of her friend Irene. I told him Mrs Randall was perfectly all right and living here with her husband. Tim said Irene may call herself. If she phones, whoever answers must put her off somehow and indicate that she should not phone again. I will tell my mum the same.'

They didn't have to worry if Tim had got the message. No more calls came through. Florence still asked about Tim from time to time, but as the period with no contact increased, these questions became less frequent.

Dave was now sleeping in the same room as his sham wife for two reasons: one, Florence had taken pity on him about being in the outbuilding, as it was beginning to get colder; and two, they all wanted to make it look right when the German patrols visited—and the Germans definitely didn't give any prior warning. Florence had not invited Dave into her bed, as she was still dreaming about Tim, but she knew Dave really fancied her. She resigned herself to the inevitable after not hearing from Tim.

Dave had been in her room for a week when she said one evening, 'If you make yourself nice and clean with some nice aftershave, you can sleep in my bed tonight. If you want to sleep in my bed, you must always be clean.' She told him this because she had noticed he sometimes smelled a bit at night. He always washed and shaved in the morning. 'From now on, you must wash and shave in the evening if you want to share my bed.'

This was a thing he was more than happy to do for the reward involved.

So that night it happened. Pregnant women can still feel a sexual urge, and Florence was no exception. She hadn't been with Tim since she conceived, and that was nearly three months ago. She was still looking radiant and her slim, lithe body was just beginning to show a slight bump. Dave was fresh and clean with nice-smelling aftershave, and Florence had scented up as she would have done for Tim.

Dave hadn't been with many women before, and he hadn't read up about women as Tim had. He wasn't as good-looking as Tim, having slightly sticking-out, large ears, but he did have an athletic body because he'd played rugby as a wing forward until recently.

Unfortunately, Dave was so overawed by Florence that he spurted his lot almost as soon as he got into bed. Florence hadn't had this happen before, but even so realised it must have been her effect on him. She just told him not to worry

The First EU

and cuddled him as they fell asleep. She was a bit frustrated, not having had him inside her.

Early next morning she woke him, as she had sometimes done with Tim if she felt sexy. Bringing him up and taking off her panties, she said, 'Can you gently and slowly put it in, and let me do the moving?'

Dave was absolutely ecstatic. He could hardly believe this was happening to him.

Florence rolled over to be on top. 'Please control yourself for a few more minutes, while I reach my climax.' She moved her body up and down on him with faster and faster thrusts. Finally she gave several long gasps and locked tightly on to him, aligning her hips for maximum penetration. She kissed Dave desperately through her climax.

Dave had been almost delirious throughout, but he did know that Florence was satisfied. He let himself go, reaching his climax a few moments later.

When he'd caught his breath, he said, 'That was unbelievable. I've never been so well satisfied in my entire life, my darling Florence.'

'You were better than I thought you would be. Last night you were too excited. I didn't realise I would have such an effect on you. Now I'm happy. We will have to learn to make love carefully from now on, sweetheart.'

CHAPTER 34

PEOPLE ON THE OAT FARM

Florence and Dave were so radiant that even though they tried to hide their obvious glow, the rest of the household, including Auntie Joyce, knew what had happened. No one mentioned anything at breakfast, but Andy and John did make a joke to Dave later in the day. They were happy for him and Florence.

As far as Florence was concerned, she believed that although Dave was a bit inept, he could improve with guidance. Tim had told her how he had studied to satisfy women, and she could only assume Dave had not read the same books. Nevertheless, Dave would make a good stand-in. If Tim ever came back onto the scene, she didn't know what would happen. For now, she was more settled than she had been for a while.

The brothers' farm was planted with oats. This crop grew well in the colder areas of the United Kingdom. They had sold their crop just before the fighting started, so they were flush with money. The German patrol hadn't bothered them. The Germans could see that the farm was run on an efficient basis. English-speaking farming experts went

The First EU

through the farm with a checklist and suggestions. They made a report and explained their procedures. The report was a standard form with different sections covering all farms that were likely to be found in the United Kingdom.

Unfortunately for the Germans, most farmers were not well educated, some being almost illiterate. In the case of the Oat Farm, the owner-brothers had both been to university. They had studied engineering and business management and knew how to handle the paperwork for projects. It was easy for them to communicate with the German experts.

Dave was also involved. He was even more knowledgeable about projects and procedures, but no one mentioned that. The story was that he got his knowledge from working in a car-exhaust factory.

The British men gained respect and the friendship of the Germans administering the efficiency programme, who spent a lot of time on the farm, one of the largest in the area. They needn't have spent that much time there, as it was already being well run. Everyone knew the Germans were sniffing around the three beautiful women there.

The women, being a bit bothered about the Germans, arranged for other girls from the village to be on the farm the next time the Germans would be there. When this happened, Florence asked the patrol if they could give the village ladies a lift back. After this, the farm women didn't see so much of the Germans. It seems the male attention had been deflected a bit.

The Germans battled with most of the farmers to get them to understand and carry out improvements. They asked the young men on the Oat Farm if they could call a meeting of all the local farmers, explain what was going on, and tell them how to handle the procedures and paperwork. Andy and John held this meeting and received a lot of unpleasantness and resistance from their fellow farmers—so much so that they were called collaborators.

This was distasteful, especially for men who had fought gallantly in the war. They mentioned to the Germans they were not happy, saying they had fought in the war. 'The war is over,' said the German captain in charge. 'Whatever happened is history. You can tell your farming friends about your war exploits, and we hope you will receive their goodwill. But we need to do something about compliance. The district commander is getting frustrated, and I don't want any trouble for the older farmers.'

The three young men on the Oat Farm were also feeling frustrated with the local farmers, and they also wanted to see the efficiency improvements acted upon. It was in their training to run their own farm well.

On hearing the exploits of the brothers' service, the attitude of the older farmers changed a bit. Andy and John were asked details of their exploits. They said only that they had been armoured car commanders and fixed the roads for the heavy equipment. They didn't want to go into too much detail, as they knew the anti-aircraft cannon mounted on their vehicles had caused the deaths of many German airmen. The local farmers started to warm to the brothers.

Now the Germans wanted them and Dave to take the lead in the local area. What could they do? They were naturally interested in farm efficiency. It has been part of their training. Even Dave had similar schooling, although he didn't have the farming background. The methods the Germans wanted to use were the same for project work in most fields.

Chapter 35

ASSASSINATION AN IDEA

The original idea of organising an armed resistance was disappearing. The military defeat of the United Kingdom had been decisive, and in most areas the Germans were on a charm offensive. This was the directive from high command to their occupational forces.

The only thing that the three young men at the Oat Farm were considering was the assassination of Hitler and his senior cohorts. But they couldn't see how this could be achieved.

The brothers had two specialised sniper rifles with ammunition, taken from a German patrol car they had come across in the recent fighting. They had killed the car's four occupants. The day after, they had driven their armoured cars as far towards the Oat Farm as they could with the fuel they had. They told their men it was every man for himself, and they could get off wherever they wanted. The brothers ultimately made their way back to the farm on foot, avoiding German and British forces and carrying the sniper rifles. They didn't tell anybody about the rifles, which they buried in the middle of a ploughed oat field. Not even Dave had been told.

Andy and John were glad they pulled out. Some who fought to the last man didn't survive. Since then, the brothers had had contact with only a few of their eighteen former comrades. They believed the ones they couldn't find were slave labourers already.

There was great consternation when Heydrich ordered the execution of two hundred slave labourers. It led to a lot of trouble around the country and caused deaths on both sides. This didn't worry Heydrich, of course. But other German leaders were concerned.

The main population centres, where slave-labour round-ups were commonplace, were where most of the trouble occurred. As with the Dale Farm area, the charm offensive was having a good effect in the area of the Oat Farm, and people weren't so anti-German.

The brothers and Dave were becoming German favourites. They were given a lot of privileges, especially as they had agreed to work with the local farmers.

The area around the Oat Farm was sparsely occupied. The nearest Germans were formally garrisoned eight miles away, towards Dumfries. But because two were now attached to local girls, they had commandeered an empty house in the village and made it habitable. Six of them with work and contacts in the area had started living there.

Dave had originally told everyone in the local pub that he was travelling to Glasgow for a job offer. The farmers spoke to the barman, saying that Dave had come looking for his wife all along. She had heard the Gestapo was looking

The First EU

for him and didn't want to get involved again, as she hadn't seen him since she conceived his baby. They had met later and sorted everything out. Now all was well and he was no longer being chased by the Gestapo. There had been some problems between Dave and his wife that the brothers weren't quite sure about—some affair. Anyway, everything seemed to be OK now.

Dave and Florence were becoming part of the Oat Farm family in the local community. Auntie Joyce was happy that Florence was pregnant. The older woman fussed about like a mother hen.

Florence got a letter to her parents saying everything was OK. The letter was given to someone going to Glasgow to post there, to disguise Florence's location. Florence still didn't know anything about Tim or the situation regarding the research centre, and there was also the matter of her false ID to conceal. She did say she was staying with Auntie Joyce, her mother's sister. Her mother had known she was going there anyway. Her parents had been approached by German security once, but that had been over a month ago and there had been nothing lately.

Chapter 36

A CAMPAIGN IN THE VILLAGE

Molly was cooperating with the German media people. They had even hired an advisor for her make-up and clothing. She was becoming a bit of a star and had quite a schedule. Needless to say, Molly was getting a lot of attention from a number of young German soldiers. But she was still missing her Tim and hadn't presented her body to Dieter or anyone else yet. She saw Tim from time to time as he was attending the village on business with the captain.

Tim, as Tom, was also involved with the media campaign, and they met sometimes, stealing a few words. He knew Molly was still smitten by him, but because he was spending all his time with Irene, he was feeling more for Irene nowadays. He assumed Molly was engaging with Dieter in the same way he was with Irene.

Tom and Molly crossed paths during a mid-afternoon refreshment break. 'Excuse me, Molly,' Tom said, as if they were mere acquaintances, 'do you like working for Olaf?'

'Oh yes! He is very kind. He has given me some lovely new clothes for the filming and said I can keep them. Are you happy working with the media people?'

'Well, yes. I'm just helping with the farm efficiency drive. I will be making a movie about it soon which will be broadcast to the whole country.'

'I see. My photos with Dieter have already been in the new magazine called *Friendship*, being distributed free by the Germans all over the country. We are making a movie too.'

Tom glanced around. No one was near. Lowering his voice, he said, 'Soon everyone who knows us will see we are working with the occupiers.'

'What can we do?' Molly replied. Then she broke off as she saw Olaf approaching.

Tom said, 'We must talk again.'

She nodded.

'Hello you two!" said Olaf. 'You make a good-looking couple.'

'I'm sure there must be many German young men who will line up if Dieter has to leave the scene,' Tom said.

'You are right there. How is your work with the farmers going?'

'It's going well. As you probably know, we're making a movie with your people to promote the efficiency drive.'

'Keep it up! I think it would be an idea to include Molly in that.'

'It may well,' said Tom. 'It's always effective to have a pretty girl in an instructional film mainly aimed at men.'

'What do you say, Molly?'

'I'll do whatever you say, sir. It definitely sounds exciting. Will you have to buy me some farming clothes then?'

'You have got ahead of me, my dear. I'll discuss this with Tom's media team.'

'Great. I'm up for it.'

'That's good.'

Molly looked back at Tom as she hurried away with Olaf. Tom knew from that look that there was some lingering love.

Molly told him in a later stolen conversation that she wasn't sleeping with Dieter or anyone else because she still had feelings for him. This information made things difficult. His life regarding women was becoming rather complicated, to say the least.

CHAPTER 37

THE SNIPER RIFLES

In southern Scotland, an interesting turn of events had taken place. Andy, the elder farm brother, was told that a very important person was going to be visiting Scotland soon. When he indiscreetly inquired again a few days later, he was told under pain of death that the person was none other than SS group leader, Reinhard Heydrich.

Andy didn't learn the exact details because security was high. Heydrich had been badly injured in an assassination attempt in Czechoslovakia. In the days that followed, the chatter among the German soldiers was about Heydrich's visit. They were excited and couldn't contain themselves. Young soldiers thought Heydrich was a hero for the way he had fought off the assassins. But because of his ruthless ways with occupied people, he wasn't liked so much by older Germans who were looking for a peaceful occupation.

With this information, the brothers decided they should dig up the two sniper rifles. They also had a box of one hundred rounds of ammunition for the rifles. The

Germans weren't always on the farm, and nowadays the brothers normally knew when they would be arriving, so uncovering the rifles wasn't that dangerous. The field had just been planted for an early oat crop the following year, so it was easy to disguise the disturbance on the surface. They had the firearms out of the ground and the surface replanted in an hour.

They decided to conceal the rifles in the hidey-hole in their well. They put the waterproof rifle case in there for the time being, while they planned what to do.

Andy and John, as junior officers in the British army, had trained with British, German, and French weapons. They hadn't handled this particular sniper rifle, but even so, they had an idea of how to fire it. The guns were identical and had come with lightweight tripods.

Dave was the only other person on the farm who knew about the rifles. The men didn't want to get the women involved. As for inquisitive outsiders, the farm's location gave the brothers a five-minute warning of approaching vehicles. This was more than enough time to place the guns safely in the well hiding place.

At some stage, however, they would have to practise-fire them, and this was a bit of a problem. The noise would be heard, and they were not supposed to have any guns. The Germans had required all guns, even shotguns, to be handed in. Andy and John had complied with this order.

The brothers found some shotgun cartridges and exploded one inside a pipe. It made the normal sound of a gun, and this was what they wanted. If the ladies of the house or anyone else heard the noise, the brothers could say it came from a device rigged up for scaring the crows and pigeons.

The First EU

So the three men studied the guns for a while: the magazine, the way the ammunition loaded, the safety catch, the telescopic sights, and so on. They decided to do some target shooting at the barn across the back field, putting some old blankets and straw bales around the gun to limit the noise. The target was a paper sheet pinned to a thick plank.

Andy fired the gun. Its small kickback, accuracy, and explosive force from four hundred yards surprised him. He fired two single shots and then a burst of three per gun, adjusting them for repeated strikes inside an eight-inch diameter target. After that, he marked the gun he preferred and put them both back down the well. The following day, making sure no one was around, the brothers buried the non-preferred gun in a new place, along with half the ammunition.

'What was all the noise, then, Dave?' asked Florence the night after the target practise.

'Oh, we were just testing some old cartridges to scare the birds away. The scarecrows are not doing a good job any more.'

'Don't forget to have a good wash. I feel sexy, and you have been away for three days.'

Being pregnant seemed to affect Florence in that way. She was three and a half months now, and looking even better. She had put on a little weight all round, but her bump was not yet very noticeable.

Dave knew that Florence was still thinking about Tim. He hoped Tim would never come back on the scene, as Dave had fallen deeply in love with his sham wife. He told her he was going to look after her and consider the baby as his own.

They didn't discuss Tim. Both knew it would only lead to arguments, which would affect the harmony they had and consequently their lovemaking.

At the moment, Florence only knew what she had heard from Dave: that Tim had gone into hiding with Molly. She had no reason not to believe him, as she already knew Tim had been having an affair with Molly for some time.

Chapter 38

GETTING TO EDINBURGH

Dave and Florence had a great night of lovemaking. Dave had learned to control himself now after a little practise and Florence was showing him other things she knew. She had learned some of them from Tim. She had been nineteen when she first met him and had only been with one other man before then. Her first love had lasted six months, when she was eighteen.

The local girl who was living with John worked in the village post office. She rode her bike into the village and back every day. This was only two miles. Jean, Andy's friend, was from Edinburgh and didn't know anyone locally. She spent most of her time on the farm, or sometimes at the village inn with Andy or John.

Jean was from a well-established Scottish family and, being rather academic, didn't get on that well with Auntie Joyce, although she was definitely on the same wavelength as Andy. They had lived together while at the university. A bit bored in the isolated farmhouse, she took on the garden.

She couldn't plant much because of the time of year, but she planned for the next season and got things in order. She also purchased a hundred pullets and arranged for the chicken shed to be enlarged and improved with better fox-proofing.

Andy wouldn't have protested the cost, as it was keeping her busy, but Jean insisted on paying for everything. She had her own little car, having managed to drive south from Edinburgh a week or so after the fighting stopped, when things were still in disarray. The farm had a supply of fuel she could use, and she often ran people to the village.

Jean was twenty-three years old and well built, standing five feet five. When she swayed to and fro at the local dance, in her university sort of way, heads definitely turned. She seemed to bewitch some of the local lads and German soldiers. But she was happy with Andy.

One night, Jean asked, 'Andy, is there anything bothering you? You are very quiet lately.'

Andy was thinking about the assassination, but couldn't say anything of course. 'I'm fine. I was just thinking about my men who have disappeared, probably to slave labour. There are so many I can't get hold of, and now I'm such a collaborator.'

'It's not your fault, darling. Don't think too much. Come on, let's make love.'

John had a safe phone contact to a resistance fighter friend in Edinburgh. He learned that Heydrich would be staying at Edinburgh Castle—and a plot to assassinate him was hatched.

It was decided that Andy would attempt to assassinate Heydrich while he was in Edinburgh. Arrangements were made through contacts in the resistance for Andy to be transported to Edinburgh by a fishing boat, which would pick him up from a secluded bay near Eyemouth. The pickup point being twenty miles from the farm, Andy decided to ride this distance on his bicycle at night, carrying his preferred rifle with half the ammunition.

They assumed that Heydrich would walk about on the castle parade ground, and a spot about three hundred yards away was identified. From it, Andy would have a clear sight of nearly the entire ground. It was just a matter of getting there and waiting.

The biggest problem was how to explain Andy's absence from the farm. He was working with the Germans on a daily basis. It was worth the risk because it was so important to kill Heydrich, though the momentous act would undoubtedly have terrible consequences.

Heydrich would be at the castle in a few days' time, so Andy made arrangements to leave the following night. In a determined and solemn way, he made his farewell. 'My brother John and dear friend Dave, I'm going to kill Heydrich. Tell the ladies of the house I've gone to see a friend who is gravely ill and will be back in a few days. Jean doesn't know anyone near Dunbar, so she won't come looking for me. I'm going to try and get away with it, but in the worst-case scenario, I'm not going to put this farm in danger.' Then he hugged them both.

The two men left behind were almost in tears as he disappeared down the lane that day in late October, the gun strapped to his back. They knew he meant what he said about not putting the farm in danger, although his disappearance—if it came to that—would create much suspicion.

Andy's bicycle ride to the coast was uneventful. He used back roads, knowing the area well. He got there one hour early. The fishing boat arrived on time and gave the correct prearranged torch signal. Andy gave the correct signals back and then waded into the sea. He held the gun and ammunition above his head as he pulled the bike through the water.

Once aboard, he had to stay below decks, as there were patrols in the area. This didn't do much for his seasickness. As soon as they got into deep water, they discarded the bicycle over the side.

It was good that he was concealed. They soon met a patrol. The owner of the boat convinced the Germans they were just motoring back from the fishing grounds. If they had been searched, Andy and the gun would have hidden under a hold full of freshly caught fish. The catch was about two tons of cod, and it was pretty smelly.

'Have you got any fish to spare for us?' shouted one of the Germans.

The skipper had been approached like this before. 'We only have cod on board. All right?'

'Yes, we would like a few, thanks.'

The patrol boat came alongside, and the skipper handed over six good-sized fish.

'That's great!' shouted an English-speaking soldier.

'Unfortunately, they're not gutted and scaled.'

'No problem!' The patrol boat pulled away under full power.

On arrival at the Edinburgh fishing harbour, the resistance people took charge of the gun. Andy was taken to a safe house to clean up and get some sleep.

The First EU

The following day, avoiding certain areas, they went to the pre-chosen position with a view of the castle and parade ground. It was the tower where the camera obscurer was housed. The camera obscurer was a rotating, angled mirror at the apex of the roof, which projected an image of the landscape onto a horizontal surface inside.

'This is where you will have to stay until the deed is done—or not,' said the resistance leader.

Chapter 39

THE TOWER EMPLACEMENT

The area around the tower was searched by German security on a regular basis, so utmost care had to be taken. The gun was kept hidden there, but because of the checks, the resistance leader changed his mind and decided Andy could not stay in the tower. He would be put up in the safe house.

Heydrich arrived that day. The following day, unbelievably, Himmler turned up. A ceremony was held to award honours to the soldiers who had been heroic in the recent fighting.

A tunnel had been built at the time of the Scottish kings; it led from near the base of the tower to the fishing harbour. This was made ready.

The general public didn't know these key Nazis were in Edinburgh, but the resistance did. Their instruction to Andy was to take either one of them out, and preferably both. No other Germans were to be targeted.

After the shooting, Andy, with the guidance of a resistance fighter who would always be with him, would flee along the secret tunnel. The same fishing boat that had dropped him off would be ready in the harbour. Once on the boat, Andy would be dressed as a crew member. If there was any chance of them being apprehended, the gun would be ditched over the unsighted side of the boat.

The following morning, the word was that there would be a ceremony starting at ten thirty. Andy was taken to the tower just after the Germans had done their rounds at ten o'clock. He waited, setting up his gun out of sight. As he had been told the distance was three hundred yards, he adjusted the sights accordingly. The resistance fighter, Jonnie, checked with binoculars.

The crucial time arrived. Luck was on their side; Heydrich and Himmler were walking together. Andy acted quickly, since the opportunity might not present itself again. The ceremony started; Heydrich and Himmler stood side by side. Andy set the rifle to automatic and took aim. He had two magazines, but hoped he could do the deed with just one.

He squeezed the trigger.

The gun was shielded for noise but still made a loud report. Andy kept his finger on the trigger. After a dozen shots hit Heydrich, he swung the gun slightly to aim at Himmler, who was moving towards his Nazi associate, probably in reaction to seeing the volley of shots hit home. The remaining rounds went into Himmler's upper body.

Andy saw in his sights that both Nazis had fallen. With the euphoria of a successful kill, he shouted, 'My God, they are both down! Let's go!' With Jonnie carrying the gun and magazine, they sprinted down the stairs for the escape tunnel.

The Germans were in disarray, and there were no roadblocks or checks at the end of the tunnel near the fishing harbour. Other fighters sealed up the exit. 'Good-bye, my friend, and good fortune be with you,' Jonnie called.

'Jonnie, you may need more luck than me!' With that, Andy boarded the fishing boat. He changed into working clothes below deck straight away.

Everything seemed to be going well until, about a mile out, they saw a patrol boat approaching at speed. Over the unsighted side of the boat, they ditched the rifle ammunition and Andy's shooting clothes wrapped around the rifle. The next few minutes would be critical. Andy dirtied himself as much as he could, and they waited for the patrol vessel.

When it caught them up, they saw it was the same boat they had seen on their inward journey. The German captain shouted, 'We have orders to search your boat and check everyone's papers!'

Three of the German crew came on board and gave the fishing boat a thorough going-over. Nothing was found. Then they checked all the crew's papers, Andy looked slightly different to the photo on his ID papers, but the Germans accepted it.

One of the Germans who could speak English said, 'There's been big trouble in Edinburgh today because of an assassination attempt. I don't know the details. You had better be careful. When are you returning?'

'In a few days,' said the skipper.

'Great. Maybe you will have some more fish for us.'

'I'm sure we will.'

As the skipper held the boat steady, the Germans scrambled back on board their patrol boat, waving as it sped away.

Chapter 40

ESCAPE AND EFFECTS

Heydrich had died immediately from seven hits to his upper body. Himmler had been hit four times, once in the neck; he died twelve hours later. Hitler went berserk, ordering the immediate execution of two thousand British slave labourers.

There was a separate plot afoot to assassinate Hitler and replace him with a respected member of the German establishment. With the removal of two of the most aggressive officers of the German high command, the Hitler plotters gained more confidence to put their plan into action.

The two thousand British men who were waiting to be shot were lucky; the German deputy under Heydrich delayed these executions. He didn't know about the plot against Hitler, but was a moderate and wanted the situation to settle down before doing anything. One thing he did know: the consequences of these executions would be catastrophic for relations between the German occupiers and the British population.

The whole of the United Kingdom and especially Scotland was in panic mode as the German security forces tried desperately to find the perpetrators of this terrible deed. Edinburgh was scoured from top to bottom.

It was suspected that the camera obscurer tower was the place where the shots had come from. Nothing could be found in the tower, but the tunnel was discovered. A further assessment indicated that the assassin could have escaped that way and then maybe continued on by boat. The fishing boat that had been stopped soon after the act again came under suspicion, as all the other boats in the area had been eliminated from the search.

In the early hours of the next day, a spotter plane located the fishing boat on which Andy had taken refuge. It was far out to sea, but the skipper and crew knew the game was up now. Andy decided if they were intercepted and searched again, he would jump over the unsighted side of the boat with a weight tied to him. It was a terrible thing to contemplate, but it was the only thing he could think of to protect the people at the farm from being executed—and of course the people on the boat. He hoped that in this way, the Germans would be prevented from finding out who undertook the assassinations.

The skipper was concerned. He knew Andy wasn't thinking straight. Andy's sudden disappearance would immediately cause suspicion, and all on the Oat Farm would be in grave peril. 'I can't let you do this, Andy.'

The spotter plane flew over them again. The skipper turned the boat directly towards land at full speed. They slowed a few hundred yards from the coast. By this time, Andy was thinking a bit more clearly. 'I can swim from here, Skipper, and then make my way back to the farm.'

'That's better. Good luck, my son.'

The boat sped away as soon as Andy went overboard. It headed toward a position in line with its previously spotted location.

At the end of October, the water wasn't too cold. Thermal lag created a situation in which the sea temperature dropped more slowly than the land temperature, with a little help from the Gulf Stream. It was an easy swim for Andy. He discarded all his fishing crew clothes and wore only his shorts. He made it to shore near the place he had been picked up from a few days before. He had to get back to the farm as quickly as possible—not that easy with nothing but shorts on and no bicycle for the twenty-mile return journey.

He found it colder out of the water than in, so he ran to a nearby hamlet to keep warm. Once he had to hide from what looked like a German patrol car. The route posed no difficulty; this was the area where he had been brought up. Sometimes his dad had driven the family Bentley, his pride and joy, to the seaside in the summer. Andy had also visited as a teenager on many occasions, mostly to attend dances and meet young lassies.

In the driveway of the first house he came upon, he found a lady's bike. He used this to cycle two miles further to his old girlfriend's house. At this time in the morning, there wasn't any activity on the roads to speak of. He could hear approaching vehicles from a long way off. To be on the safe side, he took cover from all three vehicles he encountered. One was a German patrol, probably the one he had seen earlier when leaving the beach. They were definitely on the lookout for something.

Chapter 41

THE PRETTY HELPER

By the time Andy arrived at his old girlfriend's, it was about seven o'clock. He knocked at the door and her mother answered it. 'What on earth have we here?' exclaimed Mrs McDonald.

'Well,' said Andy, teeth chattering, 'it's a long story.'

'I bet it is. You'd better come in. I'll call Sarah.'

When Sarah appeared, Andy pleaded, 'Please don't ask too many questions. I'll explain everything later. The first thing I must do is get this bike back to a house near St Abbs before they report it missing to the police.'

Sarah brought a blanket for Andy, which he put around himself, and then called her young brother. 'Patrick, can you do me a big favour and ride the bike out there back to St Abbs?'

'No. It's a girl's bike. What about if someone sees me?'

'Look, I will give you a pound, plus pay for your return bus fare,' Andy offered.

'Well, that sounds good, but I want the money before I leave,' said the twelve-year-old.

The First EU

'Sarah, could you lend me some money? I really will explain it all later.'

Sarah went to her room and returned momentarily. 'Here you are, you rascal,' she said, handing her brother the pound note.

'I want to go now before any of my friends see me.'

'That's great, and don't tell anyone what you're doing. Try and get the bike back before anyone notices. If it all goes well, I will give you another pound.' Andy explained where the house was. Patrick knew it because of a newspaper delivery round he'd had there before. With the extra pound in his mind, he was gone straight away.

'Now,' said Sarah, 'you need to do some explaining.'

'Well, I can't tell you the truth as it would put you in great danger. But I do ask your assistance.'

'What do you want,' said Sarah slowly, emphasising each word.

'I want you to say I have been staying with you for the last three days because I can't keep away from you.'

'Erm. The plot thickens.'

Sarah had been in love with Andy and he with her before he went to university. Their relationship hadn't survived the ravages of separation. Plus Sarah was from a poor family, her father being a general labourer. The relationship wasn't encouraged by Andy's parents, although his mother had got on well with Sarah. Andy and Sarah had both moved on from those days.

'All right. My boyfriend is away—well, I haven't heard from him since the fighting. I suppose there is no problem with what you suggest.'

Her mother came into the room with some clean clothes belonging to her husband. 'Andy, put these on. You are making me feel cold, seeing you like that.' They were slightly large, especially around the waist, but at least they gave Andy a better feeling of warmth and well-being.

'I'd like you to phone my brother John as soon as possible and ask him to come and pick me up,' Andy insisted. 'If he isn't there, you can speak to Dave. If my mum answers, don't give her any details. Just say I've been here with you and ask if you can speak with John or Dave.'

'All right,' Sarah said. 'I will go to the call box right away. When I come back, we can talk more, and I will make us some breakfast.'

'Thanks. And can you ask him to bring some clothes and money? Twenty pounds.'

He relaxed more as he started to feel normal after his recent days of exceptional turmoil and activity. He just wanted to get back to the Oat Farm. It was hard to remember that a short while ago, he had been thinking of killing himself to save his friends and family.

Sarah returned. 'I spoke to John. He seemed very relieved that you were all right. He will be here in about two hours.' She looked at Andy quizzically. 'You know, a terrible thing happened in Edinburgh yesterday. Heydrich and Himmler were shot. Heydrich is dead and Himmler is badly injured; that's what I heard from the post office man.'

'OK, I will tell you: it was me who shot them. I want you to make sure Patrick and your mother say nothing out of place. The story is that I came to see you because we are still in love and having an affair. The only people at the farm who know are Dave, who lives on my farm with his wife, and John. There are some resistance fighters in Edinburgh who know. That's all, and I'd like to keep it that way. Only your mother saw me naked so just tell her to say nothing, Patrick will just think I'm sniffing around his sister again.'

'Good God!' Sarah started to shake and cry. 'You know there are going to be terrible repercussions! Will we be safe?'

'You will be safe if you do what I say.'

'I'm frightened, Andy,' she said, still shaking.

'In the long run, we hope this will be the beginning of something better. This is the only thing we can do at this moment, with the enemy being so strong.' He looked into her eyes. 'We had good times when we were younger, Sarah. Now I need your help. I have a girl staying with me on the farm. The ladies there all think I've been to see an injured comrade, hopefully they won't find out I called in here.

I'll sort it all out. It's unfortunate I had to tell you what was going on. By the way, where is your father?'

'Oh, he's away working on a job for the Germans in Eyemouth.'

Sarah's mum had gone out to do some shopping. Patrick wouldn't be back from returning the bike until past ten o'clock, as the bus was on the Saturday timetable. Sarah and Andy had the house to themselves.

'I think we should make love, as we are supposed to be having an affair,' Sarah suggested. 'I've just finished my period, so you don't have to be careful.'

'There's nothing I would like to do more, my lovely Sarah. I wondered if you wanted to make love.'

As they had a small window of opportunity, they got straight to it. They had few hang-ups. In the rapture of old lovers, Andy found an outlet for the turmoil he had been going through.

They were right at the height of it in Sarah's bedroom when her mum returned. She knew what was going on but didn't call out to them. It was the times, and Mrs McDonald had always liked Andy.

They were glad that Sarah's mum didn't make a fuss. This gave them time to wind down and just enjoy one another briefly.

'Andy, I still love you, you know,' Sarah whispered.

'I still have feelings for you too. I remember the good times we had.'

Soon after they emerged from the bedroom, John arrived to collect his brother and take him back to the farm.

From the money John had brought, Andy handed Sarah five pounds. 'Would you buy a bike for Patrick?'

He changed out of his baggy clothes into his own that John had brought. Then Patrick arrived, and Andy gave him the additional pound he'd promised. Patrick reported, 'Some people saw me with the bike. I said I was just checking it out, as it was the type of bike I wanted for my paper round. They sort of believed me. It didn't matter anyway—what could they do? The bike was there.'

'Goodbye, Sarah,' Andy said a few minutes later, feeling that he'd like to spend much more time there. He gave her another five pounds when no one was looking.

'Goodbye, Andy.' They exchanged a gentle kiss on the lips. Sarah wanted him, but she was still frightened by his revelations. She couldn't imagine her lover as a cold-blooded killer.

'Goodbye, Mrs McDonald and Patrick. See you again sometime.'

Mrs McDonald put a packet of egg-and-bacon sandwiches in his hand.

'Goodbye,' the brothers said in unison, and they were gone.

CHAPTER 42

BACK TO THE OAT FARM

'Well,' said John as they drove, 'devastation reigns. We heard this morning that Himmler has also died.'

After ten miles, they came to a roadblock. 'Your papers, please,' said one of the German soldiers.

Another recognised Andy from the farm programme. 'Hi, Andy.'

'Oh, hi, Wilfred, how are you?'

'There has been some terrible news.'

'It's terrible indeed,' said Andy. 'We heard at the post office that Heydrich and Himmler have been shot.'

'Yes. I think we are in for a very bad time.' Wilfred was a good English speaker, self-taught by listening to the English radio and watching American movies. He had also attended night school to improve.

'We've been to see some farmers about the new procedures; we are on the way back to the farm at the moment. So what is going to happen now?'

'Well, they must find the assassins first of all. Until then, there will be severe restrictions.'

'Will we continue with the farm efficiency programme, do you think?'

'It must continue, or we will all be starving soon enough.'

'We will attend the village centre tomorrow and may see you there.'

'I hope so,' Wilfred replied seriously. 'These are dangerous times. We must remain friends.'

'Goodbye, Wilfred.'

'Ciao, Andy, John.'

As they continued back to the farm, John said, 'I told the girls that you had gone to see an old friend who was sick, and that I didn't know the details.'

'What about the Germans?'

'They didn't come around. We did the farm visits last week. I think they were happy to let us get on with our own farm work.'

'It couldn't be better. The deed is done, I'm still alive, and—as far as I know—I got away with it.'

Chapter 43

THIS COWARDLY ACT

The sun was just rising through the majestic elm trees in front of the little farm belonging to Auntie May and Uncle Albert. The cocks had already been crowing for some time. There was an expectant dread in the air.

Irene and Tom were having an early morning dalliance. After all, it was Sunday, and they might as well enjoy one another, not knowing what awful outcome the immediate future may hold. Although the farm needed daily attention, they knew Auntie and Uncle would take care of things this morning, as they usually did on Sundays before they got spruced up for the church service.

Before yesterday, it hadn't seemed to the young couple that there was a war on. They were happy, having found a deep feeling of contentment. It was a fool's paradise as they both knew, especially Tom. The film of him helping the farmers had been made and was being viewed over the whole country. No one had reported recognising him yet.

He didn't know it, but he had been recognised in Scotland, at least by the three young men on the Oat Farm. Dave especially had no doubt. But they were saying nothing. Molly had been recognised by her friends and parents, but this didn't cause a problem. Her story about running away from the research centre rang true with them. She had been a junior employee anyway.

Yesterday, the people at Dale Farm had received the news about the assassinations. Nobody knew what was going to happen, but everyone was contemplating terrible consequences. Tom wondered how Florence was getting on. She was living in southern Scotland a long way from Edinburgh. He hoped the distance would protect her.

Tom and Irene decided to attend church on this Sunday. They never normally did. But some Germans attended, and Tom especially wanted to find out what was going on. It wouldn't be good, but it was better to know.

Surprisingly Molly was there with Dieter. 'Hello, Tom, Irene. Nice to see you,' she said.

'Hi, Dieter. Hi, Molly,' said Tom.

'This is a terrible day,' said Dieter. 'The very popular commander Heydrich and our SS leader Himmler are both dead.'

'Yes. What is going to happen to us all now?' Tom asked.

'I don't know,' said Dieter, 'but we are all friends, I hope.'

'Well,' said Tom, 'the farm efficiency programme must go ahead, or we will all be starving by next year.'

'The captain said to us this morning that things must go on as usual until we are advised otherwise by the high command.'

Everyone in the church looked worried. The vicar said in his sermon, 'God will be with the families of the assassinated leaders. God does not condone the taking of human life.' That was all he mentioned about the recent events.

After the service, the captain had a word with Tom and Molly. 'I need to see you at the vicarage this evening at six. I want us to have a conversation with key people in the media campaign.'

At six o'clock, Molly, Dieter, Irene, Tom, the captain, the lieutenant, the vicar, Sally, Olaf, and Olaf's media team met in the vicarage lounge. There were a few extra soldiers and security people plus some of the local police in the entourage, and it became clear there wasn't enough room. Luckily on Sundays, the church hall was not used for other functions, so they decided to use it for this important meeting.

In the end, there were about a hundred people present. The Germans put a guard on the door. Sally organised coffee, tea, and biscuits through some of her church ladies. Olaf Franscheld stood up to address the group.

'Because of the cowardly and despicable act that took place yesterday in Edinburgh, we are in a fragile situation until the culprits are found and brought to justice. Our security police are working around the clock to this end. In Scotland, there has already been a six o'clock curfew imposed, and all men in Edinburgh, no matter who, have to present evidence to show what they were doing at the time the murders took place. Our dear leader has ordered the immediate execution of two thousand of the conscripted United Kingdom workers. This will be carried out tomorrow. All people living within a one-hundred-metre radius of the camera obscurer tower where the shots came from have been arrested for interrogation.

'We are fortunate that the German occupational policy—what you call our charm offensive—has achieved a lot of success in this area, with the cooperation of local people like you here today. Unfortunately, we will suffer just the same. You understand that Germany cannot allow something like this to happen without extreme consequences. We must stop these sorts of killings.'

There was stunned silence in the hall.

He continued, 'In the meantime, everything for us will continue as before. I don't want any let-up in the overall push to make the goodwill movies. So that is it, ladies and gentlemen. There is nothing more to be said. Good evening to you.'

The locals were so affected, they could not drink their tea or coffee. Even the Germans were affected.

Tom said to Molly and Irene, 'Tomorrow, two thousand innocent men are going to die. What will happen then? We've had a friendly situation with the Germans in this area. I don't think anywhere else in the country has had it so good. It must be pretty bad in Scotland. I know there have been some deaths in the round-ups elsewhere in Britain.'

'Remember, two hundred men have already been executed,' said Irene. 'They were killed just because the Royal Navy was not cooperating.'

There was a bit of a commotion and some loud voices when Sally the vicar's wife got up. In a loud, emotional voice, she addressed the hall. 'Mr Franscheld, how do you expect us to work with you when you are executing two thousand innocent British workers? What have they got to do with the assassinations in Scotland?'

Franscheld responded, 'Mrs Cooper, you could say that our two assassinated leaders were innocent Germans as well. You had better get used to the fact that those men are going to die. Unfortunately, there is nothing I can do to stop it. This will teach a lesson to the cowardly people who undertook this dastardly act. Good day, madam.' With that, the media chief walked out of the meeting.

Chapter 44

TARGET HITLER

At that time, no one in the village, German or British, knew about the goings-on within the German high command since the conquest of the United Kingdom. Hitler had returned to his original policies, like the persecution of the Jews. He was 'liquidating' the Roma, insane people, and political opponents again in large numbers. Jews and others were joining the British labourers in slave camps.

These policies alarmed some of the German high command. With the assassination of two of the most vicious officers in their circle, some of the others felt it could be the time to make a move.

There had been at least two attempts on Hitler's life in the last three years, and many more dating back to 1934. He was aware of the dangers, and knew that now would be a prime time for his enemies to act. Hitler had been planning to visit England, but this trip was cancelled.

Two days after the assassinations, it just so happened that a moderate group in Germany was able to get a small bomb in a briefcase onto Hitler's plane. They knew the plane was going on a three-hour flight to Italy for a meeting between Hitler and Mussolini. The bomb was timed to explode two hours into the flight.

But the flight was delayed, maybe to throw off any would-be assailant. The plane finally took off two hours late. When the bomb exploded, the plane was only fifty feet above the ground.

There was a small lake at the end of the runway. The plane broke in two, and the front part, containing Hitler inside a bomb-proof capsule, fell into the lake. Hitler was not killed, but in the confusion, it took a long time to get him out of the water. He was suffering from hypothermia and had water in his lungs.

Hitler was not a physically strong man, having suffered from all sorts of ailments and dubious treatment from his doctors. He had the best attention possible, they said. Nonetheless, he died of pneumonia and a collapsed lung three days later.

The others in the front of the plane, the two pilots, had been badly injured. The four people in the rear of the plane survived with minor injuries after that part fell into bushes on the edge of the lake.

The leaders of the military got together immediately, flying in from the far reaches of the German-occupied territories. They quickly asserted absolute control over their soldiers, who were used to stop the country from falling into anarchy.

These men, six field marshals, two admirals and the head of the airforce with his deputy represented all German men in the armed forces. They were brilliant military leaders

The First EU

but not politicians. This didn't matter because they were well respected and had the loyalty matter because they were well respected and had the loyalty of their men. They were to become the saviours of Germany.

In the swiftly convened meeting, all agreed the following: German soldiers, having pledged their lives to Hitler, would now have to pledge to whoever the new leader was going to be. Three SS leaders were still alive. They were told the SS would be integrated into the mainstream armed forces over the next three months.

The SS engineering team at the Tim's former workplace, the research centre, kept their positions in the reshuffling. The 'SS' part of their title was quietly dropped after a month or so, and they became simply the special engineering team.

The SS became history.

The two leaders who came to the fore were Rommel and Doenitz, revered for their wartime exploits. Rommel had secured a crucial source of oil for the regime in his battles against the British in the Persian Gulf. Doenitz had conducted a successful submarine campaign in the Atlantic, starving the United Kingdom of vital supplies in the years leading up to the German invasion.

The Gestapo were called in and agreed to the new regime. Discussed with them was bringing to justice the culprits in the assassinations, but it was emphasised that although this was a high priority, above that was quickly establishing stability in Germany and the occupied territories. One hundred thousand troops were drafted in from the occupied territories to secure stability in Germany. These would be in place for only a few weeks, until order was confirmed. Then the troops would be sent back to the occupied zones, as the military feared resistance groups would take advantage of the situation.

The German regime was going to change from top to bottom. There were only a few people who could bring the situation under control. When the colonies belonging to the occupied European countries were included, the Germans had a third of the world's land surface under their control. They had no intention of throwing this away.

Goebbels and some other senior hard-line Nazis were put under house arrest. Thousands of people who had been close to Hitler had to take an oath of allegiance to the new regime. Any who hesitated or became difficult were quickly dealt with— jailed or roughed up. In no time at all, people were queuing to give their pledges to the new leadership.

Hitler had run Germany in such a peculiar way that those who took over had to quickly get to grips with what was going on and sort out the tangled mess. Rommel and Doenitz were in this. A senior moderate took over the Gestapo.

The Germans, in less than three years, had successfully coerced and encouraged the countries of Europe to be good collaborators. They intended the same for the United Kingdom. The new United Kingdom leader postponed and then cancelled the execution of two thousand slave labourers in the hope that goodwill could still be rescued. The new, moderate German high command, although still wanting to find the assassins, realised the situation had played into their hands. From now on, they could follow a different path.

People like Tom and Molly were in great demand to encourage cooperation. Everyone must be taught the German way, which would be much better for all if they embraced it.

The First EU

There was one week of mourning for Hitler. His mad doctrines were put to one side. There was a hunt for the bombers, of course, but as with the hunt in Scotland, it was deemed slightly lower in priority than the rescue of the situation as a whole. There were still plenty of officials in the hierarchy who wanted to persecute the Jews and continue with the termination of others they deemed undesirable, but most Germans were in favour of changing course—although until then they had turned a blind eye.

The people in the village near Dale Farm did as they were told, continuing as before. They had not heard about any executions but didn't know how they would continue cooperation if executions did happen.

Two days after the meeting in the church hall, they heard about the plane crash. Hitler was then fighting for his life in hospital, and the executions had been postponed. It was a time of great uncertainty for all, including the local Germans. Olaf Franscheld was called back to head office in London.

When it was announced that Hitler had died of pneumonia, everyone had a feeling of heightened emotion. For the farm community, that emotion was relief, although they wouldn't admit it.

There was a church service for Hitler that all the Germans attended. There were no villagers or farmers there, not even Molly or Tom. Sally's husband took the service and prayed for Hitler as a human being.

Sally was the only local woman who attended. She sat with Lieutenant Tobias Schmitt. They had a definite affair going on. Maybe it was not a physical affair, but they had been working together on a number of cooperative projects.

Sally was a part-time teacher at the junior school. Along with her role as the vicar's wife, this gave her a lot of leverage with the lieutenant in terms of gaining local cooperation. The Germans were, after all, supposed to be on a charm offensive. As far as the lieutenant and Sally were concerned, this was definitely the case.

Schmitt, like Sally, was married. They tried to keep their feelings under control, but people could see and were starting to talk. They made a striking couple when dancing at the dances in the church hall. The lieutenant was an accomplished dancer and helped Sally, who was a bit rusty although she had been a good dancer in her youth.

Word had got around about the dances, and the Saturday gatherings had become so popular that they were held on Fridays now as well. German soldiers were limited to just one dance day a week because they were coming in from as far as fifteen miles away.

Chapter 45

THE CARROT AND STICK

In Britain, the German authorities had to be firm but reasonable. The rise of the moderates didn't mean that they were going to pull out of any of their hard-won territories. The idea was to consolidate in a way that the local people could benefit from greatly if they cooperated. But if the locals resisted, they were to be pounded on with an iron fist. To this end, it would be necessary to keep German security forces and the Gestapo well manned. Troops were stationed where they could easily be deployed to trouble spots.

Special people like Tom and Molly in the Midlands and Dave, Andy, and John in Scotland gained great benefit by their cooperation. Their media shows encouraged and showed the population what they should be doing to become efficient and learn to speak German. Germany had been working like this in Europe for two years, and even with Hitler in charge, they had been quite successful.

There was a lot of work to do to convert British farms and factories to German methods, so there was no unemployment in the United Kingdom. In fact, everyone had to report to centralised bureaus, where they were allocated to a work programme. The Germans were ones for procedure and efficiency and cooperation. The old class system in the United Kingdom didn't apply; it was a meritocracy now. All the stately homes were commandeered. Many ordinary people who had been annoyed with the establishment for years were being given more recognition. They were treated better by the Germans than they had been by their own ruling classes.

The farming programme and Molly's engagement agenda were ticking over. Eight days after Hitler's plane crash, on a Wednesday, a new head of media arrived in the village from London. Olaf Franscheld had been replaced. He was a member of the SS and definitely not a moderate.

All involved in media outreach were called to the church hall as normal at six o'clock. Introducing himself, the new man started.

CHAPTER 46

COOPERATION IN THE VILLAGE

'Good evening, ladies and gentlemen. My name is Horst Geissler, I will be your new head of media, pursuing the same line as Olaf Franscheld, who is now working on another assignment.

'The dire events of the past week must be put behind us, though of course the perpetrators will be pursued and brought to justice. We want to bring Britain into our European community, which will be the most successful group of nations the world has ever known. We have our way of doing things and hope you can embrace them. In some cases, you may think you can improve our methods, and we are always willing to listen. The main thing is now we will be much more lenient on people in general so that there can be as much cooperation as possible.

'You in this area have been at the forefront of cooperation, which is why we have our Molly here demonstrating friendship and Tom, who has shown that he can understand our procedures and run with them. We hope these examples will convince the older generation to implement change. This will improve the efficiency of your farms. From next year, there should never be a food shortage again, and the variety of food will also be wider than you could ever imagine.

'Rather than you working for us, I emphasise that we will be working together, especially regarding the farm programme. We want to make Molly even more of a star, if she is in agreement. I believe Molly's German is coming along well, and we want to send her to drama tuition. At still only nineteen, she has much in front of her. I didn't mean that in the wrong way, of course,' he hastily added as some people started to laugh.

'I want to say lastly that anyone who wants to help us in our efforts for the efficiency drive and the cooperation of our great peoples can call in to this church hall to see us. We will have a presence every weekday from eight thirty in the morning until seven in the evening. When the children's classes are running, our desk will be in the alcove. One more thing to mention: we would like all young people at least to learn to speak German. Thank you and good night, ladies and gentlemen.'

With that, he stepped down to take his seat at the front, next to Tom. 'Can you give a response to my speech, Tom?'

Tom was rather taken aback, as he had not been warned he would have to say anything and hadn't prepared. Yet he couldn't refuse. He stepped up on the stage.

'Ladies and gentlemen, I didn't expect to be making a speech tonight, so it will not sound polished—although I know what I want to say. Firstly I would like to acknowledge our new media chief, Horst Geissler, and thank him for his address. I look forward to the new direction of our collaboration, with more leniency and friendship. I encourage people to attend the recruitment office in the church hall, mentioned by Mr Geissler. I would say to everyone that if you can't beat them, you might as well join them, and that is my policy. I honestly look forward to further success for our efficiency and cooperation programmes.

'Molly and I have started learning German. I'm not at her level, but I'm working hard at it. After all, most of the Germans here can speak at least a bit of English, and all the German people I deal with are good English speakers.

'I'm so glad that the execution of the two thousand workers has been rescinded. I don't know how I would have been able to continue with cooperation otherwise. Now I think the good times of joint prosperity will be here soon enough. So, ladies and gentlemen, that is it. Good evening to you all.'

To Tom's surprise, everyone clapped, led by Horst Geissler.

***

This quiet area north of Birmingham had been relatively unaffected by the violence happening in the rest of the country. There had been a lot of deaths especially from the rounding up of slave workers. In all, about five thousand people had been killed. Most were prominent academics, resistance fighters, and forces people who hadn't stopped fighting quickly enough. People were more resentful in other areas.

With the coming to power of more moderate leaders, all British slave labourers were released. The ones on important work were retained on lenient terms and were paid. Jews were also to be treated much better, but the return of their possessions was being left to individuals. So things were improving, but there was still a lot of unhappiness.

Of course, resentment over war deaths went both ways. The British had put up a good fight, not rolled over like France. They said that over two hundred thousand German civilians had been killed by the British bombings, especially in the cities of western Germany like Aachen, Cologne, Dusseldorf, and Frankfurt. Because of their spirited resistance, the British had earned more respect from the invaders than any other of the occupied countries. The Germans wanted to use British influence around the world to help in their overall goal of world domination.

Arthur had never been sent to the ghettos like his parents and sister. He was in demand as a proficient surgeon, working on all the war casualties. There had been many wounded in the round-ups and other violent activities of the Germans, even after the surrender.

As soon as the Jews were released, they strove to return home and take up normal life. There had only been a few months of occupation in Britain, unlike in Europe; the Jewish properties in general had not been taken over. Arthur's family returned to their home and shoemaking business in East London with no problem.

Chapter 47

BACK TO THE MEETING

Horst Geisler wound up the meeting by saying, 'Ladies and gentlemen this is going to be the start of something good for both our countries. This friendly village is going to be at the centre of a media campaign that will affect the whole of the United Kingdom. I look forward to all the people here being involved and hope I can do my bit to help. I want your suggestions too, as I want you to be happy. I know we have been through some terrible times recently, but I want us to come together now. Good night and God be with you.'

Then he addressed the vicar. 'Vicar I would be grateful if we could use your living room for a more cosy meeting with the main people. I would like to have a friendly talk with them. I can provide the drinks and food.'

'Of course, Mr Geissler. You are always welcome. Sally, could you ask a couple of your ladies to help?'

'Certainly, Ray.'

The main room at the vicarage was often used for committee meetings, Bible classes, and the like. Perhaps twenty-five people could be seated there when chairs were brought in from other rooms. It was a grand room with wooden beams showing, an impressive marble fireplace, and an oak mantelpiece. The two large sash windows either side of the fireplace were covered with thick navy-blue velvet curtains.

The fire had been lit earlier, adding to the comfort of the place, as it was a cold November evening. With all the main people plus some other Germans and local councillors, the room was full. It was quite a cosy affair. Importantly, there were no local police or German security people in attendance. The normal guards from the lieutenant's patrol were stationed outside.

Captain Martin Vloch was at the vicarage with the rest. He had become friendly with Tom lately, being impressed by his knowledge on the engineering and programme management side. The captain was a family man and had not been chasing the ladies in the area, as so many of his comrades were doing. That did not mean, however, that he was unaware of the effect a beautiful woman could have.

He caught Tom near the grand fireplace by himself. 'Tom, that was a great speech. I've just been thinking—for your German knowledge, I could bring you a good-looking lady tutor from Germany. That would help you no end. They call them long-haired dictionaries.'

'Thanks for thinking of me, Captain. I just wonder what Irene would think of your suggestion.'

'Yes, I can see how Irene may have some concerns. It's just a thought.'

Chapter 48

THE GERMAN PARTY

Straight after the church hall meeting, Horst Geissler found Sally. 'My people have brought the food and drink. Can they deliver it to your kitchen?'

'Of course, Mr Geissler.'

'Please call me Horst.'

'Fine, Horst.'

A few minutes later, a worried-looking tea lady came rushing up to Sally. 'Two young German men have just delivered food to your kitchen. It's all funny German stuff, and we don't know how to serve it.'

Sally quickly found Horst. 'My ladies don't know how to serve your German food.'

'All right. I will instruct the young men who delivered it to help. They can speak some English.'

One of the tea ladies was the mother of two of the choir girls who had been seeing the German soldiers. They lived near, and popped in when they spied the German men preparing the food. They just had to get involved, although their mother tried to send them home. Luckily the vicarage kitchen was large, like the farm kitchens of old, so there was plenty of room. The young people got on well, the girls helping their mother follow instructions from the Germans.

Tom and Molly expected that at this meeting, people would discuss in more detail the strategy to be followed and what the various people's assignments would be. They were surprised by Horst Geissler's words.

'Well, people, tonight we are not going to talk about work. What I can tell you is that with the removal of the old leaders from the scene, I've been instructed to tell you that Germany is going to be following a completely new direction. The normal rule of law will be followed, applying equally to Germans and all under German occupation. We are going to stay in occupation everywhere to bring a fantastic new future that is going to mean the unification of Europe. Our union will be the greatest world power that has ever been. So that no more bad things will happen from our side, our security forces will be greatly reduced. We want to work together with everyone to aim towards this great future. There has been much suffering on both sides. We want to put this behind us. We don't expect things to run absolutely smoothly, and know there is much bitterness still. But from our side, we are really going to try our best.

'Friends, let us party.'

With that, the properly prepared German food was wheeled and carried in, and the party did indeed start. There was plenty of beer and schnapps and even some good French wine. Right at the beginning, ten bottles of champagne were opened, giving everyone a glass to toast the great future. Even Sally's two young daughters couldn't be kept away; each had a sip of champagne. Sally didn't worry on this special occasion.

The whole vicarage seemed to have a glow. There was a warm feeling about the place. People scurried about, and the drink was really beginning to flow. Some children, friends of Sally's daughters, arrived, and it seemed more villagers had turned up. Most of the lieutenant's patrol had also turned up, including the soldier friends of the choir girls.

The vicar said, 'Horst, we had better open the church hall for the overflow people, and if possible send some food and drink there.'

'I'm delighted to do so. I will order more German food and drink.'

With this, the dance music was put on. Rumour spread that the German occupation was going to be much better now, concentrating on a new way forward under a united Europe guided by Germany. The food was most welcome as everyone had been on war rations for some time. Even the German soldiers were on rations. Nearly all guessed this was special food arranged only for today, so they had better make the most of it.

Everyone was letting their hair down. There was a lot at stake for the main players. Molly and Tom had been earmarked for big roles. Originally Molly and Dieter were going to be featured as a couple, crossing the boundary between conqueror and vanquished. This hadn't worked out because Molly didn't want Dieter as her boyfriend, although she liked him.

Captain Vloch wanted to put Tom forward as a young leader in the quest for an efficient future for a unified Europe, with Germany at its centre. Tom was excited about this idea but thought he must come clean about his fraudulent personal situation. He reasoned that the risk must surely be low now; his escape from the research centre had not caused any injury or put anyone in danger.

He didn't know what to think about getting a German 'long-haired dictionary'. It seemed a novel idea but would complicate things in his love life. His German was already coming along quite well. He had been practising with the soldiers he'd been working with and was getting books from the captain and help from Molly's tutor.

Chapter 49

SALLY'S IN LOVE

Sally and the lieutenant were getting on too well, especially after a couple of drinks. They decided to walk over to the dance.

'Come here,' she whispered forcefully, pulling Schmitt through the doorway of an outbuilding.

'Oh, Sally, kiss me deeply.'

They kissed so passionately, they nearly fell over. Sally put her hand inside his trousers; he pulled her bra up so he could kiss her well-formed breasts, which were like balloons ready to burst. He pulled her dress up and put his hand inside her panties. Her wetness down there surprised her. She could hardly remember when she had been so flowing. Sally moaned, 'Oh, that's too beautiful.'

They were almost climaxing. The pent-up desires of the last weeks of working together on the media campaign added to their passion.

'Mummy, where are you?' a small voice cried out. 'I need you. Sheila has fallen over.'

Alan J Caulfield

They quickly disengaged and pulled their clothes straight. 'Oh, darling I was just going to the dance with Uncle Toby,' Sally called back as her daughter ran up. 'I'll come straight away. How did she manage to fall?'

'She fell down the stairs, Mummy.'

Daisy, Sally's younger daughter, luckily hadn't seen anything. She hadn't even seen that they were in the old brick outbuilding. Sheila had fallen down the stairs while showing off to her friends who had come over for the party. She had a bruise above her left eye. Her pride had been hurt more than anything.

The lieutenant held a cold wet flannel on the bruise. 'Thank you, Uncle Toby,' Sheila said. All was well soon enough.

Schmitt and Sally had a knowing look at one another, feeling lucky they had only been glimpsed by Sally's nine-year-old and not anyone old enough to be asking awkward questions.

'Mummy, you've got wet patch on your bottom,' said Daisy,

'Oh, have I?' said Sally, rather surprised she had forgotten. 'I must have sat in some drink someone spilled on a chair. I will have to go and change my dress.'

Sally quickly went to her bedroom to change and clean up. She wanted her Toby. Her desires were going to be the end of her, she thought. It had been good between her and Ray in the early days, but for longer than she would like to admit, there had been something missing on the sexual side of their marriage. She was a friendly person, and some would say this made her seem a bit flirty, but she had never been unfaithful to Ray. So far, that is.

The First EU

'Where have you been?' Schmitt said to Sally on her return.

'Well, you should know! It was you who caused the problem, getting my dress wet. I've just been to change it.'

'I could have helped with that.'

'That would have been great, but we will have to save it for another day, darling.'

They went over to the hall, this time not getting sidetracked. They could talk freely because so much noise was coming from the other guests, most of whom had had some drink by this time. Nothing could be overheard of an individual conversation.

CHAPTER 50

THE LANGUAGE SCHOOL

Tom told Irene about the long-haired dictionary as they were walking over to the hall. Most people from the vicarage were there now. She thought maybe if Tom acquired a long-haired dictionary, she could get a short-haired dictionary. *Not really*, she mused. *I love Tom so much.* Irene could only be an onlooker and hope she would retain Tom in the hurly-burly of the present situation.

But she had another thought. She was well educated and surely could find a position in the new, moderate German system. Not wanting to waste any time, she approached Dieter. He was looking a bit glum, what with Molly being with her German tutor.

'Hi, Dieter. Do you have a moment to talk? I have an idea.'

Dieter was more than happy to do so. Irene was wearing an enchanting dress with slits that showed off her lovely legs. The vision was alluring. 'Sure, Irene.'

'I want to be involved in the new German regime Horst Geissler spoke about tonight. I want to learn to speak

German, and at the same time I want to start a language school to teach English.'

'That sounds interesting. Tell me more.'

'I had a good education in English at a top private school for girls. Then I worked in the legal profession for a number of years, where I had to practise good English all the time, I also learned public speaking. I want to start as soon as possible. If you can help, it would be great.'

Seeing that Molly was lost in deep conversation with her tutor and Tom, he said, 'Let's go and see the captain.' His own lieutenant seemed to be taken up with Sally.

When they put Irene's credentials to Captain Vloch, he was interested, and became more so as he fixed his eyes on Irene. Also, he'd had a couple of drinks already. 'This is a good idea and exactly what we have in mind. We want people to come forward with ideas. People must do what best suits their assets, and yours are your legs—and your English knowledge, of course.'

Irene made out she was a bit embarrassed, but was flattered, as most women would be. 'Captain,' she said, 'I'm glad you like all my assets, but it's only the academic ones we are considering here, isn't it?'

'I suppose so,' said the captain. He was thirty-six, ten years older than Irene, but thought she was delightful, especially as her enthusiasm showed through for the English language project. Apart from her good looks, the proposal had a lot of merits, and he wanted to help. He wouldn't get into trouble, he thought. After all, she was with Tom, the Germans' number-one protégé.

'I want to help you. I will have to think how we can proceed. Dieter, it was good that you brought Irene to me.'

'Yes, sir. The lieutenant was busy.'

'Indeed.' They all could see the lieutenant was still talking to Sally. 'Dieter, I've heard you have a degree in the English language from Cologne University. I would like your assistance on this project as well. I will speak to Lieutenant Schmitt when he is free.'

'I would like that, Captain.'

Irene was surprised that her idea had been taken up so enthusiastically and quickly by the captain. She looked at Dieter and realised he had given up on being Molly's boyfriend. She thought a new project might cheer him up a bit. He was a sensitive person. Maybe he would meet someone else through the school.

Vloch said, 'Irene, I would like you to put a rough proposal together and discuss it with Dieter. The two of you should come and see me on Friday afternoon.'

'Certainly, Captain,'

'Now let's enjoy the party. Would you like to dance, Irene?'

'Yes.'

The lieutenant and Sally, feeling they had been together too long, decided they should find other people to talk to. Schmitt wandered over to Tom, Molly, and Molly's tutor, who were in deep conversation near the alcove.

Molly's tutor was Fritz Theyse. He was only slightly taller than Molly at five feet nine, but made up for that by being athletic. He had blue eyes, light-coloured hair, and classic features. He was also very talkative, quite the opposite of Dieter.

'Hello, may I join you?' asked the lieutenant.

'Of course' Tom, Molly, and Fritz said in unison.

The First EU

'I think I have been monopolising Sally too much tonight.'

'Why worry? If you like talking to her, you should,' said Molly.

'Anyway, what have you got to tell me?' said Schmitt.

'We have just been speaking about what Horst Geissler said this evening. We are so excited that this village is going to be at the centre of a new time of friendship and cooperation. What do you think?'

'Being friends is all very well, but the farm efficiency programme is the main thing. That's the food we need to survive. Molly, shall we dance?'

'Yes, why not?' said Molly, getting up with a flurry.

It was about eight thirty. After another half an hour had passed, all the people who had gone to the vicarage were back in the hall, either dancing or chatting. There was food and drink, and it wasn't likely the local police were going to stick to the letter of the law when it came to licensing regulations.

The hall was quite packed after word got around. The Germans had previously had a small leaflet printed off, outlining the new direction Horst Geissler had spoken about. He quickly sent for a few hundred, which were distributed at the hall. He again asked people to come forward with ideas.

Chapter 51

THE JITTERBUG

Although there had been a number of dances since Tom came back on the scene, he had been keeping a low profile, especially after showing his prowess at unarmed combat. He was dancing a bit but purposefully kept away from Molly. He had also been drinking a little. When the ebb and flow of the evening brought them together later, he said, 'If a good number we know comes up, let's dance like we used to.'

'Do you think we should, Tim? Oh, Tom—sorry.'

'Yes. Why worry? What can happen now? Let people talk.'

'Yes, let's then.'

Molly was dancing with Fritz when a fast number came up. Tom had been dancing with Irene and Sally; they could dance all right, but not like Molly. The fast number was a jitterbug which Tim and Molly had often danced to. They had belonged to a dance club in Coventry, where they had been among the best couples.

As no one else wanted to tackle this number, Tom went over to Molly. 'Let's go.'

The First EU

So they started dancing the jitterbug, and such was their performance that a space was soon cleared on the dance floor. Other couples stopped just to look. The number was over three minutes long, and at the end of it, everyone clapped, including the Germans. Irene and Dieter didn't though. Molly and Tom looked rather like an item as they wound down.

Soon after, they parted—to Irene for Tom, and to Fritz for Molly. Poor Dieter didn't get a look in, but he came over to Molly anyway, and she danced the next dance with him after she had got her breath back.

The captain looked at Tom quizzically. 'That was some dancing from both of you.'

Tom knew he shouldn't have taken the risk that his past might be found out. 'Well, Captain, Molly said she could dance. I used to dance at a club. We were talking earlier about our jitterbugging days, and I said if one came up, we would try it out.'

'I see,' said Vloch. He seemed unconvinced. 'You were very good. Truthfully, you amaze me. You are superb at unarmed combat and dancing. You have picked up our technical procedures very well. You are progressing quickly in the German language. What other things might you surprise us with?'

'Erm… I can play football as a forward? I play rugby as a wing. I can ride a motorbike and a horse after a fashion, and drive of course. That's about it. Oh, I have sailed a small boat and can swim. Not that I'm going to need much of that around here.'

'Great.' Vloch sounded less quizzical now. 'I'm glad you are working for us.'

'Thank you. I think I had better go and dance with Irene.'

'There's another interesting young lady. She was talking to me earlier about starting an English language school for the Germans. I'm going to help her, as is Dieter. They're putting a proposal to me on Friday.'

'That's fascinating. I know Irene is good at English. She helps me sometimes, and has had a good education. See you later.'

Irene was dancing with Dieter, so Tom sat down to wait. Irene was happy to see Tom waiting for her but didn't stop dancing straight away. She danced another two numbers with Dieter, keeping Tom waiting. Tom thought maybe Irene was upset with him for his earlier performance with Molly.

He shouldn't have worried. Irene was happy to see him back from Molly. 'Hello, darling,' she said after excusing herself from Dieter.

Tom called, 'Hi, Dieter, wait a minute. The captain told me you and Irene have an idea for an English language school. It sounds great. I hope you make a success of it.'

'Oh, we will,' said Dieter.

'Yes, we surely will,' said Irene. 'I'm really looking forward to working with you Dieter. It would be so good if all Germans could speak English and all English could speak German. This is what we are aiming for. We know it will never happen, but it must be our goal. I'm going to find a nice young local girl to help us, just for Dieter. And we must start interviewing candidates proficient in English.'

'Oh, you don't have to worry about me.'

'But I do, Dieter.'

Sally came over with some other good-looking ladies about her age. 'These ladies are colleagues of mine through the junior school. They have just stopped in to see what is going on.'

'Why don't you introduce them to Horst and some of his friends?' said Tom. 'I'll come over with you. They have just been sitting around talking all evening—probably about work, knowing them.'

Chapter 52

SALLY'S TEACHER FRIENDS

Horst looked up as Tom walked over with Sally and her colleagues. 'Hello, Mr Geissler,' Tom said. 'These ladies want to speak with you about your plans. Or, if you don't want to talk about business tonight, they would like to dance with you and your colleagues. They are all local teachers.'

'Thank you for introducing us,' Geissler replied, surprised. 'I think I would prefer to dance, but I will tell you I'm not very good.'

The best-looking of the ladies stepped forward. 'Well, Mr Geissler, I would like to dance with you. We can do a slow one to begin with and see how it goes.'

Horst Geissler was quite taken aback by her confidence, though it was not unappealing. She appeared to be in her early thirties; he was forty. He had not danced this evening, having just arrived with the last group from the vicarage.

'It's only ten o'clock,' she continued. 'We have more than two hours to get to know one another. My name is Kathryn. You can call me Katie.'

'My name is Horst, Katie.'

Horst was, as always, with his two senior media people, and there were two other ladies of similar age who wanted to dance. That took care of the three media men; they couldn't back down now.

Chapter 53

NO SUSPICIONS IN SCOTLAND

Back in Scotland, the sun was shining through the majestic oaks planted around the farmhouse by Andy and John's forefathers. They drew near in the little car that belonged to Jean. Andy knew he would be interrogated by the ladies of the house—not least his girlfriend. It was difficult to contemplate. What made it more serious was that, in the hurly-burly of the last few days, he hadn't thought about the story he would tell.

He had to trust Sarah implicitly. There was no choice about that, but he wanted to get as few people involved as possible. Even among the resistance people, few knew his true identity. No one on the boat or at the tower had known his surname. There was no problem with him using Andy, as there were so many in Scotland.

The escape boat had been searched by another large German patrol far out to sea. It had found the fishermen from the position given by the spotter plane. Luckily, the spotters had not got an accurate count of the crew members on the fishing vessel. If the original patrol boat had checked, they would have realised one man was missing.

So all was well. The Germans were taking their investigation to ridiculous extremes, which became more evident as time went on without firm leads. By studying the bullets retrieved from the scene, investigators had established that they were German. From the accuracy and number of shots, they deduced the use of a new automatic sniper rifle. Twenty-one bullets were found at the castle parade ground, and the Germans suspected there were more.

It was further established that two of the new guns had been issued to a four-man patrol that had been wiped out near Glasgow. Here the Germans drew a blank. British army records had been destroyed just before the Germans took over. So now they faced a countrywide interrogation of all British troops who may have been fighting near Glasgow.

Torture was used at the beginning, but after Hitler's death, there was some respite while the Germans took stock. When the new, more moderate leadership came in, torture was dropped.

On the same day Hitler was attacked, Andy and John were interrogated. They had been combatants and were fighting in the area where the guns went missing. They held to their story, and because the leader of the farm efficiency drive put a good word in for them, that was all that happened. It seemed that Andy had got away with it.

He had told the ladies at home that he had gone to see a friend who was injured and lived towards Edinburgh. He had such a friend who lived on the coast between Eyemouth and Dunbar. The friend had been a corporal in his patrol and was also named Andy. He contacted the corporal, who was nearly recovered, and filled him in on the ruse in case anyone should check.

After the week of mourning for Hitler, the investigation was toned down. It was quite convenient that two stalwarts of the old regime as well as Hitler had been eliminated. Now the moderates in the German command could continue with their aim of world domination.

Andy's friend the corporal phoned the farmhouse; it had been arranged like this. Florence answered the phone, and the corporal left a message, asking her to thank Andy for his visit and to tell him that he was much better now. This seemed to do the trick. From then on, not much was said at the Oat Farm about Andy's trip.

Andy, John, and Dave, working closely with the Germans, could see the change in their administration and attitude. The occupiers were much more inclusive and cooperative. The men from the farm had also seen the short film clip of Tim explaining how the implementation of the farm efficiency programme was going in the Midlands. The clip included Uncle Albert, Auntie May, and a young lady called Irene.

The efficiency implementation at Dale Farm had been undertaken using German procedures, with the help of the German soldiers and local farmhands, male and female. On this small farm of ninety acres, it had been decided to concentrate on egg production and raising pigs for bacon. Two cows and two horses were retained, but the bull had been taken to market and one horse went to another farm. They kept the newly planted apple orchard, but all the rest of the acreage was given over to growing things the chickens and pigs could eat. Some hedgerows were pulled up to make the fields larger, allowing for efficient mechanised ploughing by ex-military vehicles. These were well suited to travel over rough terrain, even the steep slopes on the remote farm.

All was quiet now on the Oat Farm. There wasn't much the young farmers had to change to comply with the new German procedures. Their farm was already running quite efficiently, growing oats and maintaining a modest herd of fifty milking cows.

Andy was missing Sarah and took a couple of trips to visit her. Their time together was all the sweeter because Sarah knew his story completely. She was the only woman he could talk to about the assassination. Because of this, they were becoming closer. Andy knew he could trust Sarah, but he was aware of the closeness they were generating. He didn't know what to do about it.

Florence was enjoying the sex she was having with Dave. Obviously there was no chance of her falling pregnant, and this may have had something to do with her sexual enthusiasm. Unbeknown to her, she was getting much closer to her fake partner. He, of course, was besotted with her and looking forward to the new baby. There was never talk of Tim coming back on the scene, although Dave had seen him in the promotional film. Florence thought about Tim less now than when she had first arrived on the Oat Farm.

Chapter 54

MEN'S TALK

All the three young men on the Oat Farm had been involved with helping the German farm efficiency campaign, and therefore mixed well with the Germans. It was suggested that they should learn to speak German. Most of the Germans could speak at least some English—about half of them could hold a conversation, and a quarter were fluent.

So the three young men took up the challenge. After practising with their German colleagues, they were coming along quite well. Hearing this going on, the girls on the farm also started learning German. A kind of competition developed. Florence had the advantage of having studied German for four years as one of her compulsory subjects at grammar school. The others picked German up fast. Florence helped in the tuition no end as it all came back to her. They also listened to the German armed forces broadcasts. Only poor old Auntie Joyce was left out a bit.

Midway through November, on a night when they knew there would be a lot of Germans in the local pub, they all attended. The three girls wore very revealing dresses and looked their best. When they walked in, everyone took note of this feast for the eyes. The German soldiers especially couldn't help but watch these young beauties. They started talking, not knowing that the girls had been waiting for this.

The Germans talked about the women in rather crude terms, saying that they would like to go to bed with this one or that one and what they would do once they got there. Then Jean said in German, 'What is the name of the one of you who said he wanted to go to bed with me?'

And Florence piped up, also in German, 'You can't go to bed with me. I'm pregnant, you know.'

'Well, I'm too young,' John's girlfriend Susan added—in German, of course.

The Germans looked dumbfounded at these women understanding and speaking German back to them. The senior soldier said in German, 'Well, ladies, your German is very good.'

'Yes.' Florence took over, as her German was the best. 'You had better be careful what you say. As per the recent directive that everyone should learn German, we have all been studying hard. We want to become fluent. We listen to your armed forces radio programmes to help us.'

'Well, ladies, we promise we won't talk about you any more. Please accept our apologies and a drink from us. Whatever you want,' said the senior man. 'My name is Hans Gerard, and I'm pleased to meet you.'

'And I am Florence,' she said, offering her hand to shake.

'My name is Jean, and I'm pleased to meet you," said Andy's girlfriend. 'We will have to order our drinks in English because we don't want to get that wrong.'

'Fine. We will allow you to do that, but for the rest of the evening we will speak in German.'

'Well, we will try,' said Susan. 'Remember we have only been learning German for a month or so.'

The three men from the farm left the women with their new-found friends. Among the twelve soldiers were some from the efficiency campaign who were known to the farmers.

Maybe Andy shouldn't have left Jean with Hans. After a few drinks, they were getting on far too well. Florence and Susan were not as confident as Jean and didn't throw themselves into the conversation as much. Even so, they had a good chat with the Germans.

Hans Gerard was impressed with them and wanted their help to get other locals enthusiastic about learning German. There were no media people at his beck and call.

He asked Jean if she and the other two ladies could accompany him to some of the local villages, as far as Dumfries to the west and Eyemouth to the east. Jean called Andy over. 'Andy, this is Hans.'

'Pleased to meet you, Hans,' Andy responded in German.

Hans said, 'Likewise. I wanted to tell you how impressed I am with the level of German your ladies have reached in just two months.'

'We have all been practising at home among ourselves,' Andy said.

'I would like you to come with us to town halls and tell the people how they might achieve your fluency. It will help their general well-being and job prospects to learn German in this new German-guided Europe that one day is going to rule the world.'

'I would be more than willing,' Andy said. Then he had to switch to English, because his vocabulary in German only went so far. 'But what with the farm efficiency programme and then the work we need to do on our own farm, there isn't much spare time for us to help. If I'm free, I don't mind coming along, and I'm sure my brother and Dave would also attend. I certainly don't mind if the ladies want to help you.'

'All right. I know you are working on the efficiency programme, and I wouldn't want to put that in jeopardy. We will leave it at that. I'm happy you don't mind the ladies helping out.'

'I should have said, I don't mind Jean helping. You will have to ask John and Dave about their ladies.'

Chapter 55

THE GERMAN LANGUAGE SHOW

In the event, John and Dave didn't mind, and the captain started organising the town hall meetings, helped by Jean.

Hans Gerard was a captain and quite young for it, having just turned thirty. He had no family so far, although he had a girlfriend in Germany—when he was there. When he was absent, he heard rumours. He was of average build with typically blue-eyed German looks.

The captain and Jean took the lead in this venture. His day job was managing the adaptation of German and British army vehicles for civilian use. They were much needed in the farm efficiency programme. He took the ladies to see the group leader for the extended area and explained what he wanted to do.

Jean was very forthcoming. The group leader was suitably impressed and gave the captain a free hand to take as much time as he wanted on the German language project. The condition was that he didn't neglect the vehicle upgrade assignment. He was given another man, a lieutenant just over from Germany, to help him with whatever he wanted.

It became apparent that Jean and the captain were spending more and more time together. They didn't realise that they were falling for one another, and people were beginning to talk. Florence and Susan could see what was going on. In the end, Florence decided she should have a word with Jean.

Florence managed to get Jean by herself in the ladies' toilet at the town hall of a village they were visiting. 'Jean, I thought I'd better let you know that people are talking about you and Hans.'

'In what way?' said Jean a bit defensively.

'What do you think? It's obvious, isn't it? You're supposed to be with Andy, as you do live with him on the farm, but you are spending all your time with the captain. You seem to be getting very familiar with one another and very close.'

'It's only you who have concerns, Florence.'

'No, it isn't. You can ask Susan or any of the people we work with.'

'Well, it's none of their business. I will do what I want. It's only Andy who need be concerned, and so I would appreciate it if you didn't bring this up again.'

'Fine. It's your life. I will not mention it again.'

After that, the women on the Oat Farm were never as carefree and easy-going with one another as they had been. It was a wake-up call for Jean. She wasn't so free and easy with Hans, either—in public anyway.

The presentations were so successful that their team was asked to give some presentations in Edinburgh. It was almost billed as 'The Hans and his Three Girls Show'.

Coming up to Christmas, the team had been in Edinburgh for nearly a week, going around to all the centres with their presentation. They stayed in the best hotel in town. Florence and Susan shared one room and Jean had her own. Florence and Susan didn't think about it, but Jean had arranged it like this, so the captain could visit her or she him without anyone knowing.

Their affair seemed to improve the performance of the presentation. Audiences were enthusiastic, and more and more places wanted to see them. They performed until two days before Christmas, at which time Susan and Florence, although they were enjoying the limelight, made it plain they wanted to go home. They had been away for ten days. By this time it was obvious to everyone that the captain and Jean were having a full-blown love affair.

When they returned to the Oat Farm, Jean told Andy she was going to move out. Andy had already been warned about Jean and the captain. 'Where are you going to go?' he asked.

'I'm going back to my parents in Edinburgh. I want to have time to think.'

'All right. Will you be returning here?'

'I don't know.'

'Well, I'm not going to live like a monk over the festive season. I've heard you have been enjoying yourself recently.'

'Oh. I suppose Florence told you.'

'No, I heard from others.'

'Who?'

'The two Germans helping Hans on the trip. I know them from the efficiency programme.'

The First EU

Jean didn't say anything more. She collected her possessions, put them in her little car, and drove away, not even saying goodbye to Auntie Joyce.

Jean never lived on the farm again, but she continued in the German language show. She returned to apologise to Auntie Joyce and the rest of them for walking out without saying goodbye, and brought Auntie Joyce an expensive angora coat. All was forgiven. The other women realised that Andy had already gone his own way before then.

Chapter 56

SARAH'S RETURN

There was no question that Andy had been thinking of Sarah more and more. He went back to her the day before Christmas. Although she had recently started a new relationship, it hadn't been consummated. Sarah gladly ran into Andy's arms, dumping her boyfriend, and spent the Christmas and New Year on the Oat Farm. Being a down-to-earth girl she got on well with Auntie Joyce and was much more sociable than Jean.

Although Florence was five months pregnant, she was still feeling sexy and very pleased to see Dave. He was surprised she was so amorous but wasn't complaining. She looked gorgeous, and her previously nice-sized breasts were filling out even more. He practised all the things she had shown him that she liked. One of his Christmas presents to her was three sets of sexy ladies' underwear. This helped their pleasure no end.

It was a happy farmhouse over that Christmas of 1942. Both young women doing the German language presentation

The First EU

were well paid. Florence and Susan could hardly believe how much they were receiving, although Jean didn't seem to think it was anything out of the ordinary. Unfortunately, Florence would soon have to wind down on the work side. Dave was becoming very concerned and protective. She knew he was right, so she didn't argue too much.

He was persuaded to let her take part in the show for a further month in the new year if she did the presentation sitting down and the German people involved made sure she didn't overdo things. They were trying to find someone to take her place, but the three women had a rapport and their German had become fluent. It was quite a search.

In the end, they found someone living in Dumfries: a nineteen-year-old girl whose mother was German, although that had been kept quiet until recently. Her father was the one in the Dumfries civic administration who had organised false papers for Florence and then Dave.

CHAPTER 57

RETURN OF THE CHILDREN

It was a cold November morning when the postman delivered a letter to Uncle Albert and Auntie May at Dale Farm. It had a Birmingham postmark, and the farm address had been written in a scrappy hand. It was from the mother of the three children who had stayed at the farm after being evacuated. She was having a bad time; her husband had been rounded up for slave labour after leaving the army. She asked if the children could come and stay over the festive season. Auntie May thought, reading between the lines, that the mother would like them to come back full-time.

'What do you think, Albert?' she said after they had both read the letter.

Uncle Albert remembered that the eldest, a boy, had become difficult towards the end, and he couldn't control him. 'I don't know. The younger ones are no problem, but that boy … I just don't know. Let's ask Tom and Irene.'

'We can't split the children up.'

'We'll explain it all to Tom and Irene tonight, May.'

The First EU

Tom arrived back first, driving his small patrol car. It had been given to him by the Germans, as his time was precious to them.

'Tom,' said Auntie May, 'we received a letter today from the mother of the children who stayed here during the evacuation. She asked to send them for a visit, and reading between the lines, we think she wants them to live here permanently. The problem is that Uncle Albert couldn't control the boy, who is a big fourteen—sorry, fifteen-year-old now.'

'No worries,' said Tom. 'I should be able to help with that. I would like children to be here. Let's just ask Irene, all right? I'm sure she'll say yes. We can make use of the third bedroom, where they stayed before, and the boy can go into one of the attic rooms.'

Irene got back quite late, driving the farm lorry in from town. After all had been explained to her, she said, 'I think it would be a great idea and so nice to have children here for Christmas.'

'We'll do it then,' said Uncle Albert. 'But Tom, you must help me with that young lad. He attended the local school but didn't get on with the kids. I think he was being bullied.'

'Of course.'

There was no telephone number in the letter, so they sent another letter back, saying it was fine for the children to visit and she should send a telephone number if possible. In the reply, there was still no telephone number. The mother just said her three children, would be arriving on Tuesday, 24 November, well before the schools broke up, on the three o'clock bus from Lichfield. In addition to the teenage boy, there were two girls of ten and twelve.

Molly, having had a few to drink with Fritz on the night of the big media announcement, took him to her bed. Unfortunately, she found he was useless. It may have been the drink or the overexcitement. He wasn't any good the following morning either.

He continued in his job as tutor to Molly, in a businesslike way. Molly was learning German quite well, though she had no one to speak it with at home. In the day, she was always with Germans who were more than willing to speak their language with her. After a month, Molly could just about hold a conversation in German. She was still trying to keep up but needed more encouragement. She was a little on her own. Of course, the Germans had all sorts of advertising roles for her.

Horst Geissler, the head of media, realised that Molly was getting a bit lonely. He brought in a German girl of the same age to help. She was another beauty of similar build. They hit it off straight away. From then on Molly was a different person. The two made a real bond of friendship, helping one another with their German and English respectively. Angela Braun was the German girl's name. She was put up in one of the other three guest rooms at the vicarage.

The girls couldn't be separated. They were much in demand and known as the gorgeous duo. Angela was as good as Molly at dancing and soon picked up Molly's unarmed combat moves too.

Chapter 58

THE CHILDREN ARRIVE

At three o'clock on 24 November, three ragged children turned up at the village bus terminal with their scruffy bags. Irene, who knew the children well, was there to pick them up and transport them back to the farm.

Irene was surprised at the state of them. There was nothing she could do apart from run them back to the farm. On the way, they told her an alarming story of poverty and violence in their broken family. Their father had been taken away. Even before then, he had never given any of his soldier's pay to their mother for keeping them. The only help they got was from kindly neighbours.

When they got to the farm, all the children seemed rather worried that they would be turned away. 'Hello, Auntie May and Uncle Albert,' they said in unison.

'Well, children, you all look rather cold!' exclaimed Auntie May. 'Come in. Let's get some warmth into you.'

The boy had a letter for the farmer. He didn't know what was in it. Uncle Albert read it silently. 'Your mum says she hasn't got any money to look after you, and could we take you in until she sorts herself out. This is a serious situation. We will take you until after the New Year, and then see what we can do.'

'Thank you,' said the children, again together.

Irene took over. 'You all need a clean-up. Show me what clothes you have.'

The children got a few clothes out of their bags. They were summer clothes and worn out, although clean. Clearly they were wearing the only winter clothing they had.

'All right. We have some hot soup and bread to warm you up. Then you can each have a hot bath.' Irene made sure they scrubbed themselves and thoroughly washed their hair. The teenager was rather embarrassed about showing himself, but a large towel solved that problem.

'Now we must sort out your sleeping arrangements,' Irene told them. The two girls were put in the middle large bedroom downstairs, and the boy was put in the attic bedroom above the farmer's bedroom, where Molly used to sleep. It was the larger of the two attic rooms. The access ladder was in place all the time now. The rooms had been made nice with warm bedding: sheets, a few blankets, and a quilt.

The children seemed tired, so Irene said, 'Fine. Tomorrow we will go into the village. Go to sleep now.'

'Thank you, Auntie,' the girls said.

'And you, Jamie,' Irene said to the teenager.

'Yes, Miss Irene, but can I have a light so I can read my book?'

'I'll get out a paraffin lamp for you, but don't read too long. What are you reading?'

'Oh, it's a story about travelling on a motorbike.'

The First EU

'That's nice. Here's the lamp. Turn it out before you go to sleep. You turn it here, all the way.'

'Thank you, Miss Irene.' Jamie looked a bit worried.

'What's the matter?'

'I'm worried about my mum, miss.'

'We'll talk about it tomorrow. There's nothing we can do right now. You have a good sleep.'

Tom arrived back about ten thirty, having eaten at work quite late. He was busy nowadays on the efficiency drive, and enthusiastic about it. Irene told Tom all about the children, whom he had not seen before.

'They must be so poor,' Irene lamented. 'You know, we have enough money. I will sort the girls out, and you can take care of the boy. Is that all right, Tom?'

'Of course. I'm earning good money now and have a lot still left over from my Coventry days. If you want any more, I have plenty. Let's spoil these poor kids.'

'Yes, let's. We'll get them two sets of good clothes and a set of Sunday best, plus warm coats. We'll have a good shopping day tomorrow.'

Tom suggested, 'The Germans have good sources. I must go in early tomorrow and ask them about kids clothing. Bring the children along later.'

'Yes. I also have to attend work. I'll bring the kids with me about ten o'clock.'

After a moment, Irene added, 'The boy is worried about his mother.'

'Oh, more problems,'

'Tom, look at me.' She fell back on the bed with her legs wide open. 'Come now, my darling. I want our own family. I love children.'

'Thinking about these kids makes you look so sexy.'

He grabbed her hard. She gave a little yell. Her legs always turned him on. He pulled down her panties and spread her legs again, kissing her all over. But he was thinking, *Whatever you may want, I don't want you to fall pregnant.* Florence doing so a few months ago had complicated his life no end. He was not going to get out of control in his lovemaking tonight.

'Oh, darling. I love this, you know.' She was fast in reaching her climax and just let it go, trying to stay quiet because of the kids. They made love a second time, reaching their climax at the same time. Tim withdrew at the crisis, as he didn't know the time in her cycle. They wound down in one another's arms. After a while, they realised it was getting a bit cold, so they slipped below the bedclothes and embraced again, still naked.

'Why don't we start a family?' Irene persisted.

'I would like to leave it a bit. You know I've got this problem with Florence. I didn't want her to fall pregnant. I was tricked into it, actually. When things calm down a bit, we can talk again. I will enjoy you, Irene, as I do. If you accidentally fall pregnant, I will never ask you to terminate. I don't believe in that. It's bad for women. We will play it by ear as we go along, my darling. It will all work out in the end.'

Soon they fell asleep.

The following morning, Tom left before the children awoke. Irene and Auntie May got them fed and ready to visit the village. The first stop was to visit the doctor and then the dentist.

The doctor found them reasonably OK, although a bit undernourished. He checked them for tuberculosis and lice, and on both these counts, they were clear. The dentist found a few fillings that needed to be attended to, and Jamie needed an extraction of a side tooth that was beyond repair. Irene arranged for this work to be completed over the next few days.

Irene found Tom at the headquarters, where she was also working with Dieter. Her new English school was in one of the rooms. 'The kids are in the lorry.'

'Yes. I've inquired about getting clothes. Because there are no German children here yet, it will take time to get access to the special allocations they have for their children. Captain Vloch's wife is coming here to live this weekend with their three children, and then we can see. In the meantime, we can buy one set of clothes for each of them. There are four shops in the village that carry children's clothing. We can negotiate the best price among them, or we could wait for the market on Saturday. That's only three days away.'

'Absolutely, that's good sense. I'm going to see Sally about getting them into the school. It will be good that they are in before Christmas, as they will be able to join in all the school festivities.'

'That sounds great.'

Irene approached Sally, who went to the headmasters of the junior and senior schools. The girls were fine, but there were problems with Jamie. It was an administrative issue, they said, but the real problem soon became apparent. It was Jamie's troubled history.

Tom came over and assured the senior headmaster that he would control Jamie. The headmaster relented. Tom's prowess at unarmed combat seemed to do the trick.

Chapter 59

THE GERMAN FAMILY

Captain Vloch's wife flew in from Germany with their three girls on Wednesday morning, 25 November. They had an open invitation to attend the vicarage. After getting settled in their allocated house, the whole family went over to see Sally and her girls.

Sally's children had been told to be nice to the German children, as the war was over and everyone must be friends now. This was easy for them; their father was the vicar and a man of peace. Hanna, the eldest Vloch daughter, was fourteen, and her sisters were similar ages to Sally's daughters.

It happened that the kids from Dale Farm were also in the village, getting their teeth sorted out. They popped into the vicarage on the way back, as Irene had been told the German children were there.

As Sally had done, Irene told her charges, 'You must be nice to these German children because we all must be friends now.' She hoped it would be OK. She knew their father had been in the army.

Jamie fixed his eyes on Hanna. They were going to be in the same class at the senior school.

Although the German children had been taught some English, it was still early days and they were rather shy. All the children were told to say hello.

'Hello, my name is Jamie,' Jamie said softly because of his teeth.

'Hello, my name is Hanna.'

'Pleased to meet you, Hanna. Will you be at the party on Saturday?'

Hanna looked a little confused. '*Ja, ich denken.*'

'Yes, she will be,' Irene interpreted.

When they had all introduced themselves, Irene gathered her flock. 'Jamie, Jennifer, Wendy, come. We are going back to the farm now. You must get some rest after your dental work—just soup and bread for you today, nothing hard to eat.'

'Can't we stay, Miss Irene?' pleaded Wendy.

'Well, if Auntie Sally doesn't mind, you can stay half an hour while I go to my office.'

'That's fine,' Sally assured her.

In the event, it was over an hour before Irene returned, carrying three English/German dictionaries for the German girls. By this time the children were getting on well, the German girls having lost their shyness.

'I've made some soup,' said Sally. 'Is it OK for them to have some?'

'You shouldn't have bothered,' said Irene.

'Well, it's done now, and the others are tucking into it.'

'Can I be another half an hour then?'

'Sure.'

'I'm with the captain and his wife, plus Dieter and Fritz, at the village centre; we are discussing how to teach the Vloch girls English. There are some other German children arriving soon as well, I believe.'

'One of the best ways children learn is just by letting them get on with it like they all are now. Look at them with the three dictionaries you brought.'

'You're right. I'll bring some more dictionaries when I come back for our kids.'

It was another hour before Irene came back, and when she did, it was with the captain and his wife.

Chapter 60

JAMIE AND THE SWASTIKA

As soon as Jamie saw the German uniform with the swastika on the arm, he looked terrified. He got up straight away to stand by Irene. The sight didn't affect his sisters Wendy and Jennifer so much.

Irene had three more dictionaries, giving one to Sally's two girls, one to Wendy and Jennifer, and one to Jamie. 'Children, we absolutely must go now. Thank Auntie Sally for the nice food and say goodbye.'

'Thank you, Auntie Sally. See you on Saturday,' said the Dale Farm children. The girls were completely over their dental work, but Jamie still seemed a bit subdued. Whether it was his tooth or the German uniform he had just seen, it was hard to say. Hanna looked coyly at him as they departed.

Auntie May was happy to see the children return. She had made more soup and baked some nice bread. It smelled so good that the kids had another supper. They needed the extra nourishment.

Alan J Caulfield

It was arranged that the Dale Farm children would start school on Monday, the same day the three German girls would be starting. They had a party on Saturday and a Sunday church service to attend before then.

The farm children, with not much to do, managed to sneak into the village with Tom on Friday morning. Initially, they landed at the village centre. When the captain's wife found out they were at the centre, she brought her children over also. The children talked to one another without any urging. After lunch at the captain's house, they all ended up at the vicarage again. At six o'clock the farm children were driven back for their evening meal. The captain's children stayed on at the vicarage, where they were joined by Molly's tutor, Fritz.

After looking briefly in the local shops for clothes, Tom and Irene had decided to wait until the Saturday market. Irene took the girls. They were sorted out reasonably quickly with nice winter outfits, although there was some haggling from Jennifer over colour matching.

As far as Jamie was concerned, it took ages. He wanted the latest in fashion and was very particular. Meeting his demands was not that easy because of the times, and not that cheap either. But Tom patiently negotiated the best price with the market man, and they were all happy in the end.

Everyone went along to the village bathhouse for a good scrub-up before donning their new clothes. They looked healthy, radiant, and smart—very different to how they had looked on arrival.

At the vicarage at three o'clock, they took out pencils and paper and English/German dictionaries. Jamie looked

The First EU

for Hanna, but she wasn't anywhere to be seen. It transpired that the captain didn't want Hanna to study English with a boy. He thought it inappropriate.

But Hanna, being a teenager, worried at her dad so much that in the end he relented. His condition was that she talk to other people besides Jamie. That was difficult, as the other children were much younger. At that age, a couple years really mattered.

When Hanna arrived at four o'clock, Jamie couldn't disguise his delight. They really hit it off and were together the whole time.

Jamie told Hanna that he was frightened of her father when he wore his uniform with the swastika on it.

'Oh, Jamie, *mein vader ist gut.*'

'Fine. I won't worry.'

'*Meine mutter und mein vader* like *de Englische menschen, peple Ich denke.*'

'I must teach you English. You will be living here—I will not be living in Germany.'

'*Ja*, you must.'

Fritz and Dieter popped in on the party, at the request of the captain, and were impressed with how everyone was getting on. Fritz was only twenty-two and looked younger; he caught the eye of Hanna. He didn't know he so impressed her. He was just trying to help with her tuition.

He said to her in German, 'Remember what I said last night. You shouldn't be shy, and even if it doesn't sound right, you should always try to say the word. In the dictionaries, it shows how to pronounce all the words. You should practise with someone, like Jamie.'

The younger girls were all getting on well. Dieter said to the British girls in English, 'You must help Eva and Helga with their English, because they have come to live here. Later on, you can all learn German. It will be good if you can speak German when you get older.'

In German, he gave the captain's daughters the same advice Fritz had just delivered: 'Remember what I said yesterday. You must always try and say the word. Don't worry if it doesn't sound right at first.'

Chapter 61

THE CHILDREN'S MEETING

When it came to it later on, the children decided they wanted to sleep over at the vicarage that night. Sally didn't mind. Nor did Irene, as new nightclothes had been purchased for her brood.

It was to be expected that the captain wasn't too keen on Hanna being involved if Jamie was there. But there was so much pleading from the girls that it was agreed. Jamie was given the remaining guest room at the vicarage.

With the excitement of the evening, it was gone twelve before the girls sleeping in the lounge finally stopped talking. Their eyes rolling back, it was time for sleeping. Hanna and Jamie were also sleepy, and Jamie was ushered to his designated room. Sally had promised the captain and his wife there would be no unruliness and took charge of the teenagers. All of them had got valuable English practise and enjoyed themselves at the same time.

The village had suffered minimal bad effects from the war, but there had still been an impact. Like Albert Black's sons, other men from the village had been killed or gone missing in the fighting, including fathers of children who attended the local schools. The captain's children were the first German children to attend there.

Knowing this, the school and church people had to make sure the children were protected. The church service at eleven that Sunday was advertised as a service of forgiveness, and all were encouraged to attend. There was such a turnout that to get everyone in, only the sick were allowed a seat. Most pews had to be moved outside to make room for everyone else to stand.

The vicar preached about forgiveness, mentioning the story of the Good Samaritan and other stories from the Bible.

Lieutenant Schmitt gave a talk about all the German men who had been killed in the fighting, along with the men, women, and children who had been killed in the bombing of civilian areas by the British. He drew a parallel with the civilian deaths in Britain, emphasising that there was sadness all around, but now was a time for healing. 'We know some of our leaders have not been correct in their actions, but they are no more. A new, moderate leadership is in charge now. If we all work together, this will be the dawning of a great future which will be unending. We are all Christians and must pray together that our great new future will come to pass.'

Then the vicar led a short prayer.

The children sat together in the service; neither Sally nor Irene could separate them. Uncle Albert and Auntie May also attended the service and invited all the children back to Dale Farm for Sunday lunch. This was agreed by all the parents involved, with the proviso by the captain and his wife that their children must be back by mid-afternoon so they could settle down and get ready for their first big day at school.

Irene drove them in the farm lorry from the service to Dale Farm. Hanna and Jamie sat in the front and the rest in the back. A cover was put in the back so the girls didn't get too dirty.

The children were not encouraged to go outside at the farm. It was cold and wet and muddy. The five village children were run back to the village at three thirty. Irene and Auntie May insisted that the three children at Dale Farm settle down.

In this quieter time, Jamie and the girls started talking and worrying about their mother. She was in an abusive relationship with another man, not her husband. They knew her address, which was near where Irene had been brought up. But there was no telephone, so all they could do was send a letter.

Although poor, with a drunken husband, the children's mother had been in a better position before. She had got herself a job after the children were first evacuated, and sent money to Uncle Albert on a regular basis.

What had happened in the time the children had been back with their mother, Irene and Auntie May didn't know. But obviously some bad things had been going on, and Jamie was worried.

Uncle Albert wanted to contact the police where she lived, but was persuaded not to until they found out more. Auntie May sent her a letter to say that the children were well, but were worried about her. Could she please send a telephone number?

This satisfied the children. The adults left it at that, waiting for a reply to the letter.

Chapter 62

FIRST DAY AT SCHOOL

The following day, Irene ran the children in to school before she went on to work. All the German girls were there. The junior and senior schools were next to one another.

Jamie was returning to the class he had been in a few months before. Because of his poor background and the fact that he didn't have a father, he attracted some bullying. His resentment had led to him seeming uncontrollable, at least as far as Uncle Albert was concerned. Though Jamie wasn't a violent person, the bullying caused some fighting. He had to stand up for himself. He inevitably got the blame, since it always seemed to be him involved. This had been why the headmaster was hesitant to take him back.

Another boy hailed him. 'Hi, Jamie! Wow, are you coming back to school then?'

'Hi, Gordon. Yes, I'm back. I hope we don't have all the problems of the past and can be friends.'

'What do you mean, we were friends before?'

'Yes, fine, Gordon.'

The First EU

'What about your friend then?'

'Her name is Hanna.'

'Well, I like Hanna.'

The teacher entered the room. 'All right, class, we have two new pupils today: Jamie, whom you will know from before, and then Hanna, who has just arrived from Germany. Hanna can't speak English very well, so I want a girl to volunteer to help her.'

No one put their hand up.

'I will have to allocate someone if you don't volunteer.'

'I will, sir,' Jamie said, putting his hand up.

'Well, Jamie, I really wanted another girl. But as you seem so enthusiastic, I will let you do it for now. We will see how it goes. You can sit together then. Hanna needs to learn English as soon as possible.' The teacher remembered that Jamie wasn't that good at English, and hoped one of the girls would volunteer soon.

'Now, children, the war is over, and we all have to get on together. I want you to be nice to Hanna and help her whenever you can, especially with her English.'

At lunchtime, one of the girls who was top in the class for English came over. 'Hi, Jamie. Can I help your friend Hanna?'

'Well, Ruth why didn't you volunteer then?'

'I didn't want to do it all the time.'

'Dank you for help,' Hanna said to Ruth.

'I will try and get you a German/English dictionary,' said Jamie grudgingly.

'Thanks. That should help.'

'Hello, Hanna,' Gordon said, approaching with a couple of friends. 'You don't want to be with this loser.'

'Are you starting to pick on me again?' said Jamie.

Ruth said, 'It's just like it was before, isn't it, Gordon? You've started bullying again. I'm going to tell Sir if you don't stop it.'

Gordon slunk away. Hanna could see there were some problems.

Chapter 63

TO STOP THE BULLYING

After school, Jamie went to the unarmed training session, as he had been told to meet Irene there. Tom was there as well.

'Hello, Jamie,' said Tom. 'Thinking about taking up unarmed combat?'

'I'm not very good, Uncle.'

'This will make you good. And you won't have to worry about other kids picking on you.'

'I'll give it a try then.'

'Have you got shorts and training shoes?'

'I've some at the farm. They're not very good.'

'I'll see if one of the Germans can lend you gear. I'll order you more through the German allocation soon, with some other clothes.'

Jamie was almost adult size and could wear practise clothing borrowed from one of the soldiers. Molly and Angela attended the training and gave lessons. That was enough to keep him interested. He was a bit awkward at first. After the first day, he acquired his own gear, which fitted better. He soon picked up the basic moves. Molly continued to floor him quite easily, but he was able to give Angela a hard time after a couple of weeks.

Hanna also started attending after school. Although she was rather petite, she could give good account of herself after a few weeks. This encouraged more of the children in their class to join. The soldiers had a lot of fun with the children at these sessions. This helped ease difficulties that some of the children had. Of course, it would never break down all barriers, especially with the children who had lost fathers.

Because of Tom and Irene, the children from Dale Farm now had a better position in the school pecking order. Tom was well known throughout the village because of his unarmed combat and dancing skills, plus the films he was making for the farm efficiency programme. Irene was well known for her new language school. Both had German friends in high places. Jamie was less picked on, especially after he floored Gordon a couple of times.

Jamie attracted other girls but remained fond of Hanna—as were some of the other boys in his class, including Gordon. Hanna had a puppy love for Fritz, who was asked by the captain to help her with English. Hanna's mother was aware of her feelings for Fritz and therefore encouraged her friendship with Jamie.

The bad effects of the times caused some of the local children to pick on the German children and call them names. This was quickly stamped on by the school, the church, and the police. Some of the culprits were from families made fatherless by the war. It wasn't easy for the German authorities to get the cooperation they needed when there had been so much killing.

Chapter 64

CHILDREN AND THE MEDIA

There were always German media people in the village, filming with Molly, Tom, and lately Irene and her language school. It was easy for them to consider filming the children. This was discussed with the captain before Horst Geissler returned to his head office in London. The captain was in agreement, but he stipulated that he had to have his children in sight.

The two younger girls were in favour of the plan, but Hanna was a bit hesitant. Her sisters' good friends from Dale Farm and the vicarage gladly entered into all the activities, like the nativity plays and choirs. The filming was just one more activity to get excited about, which improved their performances. As Hanna did not yet participate in school activities, the film crew sought to film her normal school and living activities. She reluctantly agreed, as long as she could include Jamie.

All this filming was for both German and English viewing. The choirs practised a German number. Dieter and Fritz helped with the German. Irene's language school was used by the captain for teaching his children English. From the new year, German language teaching was going to be compulsory all over the country, and of course, this village was taking the lead.

The media people were very popular with the children. They brought little treats every day—sweets, cakes, pencils, diaries, and so on. A film of the choir singing carols was to be distributed in Germany and the United Kingdom before Christmas. A lot of hard work for the children was involved, but the extra work didn't worry them.

Other film sequences were added in general news broadcasts initially. Because of their popularity, separate, longer features were brought out before Christmas too, meaning more shooting and work in the cutting room had to be quickly undertaken. This was managed, and the features were popular in both countries.

Horst Geissler was also pleased. He returned to the village and spent Christmas with Sally's teacher friend, Katie.

The film crew was so busy with the younger girls, they didn't film anything with Hanna until a week before Christmas, when they managed to film Hanna with Jamie at the farm. The farm was quite photogenic despite the winter weather, being in the heart of the country. Hanna was definitely a treat to the eyes. Jamie was not bad-looking, tall and gawky as happened sometimes at that age. This didn't seem to worry Hanna, who was quite attached to him. She had got over her infatuation with Fritz after he started a relationship with a pretty local girl.

The First EU

The film featuring Hanna was popular. A longer movie was made straight away. It showed Hanna at a dance organised for the older children at the senior school. She was shown dancing with Jamie and some other boys, plus talking to girls her own age. It also showed the Christmas decorations of village houses: the vicarage, Dale Farm, and the captain's house.

The filming was finished by Boxing Day, and it was in the cinemas before the new year. It was thirty minutes long and an unqualified success. The film crew said that success was probably because of Hanna and Jamie. Their adolescent shyness came over as an unusual characteristic in the movie business. Audiences could see the truth in it all and the natural sentiments portrayed.

The young couple started to get fan mail from both countries. They were not sure they would have received so much if they had been described as a couple. It had been the express wish of Hanna's father that the film not show them like this.

Hanna's mother, with Sally's help, managed the young couple's fame. All mail had to go through them. In the end, most of the letters were answered with a photo and a standard copied reply. Any letters from people they knew, like old friends and classmates, were shown to Hanna and Jamie.

Chapter 65

A PROUD MOTHER

The mother of the evacuees came to see her children just before Christmas, and brought some presents. She was happy that her children were getting on so well and looked so healthy. She met everyone involved in helping them and gave some money to Auntie May for the children's keep. 'They've all got new clothes and look so well.'

'Well,' said Auntie May, 'you must thank Tom and Irene for that. They live on the farm and have purchased a lot of new clothes for the children.'

Jamie was happy to see his mother and introduced her to Hanna. Hanna was doing well with her English, probably because of the care and attention she was getting from Jamie.

His mother said, 'You know, Jamie, I'm very proud of you.'

'Are you all right, Mum? I'm really missing you.'

'Oh I'm all right, but it's best you stay here for now. Uncle Les is still at home, and you know you don't get on so well with him.'

At the village centre, she saw the movies her girls were in, which were just about to be released. 'Girls, I'm so proud of you! I will tell all my friends to look out for your film. What about you, Jamie? When will you be in a film?'

'After Christmas, but it's not going to be about me. It's going to be about Hanna and how she is settling down in England. The other film is also about the German girls.'

'Yes, but you children feature very much in the film I saw of Dale Farm.'

'Have you seen Dad lately?'

'No, I haven't.'

This was not quite correct; his father, whom Jamie had been close to when he was younger, unfortunately was still drinking. Because he had no regular job, he had been put in a labour camp. The Germans didn't let anyone off when it came to working, including drunks.

It really was a tonic for the children to see their mother. She stayed in the vicarage for two nights and accompanied the children to combat training. She had meetings with all their teachers arranged by Sally. In them, she found they were all doing well. Leaving them was sad for her and the children, but she knew they were much better off at Dale Farm than they would be back in Birmingham, living in her fractured home.

'Thank you very much from the bottom of my heart,' she said to Uncle Albert, Auntie May, Tom, and Irene. 'I don't know how I can repay you.'

They replied that it was a pleasure to help and her children were easy to live with. She took the bus back to Birmingham the next day.

Chapter 66

THE GESTAPO IN SCOTLAND

After the assassination of Heydrich and Himmler, the Gestapo in Scotland were almost out of control. They had their ways which included torture until death in some cases. But no one they seriously questioned knew anything.

There were some summary executions of Scottish suspects in the days following the killings. But after the death of Hitler, the investigation was scaled down and followed normal procedures. It was noted that the assassins could have killed many more senior German army personnel, but had not done so. Himmler and Heydrich had been specifically targeted.

The weapon used in the assassination was thought to be one of the two missing from a four-man German patrol that had been killed near Glasgow. Through painstaking questioning of innumerable German soldiers, it had been determined that two British armoured cars had been operating in the area at the time of those killings. One such vehicle had been found forty miles south of Glasgow, completely cleared of all information. It had been placed in the vehicle pool, to be adapted for use in the farm efficiency drive. The Gestapo were convinced that these vehicles—and the British soldiers who had operated them—were the key to solving the crime.

The resistance in Scotland was in its infancy and, so far, not well organised. It hadn't been infiltrated by the Germans. It consisted mainly of sleeper cells and small arms caches. They knew there wasn't anything they could do at the moment with the enemy being so strong. There was the talk of action against collaborators, especially those working for the German media in the charm offensive.

Only a handful of people in the resistance knew who the Scottish assassin was. One reason was because the scheme had been very hastily arranged. Luckily, the new moderate regime coming in disrupted the whole of the German establishment, especially the security services. This played a role in keeping Andy safe for the time being. The Gestapo were more interested in saving their own jobs than solving crimes, it seemed.

Chapter 67

FLORENCE SEES TIM

The young men on the Oat Farm had seen Tim in the farm efficiency films. Dave especially didn't want Florence to see these, as she would surely recognise her husband. He had also picked out Molly but didn't think Florence would recognise her, as they probably had never met.

The secrecy came to an end just after Christmas, when they attended the local hall to see the media campaign films. Of course, the one on farm efficiency was shown. Florence exclaimed, 'Oh, my God, that's Tim!' She could hardly control herself.

Dave admitted, 'Yes. This film has been circulating for a few weeks. I have seen it already.'

'Why didn't you tell me then?'

'I didn't want you to get upset.'

'Well, I am very upset now, Dave! How could you think I didn't want to know about the father of my child? I would be a strange woman if I didn't want to know that! I would like you to run me home, if you please.'

The First EU

But they didn't leave straight away, because just then Tim appeared in another film about German children settling down in England. Florence watched this too, then said, 'I'm so disturbed about this. I just want to leave. I must contact my husband.'

'All right, Florence. Don't get stressed. We will contact Tim. But keep in mind, we have false identities, and so does he. Tim is now called Tom.'

She looked worried. 'Please, let's go.'

The brothers from the Oat Farm could see Florence was distressed and guessed why after they too saw the films of Tim.

Dave had no choice but to help Florence find her husband. Through the film, he knew that the place featured was a large village north of Lichfield, and the farm was Dale Farm. Florence immediately wrote a letter to that address, this time posting it in Dumfries.

She wrote that she was fine and living with Dave, and that she wanted Tim to contact her. She gave her telephone number, though it hadn't changed since his last call. She also gave the number of the local post office, just in case there were any problems. She didn't know why he hadn't phoned already.

Two days later, just before the new year, Tim made a call to the farm. This time Auntie Joyce picked it up. She covered the receiver and shouted, 'Florence! Telephone!'

Florence was there in an instant. 'Oh, Tim, I've wondered about you. How are you?'

'I'm fine, and you? I saw you in a film about learning the German language; you looked great and so proficient and confident.'

'Did you get my letter?'

'No, I didn't. I just phoned because I saw you in the film. The last time I phoned—maybe two months ago?—I think it was Andy who answered the phone. I asked for you and was told you were Mrs Randall now and were well and happy.

'My life has been very hectic, Florence. I have a new identity. I think I'm going to have to come clean soon because I'm making lots of films and will be recognised, as I already have by you.'

'I have a Mr Randall, Tim. He is your friend Dave from the research centre.'

'How did that come about?'

'It's a long story. Anyway, I'm missing you and want to see you. Are you still with Molly?'

'Molly?'

'Yes, Tim. I knew about Molly.'

'Oh. Erm, I'm not with Molly. I have another friend, Irene.'

'Oh, Tim. She sighed. 'I just want to see you.'

'I will have to see. I must make a plan. Maybe because you are doing media work, I can swing something. I will sound out the captain. He is my German boss, except when I'm making the films. Irene is running an English language school. I will ask the captain if we can get together—either we visit you or you visit us.'

'It's all such a mess. But I must see you.'

Chapter 68

TOM COMES CLEAN

Tom didn't know if any of his phone conversation had been listened to, but Britain was an informing police state now and one could never be sure. So finally he decided to tell Captain Vloch all, from the time he left the research centre. He had to be careful not to get others into trouble, like Irene and the Blacks. Molly was all right, but he spoke to her about it anyway. She agreed he could tell the truth about her. She didn't want any discrepancies and felt confident she wouldn't be punished for her fraudulent past. The big problem was the Blacks at Dale Farm. Not only had they put him up, but they had organised false papers for him afterward.

Still, Tom thought Captain Vloch was a person to trust. In the event, he was right. Tom told him that he had run away from the research centre as Molly had, and indeed he knew Molly very well. But unlike Molly, he had taken it a step further and acquired another identity.

'You know, Martin,'—Tom had been calling the captain by his Christian name for some time, at the captain's insistence— 'I was thinking I didn't want to give my expertise to the people who were invading my country and killing my countrymen. But I hadn't thought it through. I wanted to join the resistance but couldn't find them. I got stuck here. Then you came to the farm and my false identity passed the test, and you gave me the opportunity to work in a field I liked. I was happy. I'm even happier to be involved in the friendship campaign because I believe that is the only way forward. The only people around here who know anything are the Blacks and Irene at the farm plus Molly. People in the village don't know about my true past, not even Sally and the vicar.'

'I will have to think about your disclosure,' said Vloch slowly. 'You have become so useful to us that I'm sure we can sort something out. The main thing is there have been no deaths or injuries involved in your actions. You did break the law, however. We will have to see what the research centre says.'

A few days before, a couple of Tom's old colleagues at the research centre happened to see him in a farm efficiency film. The film had been put out for general release as it had proved so popular among farmers. News of the identification had spread around the centre like wildfire, and within a few days the Germans found out.

The director of German media for farm effeciency in the United Kingdom, Jochen Klos, contacted the head of the research centre to have a discussion about Tom Clark/ Tim Handle. The head didn't know the full story. He asked if they could have the conversation the following day, so he could gather the necessary information about Tim Handle.

The information was good and bad. The German team had struggled when first taking over the research centre, because more than half of the top research talent had gone AWOL. Tim had been a crucial member of the team, more so than the others. The German team thought that things were caught up now by their own experts, but they wanted Tim Handle back to debrief, just to see if there was anything he could add. The research head decided that if Tim agreed to come to the centre now for two weeks, they would allow him to leave officially and permanently, as long as he stayed on call for them.

It was an offer Tom couldn't refuse. He resumed his old name and was put up in a five-star hotel in Coventry. He was received as a bit of a hero back at the research centre.

Because Florence was with Dave and had another name, Tim did not mention his marriage.

Chapter 69

MOLLY AT THE HOTEL

After four days in the hotel without company, Tim answered a knock on his room door late at night. Molly was standing there with her travelling case. She looked quite delectable and had a pleading expression. As when Irene had come to him in his small attic room, Tim responded to her beauty. 'Come in. How did you get here?'

'I told Horst I wanted to see my mum and dad. Tim, I've missed you so much. I want to be with you.' She flung her arms around him, 'Oh, darling, I love you.'

'Molly, you know I'm with Irene now. Haven't you got a German boyfriend yet?'

'No, they are all a bit strange.' She didn't think it was worth telling him about the fiasco with her tutor Fritz.

'There must be some nice, ordinary German men. I see you are always with Angela. They call you the gorgeous duo. Has Angela got a boyfriend?'

'I think she has one in Germany.'

'It looks like you're planning to stay here?'

The First EU

'I came straight from the village. I'm supposed to be staying with my parents.'

'I think it's too late to go to them now. You will have to stay here tonight.'

Without saying another word, Molly went into the bathroom with her case.

Tim knew he didn't have to accept her. He could easily have sent her away. She had somewhere to stay. He was being weak-willed as he normally was when it came to the fairer sex. It would be impossible for him to keep away from Molly until the next morning.

A few minutes later she appeared, wearing sexy pyjamas which consisted of a frilly, black, see-through top, panties, and bra.

Tim exclaimed, 'How can I stay true to Irene when you come here like this?'

'Well, what are you going to do then?' she said, giving him a cheeky smile. She knew he would find it impossible to resist. After all, they had been passionate lovers until only three months before—and she had seen him say yes to every other offer too.

She ran into his arms and started undoing his trousers and shirt. In no time they were naked like the old days. She remembered his ways from before. He too remembered her delights. He brought her fully on, kissing her all over. The lovemaking was so sweet, he was drenched with her. 'Let's take it slow,' he urged.

'Whatever you say, darling.' She passionately French kissed him, then sighed. 'I want to go on top.'

'But darling, when you're on top, I come so quickly. Just slow down. You can get on top in a minute.'

'Oh, yes, darling, I will.'

He could feel her pushing up against him and knew she was coming.

Giving in, he gasped, 'OK. You can.'

They rolled over and Molly was on top. She just let go. Tim noted she was more athletic, slimmer, and maybe more energetic than before. With her wild movements, he was reaching his climax and couldn't help himself. 'Molly, I'm coming!'

'Come, darling, come. Don't worry. I finished my period today.' She came again as he did. They locked together in a frenzy of passion and French kissing.

They stayed embraced for some time, whispering tender words. Molly wanted Tim more than ever. Tim felt the old feelings coming back for her and didn't know what was going to happen now. Why was his love life so complicated? But he had enjoyed Molly. He knew she was hot for him. He thought smugly of all the men who had seen her films and would give anything to get Molly into bed.

He had an early meeting next morning, so he left Molly in the room. She tried to delay him in the usual way, but he was firm, remembering the time he had been reprimanded for being tired at work when he first started going out with her. That seemed so long ago.

'I'll be here for you when you get back, darling,' she promised. He just nodded. He had some problems at work on his mind.

As he exited the room, he was surprised to see a German he recognised from the village, sitting in a chair near the lift. 'Hello,' Tim said.

'Good morning, Mr Handle. I'm here as Molly's bodyguard and driver. I'm very worried. Molly should be with her parents, but insisted I bring her here. She has asked me to let her parents know where she is, but I'm not going to leave her. I'll be in big trouble if she goes missing. Can you let them know?'

'Yes, I will let them know on my way to work.'

'Thank you, sir.'

Tim was still driving the patrol car he had been given in the village, and had as much fuel as he needed. It was no problem to stop round at Molly's parents.

There was excitement in the hotel as news got around that Molly was there. People wanted her autograph and photograph. She wasn't so lionized back in the village, where everyone knew her and she was able to lead a normal life.

Molly came down for breakfast quite late, about ten o'clock, and was surprised by all the fuss. Her bodyguard Rolf was in the midst of the hubbub and was getting quite agitated. Molly called the hotel manager and asked if she could have a bit of peace and quiet so she could eat her breakfast.

'Certainly, Miss Brooks. Whatever you want. We are honoured to have you staying at the hotel.'

'Rolf, when I have finished breakfast, you can let people take photographs and talk to me as long as there aren't too many of them.' Molly called after the hotel manager, 'Can you please help Rolf with the people who want to take photos?'

'Certainly, Miss Brooks.'

'And please get hold of Tim Handle on the phone for me.'

'Yes, Miss Brooks,'

The previous night, Molly had come to the hotel with Rolf and asked for Tim's room number. She wanted to go to the room and knock on his door personally. The hotel porter said this was not possible and that she must phone first, Molly created a fuss. Hearing this, the night manager had come over and recognised her as the star of the German propaganda films. He shushed the porter and said, 'You can go to the room, Miss Brooks.'

'Can you please find a room for my driver?' she asked. 'I will sort out the payment.'

'Miss Molly!' Rolf exclaimed. 'You must tell me who is in the room. I must stay in the hall, on your floor.'

'It's Tim Handle, Rolf.'

'Fine. And?'

'There are comfortable lounge chairs in the hallway near the lift, only twenty yards from the room,' suggested the night manager. 'There will be no charge, Miss Brooks.'

'Thanks for being so helpful,' said Molly. pressing the button for the fourth floor.

***

Tim phoned her at lunchtime. 'I saw your parents this morning, Molly. they really want to see you.'

'All right, I'll ask Rolf to run me there this afternoon. I want to see you this evening after work. Maybe we could see some of our old friends. Tonight is unarmed combat training for the Coventry squad.'

'If I have time, why not?'

'Mm, I'm missing you, Tim darling.'

The First EU

'Don't say it like that. Look, ask your bodyguard to run you to the hall. We can see some of our friends there. I'll tell the people at work we will be there tonight. I'll see you at six o'clock then, at the hall.'

'I'll be there, darling. See you later.'

CHAPTER 70

ANGER TOWARDS MOLLY

Coventry had an industrial base that had been decimated in the wartime bombing. There was a lot of animosity towards the Germans, and soldiers always went around in groups. There wasn't a free and easy atmosphere like in the village. When it became known that Molly was in town, some people were not happy to see her, saying she was a German whore.

Tim was heavily denounced for his collaboration by some people at the research centre and around Coventry. He became for the first time concerned for his safety. There weren't many, but the ones against him and Molly were very vocal. These same people were also against the Germans of course, and faced the possibility of being arrested and even worse.

Tim was aware of these feelings but didn't think there would be any problems at the unarmed combat training. Unfortunately, he was wrong. There was a small group who were not happy with Tim's and Molly's friendships with the hated occupiers. As all these people had lost friends and family, this could be understood.

When Molly arrived, Tim was already at the hall. He was aware of tension from a group of about six people, one or two of whom he knew from his working days before the ceasefire, nearly six months earlier.

Molly had Rolf in attendance, and he stood out in his uniform. The disaffected group shouted, 'German whore!' and booed.

Tim approached them. 'What do you want?'

'We want you and your German loving whore to f— off,' said the spokesman of the group.

'We will not. We are here to meet old friends.'

'You haven't got any friends here.'

Tim ignored them and continued to walk towards his old friends. Once he got to them, he turned around to the jeering group and said, 'Molly and I decided to collaborate because, looking at the situation with common sense, there was no point in fighting against such an overwhelming situation. We were well and truly beaten. Unless we can get massive outside help, nothing will change. Russia and the USA are not going to lose countless men fighting to liberate us. When the new, more moderate German regime came to pass after the assassinations, there was even more reason to collaborate. People on both sides have lost loved ones. We can bring Germans to you who have lost family in the bombing of their cities by the RAF.'

'The United Kingdom will not be ruled by Germany!'

'No, not only Germany. It is going to be a joint affair, with Germany leading things. I'm impressed with the German way of working. You will see the outcome of their farm efficiency campaign next year, in the increased yields of next season's crops.'

'Well, I don't know about that.'

'Well, I do, because I have been working on the farm efficiency programme over the last few months. We don't produce enough food to support ourselves in this country. From now on, we will. All farms will produce what they are best at; therefore yields will improve. If you want to do well, you must learn the German language and their way of doing things. Then you will progress to good positions within the system.'

'That's what you are doing, just looking after yourself.'

'What are you going to do? if you fight this system, you will end up dead. If you cooperate, you can do well for yourself. It's a logical choice and doesn't take much thinking about. As far as I'm concerned, it will help the rest of the population also.'

'You aren't welcome here!'

'Look, why don't I bring over some Germans. Angela, Molly's friend, lost her parents to RAF bombing last year, for example. We can have an evening of practise and a party afterwards to get to know one another. All food and drink will be provided.'

The leader was pushed by the other dissenters to agree.

'Molly, have you got a photo of you and Angela?' Tim asked.

'Yes, in the car. Rolf, could you please fetch my handbag?'

Rolf had been rather agitated through this whole confrontation, and even released his gun holster. Fortunately nobody seemed to notice. After Molly showed the photo, there was nothing left to say. They agreed to have a friendly evening.

Chapter 71

A DAY'S HONEYMOON

Some of the tension had been taken out of the evening, but the confrontation still left a bit of a bad atmosphere. Tim and Molly's friends were happy to see them, and Tim took them to the local pub for drinks. He bought more drinks for the dissenters when they arrived later. Things were looking a bit better then. Rolf could see there was some lingering hostility. He wanted to call in local soldiers he had already made contact with, but Tim told him not to. Luckily, no policing turned out to be necessary.

Tim and Molly went back to the hotel not too late and had a quiet drink in the bar. The night manager kindly kept local people from bothering Molly, but there were some Germans in the bar, engineers on a project. Recognising Molly, they came over for a friendly chat in German and were pleasantly surprised at how good her German really was.

Molly always liked to get German practise and was showing off to Tim, who wasn't as good. The local girls who had been keeping company with the soldiers weren't happy to lose their German partners, but all was resolved when Molly and Tim bade their new friends goodnight.

Tim wasn't required at the research centre the next day. The team leader had said he could take a day off. He didn't know why. In actual fact, the whole of the centre had found out about Tim and Molly and decided to give them a day's honeymoon.

It was perfect for them. After the confrontation, they were a bit subdued that night. Tim didn't want to make love; he just wanted to be quiet and relax with Molly. In the end they did, but it wasn't a wild affair.

Rolf had his own room, as he wasn't needed as a bodyguard. Tim carried a Luger for protection. He practised at the firing range with the Germans and had had basic firearms training in his army cadet days. He wasn't sure what would happen if he had to pull the trigger in anger though.

The following morning, Tim and Molly had a loving session. Molly was insatiable, and they kept going until Tim couldn't keep it up any more. They ordered a champagne breakfast in bed and had another session later. The champagne helped them along.

In the afternoon, they took a leisurely walk about Kenilworth, a small town nearby. If they had done the same in Coventry, it would have been likely that Molly would be recognised. Rolf was shadowing them, of course.

When Tim arrived at work the next day, the whole centre seemed to know what he had been doing. He had a happy sort of look about him. Some of his colleagues jokingly praised him for being so lucky in having the

The First EU

national pin-up girl in his hotel room. He hadn't realised that the whole centre knew about it. It was too late now. He just had to accept all the ribbing. It soon stopped as he got involved with the problems of the day.

Chapter 72

THE FRIENDSHIP WEEKEND

It was mid-January 1943. The friendship evening Tim had negotiated was renewed as a friendship weekend, and the coming weekend was earmarked. Angela and two other attractive German girls attended. The two recent additions were hastily chosen from among dozens who had volunteered. English proficiency and good looks were the criteria. The function started on Friday at about five.

Horst Geissler attended and gave a similar speech to the one he had given in the village. The leader of the dissidents, Bill, was bowled over by Angela. Bill had lost his father, whose merchant ship was sunk by submarine action in the North Atlantic. With sad wartime losses in common, they found plenty to talk about all evening.

About three hundred people in all were invited, including two combat training groups, two modern dance groups, and eighty soldiers. The German commanders had given preference to the men who spoke at least a bit of English. In the end, another fifty people, mainly English

The First EU

but some German, also got entry. Although it was a large hall, this really pushed its capacity. A joint German/English team checked attendees for weapons and drink.

After speeches by Horst and Tim, the party started with free food and drink. It had a good effect and a lot of friendly contacts were made, especially between soldiers and local girls. Although not everyone was happy about the fraternisation, it was the start of things to come. The British would have to accept German rule in the United Kingdom. The ones who wanted to help would be treated well, and the ones who resisted were in for a very hard time.

The following day, German administrators put something on for the children who wanted to learn unarmed combat and dancing. This started at one o'clock and went on all afternoon. A lot of parents came. Seventeen children from the village were drafted in, including Wendy and Jennifer from the farm, Sally's daughters, the German girls, and Hanna's school friend Ruth. Of course, Jamie came as well.

The village kids showed their prowess in German, and the German children spoke English. Some of the Coventry children called out bad things to the Germans. But this soon stopped when they saw the Germans were well supported by the village children.

The children's afternoon went off well, helped by good food—especially cakes, which were not normally available in this time of severe rationing. There was much interest in Hanna among the Coventry boys, but Jamie was in close attendance. He was becoming quite a strapping lad, and Hanna was happy with his attention.

That night, another function for the adults took place, including as many different groups as possible. Molly's mum and dad attended. They were proud of her, albeit in a bewildered way and with some reservations.

Sunday was given over to Sunday school and church for those who wanted it. As a whole, this weekend in Coventry went down very well. It was the first of many similar events all over the country.

As well as spending time with her parents, Molly attended the research centre on three separate days. She was treated as a celebrity. There was no dissent among her former colleagues. She brought Angela with her on the second day. They hosted a question-and-answer session in the canteen. Both gave their personal histories before questions were taken.

Molly even got Rolf involved, because people wanted to know about him. His English was reasonable, and Molly helped him along. His history was that he had lost a younger brother who had fought with Rommel in the Middle East. Folks wanted to know what it was like in Germany. He told them in his home city of Frankfurt, everyone had been frightened by the British bombing. Rolf's parents were not bombed, luckily. When the audience learned that Angela, who was only nineteen, had lost her parents and sister to British bombing, the questions to her became more subdued.

This session was so popular, the girls hosted another the following day. Molly was in demand for her media work, however, and after putting her media bosses off for so long, she had to return to the village. Angela returned with her. By then Molly had spent twelve days with Tim on an original one-week leave to see her parents.

On the farm, Uncle Albert and Auntie May were really missing Tim. A team of people were working on the farm's efficiency improvements. One of the Germans had started staying in the outbuilding, which had been made more habitable. He was a happy, good-looking man, maybe a few years older than Tim. He wanted Irene to help him with his English, which needed a lot of improvement. The children helped him too, and he helped them with their German, which they were picking up quickly, as kids do.

Jamie and Hanna could hardly be separated. The adults were concerned that their puppy love may be affecting their schoolwork, but it didn't seem to. They were both doing well. Tim had already had a chat to Jamie about the birds and the bees and pregnancy. He hoped Jamie had heeded it. There was little the adults could do if the youngsters were determined to get together on a sexual basis. Captain Vloch wasn't always happy about Jamie, but his wife calmed him down. She said it was better Hanna had someone of her own age and told him about their daughter's prior infatuation with Fritz.

'What? Fritz!' exclaimed the captain. 'I will have him court-martialled.'

'No, darling. Fritz probably doesn't know anything about her feelings. It was just one of those teenage crushes.'

'Oh, I see. Ah, yes.'

Tim was getting very much involved in the jet propulsion project. He pointed out a number of things that were incorrect in the set-up and seemed to be leading the young team. He dealt directly with the older designers he knew, who had the original idea but under British rule couldn't get enough ongoing government funding. Now there was unlimited funding and German equipment. Of course, Tim's knowledge of German helped no end, as the German experts didn't always have the language skills.

At the end of his initial two weeks, the centre asked him to stay for another two weeks. He agreed, but said they must find someone else to take over by then. He thought it could be a young German engineer, Gerald Baermann, if the British team would accept him.

Gerald was proficient in English and a competent engineer, a year older than Tim. He had the respect of most of his colleagues as a hard-drinking, hard-working individual, very knowledgeable and enthusiastic. Gerald led the light-hearted teasing when it was found Molly had stayed in Tim's hotel room.

The younger people accepted Gerald with no problems. Only some of the older English and, surprisingly, German employees seemed a bit hesitant. In the end, with Tim's endorsement, Gerald was accepted.

Finally, after being in Coventry for four weeks, Tim was allowed to return to the village. He had some soul searching to do and decisions to make regarding his personal life, which would affect a number of people quite dramatically.

Chapter 73

TIM'S THREE LADIES

In Scotland on the Oat Farm, Florence waited for a call from Tim. He made that call when he arrived in Coventry. It was a few days into the new year. Tim didn't have to hide anything now, so he didn't worry about being listened to—but of course, he had to be careful regarding Florence and her false identity.

'Florence, I've told them everything except that I'm married. They said if I came back to the centre for two weeks, I could go back to working on the media and farm efficiency projects permanently afterward. I haven't mentioned anything about you yet because you told me you are with Dave, and I didn't know what was going on.'

'Oh, Tim, it's all so complicated. I had to be Dave's wife to help his story and give him an identity that would be credible. And I'd heard you went into hiding with Molly. What could I do? I really want to see you now; I will be having your baby in less than four months.'

'I want to see you also, but I must finish here at the centre first. Then I will have to see what I can organise. So much has happened, Florence. Some good, some bad. But we are alive, so we must be lucky. I will call you.'

'I will wait for your call, my darling husband.'

Molly hadn't yet arrived at the hotel when he made this first call, but Molly was with him when he was told the centre wanted him for another two weeks. He made another quick call one evening after Molly had left for her last media show in Coventry.

'Hello, Auntie Joyce. It's Tim here—Florence's husband.'

'Oh my word, the world is becoming so bewildering. Florence is not here. She's away with the German language show.'

'Yes, things must seem complicated, Auntie Joyce. I would be grateful if you could tell Florence I will be at the centre for another two weeks. I will contact her when I return to the farm in the Midlands where I've been living. If Florence wants to contact me, I can give you the number of my works.'

'Wait till I get a pencil.' She returned in a few moments. 'Fire away.'

Tim rattled off his work number and rang off with 'Thanks, Auntie Joyce.'

Tim had also been in contact with Irene. He called her at her work in the village, as they still didn't have a telephone at Dale Farm.

Irene had found out from Sally that Tim had had Molly in his hotel room in Coventry. Sally found out from Lieutenant Schmitt, who found out from Captain Vloch, who found out from Molly's bodyguard Rolf. Molly hadn't tried to keep the situation a secret. She had no reason to; she wanted to be Tim's girl now.

When she heard the gossip, Irene was so upset that she went straight back to the farm and wouldn't come out of her bedroom. There was nothing Auntie May and Uncle Albert could do. She had known grief and pain already in love, and while sobbing in her bedroom, she had a good think about her relationship with Tim. She knew Tim had low willpower when it came to women, with three on a string already. If she stayed with him, she would only get more of the same.

The following day Irene took Tim's call. Cutting through his small talk, she said, 'Tim, I loved Tom, but he has gone. You must go to Molly. I don't want to be with you any more. You must find somewhere else to stay.'

Tim was silent for a moment. 'I understand. You are upset.'

'I'm not upset any more. I just want you out of my life as soon as possible.'

Tim was silent again. Finally he said, 'I will collect my stuff when I return to the village in a week's time.'

Irene put the phone down. She had already made up her mind that she was going to stay on the farm. She knew the Blacks would allow her to stay. They needed her more than ever now, what with the children and all the other changes. Irene was also determined to make her language school a success. She had no intention of wasting more time on romantic involvement.

For Tim, this was a sad but necessary conclusion to part of his problem. In a way, it let him off the hook. He was by himself in the hotel and could think about sorting out his private life. It couldn't continue in the same chaotic way.

He wanted to make sure Irene was all right, but he didn't worry about her too much. Irene was not a teenager. Given her experiences in life, he knew she would survive.

Irene told everyone in the village of her decision, so there was no confusion. Of course, Molly was one of the first to find out. The two women often came in contact at the media centre which the Germans had set up in the local council offices. Molly knew there was nothing she could say. Irene said to Molly, 'You can have him. I don't want him anymore.' Nothing more was said, and life and business continued as usual.

The situation posed a bit of a dilemma for the German media people. They had hoped in the first place that Molly would go off with Dieter, and if not him, then another of the young German men around her. Now it was apparent Molly had been besotted with Tim all along.

A good story had started with Jamie and Hanna, but they were not adults. Angela had turned down Bill, the angry guy in Coventry. The faint hope of a German-English romance was kept alive by the fact that Angela had subsequently met one of the English researchers at the Coventry centre.

Her new friend was Brian, who was twenty-two. He hadn't lost anyone to the war. The media people asked the research centre if they would allow Brian to come and see Angela at the village. The centre said yes and chose another two engineers to join the visit. The media team sent them on a blind date with two girls from Germany, to see what might happen there.

Tim had a few things to sort out when he returned to the village. He picked his stuff up from Dale Farm—clothes,

The First EU

books, and a few miscellaneous items. It all fitted in two large suitcases and a toolbox. Irene didn't say anything.

'Oh, Uncle Tom, why are you leaving? We love you being here!' lamented Wendy, the youngest child.

Jamie looked sad as well. Tim said to him, 'Look, don't worry. It's just that Irene and I have had a parting of the ways. It was my fault. If you want me, I will always be around to help you. You can see me in the village any time.' Then a passer-by caught Tim's attention. 'Who's that?'

'Oh that's Klaus, one of the German soldiers. He's really nice.'

Tim called to the man and stuck out his hand. 'Hello, my name is Tim Handle.'

'Oh, hello. My name is Klaus Staffel.' The two men shook hands. 'I'm helping with the implementation of the efficiency programme on Dale Farm. Farmer Black gave me permission to live in the outbuilding.'

'I see. It is quite habitable. It looks like you have added a wood-burning stove?'

'Yes. I need it at this time of year. We have plenty of wood after the clearing of some hedgerows.'

'The kids seem to know you quite well.'

'Oh yes. They are teaching me English, and I'm helping them with their German. They are picking it up fast. Of course, Jamie has got Hanna to help him. I try and help Uncle Albert and Auntie May with anything I can. Considering they have lost their sons in the war, they are very friendly to me.'

'I've just come to pick up my stuff.'

'I heard you and Irene are not together any more.'

'That's right. I've been stupid. Irene is a wonderful woman, too good for me.'

Klaus looked a bit embarrassed. 'She is nice to me and is also helping me with my English. She has opened a school, you know, and I go to lessons twice a week. Dieter is also helping with the school because he is qualified in the English language.'

Tim said his sad farewells to the Blacks next. 'Uncle Albert and Auntie May, I've been foolish, but I'm not leaving for good. If you ever need my help, I will always be here for you. I promise to help you with anything. Thank you so much for hiding me. But for you, I wouldn't be where I am. I really feel bad about leaving.'

'We hope to see you often, Tom, and that's sincere,' said Uncle Albert. 'Goodbye for now and good luck.'

With that, Tim was gone.

CHAPTER 74

THE HOLLYHURST HOTEL

Horst Geissler returned to the village when he heard Tim would be back. Tim was becoming quite a star in the farm efficiency instructional films, and Horst's people knew how to work with him. In these times, it would be difficult to get someone of Tim's calibre and enthusiasm to start from scratch.

Horst was not surprised to hear about Tim's breakup with Irene. He arranged for Tim to be put up in the only proper hotel in the village, called the Hollyhurst. Realising that Molly may want to stay with him, Horst reserved a room nicknamed the honeymoon suite, just above the main entrance. Everyone knew about Molly being with Tim in Coventry, so it was rather appropriate, they thought.

The Hollyhurst Hotel was about two hundred yards from the village centre. The honeymoon suite was the largest and most luxurious room in the hotel, with a large bath, a separate shower, and good washing facilities. There was an alcove set up as a living area, with chairs, a large desk, and a dining table. There was even a modern wireless set. One person could sleep undisturbed if the other was working.

The two new German girls, Heidi and Myrtle, obtained rooms in the vicarage with Angela, since Molly had vacated. Sally was getting good money for their rooms and was able to employ a housekeeper. This helped her domestic situation, as Sally had teaching work to attend to.

The three Coventry engineers, as prospective suitors, were put up separately in the Hollyhurst Hotel. A meal was arranged for them at the vicarage, at a time which happened to coincide with a sleepover among the junior set, including Jamie and Hanna. Everyone liked the vicarage. Sally had made it into a happy place where everyone was welcome.

Sally didn't realise until it was too late to change that she had forgotten about the sleepover. In all this crush of guests, where would Jamie sleep? There was no empty third room any more. Maybe Hanna would be able to sleep in with one of the German girls?

She approached Angela first. 'The kids are having a sleepover tonight, and I promised the captain I would keep Jamie separate. Do you think Hanna could sleep with you or one of your friends?'

'I've only got one bed in my room. Heidi has two in hers.'

Angela called Heidi over and addressed her in rapid German, which Sally could not follow. 'Heidi, may Hanna sleep on the spare bed in your room tonight? She is Captain Vloch's eldest daughter, a very nice girl.'

'Of course, as long as my date doesn't want some extra amorous attention.'

'You're a fast one. Go to the hotel for that.'

The First EU

Sally didn't understand the exchange but suspected something interesting.

Angela said to her in English, 'Yes, that will be OK, Sally.'

'Great. That's another problem solved.'

The three suitors duly arrived for dinner at the vicarage at six o'clock. Angela already knew her young man, Brian. It wasn't a case of love at first sight, but she liked him, and he was certainly good-looking. Angela was quite sad that she had lost her parents and younger sister in the British bombing. Brian had lost no one and came from a close, loving family. Maybe, she thought, it would help to be part of such a family.

Nothing came of the other dates, at least so far as the media team was concerned. There was no telling when it came to relationships. All three girls stayed on in the village, teaching English and appearing in public relations events like the friendship weekends. The German soldiers were always asking Heidi and Myrtle on dates, and eventually the girls developed steady relationships among these men. Not what the media people wanted—but what could they do?

Chapter 75

THE ENGLISH REPORTER

A reporter based in Coventry, Tony, had a friend at the research centre, Colin, who gossiped about Tim and Molly one evening. 'You know,' said Colin, 'I'm sure Tim used to have a wife who lived in Dagenham. When he first arrived at the centre, she visited him here a couple of times. Quite a looker. But after his affair with Molly started, we never saw her again. He claimed that he went home to Dagenham every so often.'

Tony was intrigued. 'Can you do me a favour? I could make a story out of that. Can you get more information on Tim's wife? I will make it worth your while. It could be big.'

'I should be able to find something out. I'm sure his wife was friendly with someone when she visited. I'll contact you as soon as I have something.'

Two days later, Colin phoned. 'Hi, Tony. I've found out about Florence Handle—that's Tim's wife. Yes, he definitely had a wife. She fled to Scotland a week or so after surrender day. It's rumoured she was pregnant at the time. I inquired extensively and didn't find anyone who has been in contact with her after that. I got the address of her parents, though. It's 34 Bolton Road, Dagenham, Essex.'

'Thanks, Colin. I'll see you all right.'

'One more thing—I spoke with a friend of hers. She said other people had seen a German language show from Scotland. They were convinced it featured Florence, but said she was introduced as Rita.'

'That's interesting; I'll let you know what I find.'

Tony, as a reporter, was able to get permission to travel more easily than the ordinary person. He gave a false reason for his trip. He didn't want the German authorities to find out his true quest. He travelled south to Dagenham. When he called on Florence's parents he came up against a stone wall. He was sure they had been in contact with Florence—she was their only daughter—but he couldn't get them to budge.

So he went the other way and tried to find out about the German films being made in Scotland. He found the film centre was in Edinburgh. He wanted to go, but his newspaper insisted their associated office in Edinburgh could make the initial inquiries. If it looked promising, they would let him handle it.

Inquiries made there found all the women in the film in question had come from a village in a sparsely populated part of southern Scotland. The name Rita Randall was a stage name; the performer's real name was Mrs Florence Randall. She was five months pregnant with her first baby.

Tony's editor called him into his office. 'Look at this report. You'd better get up there. This seems like a story.'

'Fine, boss. Can you arrange the passes and tickets?'

'On it. You should be all right to leave tomorrow, as long as you complete that story for the German media team before you go.'

'Will do, boss.'

Chapter 76

THE PRESS MAN IN SCOTLAND

Two days later, Tony arrived in Edinburgh. The Germans were filming the last language show with Florence before she had to go into confinement. After booking into a hotel near the studio, Tony walked the short distance to the venue. As a pressman, he got in by showing his pass; no one suspected anything.

Tony had never been one for tact, so the moment he saw Florence, he said, 'Hi, Florence. You are Florence Handle, aren't you?'

Florence was so taken aback, she had to sit down. As she was in the middle of filming, the German media people were not happy with this intervention. A captain in uniform, who looked rather menacing, rushed over. Florence was almost fainting.

The captain shouted, 'Who are you, sir? In fact, I don't need to know. Leave immediately. If you come back or worry Florence again, I will have you arrested. Now go!'

'But—'

'Do I have to call security?' The captain gestured to a soldier. 'See him out. Sir, if you come back, you'll be in big trouble. Go.'

Tony went, escorted closely by the soldier.

'Are you all right, Florence? What was that all about?' asked the captain.

'He was … from my past. He said something bad about an old boyfriend.'

The captain patted her hand comfortingly. 'I just want you to be happy so we can finish this last film. I think it will be fantastic. The people love you even more because you are pregnant. Do you want us to make sure this guy doesn't come back?'

'Don't do anything bad to him, but I don't want to see him again.'

'Fine.' The captain said in German to another soldier, 'Follow those two. Be rough when you throw the intruder out. No permanent damage—just make sure he doesn't come back.'

'Yes, Captain.' The burly soldier had seen what had happened. He liked Florence, as he liked all the young ladies in the show.

Tony was indeed roughly handled. By the time he exited the building, he had a bloody nose, a black eye, and damaged ribs. He had not been in the armed forces and hadn't known violence in his life. He visited the local hospital and told them he had fallen down some stairs. Once he was patched up, he went back to his hotel, still rather shaken.

That was the end of that avenue of inquiry. He knew he must get results; his boss would not be happy if he didn't come up with something.

The First EU

Over a whisky and soda, he started talking to the barman about the German language show. 'Yes, those ladies are beauties,' said the barman. 'There is a new one who will be taking over when Rita leaves. She is pregnant, you know. The ladies come in this bar sometimes. They stay in that five-star hotel just down the road.'

'Where do they come from?'

'You are asking a lot of questions, friend. It also looks like you have had an argument with a bear. What has happened to you?'

'Oh, I was mugged earlier today.'

'Have you contacted the police?'

'I suppose I better. I went to the hospital already.'

'Yes, I think that would be a good idea.'

'I'm from down south. I saw the language show and couldn't help hearing one of them sounded like a Londoner.'

'Yes, that's Rita. Look, it's common knowledge they all stay on a farm near Eccles, on the English border.'

'Oh, I see,' said Tony, making out he wasn't that interested.

The barman continued, 'You know, we had a terrible time here in Scotland, especially Edinburgh, after the assassinations of Himmler and Heydrich. There are people who say these girls and their men are collaborators and should be taken out.'

'I don't know anything about that, and I don't like talking like that,' said Tony.

'It's not me.'

'Rather tell people not to talk like that. Since Hitler has gone, we have a much more moderate regime here.'

'I suppose we have.'

Tony went to the main railway station in Edinburgh to find out how to get to Eccles. He found he must get a train to Tweedmouth and then a local train to Keslo. He hoped he could get a bus from there to Eccles. The station didn't have that information, but the stationmaster said he was almost one hundred per cent certain there would be.

Then Tony found that the girls taking part in the show were finishing on the coming Friday and returning home. This was the twenty-ninth of January. He thought he had better not make too many inquiries in Edinburgh if he valued his life. It being Wednesday, he would start travelling the following morning.

On his way back to his hotel, he was stopped in a security check. There was some suspicion because of his black eye and swollen lip. He was taken to the police station and had to phone his editor, who spoke to the Scottish police. The editor told them that Tony was on a story about the German language show. This seemed to satisfy the police, although they asked him about his black eye.

'Someone attacked me in the street and ran off. Maybe they heard my southern accent and thought I was a soft touch, Sergeant.'

'Well, laddie, you had better be careful. There are plenty of funny people around here, especially with the times we live in. Be along with you now.'

'Yes, Sergeant. Thank you, Sergeant.'

Tony received a signed clearance paper in case he was stopped again.

It was an uneventful journey to Eccles, which Tony was happy about. He booked into the local inn, the only place to stay in Eccles. It had four rooms above the bar.

The First EU

This was where Florence had met Dave and where Dave had stayed before his pickup in Dumfries. Tony went to the bar. Manning it was the same barman who had welcomed Dave a few months before.

'Hi, barman. It's quiet around here, isn't it?'

'Most of the time, I suppose. The name's Jock.'

'Oh, sorry. My name is Tony.'

'Pleased to meet you.'

'I'm from the press and looking for a story on the German media shows. I believe there are people in the area who are stars in these shows.'

'Yes, there certainly are—the ladies working on the German language shows and the men working on the farm efficiency programmes. The real stars are the ladies. They explain how everyone can and should learn German, as it's going to be the main language and will help with getting on in life. They are all really good-looking. One of them, Florence, or she calls herself Rita, is a few months pregnant.'

Chapter 77

TONY AT THE OAT FARM

'The ladies would be very interested if they knew a British newspaper was writing a story about them. You should go round the farm where they all stay.'

'Where's that?' Tony asked.

'It's just up the hill. The Oat Farm.'

Tony reached the farm in the late afternoon via a taxi run by the local garage. He knocked on the farmhouse door. It was answered by a middle-aged woman. 'Hello, my name is Tony,' he said. 'I'm from the *Coventry Messenger*, and we are writing a story about three ladies who star in the German language show.'

'Oh, that's lovely,' declared the woman, who was Auntie Joyce. 'My sons will be back soon. You must talk to one of them. Do you want a cup of tea?'

'Yes, that would be nice, what is your name?'

'Oh, you can call me Auntie Joyce.'

'Thank you, Auntie Joyce.'

'You look as if you've been in the wars.'

'Yes. Someone tried to mug me in Edinburgh.'

'It's terrible times we live in.'

Soon enough, Andy arrived. Auntie Joyce said, 'Andy, this is Tony. He is writing an article on the language show the girls are doing.'

'I see.'

'He got mugged in Edinburgh.'

'Yes, you look a bit knocked about.' Andy looking Tony over. 'What do you want from us and what newspaper are you from?'

'I'm from a small provincial paper, the *Coventry Messenger*.'

Immediately alarm bells rang for Andy. 'What sort of story are you writing, and why is a small provincial newspaper writing an article about Scotland?'

'Well, I will tell you the truth.'

'Yes I think you had better. It seems rather strange that a small newspaper would be doing this story. Are you working with a London paper?'

'No, we are not.'

'"We", you say.'

'My editor and people from the research centre in Coventry know I'm here. The reason for my inquiries is that people at the research centre have identified Rita or Florence Randall as possibly living under an alias. They say she is Florence Handle, the wife of Tim Handle, who was a key engineer at the jet propulsion research centre near Coventry. My information is that she was pregnant and fled to Scotland soon after the surrender on 20 August. Tim Handle is now participating in German media shows promoting farm efficiency. You may have seen him in them yourself.

'The story I have is that Tim Handle, although he had a wife near London, was having an affair with a young woman at his work, called Molly Brooks. She is now a national celebrity for the charm offensive being run by the Germans. So, you see, the plot thickens.

'I'm not very tactful. I went into the film studio; they let me in because of my press pass. I went up to Florence and asked her if she was Mrs Florence Handle. She almost fainted with that question. A German captain had me thrown out. So I came here.'

'And you may not get any better treatment here. You must stay where you are until everyone comes home, including Florence's husband. That should be in the next hour. I can't help you until the others arrive.'

In another half an hour, at five thirty, Dave and John arrived back from their media work with the Germans.

'Tony, wait here,' Andy said. 'I want to talk to the others first.'

Andy stepped out of the lounge and met the others in the corridor, where he explained what Tony was after.

'Well,' said Dave, 'I don't want to do anything that will upset Florence.'

'So what do you suggest then?'

'I don't know what to do.'

Andy said, 'Look, Dave, this problem was bound to have come up sooner or later. This guy is not going to go away. We have a problem and must solve it as soon as possible—definitely before the girls come back tomorrow evening. We will tell him he must stay here tonight. We will discuss the issue with him and tell him that he mustn't phone his editor. It will be an exclusive story for him and he should be grateful. But he mustn't say anything to anybody before we get our story straight. John, you are not heavily involved in this. Can you run him into the village to get his stuff, making sure he doesn't make any phone calls?'

'Yes, I'll do that.'

Andy thought some more. 'Dave, we know from Florence's contacts with Tim that he has been treated well after coming clean regarding his absence from the research centre. There is no reason why you should be treated any differently. You may have to attend the centre like Tim did, to give your knowledge to the team there. But as you are also working on the farm efficiency programme, you should be able to come back here and resume your normal life. I think we must get the Germans involved. The ones we think we can trust, the same as Tim did. What do you think?'

'I'll do anything as long as Florence is all right. I desperately want to keep her as my wife.'

'I know you do, but that is something you, Florence, and Tim must sort out. It is a side issue to coming clean about your false identity. You are one of the few who knows about the assassinations, and that is another reason why it will be best to get everything out in the open. I don't like this spotlight on us. This reporter could be a big problem. Before anything is published, it must go through the German media people. I'm going to phone the Germans right now. The friendliest is Captain Gerard, even if he did run off with my girlfriend.'

Andy placed a call to Hans Gerard without further loss of time. 'Hi, Captain. We have a reporter at the farm from the Coventry Messenger …' He explained the detail of Tony's story.

'This is a curious story, Andy. If this reporter is the same man who was at the studio, I remember him well. Two things you must do. One, keep the reporter with you. We must not let this story get out. Two, do not mention anything to Florence. We hope to be finished tomorrow, and that will be the last time Florence is on film for now.'

'The story will come out sooner or later, Captain. We must get our version of it straight, covering whatever is best for the media campaign.'

'Yes, you are right. I will discuss it tonight with the media people here. Stay at home in case I need to speak to you or Dave—that is his name, isn't it?'

'Dave is his name, but his surname is false. He is from the same research centre as Tim Handle and also absconded before the SS took over. That's something needing to be sorted out also.'

'It sounds complex. I'm sure I will be speaking to you again later.'

John took Tony back to the inn. Tony insisted he must call his editor from the pay phone at the bar. John said no, and a bit of a fracas ensued. Tony was a heavy man, if not that fit, and was difficult to subdue. Luckily there were a couple of German soldiers in the bar whom John knew. They helped Andy get Tony into the car again and back to the farm.

John wasn't needed in Andy's discussions, so he ran the Germans back to the inn and bought them a round. He told them, in his much improved but still basic German, that Tony was a reporter who was going to write a bad story about the language show. The soldiers didn't fully understand, but they liked the extra beer.

Back at the farm, Andy said, 'All right, Tony. If you are still not happy, we are going to contact German security and have you locked up.'

'You can't do that!'

'If you think I can't, watch me make the phone call. You will be locked up for sure.'

'All right. It seems you have connections. I'll not protest any more.'

'You will get your story, but it will have to go through the Germans first. I can tell you nothing is going to happen before Florence has finished her last film. You have found a story which is true, involving people who are valuable to the Germans for their media campaign. This is why they must be involved. We would all be in big trouble if you put this story out without their consent—and I mean *big* trouble. Your treatment in Edinburgh is child's play compared to what could happen.

'Senior German media people are discussing this in Edinburgh this evening and may phone if they need more information. They know all about Tim and Florence. We know we must all seem like unbelievable collaborators to you, but we have decided this is the way to go.'

No more was said between Andy and Tony. The German media people phoned up Andy to clarify some details. They mentioned the head office in London was involved, along with the office in the village near Dale Farm. It was such an intriguing story, the Germans were convinced they could turn it to their advantage. But of course, it all hinged around the feelings and decisions of the four young people involved: Florence, Molly, Tim, and Dave.

Florence's filming ran over to the Saturday. In the meantime, the German authorities sent two security men to the farm to look after Tony, who was still not allowed to phone his editor. The security men and Tony shared Florence and Dave's bedroom. Dave slept in with John, as John's girlfriend Susan was still working on the language show in Edinburgh with Florence.

By now Tim had been told what was going on with Tony. The men decided not to tell Molly at this stage. Tim had a long chat with Dave on the phone. He found that Dave's meeting with Florence had been quite accidental. When Florence told Tim she was with Dave now, Tim had had a nagging feeling that Dave had always fancied his wife and had purposely found her. Not so—but now Dave was very much in love with Florence and wanted to stay with her.

Chapter 78

TIM'S TURN TO DECIDE

Florence and Molly knew nothing of what was going on, and Tim felt it was up to him to make a decision that would sort everything out.

Before he did so, however, he wanted to have a long conversation with Florence. He wanted to be absolutely honest with her about everything, and then allow time for them both to think.

On Saturday afternoon, when Florence got back to the farm, Tim made the call. 'Florence? It's Tim here. How are you keeping? How is your baby?'

'I'm well, Tim, and missing you so much. And it's *our* baby.'

Clearly his small talk wasn't up to snuff, so Tim got straight to it. 'The day after I called you from my hotel in Coventry, Molly came to my room, and we have been together ever since. Irene, whom I lived with on Dale Farm, has kicked me out. I live with Molly in the Hollyhurst Hotel, in the village featured in my films for the German media.'

'Oh, Tim. Why are you doing this to me? I'm so upset. It's not good for our baby.'

'I'm sorry, Florence. I don't know why you like me so much when I've been so horrible to you.'

'You have a way with the ladies.' She sighed. 'I wish you could just control yourself sometimes.'

'Molly is the girl who appears in the friendship shows. You may have seen her.'

'Oh is it that your Molly? She is so beautiful. How can I compete?'

'You are also very good-looking. You look radiant in the German language show.'

'So they tell me. We have just finished the final show with me in. It will be out in a week or so. They say this one is the best.'

'You are so talented.'

'Am I? But what can I do now? Dave is really in love with me, and he hasn't got a roving eye like you do, but you are the father of our child.'

'What does Dave say about that?'

'He says he is going to look after the baby like it was his own, and he wants to take care of me.'

'What do *you* want, Florence?'

'I don't know. I just don't know what to think,' she said, almost crying.

'These decisions will have to be made by us. Have a talk with Dave, and I'll have a talk with Molly. You know this is going to be a big story. We are all celebrities now, and the German media are involved. I think Dave will have to go and work in Coventry like I did, and then he should be fine. We will all revert back to our original identities.'

The First EU

'Yes, and that means I will be your wife.'

Tim didn't answer that. He just said, 'I'll phone you tomorrow.'

'I love you, Tim.' With that, Florence put the phone down.

Tim told Molly what was going on.

'Oh, Tim, don't leave me again! I don't know what I will do without you.' Molly was pleading and beautiful.

Tim kept wondering why he was in such a position. He thought the best thing to do at the moment was to let the situation be. 'I won't leave you, Molly,' he said. They made slow, gentle love and then fell into a contented sleep.

Chapter 79

TONY'S EXCLUSIVE STORY

The story wasn't extraordinary; it just reflected the truth. The German media used it to show how lenient they were being on the perpetrators of these deceptions. They wanted to remind people who hadn't been involved in serious crimes that minor transgressions could be pardoned. The four young people involved had risen to great heights in the German charm offensive. It made a good story because the characters were all good-looking, especially the women. After the story was checked and authorised, the Germans let Tony have his choice among all the photos they had of Molly and Florence.

Of course, there were other people who also had to be pardoned. Auntie May and Uncle Albert on Dale Farm had already been excused. The same treatment was granted to Andy, John, and Auntie Joyce on the Oat Farm, not to mention all the people who had supplied false documents. In the end, the Germans overlooked all these indiscretions because the main people involved were too important to them.

The First EU

After the story broke, Tim, Molly, and Florence got a lot more mail, and it wasn't all nice. Many letters were death threats, so extra protection was put in place. Tim had his Luger pistol on him all the time and went for more training and practise. When not with Tim, Molly had a bodyguard. Florence was encouraged to stay on the Oat Farm. Her mother would travel up to stay at the time of the birth.

Now that Molly was a star, she could see her parents whenever she wanted. Her mother travelled to see her and stayed in the same hotel. It was clear that Molly was happy with Tim. Her mother knew their relationship had been going on for some time, so she didn't say anything, although she thought a lot about him being married. She had read the full story about these German media celebrities and could only wonder at their fame.

The media people wanted Dave to stay with Florence, mostly because they wanted Tim to stay with Molly. So Dave wasn't sent to the research centre in Coventry.

Tony got his exclusive story and an offer from the German media team to help with their reporting. He had to take a crash course in German with Fritz and the three German girls. He loved working with the girls and picked up basic German quite quickly. The German girls joked a lot with him. He was a bit portly for age twenty-seven. Tony still worked for the *Coventry Messenger* but spent more and more time in the village at the German media centre.

Irene kept herself to herself and concentrated on her English language school. Tim often visited Dale Farm to see the kids. He couldn't help noticing that Klaus was becoming part of the farm family. The children talked to him all the time. Uncle Albert and Auntie May called to him if they wanted this or that. The friendliness was obvious. So Tim wondered if Irene was also involved. It was none of his business of course. But he was curious.

There wasn't a lot of emphasis on the farm at this time of year. The Germans had taken 'before' photos and films and had to wait for the 'after' photos and films. It wasn't any good for the village kids to visit either. It wasn't nice outside this time of year, just cold and wet.

Captain Vloch's household as well as the vicarage were often used for sleepovers. The children all loved this. Other parents, seeing how beneficial learning German and being friendly with Germans could be, were getting involved.

The media team still hosted plenty of friendly gatherings with mixed groups to make films of, and the village was still the hub of the German media charm offensive, which was beginning to show positive results in the rest of the country. The captain's girls were almost fluent in their English speaking. Reading and writing would take longer. They attended Irene's language school every day after regular school. Their father made sure they did.

Irene was working closely with Dieter. She found she got on well with him and received much mental stimulation in this way. They were getting to know one another well, but Irene wasn't looking for anything more. She was still hurting a little from the breakup with Tim. Klaus was a good-looking man and could have turned Irene on if she had been looking for that sort of gratification, but she wasn't. Irene didn't want a man, but it was nice to have two in tow, each with his own particular qualities and charms.

Chapter 80

AFTER THE ASSASSINATIONS

The new regime still dealt with resistance brutally, although the SS was now part of the army. The Gestapo were much in evidence. There were no mass executions, but anyone proved or even suspected of being in the resistance was incarcerated. Anyone found guilty of killing German soldiers was executed. However, there were no more ideological executions of British academics and prominent people. This was a great relief to the whole nation. Many people who had gone into hiding could relax. Of course, they had to be careful that they weren't suspected of anything to do with the resistance.

The Germans wanted to show everyone that cooperation was well rewarded, but resistance incurred high penalties. German was made the first language of Europe and English the second, because of its world coverage. Each country could speak its own language internally, but where possible, German was used for imperial meetings, politics, legal matters, and business. German-language schools were set up everywhere, and an English-speaking officer was placed in every school—primary, junior, and senior. Rewards and punishment were meted out for success and failure respectively.

Before the assassinations, there were many people determined to resist the German occupation. Resistance cells were secretly established everywhere, some more hostile than others. This quieted a bit after the assassinations. But some resisters thought that the rise of the moderates marked the time to act, because the regime was becoming soft.

One of the more hostile cells decided they must liquidate all people involved in the media promotion of German English cooperation. As well as Tim, Molly, and the inhabitants of their village, the kill list included the young farmers in Scotland and their partners involved in the German language shows. The resistance thought these people represented the worst form of complete collaboration and must be annihilated.

Other groups were not so hostile. The view was put forward that although Tim, Molly, and company represented collaboration, the population would take their murders very badly, having seen so much of them. The aims of the resistance could backfire.

Chapter 81

THE WARNING

Nobody noticed a shadowy figure entering the public bar at the Eccles Inn. A few minutes later, the barman saw a letter on the counter. It was addressed to Andy and John.

Jock the barman spoke to all in the bar: 'Did anyone see who left this letter?'

Someone said they thought it may have been someone coming out of the toilet, but hadn't been paying that much attention.

The farm was phoned. Andy picked up. Jock, recognising his voice, said, 'Andy, someone has left a letter here for you and John.'

'Who left it?'

'Don't know.'

'That's funny. I better come down.'

Andy drove to the Eccles Inn with his brother, and the barman handed him the letter. 'Thanks, Jock,' Andy said. 'Does anyone know yet who left it?'

'No, no one is clear about that. What do you think it is then, boys?'

'We'll let you know if it's anything important.' They thanked the barman again and were gone.

John opened the letter in the car and read it. 'My God, the resistance want to kill the lot of us.'

'What do you mean, "the lot of us"?'

'All of us working on the German media campaign. The letter says preparations are well advanced and we should be ultra-careful. It says here that the kill list not only includes the people in Scotland presenting the German language show and farm efficiency campaign, but all the people working on the German charm offensive in the village where Tim and Molly live, plus others all over the country.'

Back at the Oat Farm, they called in Dave and the three had a discussion. They decided it would be unfair not to tell the girls, because they also had to take precautions without delay.

Once the girls were briefed, Andy said, 'Florence, can you please phone Tim? I need to speak to him.'

'Yes, straight away.'

Florence got through to the Hollyhurst Hotel and was then put through to Tim and Molly's room. It was already nine thirty. Molly answered, 'Hello?'

'It's Florence. Is Tim there?'

'He's in the shower.'

'It's very urgent. We need to speak to him.' When Molly continued to hesitate, Florence snapped, 'It's a matter of life and death!'

Andy took the phone. In a moment, Tim was out of the shower. Andy said, 'I received a letter just a few minutes ago,

The First EU

informing us there is a resistance plot to assassinate all the Brits involved in the German media campaign. It includes everyone on the farm here, plus many people where you live and others all over the country. The letter says they are well advanced in their planning. Be careful. Keep someone near the phone in case I get more news.'

'Thanks, Andy. Molly will be by the phone. I'm going to tell my friendly German captain straight away.' With that, Tim put the phone down.

Andy thought he better tell his friendly Germans as soon as possible also. Captain Gerard would give them protection and warn others.

Molly overheard the conversation. Her voice was alarmed. 'What can we do, Tim?' He was already looking up the home number of Captain Vloch.

On the Oat Farm, they sent Dave to the bar to look around and have another chat with Jock. 'Hi, Jock. A beer, please.'

'Right away.'

Dave, talking in a low voice, continued, 'Bad news. Keep that letter hush-hush.'

The barman leaned over conspiratorially. 'Of course, Dave.'

'Firstly, have you got any information yet on who left the letter?'

'No.'

'Right. Well, the letter contained a kill list of media figures being targeted by the resistance for assassination.'

'Wow.'

'Indeed. We will have to tell the Germans, so they might come here asking questions. Andy and John are home, protecting the women. Have you got some change? I must use the phone here.'

'Yes, sure.'

Dave rang the farm. 'Hi, Andy. I've told Jock what was in the letter. No info yet on who left it. I'm coming straight back.'

'Be careful,' was Andy's comment as he hung up.

Dave hung up as well and waved to the barman. 'See you, Jock. Be careful.'

'Yes, I'll be that for sure,' said Jock, looking rather anxious.

The Germans had once before offered the protection of soldiers stationed on the farm, but the women hadn't been too keen on the idea. The men had been given Lugers and training. The brothers didn't need much, as they were familiar with handguns from their army days. Dave needed training, but he was never happy with his gun and usually kept it locked away.

More than five minutes after he started looking, Andy finally found Captain Gerard's number and put the call through. He felt no awkwardness about it. The affair between Andy's former girlfriend and the captain had been put behind them now. Andy had a nice replacement in Sarah, who lived at the farm more often than not nowadays.

'Hi, Captain. It's Andy here. I thought I should let you know John and I have received a letter warning us that the resistance is well advanced in plans to assassinate all the British people involved in the German media programmes. We only got the letter tonight. It was left for John and I in the bar at the Eccles Inn. We have already contacted

The First EU

Tim Handle down south. He is going to be contacting the Germans in that area.'

'This is a serious situation,' the captain replied. 'I'm going to send a patrol vehicle with six men to the farm straight away. I'll let the high command know so they can contact the local commanders elsewhere. Have the letter and source been verified?'

'We couldn't find out who left the letter in the pub. Someone thought they saw a stranger come out of the toilet. That may have been the person who left it on the bar. We told the barman what was in the letter, but no one else. Your people can stay in the outbuildings here; we haven't got any room in the house. I can put paraffin heaters out there, and we can sort some mattresses out. Make sure your men have sleeping bags.'

'They will be there in thirty minutes.'

Andy hung up and greeted Dave, who had just returned from the Eccles Inn. 'The Germans are sending six men who will be quartered in the outbuildings. Can you organise two paraffin heaters?'

'Right away, Andy.'

'I'll see about some mattresses.'

Chapter 82

GUNFIGHT AT DALE FARM

On Monday, 8 February 1943, coming up to ten thirty at night, six resistance fighters traversed the brow of a hill overlooking Dale Farm. They carried rifles, Sten guns, and hand grenades. The farmhouse on this moonlit night was silhouetted in the valley.

When they were within a hundred yards of the house, a small dog started barking. A large dog joined in. This alerted Klaus, who immediately got his rifle, handgun, and ammunition. Running to the house, he got the girls, Irene, and Auntie May up into the attic. This had been pre-planned and practised already. The ladder was soon pulled up and the hatch in place.

Jamie was supposed to be up there also, but he refused, and there was nothing Klaus could do about it in the circumstances. Jamie was in the kitchen with a double-barrelled rabbit gun and extra ammunition. Uncle Albert had two twelve-bore double-barrelled shotguns with extra cartridges. All they could do was defend the farmhouse and try and stop anyone entering.

The dogs, sensing danger, were going mad. An initial shot was followed by agonised howls; the large dog had been hit. After the second shot, there was immediate silence.

The shots at the dogs had given the position of at least one of the attackers. They had obviously fanned out and surrounded the house, as stealthy sounds could be heard at the back. Those inside didn't know how many there were outside.

There was a deafening explosion. A grenade had been thrown at the front door, which was completely blown in. Klaus, standing next to the door, was slightly injured but fought on. He shouted, 'Shoot to kill!'

Uncle Albert was manning the back door. Jamie was covering the windows. One of the girls sobbed quietly in the loft, but this quickly stopped.

Tim and Captain Vloch, with four armed soldiers, were driving towards the farm. They heard the first shot, and then thought they heard the howling. They definitely heard the second shot.

'Speed up, driver!' shouted the captain. The patrol car left the road after the humpback bridge, a mile from the farm.

Then they heard the explosion.

'What the hell?' pronounced Tim, who had never been in a real combat situation in his life. He was armed with a Luger and two extra clips. The others, including the captain, had rifles as well as handguns. There were no hand grenades.

Things were happening fast on the farm. The attackers at the back were shooting through the windows and the door. Jamie was grazed on his right arm above the elbow, and quickly took cover as much as he could. Shots were coming in from all sides. Two attackers were at the front door.

'Look out, Klaus!' Jamie shouted.

Straight away, Klaus was shot at point-blank range in the chest.

Jamie and Uncle Albert let rip with their shotguns. The two attackers at the front were shredded by this fusillade. Klaus was still moving but gravely wounded.

Another grenade exploded at the back door. The girls screamed but somehow stopped again. The percussions of grenades and guns affected all the people in the farmhouse, especially Jamie, who was faltering. But the adrenaline was pumping and this was overcoming all. The smell of cordite was thick in the air.

The patrol car was still half a mile away, but travelling at speed. 'Fire your rifles, men,' the captain ordered. 'Let them know we are coming.' Everyone, including Tim, started firing their guns towards the farm. Although well out of range, they could definitely be heard.

'The Germans are coming!' shouted one of the attackers, and they all began to run.

Of the two who had been shredded, only one was mobile enough to make a move. He fired a continuous burst from his Sten gun into the part of the ceiling where he had heard the screaming earlier. He knew someone was up there.

It was too late when he saw Jamie rise from behind the settee—the last thing he ever saw. A heavy shot from the first barrel blew half his face away. The second was placed against his heart.

By now the farmer had reloaded and was firing at the fleeing attackers. He must have hit at least one of them, as a loud cry was heard. Hysterical screaming was coming from the attic.

'Someone has been hit!' Uncle Albert yelled.

The attacker lying in the doorway was somehow still alive. Klaus, staggering, shot him in the head. '*Du Scheisse*,' he muttered, then passed out.

'The Germans are here!' shouted Jamie.

As the patrol car screeched to a halt, the Germans jumped out. The farmer warned, 'They're escaping across the fields at the back!'

As Tim got to the house, Jamie shouted, 'The girls are all in the attic!'

'Get the ladder down,' Tim ordered.

'Auntie May and Wendy have been hit!' screamed Irene. 'Auntie May has fallen on the hatch and is unconscious.'

Tim shouted back, 'I'm going up on the kitchen roof and through the thatch!'

'Quickly!' cried Irene.

Wendy was screaming, 'I want my mum, oh my mum, oh no!'

Tim broke through the thatch. The attic was like a battle scene, with Auntie May unconscious and slumped over the hatch.

'She's got a head wound. The top of her head is missing,' cried Irene, who also had blood coming from her upper arm and leg. The only one unscathed, as far as Tim could see, was Jennifer.

'Jennifer, come through here. Stand on the roof. Take my coat,' he instructed.

The captain shouted to his men, 'Stay together, and shoot anything that moves!'

With this, they shot a man dead whom they discovered trying to escape. He had been wounded by one of Uncle Albert's shots. As the four soldiers sought the other attackers, it was clear they might have got away.

Before they went too far, the captain ran after his men, shouting, 'Men, come back! I want to regroup.' He had used the field radio to send for another patrol car with at least six men, and two ambulances with medics.

Surveying the situation, he realised that casualties were high for a few minutes' work. Three of the attackers were dead. Auntie May was dead. Klaus and Wendy were critically injured. Irene and Jamie were walking wounded, with Irene in the worse case.

The captain shouted to one of his men, 'Use the radio. I want at least twenty men in the area immediately. We must capture these murderers.'

Tim was trained in first aid, and two of the soldiers had extensive medical training. They took over until the ambulance arrived. 'Don't worry, little one. I will keep you alive,' whispered one of the soldiers to Wendy. They were succeeding in keeping her warm and stemming the loss of blood. She had been hit in the thigh and in the lower leg on the opposite side. She would live, though she might be crippled.

It was unlikely that Klaus was going to live. Slowing his loss of blood and keeping his breathing going were all that could be done at this stage. Although the bullet had missed his heart, it had blown the opposite shoulder away and probably shattered his spine.

Irene screamed when she saw the half-blown-away face of the attacker slumped over the settee. 'Oh my God, it's Steve!' He was her abusive lover from Birmingham, from whom she had fled nearly three years before.

Chapter 83

DETAILS OF THE ATTACK

There had been coordinated action this fateful evening all over the country. The late message to the men on the Oat Farm had been the only warning. As there had been dozens of attacks, some did get through.

Soldiers were quickly dispatched to the Oat Farm, and there was no attack there. The attackers had probably seen the soldiers. Andy's old girlfriend Jean had been told, and her sometime lover, Captain Gerard, arranged for four soldiers who reached her just in time. The would-be assassins disappeared into the backstreets of Edinburgh without being captured.

Although some German officials acted on the warning, there were some in the high command who were initially sceptical. This resulted in a number of unnecessary British deaths.

Luckily, the warning had been taken seriously at the village near Dale Farm. There were at least forty resistance fighters deployed against its residents, and soldiers were counter-deployed just in the nick of time. Otherwise, it would have been carnage. One of the choir girls was killed in the village's outskirts, and two others. This made the total deaths in the village five, with double that number hospitalised.

The resistance fighters, realising their plot had been uncovered, made a hasty retreat. A number were apprehended at roadblocks, and some went into hiding. This was precarious, as there was little help from the locals. When daylight came, most fugitives were exposed to the Germans combing the area. Only a few escaped.

The total number of British civilians killed that night approached eighty, with twice that number wounded. This started a massive debate in the country—and in a way, the Germans took a backseat.

The attack hadn't been endorsed by all in the resistance movement, but a hard core had finally persuaded the rest that it was the thing to do. In Scotland, it had been an unpopular move, which had resulted in the written warning being left in the pub. People didn't want to see three beautiful film stars taken out.

After the assassinations of Heydrich and Himmler, Andy and John had agreed privately not to have any contact with the resistance for a few months. By the time of the general attack, the brothers weren't active in the movement at all. But of course, a couple of high-ranking members of the resistance knew Andy was the assassin. That was probably another reason the warning went out.

Steve, Irene's abuser, belonged to the Midlands resistance. He had been trying to find out where Irene fled to with no success. Then, early in the new year, he saw her in one of the media shows. When the opportunity came up to take part in the attacks, he volunteered for the Dale Farm group. He wanted to punish Irene for leaving him.

After the attacks, the German army went on full alert and a curfew was imposed. Many resistance fighters were captured and many more were shot trying to escape—or so the Germans said. People knew this was another way of carrying out executions. Quite a number of non-resistance civilians were unfortunately killed by mistake. This could hardly have been avoided. After the initial gunfights and skirmishes, the death toll rose into the hundreds. The Germans also lost dozens of men, Klaus being one of them.

Tim, on behalf of all young British leaders, made a request to stop the unofficial executions from the German side and any further resistance killings of Germans. Afterwards, the killings overall went down to one or two a day, whereas before they had been running at ten or so a day. German deaths virtually ceased. This was good, as it meant someone in the resistance was listening. The German military took note.

Chapter 84

MATTERS BEFORE THE ATTACK

At the time of the resistance attack, many other issues were coming to a conclusion.

Florence and Dave had admitted their identity deception and Tony the newspaper man had his story. Florence had finished her last German Language show before going into confinement for the birth of Tim's baby.

Tim had also admitted his deception. Completed four weeks at the development centre and returned to The Village with Molly in tow. They were now living together in the Hollyhurst Hotel, Irene having woefully finished with Tim for good. The Media people were working on a story to be screened showing all the deceptions and how lenient the German authorities were being.

The Farm and German children were settling into the community and school, with a young romance developing between Hanna and Jamie and the friendship between the other girls from the farm and vicarage helping the German girl's integration. The media people had made good use of this situation.

The Friendship weekend in Coventry was a great success and similar events were taking place in many parts of the country.

Dale Farm was in the process of being upgraded for the efficiency campaign. Irene and Dieter were getting on well with their English Language school and franchising their methods to the rest of the country. The Captain was also heavily involved in this. Irene employed a good looking, unattached well educated twenty-two-year-old girl to work in The Village with them. She had in mind a romance for Dieter, but Dieter had his eyes on her.

The romance between Lieutenant Schmitt and Sally had come to a bit of a stalemate. Sally had got cold feet after their night of passion the previous year. Considering the impact of an affair on her young girls, especially if it was discovered, she tried to resurrect her sex life with her husband Ray. The first thing he had to do was lose weight, but this couldn't be done overnight. It was difficult. He tried, as he suspected her infatuation with the lieutenant, and there were some positive results.

The hunt for the assassin in Scotland reached a dead end. Several of the senior army and administration people felt it had helped the occupational situation no end to have the despots out of the way. They thanked their luck that the resistance assassin had been so disciplined—particularly those who had been in the potential line of fire.

The whole story had now come out about Tim and his three 'wives'. Not everyone was happy about this. Some people just thought he was an immoral womaniser. The Germans were worried that it would affect his standing as an icon in the farm efficiency programme, but they were willing to wait and see how it all panned out.

Chapter 85

THE PRIME MINISTER

After the resistance attacks, the political leadership realised the country was still much divided. They approached the young people in the German media shows. Molly and Tim were probably better known than the leadership, and the girls in Scotland were also very much in the national spotlight. The village near Dale Farm had become the most photographed place in the United Kingdom. And with this latest attack, it had become almost legendary.

A few days after the attacks, the Prime Minister phoned Tim. He was put straight through. The hotel concierge announced, 'This is the Prime Minister for you.'

Tim, of course, took the call. 'Good evening, Prime Minister.'

'Tim, my boy, we desperately need your help to bring the country together. I'm going to send my man to speak to you with instructions on what to do.'

'I'm very honoured to be phoned by you, sir, but please don't send your man yet. I want a private meeting with my friends and relations here and in Scotland to make my mind up on what action I can take.'

'Oh, ah, all right. But the situation is very serious, you know.'

'I know, sir. I will do my best to get back to you quickly. I must speak to my German friends; nothing can happen without them.'

'Thank you, Tim,' said the Prime Minister, sounding tired and a little rattled as he hung up.

'That was the Prime Minister,' Tim said to Molly unnecessarily.

'You are remarkable, Tim Handle. What are you going to do now?' she said.

'You and I are closer to the German leadership than any of our British politicians. They have never approached us before. We in fact are the British leaders; our choices will determine the future now. I'm going to speak to Captain Vloch and then Andy. I want to have a meeting at the Oat Farm in Scotland. Or it can be at the town hall here in the village; they can come down and stay for a few days. I don't want any of the Prime Minister's men involved yet. The only British media person I want is Tony. Of course, we will have to allow the German media people. Nothing will happen without their say-so.'

Tim knew the Prime Minister had been an appeaser before the war. He had become the leader after Winston Churchill's death and had negotiated the ill-fated armistice the previous summer. Tim thought he wasn't the sort who could handle the Germans. It needed someone like Churchill, much tougher. The Germans appreciated strength.

CHAPTER 86

THE YOUNG LEADERS

Tim phoned Vloch. 'Captain, I need to talk to you urgently.'

'I will come to the hotel. There are two senior people from Berlin I want you to meet.'

Then Tim got through to Scotland. 'Andy, the Prime Minister phoned me a few minutes ago. He wants me, you, and all the people in the media campaigns to help bring the country together. I told him I wanted a meeting with my friends before doing anything. Would you be interested in attending a meeting here? We really need to talk. What do you think?'

'It's an excellent idea,' said Andy in an enthusiastic tone.

'Fine. I'm meeting the Germans shortly, and if they agree, I will ask them to arrange transport. Phone me at the hotel when you are sure you are coming. Florence knows the number. I personally want you, John, and the girls all involved.' He heard a bit of a commotion in the hotel lobby. 'The Germans have just arrived. Talk later. Give me thirty minutes.'

The First EU

'I hope you can pull this off.'

As Tim walked down the main stairs, he could see the captain with two Germans he'd never seen before. At this stage, he didn't know if they knew about the call from the Prime Minister. He thought maybe they did.

Vloch said, 'Tim, I want to introduce you to Ottomar Weiss and Theo Severin. They flew in from Berlin this morning to solve the political problems in this country.'

'Please to meet you, gentlemen,' Tim said, shaking their hands. 'So what do you want?'

'We need to know what it is that you want, Tim,' said Ottomar Weiss, who seemed to be the senior person of the two.

'As you may or may not know, the Prime Minister phoned me a few minutes ago. He wants help to bring the country together. I told him he must wait until I've spoken to the other British media people here and in Scotland, plus my German friends. He didn't sound happy about that.'

He continued, 'For my own part, I would like all executions to cease immediately. I would like transport for my people to come from Scotland to a meeting in this village. We need to discuss a plan of action—or, as we say in engineering, a roadmap—for a successful future in this country.'

'The second request is not a problem,' Weiss responded. 'We can arrange one of our short take-off transport planes straight away. As far as the request to stop the executions, that is more difficult. Many captured resistance fighters have been proved without doubt to be murderers, of your people as well as ours.'

'Still, that is my request. It would be a fantastic way to get the divided people of this country together. You may know my story. I wanted to be a resistance fighter originally and left my key job at the jet engine research centre. But because of the German charm offensive in this village and German people like the captain, I started working with the Germans. I was very impressed, and everything changed. From a would-be resistance fighter, I became an arch collaborator, fronting the farm efficiency campaign.

'I can assure you, as the captain knows, that I would not have continued if the two thousand slave labourers had been shot after the killings of Himmler and Heydrich. I'm not saying the fighters who committed the recent killings should not be brought to justice, but for the time being, their punishment should be delayed.

'The people in Scotland will be phoning me soon. They are keen for a meeting with us. After we have had our meeting, we hope you can have a conference with us.'

'What about the call from your Prime Minister?' Weiss asked.

'Molly, and I to a lesser extent, are better known in the United Kingdom than the Prime Minister is. Yet no one from the British government has ever contacted any of us until now. He can wait. We feel that what is best for the country is some sort of collaboration. We are the young who will be living in the future. The Prime Minister can be brought in after we have had our meeting. I don't want to be disrespectful to him and the older population.'

The four men had not even sat down yet when Tim was called to the phone at the front desk. it was Andy. 'Hi, Tim. What's the story? There are about twelve of us up here, ready to go.'

'Hang on.' Tim covered the receiver and turned. 'Mr Weiss, when can my people be transported? The place is in southern Scotland, Dumfries. There are about twelve people.'

'We will be able to get a plane there about ten o'clock tomorrow morning. Give me the contact numbers of your people and I will arrange things.'

Tim turned back to the phone. 'Andy, you will be contacted by phone. The plane will land somewhere near Dumfries tomorrow morning about ten o'clock. I believe there is an aerodrome there. See you tomorrow. Oh, will Florence be attending?'

'We couldn't keep her away. Your life is interesting, Tim. See you tomorrow.'

'I look forward to it. It's been a long time.' He hung up the phone and returned to his group. 'Thank you, Mr Weiss. Here is the number of the person in Scotland. His name is Andy.' Tim tore a page out of a small notebook and handed it to him.

'Please, call me Ottomar. We will organise the flight.' The German gave Tim a quizzical glance, 'I must say you have a complex private life. I will have to phone Berlin about delaying the executions. They are an hour ahead there, so it's unlikely we will have an answer before tomorrow. I will do my best.'

'Thank you, Ottomar.'

Chapter 87

THE SILVER BIRD

At nine o'clock in the morning, there was a motley group of just over forty people standing on the former RAF runway near Dumfries. An excited babble arose when a massive silver passenger plane came into view, propelled by four powerful BMW engines. The sound was amazing as the four props were feathered and the plane was slowed by its braking parachute. It took about twenty minutes for the parachute to be stowed and fuel taken on board before it taxied over to the waiting passengers: the contingent from the Oat Farm, a handful of resistance representatives, the Germans' Edinburgh media team, and, of course, soldiers.

Surprisingly, there were also four British naval officers from the surviving destroyer which had been in the king's flotilla. They had been chosen especially for their academic qualifications, cooperation, and management skills, plus they were young and proficient in or learning German.

There were sixty luxury seats inside the plane, with a galley at the rear. This plane, specially flown in from

Berlin, was used for VIPs, and already had four high-ranking Germans on board. There was a complement of four guards responsible for the well-being of the plane. This meant they were familiar with all the safety equipment and had to check everything coming on board. Their main task was the protection of the passengers. Their leader was a junior officer.

Most of the group, including the Germans, were in awe as they mounted the stairs and stepped on board. It's doubtful if any had been on such a plane before.

'My, oh my, oh my, oh my,' pronounced Auntie Joyce as she entered the plane, 'what have you boys got me into?'

'Don't worry, Mum. Just sit back and enjoy it. Everything is out of your control, so you can just relax.'

'It's very well for you, John. How can I relax on this monster?'

Seeing his mother was becoming quite agitated, John spoke to one of the stewardesses. 'Could you please bring a large whisky, Fraulein?'

'Make it two,' said her vicar friend.

Within a minute, two large whiskies were delivered. That seemed to calm his mum down a bit. Florence was sitting on one side of Auntie Joyce, trying to pacify her as well. The brothers would not have asked their mother along normally, but Florence wanted her, as Auntie Joyce knew about pregnancy.

As soon as everyone was seated, the plane taxied to the end of the runway. The pilot revved its engines until the plane trembled, straining against its brakes. As these were released, it shot forward with a short take-off. The plane was airborne and steeply climbing. Auntie Joyce gripped her seat so tightly, her knuckles went white.

The noise wasn't too high as the engines strained to reach the plane's cruising height. There, the sound lessened to a drone soft enough for easy conversation. Light refreshments were served by the plane's three hostesses. Auntie Joyce became more settled.

Because one of the engines was playing up, the plane had to be diverted to an airbase with a longer runway, as it would have less slowing power on landing without the one feathered prop. Originally meant to land just outside Lichfield, now it landed further south, near Birmingham. This problem was known well beforehand, and there were various buses and cars waiting for them. The Scottish contingent was transported to the village in one bus. The Germans went to Lichfield in various vehicles.

Dave was slightly put out, having been left to his own devices for most of the trip. This didn't help his anxiety about Florence meeting Tim again. Florence didn't know what to expect. She was aware that momentous things seemed to be happening; the Germans appeared willing to take this group of young people and set them up as the new leaders. She didn't want any emotional outburst to hinder this ambition for the good of the whole country. To keep Dave in his place, she decided to share a room with Auntie Joyce. Dave had to be content to share with John.

When the bus reached the village, the visitors found a village in mourning. All flags were at half-mast, and extra flags had been put out for the purpose. Florence and Auntie Joyce stayed at the vicarage in Heidi's room, which had two beds, Heidi had returned to Germany. Most of the rest were staying at the main hotel, where Tim and Molly resided.

After everyone was settled in their rooms, a quick meeting was called in the vicarage living room.

Chapter 88

THE MEMORIAL SPEECH

The main room in the vicarage was rather full when Sally's husband opened the meeting. He offered a memorial speech for those who had fallen in the recent resistance attack.

'Ladies and gentlemen, we all know the last few days have been a terrible time in our village. Our people have been at the forefront of the friendship campaign supported by Germans, showing an example to the rest of the country in good relations. There is no other way forward that any Christian person can see.'

He reviewed the list of local casualties and concluded, 'God bless all who have been killed or injured from whatever side. The ones dead have gone to another place. I ask you to accompany me in the Lord's Prayer and then observe one minute's silence. Our Father who art in heaven …'

After the minute's silence, the vicar sat down. No one else got up to talk. Given the list of carnage, people were preoccupied with their own thoughts.

Finally, Captain Vloch rose and said, 'Most in this room have taken part in at least one of the German media campaigns to bring our peoples together. You are better known in this case than your politicians. In fact, Tim got a call yesterday from your Prime Minister, asking him to help bring the country together. Tim told him nothing can happen without German help. Any sensible person should know this, and we are willing to give this help. Tim told him he would make contact after our discussions.

'We want to bring young, well-educated people into the leadership. We have some senior German administration members here, just in from Berlin, for discussions over the next few days. They have spoken to Tim already. It's the young people who have the future to contend with, and it's the young people mostly who have sacrificed their lives in this conflict. If we can come up with a workable plan, you will get our full support.

'Tim has asked for the executions to stop, and I can tell you that they ceased temporarily this morning. We have captured a lot of resistance fighters who are in custody at present. We have only postponed their reckoning.

'Now we will leave you to have a chat together. I hope you can come up with a strategy. We can start our discussions with you tomorrow. Of course, we have conditions also. Is there a hall we can use that can comfortably hold forty?'

'There is the church hall, but it is a bit draughty. Then there is the restaurant in the hotel where some of you are staying. That is probably the most comfortable,' said the vicar.

'Can it be arranged?'

'I'm sure it will not be a problem if you want it for the meeting. The normal procedure should be followed for payment.'

Captain Vloch said, 'Although my men are still busy after the resistance attacks, I will detail eight to you this afternoon including Dieter and some others who speak a bit of English. I hope we see you all at nine thirty tomorrow morning in the hotel. I'll leave you alone now.' He and his men left with the captain from Edinburgh.

The people in the room were still a bit shell-shocked. 'I would like to visit Irene in the clinic later,' said Tim. He pulled Sally aside. 'Would it be possible to eat here tonight? I'll get the formal requisition through later.'

'Of course. I'll get my cook in. How many will there be?'

'I make it fifteen. I would say cater for a few more just in case.'

'Yes, we can do that. I'll have to rearrange the furniture a bit and get another table in. We will eat at seven thirty, if that's OK. Just good English food, nothing fancy.'

'Also—sorry for being such a pain—is it possible to get tea and a few sandwiches for the people now? The Scottish contingent haven't eaten since they were on the plane.'

'Yes, certainly. I was going to suggest that, I was feeling a bit peckish myself,'

'At six thirty, we will visit Irene at the clinic. Can you ask Ray to tell the Hollyhurst Hotel about their restaurant being used for the meeting tomorrow? Nine thirty in the morning, for forty people. Soldiers will be there at five today to help with any work. Finally, tell them we will not be eating there tonight. Tomorrow's breakfast service must finish by nine to allow time to get the room ready.'

The First EU

'Tim, we will leave you youngsters alone now,' said Auntie Joyce. She and her Scottish vicar were going to stay in the other hotel in the village, where Uncle Albert was also staying after the farm attack. They hoped to see him. If not, they would visit the church for prayer. A couple of German soldiers were helping him with the farm, but he was in a bad state, almost having lost the will to live.

Chapter 89

THE PERFECT SOCIETY LIST

After a bit of discussion, the group of young people who remained itemised the following list:

- A democracy based on common sense laws with protection for minorities
- Proportional representation in voting
- A caring society
- A just society
- A meritocracy
- State education equally for all, the selling of education to be limited
- No aristocratic privileges
- An amnesty for all resistance fighters who come clean and want to support the new society
- The death penalty to be abolished, keeping hard labour for life for certain crimes
- No soft touch prisons
- All war crimes, whether killings by the German army or bombing by the British, not to be pursued

The First EU

- No more persecution of any race, whether Jews, Roma, or others
- All Nuremberg decrees and laws of 1935 to be abolished
- The Christian religion to be encouraged throughout the world and especially in Europe
- Everyone to work and a survival minimum wage to be enforced
- A national health care for the poor, with private health care to continue
- A parliamentary democracy to be worked out and implemented with elections within two years
- The Lords upper house to be abolished immediately
- The country to continue under German administration, phasing back to British administration under the new methods before the elections
- Proper recognition for engineers, who must be at the forefront of rebuilding society, using cooperation, common sense, and properly worked-out procedures to solve all problems
- The British Empire to be ruled jointly by Germany and the United Kingdom, using English as the common language
- English to be the second language of Europe, as it is the language of the USA, the most economically powerful country in the world
- Endeavour to support a united Europe with German as the major language having a common currency and banking system, initially just among the major industrial powers;

- Endeavour to take complete control of all of the countries comprising the empires of Europe, including those in the Far East and Australasia, which may be disputed with Japan and the USA

A number of copies were made for the morning meeting. These were dreams, but with the occupiers behind them, a lot of these proposals could be realised.

At six thirty, the group made their way to the clinic to see Irene.

Chapter 90

IRENE IN THE CLINIC

Tim entered Irene's room first. 'Hi, Irene. We've come to wish you a speedy recovery.'

'Oh, hello, Tim. I didn't want anyone to see me like this. Can you ask the others to come again in a day or so? You can come back after you have told them. I'm too unwell to see anyone else.'

'All right.'

Tim sent the group away and went back in, much to Molly's annoyance. But she had copies of the list to arrange for and hurried off to her typewriter at the centre.

'Tell me what has been going on,' Irene said with that loving look Tim knew so well. He wasn't going to be nasty; she had been through a lot. Pulling up a chair, he told her all the vicar had related regarding the injuries and deaths. 'I didn't know about Klaus,' she said softly. 'He saved our lives, you know.'

'Unfortunately, Klaus never regained consciousness. He died two days after the attack.'

'Oh, Tim,' she wept. 'Klaus was such a nice man. I was beginning to get quite fond of him, and he was so good with the children.' She was crying almost uncontrollably. 'I must let his family know how he saved us and how good he was with us. What is this world coming to?'

He was holding her as she shook, the tears streaming from her eyes. This went on for a few minutes. He thought maybe this was why they had not told her anything, and also that maybe she had become more than just fond of Klaus. What a cruel turn of fate for Irene.

When she had calmed down, Tim said, 'It's terrible, I know. He was a good man. The latest from the hospital is that Wendy will be all right, but may have a limp for a year or so.'

'Oh, that's fantastic news. And what about you?'

He had always been able to talk easily to Irene, and he could feel that warmth coming back. Irene looked tired and tear-stained, but lovely nevertheless.

'The Prime Minister phoned me the other day, asking me to help bring the country together. I didn't like the way he talked down to me. I said I would come back to him after I had spoken to the Germans. They flew these top guys in from Berlin and they have complied with all that I've asked so far. They sent a plane to transport the people from Scotland for a meeting here, and even better, they have stopped the executions. They have only been put on hold. I don't know if I can swing that one for long. We start negotiations tomorrow with the Germans.'

'Tim, you are amazing.'

'I haven't had a chance to speak with Florence, but she looks well. She isn't sleeping in the same room as Dave, but with her Auntie Joyce. Dave is sleeping in another hotel.'

Irene said nothing.

Tim cast about for another topic. 'I hear Jamie is quite a hero.'

'You know he killed Steve, my old abuser? Steve was shooting up into the loft at the time. It was he who killed Auntie May and injured Wendy and me.'

They reminisced about their time on the farm. Then Tim looked at the clock, suddenly seeing it had gone seven thirty. 'Oh, Irene, I must leave you now. I'm late for the evening meal at the vicarage.'

'Come and see me again,' she pleaded.

'You just get better, Irene.' He kissed her on the forehead. She raised her head and pulled him down with her good arm, locking her lips onto his and giving him a long French kiss. He couldn't help but respond to it, of course. He could taste the salt from her tears, but it was still nice.

'See you,' he said when she released him.

'Love you, Tim,' she replied, and he was gone.

Chapter 91

WHERE HAS TIM BEEN

'Where have you been?' pronounced Florence as Tim entered the room,

'I was just giving Irene all the news. They hadn't told her anything. She didn't even know about Klaus dying.'

Molly, also late back from organising the copies, didn't say anything but looked suspiciously unhappy.

'We were waiting for you, Tim. Make sure your glasses are full, everyone. We are going to have a toast to the success of our mission,' said Andy.

'To the success of our mission!' they all called out and drank from their glasses.

Uncle Albert looked very despondent still, like a zombie. Tim had never seen him like this. But he did drink the toast. There were a couple of widows in the village who had called to see him and were trying to pull him out of his grief. He wasn't a bad-looking man for his age of fifty.

For the previous few days, Tim had been trying to contact Arthur his boyhood friend from West Ham Grammar School

The First EU

who had been training to be a surgeon. He finally found the hospital Arthur was working at and got him on the phone. 'Arthur it's Tim Handle here. How are you? Fine, I hope.'

'Tim, it's good to hear from you. I hope you are well. I've seen you at the cinema.'

'Yes, it's a long story. I live in a village north of Birmingham now. It's featured in most of the German films.'

'I'm all right because I was needed very much for my skills as a surgeon. But if Heydrich were alive, I don't know how long that would have lasted. My father was assaulted and my sister molested when they were rounded up and taken to the ghetto in Whitechapel.'

'That is very bad. I hope they are fine now. The Germans are looking for young people to come up with a plan to run the country and have asked me. I would be honoured if you would agree to be part of it, but would also understand if you declined.'

'I appreciate being asked, but I think I will have to give it a miss. I just don't want to have to work too closely with the German leadership for the time being. I'd like to finish my training as a surgeon. I have another year as an intern.'

'I understand. But please remember, if you ever want to join us, you will always be welcome. I'm not saying this lightly. I can tell you the Prime Minister phoned me recently and I have the ear of very senior Germans. You will see me in the news, Arthur I'm sure. I was close to being killed in the resistance attacks recently.'

'Yes, those attacks gave me a lot of work. All I can say is I wish you luck, Tim. I must go now.'

'It will be good for the nation if we can get this right. Good luck to you too. I will keep in contact.'

With that, they hung up.

Tim got the impression Arthur was holding back a bit. He was not his usual friendly self. Maybe, Tim thought, he would get this reaction from many old friends in future. But there again, the Jews had been treated especially terribly. Tim thought the Germans must show they had changed their ways for this new project to work.

After his call to Arthur another item, agreed by all, was added to the list:

- The occupational forces must treat the British people with respect and as equals. There must be no national or racial discrimination

The young men had a long discussion in the hotel bar that night, in which they discussed many things. Andy took a few notes.

Tim didn't mention anything to Dave about Florence, although he knew Dave wanted to talk. At the moment, Tim wanted to concentrate on the main task. As usual, his private life was left to find its own course.

The following morning at nine-thirty, all involved assembled in the Hollyhurst Hotel dining room, which had been arranged with chairs and a blackboard at the front. The blackboard and chalk came from a local school. There were tables arranged at the rear for snacks and drink.

The list had already been sent to a few people the previous evening. Just before the meeting started, Tim handed out the updated list to all. Ottomar said, 'I see there is another item.'

'Yes. I added that with everyone's approval after speaking to my Jewish friend in London last night.'

The First EU

Ottomar looked at the new item again, then looked at Tim and nodded. 'I understand.'

Ottomar then opened proceedings. 'Ladies and gentlemen, my name is Ottomar Weiss. I've been sent by the German government. This is momentous occasion for us here, God willing, to sort out the grave situation in this country after the resistance attacks a week ago. I feel great satisfaction that it has taken so little time to set up this meeting due to the cooperation of both sides.

'Molly has organised copies of our initial discussion points. It's an impressive list, but before we start, I would like to go round the room so that we know who everyone is. Just a brief description, please, as there are so many to cover. All proceedings are being recorded by this'—he pointed to a large recording device on one of the tables— 'and are also being taken down by our two lady shorthand writers here.'

After going around the room, the group plunged into discussion. There were many general aims which were common-sense things. These were readily agreed to as aspirations. Ottomar said, 'We like the idea of a German-speaking united Europe with English as the second language. The first difficulty is an amnesty for all resistance fighters. This will be almost impossible in light of the recent events. But maybe we can reach some sort of compromise. The same applies to the death penalty. Regarding the war crimes by RAF bomber pilots, we may have some movement there. Who dropped what bombs and where is difficult to prove. We were at war at the time and our people have committed some bad things also.

'I noticed you have added another item to the list. This is another common-sense thing, and we will make sure our soldiers always act with discipline. Our instructions have been for some time now that the local population should be treated well. You wanted to say something, Tim?'

'Yes, Mr Weiss. I have a childhood friend named Arthur a young surgeon. I phoned him last night to see if he wanted to join us on our new project. He declined, saying he has another year of training to do. He told me how his family was treated when they were sent to the ghetto in Whitechapel. It didn't make very good listening, and it all happened very recently. I discussed this with the others and we decided to add that last item written in by hand.'

'Well, Tim, I know there have been bad things going on, but since the new, moderate leadership has come in, we have put all of that behind us. I can understand your concern, as these bad things were happening only a few months ago. I will make comment of your concerns to the very top, and instructions will be sent, enforcing existing orders. There are no racial laws enforced now, and we are trying to repatriate all the Jews who were displaced. We have no slave labour. The British men working in Europe are being paid, and are free to return to the United Kingdom if they want.

'We go along with a meritocracy and abolishing aristocratic privileges, including getting rid of the House of Lords.

'We also agree with the logical engineering approach to solving problems with proper procedures. As you see, we agree with most items on your list and will support those aims and aspirations. Now how do you propose we implement them with your people?'

Chapter 92

THE EXECUTION PROBLEM

Tim said, 'As some of you know, the Prime Minister phoned me a couple of days ago, asking how we could bring the country together. I told him I worked for the Germans and nothing could happen without their agreement. I told him that I would speak to them and some young British people.

'This list has come from the young people. Many of them have engineering, managerial, and accounting training. The young people are the ones who will be living in the future. How to persuade the British establishment that they must change is a problem, but I hope this is where your support will come in. We in the media team, who have already done so much to help British/German friendship, will do whatever you want. I will say this: if the executions start again, I and this young British team will find it difficult.'

Ottomar came back, 'Tim, this is just what we want, your cooperation with the media campaign. The execution problem is a difficult one, especially where we have proof of murders carried out by the resistance recently. We carry out execution in our other occupied countries where murders have been proved. You want the death penalty abolished, but this cannot happen immediately, even if we agree to it. It is a punishment in your current British legal system.'

'It is difficult, Mr Weiss. Please try and stop executions if you can, I understand the problems. Let's get on to the important subject of the campaign and the German administration's support for the list of requirements. There should be widespread support among the general population for getting rid of aristocratic privilege and the House of Lords. Equal opportunities for education should also get wide support. Of course, the money will come from increased taxation which will hit the wealthy, but they are in the minority. Basic health care will be fine, and the minimum wage will help the poor. So what do we tell the Prime Minister, and how do we handle the media presentation for the future? What will happen if the British establishment does not cooperate with our requests, especially the Lords and the aristocratic privileges part?'

'Tim, we know what you want. Some is still up for negotiation, as mentioned. The British establishment has already lost a lot of their numbers from the bad times of Heydrich. We will handle the British government. Whatever they say, I'm sure you are right about the British class system not being popular with the majority. I will tell them you are the leaders, now supported by us.'

'I wonder what they will answer to that.'

'Leave that to us. Now we must discuss the media campaign for this new way. I want all of you young people who have been chosen for your abilities to be involved. This is our joint venture, and I think we must bring in some young German people to help as well.' Dieter raised his hand. 'Yes?'

'Sir, my name is Dieter Vollmar. I help with the English language school. There were three German girls who came over before Christmas, one of whose whole family had been killed in the bombing. Two of the girls are still here. Maybe they would like to get involved.'

'Excellent. Get on it, Dieter—that's the sort of thing we want. There has been suffering on both sides. We must devise a media campaign for this so the people know what is going on.'

CHAPTER 93

THE YOUNG NAVAL OFFICERS

Horst Geissler stood up. 'We will have to do it as we have done in the other campaigns, quickly, but on a much grander scale. In this case the Prime Minister will have to be informed of what we are doing.'

'Don't you worry about the Prime Minister; I will take care of him,' interrupted Ottomar. 'He will comply with what the young people want. I also want you youngsters already in the different media campaigns to get friendly with the naval officers I invited here as our guests—firstly to see if they can add anything to your list, and secondly to introduce them to how the media people work. With their story of your king's capture by the USA and the great sea battle that was fought to try and save him, they will add much to the campaign.'

'Yes,' said Molly. 'I will definitely do my best to be friendly with them and teach them all I know, Mr Weiss.'

Weiss looked at the officers with his eyebrows raised. 'Well, it looks like you are in for a treat, gentlemen.'

The First EU

'Thank you, sir. We look forward to learning from Molly, Tim, and anyone else who can help us,' said one of the four sailors.

'Look, people, it's coming up to eleven. We know what we are going to do now. Some snacks and drinks are ready at the back. Just mix and mingle for a bit. We will start again at eleven thirty. Lunch will be at one o'clock. We have only just started and have a lot to do.' With that, Ottomar made his way over to the snacks.

A couple of the naval officers approached Tim, who was talking to Molly. 'Hi, Tim and Molly. My name is Peter Ward, and this is my colleague Terry Bassett. We would like to add something to your list regarding the Royal Navy. The German integration of the navy is not going well because of older senior German officers who can't speak much English. There have been a number of accidents and near misses, which have been unreported. We would like to recommend that anyone assigned to the British ships for integration be able to communicate at least in basic English and preferably be young, so they can pick up new ways easier.'

'Come with me, guys,' said Tim. 'Ottomar? These naval officers have got something to add to the list regarding the integration of the British and German navies.' They explained the situation again.

'Yes, that's fine. Tim, make sure this request is added to your list. It will be investigated, gentlemen.'

There were just media items to deal with now, particularly decision about the stories that would be part of the presentation.

The list was written in a better format and a copy sent telegraphically to the Prime Minister. It was sent from the young people and supported by the German supreme authority. The Prime Minister phoned Tim straight away. Tim was still in the meeting with Ottomar; He took the call even so.

'Tim, what is the meaning of this list of requests? Why wasn't I consulted beforehand?'

'Prime Minister, as I mentioned the other night, I work for the Germans. You should realise they are the ones with the supreme power. The list did not come from me alone, but from an educated group of young British people the Germans have pulled together from their media shows and elsewhere. The Germans agreed and are going to support us. There are still some negotiations to be completed on the resistance amnesty, the death penalty, and war crimes, plus the current stay of executions.

'Prime Minister, you don't hold any power now. We, the young people in the media shows, are better known than you. I hope you realise this and decide to cooperate.'

'Well, that has put me in my place. Could you keep me informed on proceedings?'

'That's not up to me. I will ask the Germans to keep you updated.'

'Thank you, Tim. Goodday,' said the Prime Minister in a rather tired voice.

CHAPTER 94

TONY AND THE BURLY SOLDIER

At this stage, only Tony had access from the British press side to sit in the initial discussions regarding the young people's new way. He was so much in demand to send dispatches that, after a few days, the Germans allowed other British press people in, on the understanding that Tony was responsible. They wanted control of these communications and knew he appreciated the consequences of not complying. They completely backed him up. In the first week, two British pressmen were roughed up and replaced. Only then did the rest acknowledge that Tony had powerful friends and what he said was to be followed.

Everything was on heightened security because of the resistance attacks that had happened so recently. There was a whole company deployed twenty-four hours a day, seven days a week, around the village, covering all the roads and fields. The Germans had been caught unawares by the resistance attacks and were taking no chances.

All who resided in the village had to apply for special security passes issued by the police. Anyone entering the village had to have passes and a reason for their visit. It was a bit inconvenient at first, but the villagers knew why these measures were being introduced and soon got used to the idea. At least it gave those in the young people's meeting some confidence. They could relax while working. There were nearly four hundred soldiers billeted in and on the outskirts of the village now to cover the security.

The celebrities featured in the media films, like Molly and Tim, had bodyguards. The captain's house had three soldiers to protect his daughters and the Dale farm children, who were staying with him temporarily. Most of the bodyguards were chosen from among the soldiers already stationed in the village and were known to their charges, although Florence and Jean hadn't met their guards before.

A mechanised brigade of two and a half thousand men was moved to the area north of Birmingham, centred around Lichfield. Because of the notoriety of the village, only four hundred soldiers were billeted in or nearby and allowed access.

The dances were still going on. Ladies were allowed to visit from outside for these, as there were not enough in the village to satisfy the large complement of extra soldiers. These ladies had to have clearances and were bussed in and out on specially arranged transport. The dances were held at the church hall on Fridays and Saturdays. Because of the twenty-four-seven security cover required, never more than one hundred soldiers were allowed to attend at any one time.

The town hall was used for live performances. A girl group from out of town performed there once a week. Dances were held there as well as the church hall.

Other soldiers had started to attend the unarmed combat training. It seemed this was becoming more popular with the soldiers than the locals. The soldiers also gave German lessons to anyone who wanted them. This was popular, as in this way the soldiers could pick up a bit of English at the same time. The people, even the old, knew it would be good to learn German. Of course, infatuations developed between teenage school girls and their German soldier tutors; this was inevitable. But as far as anyone knew, nothing bad happened.

After the resistance attacks, there had been thousands of arrests. The Germans deployed their well-known brutal methods to extract information about everyone even slightly involved. Most except the identified fighters would be released within a few weeks, as per the new young leader's conditions.

The burly soldier who had roughed up Tony in Edinburgh was purposely placed in the platoon of thirty soldiers responsible for security at the village meetings in the Midlands. Tony did meet his burly assailant, who apologised as much as any soldier could and offered to take Tony for a drink. In the end, they became friends, often drinking together, when they would chat about their families and other things.

This soldier had been learning English quite intensively ever since the days when he was protecting the three stars from the German language show. The German guards had all been eager to learn, and the three girls had been more than happy to help. Whenever he was off duty, the soldier now sought Tony out.

What made these gatherings even more popular was that sometimes Molly, Jean, Myrtle, Angela, and even Irene would join in, either at the village pub or the Hollyhurst Hotel bar. This made other soldiers more than keen to come along. Within a couple of weeks, there were gatherings nearly every day. New way projects were always discussed at these impromptu meetings.

CHAPTER 95

THE DALE FARM FILM STORY

All were getting ready for the media event. The list was rehashed again and shortened where possible, with the most contentious items that needed further talks highlighted. The list was printed and went to the newspapers, with photos of the team of young people. The six featured at the head of the list were Tim, Andy, the naval officer Terry Bassett, Molly, Jean, and Irene. Then there was an overall photo of about twenty people, Sally being the oldest.

A movie was made of Tim, Andy, and Terry Bassett talking about how they had compiled the list—thinking about the majority of the people and what they would like in a model society. Molly, Jean, and Irene also added dialogue.

After this, a short film was made concerning how to set up a model team, using Tim's team as a template. The Germans wanted to get groups all over the country involved and coordinate them. All were welcome: not only the young and educated, but the whole of the working class and anyone else, including the previously privileged if they wanted to roll their sleeves up and work as equals. The large estates were to be split up, especially those from which the people had fled or where they had been murdered in the Heydrich days. All royal land was treated in this way.

Andy and John, being large landowners, were very much involved in the project of land redistribution. All land commandeered from the aristocracy would go to the state, to be farmed in the new, efficient way. This programme would now include farms and small holdings over a hectare, meaning even properties with large gardens would come under the scheme. Of course, this would require a large workforce, which would be working with the occupying army, helping friendship and language tuition both ways. It was a bold scheme, not without its problems owing to recent fierce fighting. But everyone knew it had to work.

In the discussions at the hotel, Auntie Joyce attended initially. But along with the two vicars, both around fifty years old, she decided to excuse herself and leave it to the youngsters. This is what the Germans wanted, but they had been too polite to ask.

While the two vicars were talking over coffee, Auntie Joyce decided to visit Uncle Albert at his hotel. He was still not worrying about Dale Farm too much and still looked like a zombie. 'Albert, how are you?' she greeted him kindly. He perked up a bit, and they spoke at length.

At the end of their conversation, she said, 'I would like to see your farm. When are you going there?'

'I should be there already today. They have given me a few Germans to help repair things and tend the chickens and other animals. They are probably already there.'

'Can I come with you?'

'It's nothing much, only ninety acres.' But the farmer perked up a bit more. 'If you don't mind travelling in my old lorry …'

'Come on, let's go. Where's your lorry?'

When they arrived at the farm, it was easy to see the damage done in the fighting. The two doors had been blown in, with masonry displaced. There were bullet holes and shotgun blasts everywhere. The place appeared uninhabitable.

'Albert, what are you going to do? I want to help you.'

'I don't know. I just don't know.'

It didn't matter. Unbeknown to Uncle Albert, Dale Farm was being discussed at the highest level. Help would be coming sooner than anyone could imagine.

It was six days after the attacks when Auntie May and the other local people killed were buried in a joint service taken by Sally's husband. There was much sadness. Most of the village and many others turned out. There was only room in the church for immediate family and friends.

Uncle Albert had since begun to feel very lonely, but it seemed Auntie Joyce had taken a liking to him. In his sad state, he was glad of the attention from a smart-looking farmer's widow four years younger than him.

The media team explained to Tim and Molly their idea of running the story of Dale Farm and its various inhabitants over the last year or so. The main part of the story would start when Irene drove Tim and Molly into hiding in the old farm lorry, and run up to the resistance attacks two weeks ago.

Neither Molly nor Irene was happy about personal details being divulged. So they were asked to give their own portrayal of the events. Tim was asked to provide the same. He didn't have much spare time, so a shorthand typist was provided. Molly or Irene could have done this, but it would have caused him to hold back a bit, the media team thought.

From these three accounts, the media team put a story together. They decided not to go too far into detail, saying only that Irene had arrived to work on the farm and the kids had been there previously.

What they wanted to emphasize was that Tim and Molly had started out to join the resistance. When, by chance, they had come in contact with the German occupiers, the two fugitives had changed their minds and decided to join in the endeavour to bring the country together.

So, with a few visits to the farm, the footage was shot and the media people got to work. The movie started to take shape. It ended up over an hour long.

Then the young people's list of requests had to be distributed. The government was asked to help implement the items and coordinate cooperation groups all over the country. The Germans put pressure on the Prime Minister to get things moving, as there seemed to be some inertia in the government channels. The Prime Minister was told he would be replaced if things didn't start progressing. It was difficult for him as he had many friends in the House of Lords.

In the end, things did start to happen. Tim asked the Germans if they could become friendlier with the Prime Minister. They agreed, and he, Andy, and Terry Bassett started a dialogue, which helped the situation no end. As time went by and the requirements started to be implemented, the young people became quite fond of the kindly old Prime Minister.

The First EU

It wasn't all plain sailing, of course. There were plenty of obstacles to overcome. The abolition of the House of Lords and aristocratic privileges based on wealth were the main ones. It wasn't always clear how to deal with this. For instance, Andy and John owned a productive farm of nearly a thousand acres, making them quite rich compared to some.

The media people saw that Dale Farm had become a bigger story now than it had ever been. The German authorities wanted to knock down and rebuild the farmhouse.

Chapter 96

MATTERS AFTER THE ATTACKS

The main British characters involved with the media campaigns had no choice. They were widely known as collaborators and therefore had to continue as such. Their deceptions had all been admitted to, and the German authorities were willing to forget everything. Their misdeeds were featured in the media presentation to show others that the occupiers weren't always so harsh.

Jamie was a fresh, young hero now. Hanna was proud of her young man. Their romance seemed to go from strength to strength, and it still didn't affect their school work. The captain was considering sending his wife and children back to Germany for safety's sake, but the three girls made such a fuss against this that he gave in. Without telling them, he simply beefed up their protection.

Another reason why Hanna was becoming more possessive with Jamie was that he was in the sights of a number of lovely girls who were openly flirting with him. He loved the attention, of course, but Hanna didn't have to worry. He was quite devoted to her. They had both matured since they started seeing one another. To the captain, Jamie had gone from being a bit of an annoyance to an admirable young man. He was becoming quite fond of him. Jamie's German was coming along well, probably because of Hanna, his long-haired dictionary.

Tim was not going to solve his personal problems any time soon. He was happy living with Molly although he did feel sorry for Irene. Florence was his wife, but he hadn't been with her since their child was conceived. They didn't discuss anything.

His main push now was to get the country sorted out. He felt he was going to need all his energies for that, without distraction. He didn't care what people thought about his moral behaviour; he was quite certain he was a good person.

After five days of meetings, negotiations, and filming, some of the people who had been flown down from Scotland were flown back. Florence and Dave, Andy's brother John, and the Scottish vicar returned. Florence's mother, who was Auntie Joyce's sister, took the place of Auntie Joyce at the Oat Farm, to run the household and be with her daughter at the birth. Auntie Joyce was determined to stay in the Midlands and help Uncle Albert rebuild his farm and life.

Florence and Tim did have one more private meeting, which Florence insisted on. 'I want to join you as your wife,' said Florence tearfully.

'I don't know what is going to happen, but I must stay here for the moment. What I'm doing is too important to put at risk. You have Dave; he loves you and will take good care of you.'

'But I love you.'

'Florence, I must stay here.' Nevertheless, as he cradled her in his arms, some of that old loving feeling was coming back. 'Sorry.' He knew it wasn't good for the baby, her getting upset like this, but he was resolute as he pulled away and kissed her goodbye. 'You'll see me in the news. I have such a big job to do with all the other young leaders.'

'I wish you luck, Tim. Please come for me when all this is over.'

'Who knows where this will all end up? Just two weeks ago, we were nearly assassinated by the resistance. I want you to relax and be happy, for the baby. I must go. Goodbye, my darling.'

Irene was still recovering in the clinic. She too had strong feelings for Tim, especially now as Klaus was no more. Dieter was very attentive and was still in love with her, but she didn't reciprocate or encourage him.

Tim knew Irene was sweet on him again, but preferred to ignore it. Molly had possession, and after all, possession was nine-tenths of the law. He got on well with Molly, who had matured no end in the last few months.

Tim knew he had an important assignment, taking part in the new way the United Kingdom would be run. This was his main mission. He didn't want anything to adversely affect his work. So Dave would stay with Florence and Irene would make her own way.

To enact the new plan, the British government and civil service had to be reinstated. Most of both institutions had been dissolved after the invasion and the Germans had taken over the running of the country. It would be difficult to reverse this. The police were under the Gestapo. All schooling was controlled by the Germans.

The war, although short, had occurred in the middle of harvest season. The disruption had caused at least twenty per cent of the harvest to spoil. There was not enough food being produced anyway. The rest of Europe, which had a good harvest, sold the British some of their surplus. More was purchased from Russia. In this way, the United Kingdom made it through to the next harvest without extra rationing.

The Germans called a meeting of the expanded teams of German and British young leaders. All were under thirty and experts in their fields of engineering, management, and accountancy. For two days, these young people were shown everything there was from the German side of running things. Questions were encouraged. This gave them a good grounding for the meetings to be held over the next few weeks.

Chapter 97

THE TWO KINDLY LEADERS

There was a meeting set up in the village main hall with the Prime Minister, the chancellor of the exchequer, the home affairs minister, and one or two others from the cabinet, plus all the civil servants who were the heads of their departments. Although parliament had been closed, the Prime Minister and his cabinet had been left in place. They didn't have much to do at the present time, but the Germans could see a role for them now. The six young leaders were introduced by going around the table.

The Prime Minister had been one of the original appeasers who negotiated the armistice agreement. The young people warmed to him; he was a gentleman and had a kindly aura about him. He wasn't liked for his gambit at those negotiations, but most admitted that whoever had been negotiating, the same outcome would have occurred.

'Tim, we have come to see you and your young friends at the request of the German occupational authorities.'

The First EU

'Welcome, Prime Minister. It's good to see you rather than just speaking on the phone. As you know, we have given a list of requests.'

'Yes. It's a good list—rather radical for some, but as you seem to have the support of the supreme power, it must be.'

'To be a proper democracy, we must have an elected government. This has been promised in two years' time, with a much-changed voting and representational system. In the meantime, we want to know what is going on. How are the finances being dealt with? How are the occupational forces being paid? We have chartered accountants and other specialists, both British and German, among us, and we should be able to get to grips with all this information.'

Andy got up. 'Again, good afternoon, sir. I appreciate you coming here with your ministers.'

'We didn't have much choice, Andy.'

'Well, sir, nevertheless, you came. We all want to work together to repair our battered nation. And so I thank you. The Germans are running things at the moment, but many of their people will be returning home this year. We must get in place a new and better civil service, devoid of any aristocratic, privileged positions. To do this, we want everyone in the civil service to reapply for their jobs from the top to the bottom. We have made a list of criteria for this process.

'Other critical things include the following. First, we must produce enough food for our nation. Then we must make sure there is stability. We must clear up the destruction left by the fighting last year, including all the unexploded munitions. A new road and rail system is needed, new port facilities, and most importantly, homes for all.'

Alan J Caulfield

'There is a lot to do.'

'Yes, sir, and we have a plan devised by us and the Germans.'

'And what is this plan?'

'It is based on the engineering way of solving problems and can be followed step by step quite easily.'

'It sounds interesting.'

'You will see that it can work. We have a large team of young people from Britain and a contingent from Germany. All are highly skilled and qualified. Following the mentioned procedure, we are going to start with the heads of the civil service departments who are seated here.'

The supreme leader of the German occupation, who had taken over from Heydrich, was in attendance. He looked very German. He was the person who had put Hitler's order for two thousand executions on hold. Sitting next to him was an interpreter. Along with Ottomar and a number of other senior Germans, this leader was nodding his approval. All were most impressed with the way this Scottish farmer was handling himself.

The civil service heads thought they had been invited to give advice and were rather astounded when they found themselves being interrogated. At least two complained to the Prime Minister, not realising the truth about who was in power. They were replaced within a day. There were eleven heads of departments. Most, after the initial shock, gave a good account of themselves. Some even embraced the new way. After all, they hadn't had much to do lately.

Tim had found out that the supreme leader of the occupational forces was attending, being the well-decorated

The First EU

man sitting with Ottomar. Tim had also seen him on news clips.

Towards the end of proceedings for the day, Andy walked up to the podium. 'Ladies and gentlemen, I want to make an announcement. It is a very big thank-you to somebody here. Without him, a terrible thing would have happened.'

Ottomar was looking a bit worried. He hadn't been told about this announcement and didn't know what was coming.

'Ladies and gentlemen, Victor Gerber, the German supreme leader in the United Kingdom, is here in this room. He postponed the execution of two thousand men back in the dark days, thus saving their lives. This thank-you comes from all the young people, who insisted that I say something about this tremendous act of bravery and kindness. So from all of us, thank you, Victor Gerber, for your wonderful deed.'

The leader and the other Germans were taken by surprise and didn't know what to say or do. Applause, led by Tim and Molly, started and increased to a deafening crescendo. This went on for at least a minute.

The leader looked rather awestruck. Through his interpreter, he thanked the young people for thinking about him and wished them well with their task.

Ottomar didn't look happy. But after speaking with the leader, he seemed to calm down and finally had a smile on his face. 'Andy, please inform the other five in the young leaders group that Victor Gerber would like to have cocktails and dinner with you and them tonight.'

'We are most honoured. I will tell them straight away.' Ottomar had been going to make a complaint that Andy had done something without his approval, but didn't, as things turned out well in the end.

The meeting came to an end at about six. People drifted away, and the ones who had been invited to the dinner went to get ready.

The German leader had also invited the Prime Minister and two of his cabinet. There was also a sprinkling of young Germans, including Angela and Myrtle. The leader wanted to sit next to Andy and find out what he thought about the fighting and what he had done in the war. Andy was a bit hesitant at first, but thought this man had saved the lives of two thousand men. He would understand Andy had only been following orders.

The German leader agreed the media crew could film whatever they wanted, realising there could be very good public relations content in the dinner.

Andy had picked up a bit of German, and the chat with the senior German went well. In the end, Gerber wanted to know all about the farm efficiency drive and the girl's German language show.

Although the leader wanted most to speak with Andy, he did the rounds of the room, He spoke with Irene, still with her arm in a sling and leg bandaged. Then he went to the young naval officer, Terry Bassett. He was interested in Bassett's account of the naval battles, especially that torpedoes had been fired from a German submarine.

'Sir, I know this happened. I saw it with my own eyes. The submarine was not one of ours because it didn't make contact. It had been around all day, keeping well out of trouble. It came in close to attack the Americans and then disappeared. We never saw it again.'

The leader was silent and didn't comment.

When Gerber got to Molly and Jean, he was surprised at their proficiency in German. He also called Angela and Myrtle to join them, as the girls had all been talking together.

Finally, he spoke to Tim. Gerber had been following the exploits of Tim and Molly and was surprisingly knowledgeable about all the personal details involved. Through his interpreter, Gerber said, 'Well, Tim, I appreciate your input in the efficiency campaign and now your lead in the new way programme. But I'm also interested in your personal life, which seems very complicated. It has been virtually serialised in this country and also in Germany, I may add. There is much interest as to where it is going next.'

Tim didn't like these sorts of questions, but in this case, couldn't possibly avoid them. 'Sir, I know my private life is interesting and may have seemed chaotic in the past. I have a weakness when it comes to the fairer sex, and unfortunately, they seem to have a weakness when it comes to me. I know I don't deserve that. I've been with Molly for a long time and hope to keep it like that. My main job now is to see the new way mission through.'

'I'm glad to hear your mission is so important to you, as it is to me and the whole of the United Kingdom.' To Tim's surprise, he then asked, 'I want to see Jamie and Wendy with Irene tomorrow morning before I leave for London. Can you arrange it?'

'Jamie and Irene are available, but Wendy is still in hospital in Lichfield.'

'Fine. I will go to the hospital then, with all the survivors from Dale Farm.'

The dinner was held in the Hollyhurst Hotel. It went off splendidly. After a few drinks, people loosened up. Post-dinner conversations continued in the lounge; therefore, the leader decided to stay in the hotel. Tim and Molly gave up their room for him and his bodyguard.

The following day, everyone went back to their normal jobs. The leader met Jamie and went with him, Irene, and Jennifer to see Wendy in the Lichfield hospital. Uncle Albert didn't want to attend, giving the excuse that he was busy on the farm. The media team made great use of this public relations coup.

With the success of this meeting, another hundred well-qualified people were drafted into the new way programme. They were to interview all civil servants, many of whom had been virtually redundant since the Germans had taken over running the civil society. Those drafted in were mainly British, as qualified English-speaking Germans were comparatively scarce. Irene's English schools were destined to become very busy.

Senior and middle management posts got the most scrutiny, with a high percentage not retaining their positions. This didn't matter because the whole way of working was changing, and the existing people would have to learn everything from scratch anyway. Existing and new people would be in the same position. Some of the managerial positions were removed.

At the lower level, like police officers, teachers, and municipal workers, staff were mainly kept in place unless there was some adverse information about them. Any criticism of the German occupation, especially in the dark days before the assassinations, was tolerated. Persons with resistance leanings, if proficient, were retained.

Where positions had to be filled because of dismissals, new people were interviewed, with preference given to those who were young and good at logic and procedure.

These interviews progressed quickly. After two weeks, all the necessary changes had been made and new procedures were in place. The civil service would be taking back control on a gradual basis. Germans who wished to return to their homeland would be rotated out. Control would be in German hands for quite some time. The occupiers were more willing to give control to the young, trusting them to work in the way the Germans wanted.

Chapter 98

DECISIONS FOR YOUNG GERMANS

An interesting turn of events had happened in Germany. It was coming up to the beginning of spring now, and since the resistance attacks in the United Kingdom, there had been a constant media coverage. Although aimed at Britain, the same film clips had been shown in Germany. This included movies about the attack on Dale Farm and the films of the supreme leader talking with the young people.

Young Germans were getting very interested in the new way. Many of them, seeing the beautiful people involved, wanted to emigrate to Britain to be part of it all. They were frustrated with the set, unchanging system in Germany and signed up in their thousands to move to the United Kingdom.

This was both good and bad for the German regime. Good, because they needed these people in Britain for the Germanification process. Bad, because they could see the young in Germany were not happy with the civil and political system there. The young wanted a similar shake-up to that

The First EU

happening in the United Kingdom. Unfortunately for the young Germans, what happened in the United Kingdom was not going to happen in Germany. The establishment had to have complete control after the overthrow of Hitler's reign of terror. They couldn't risk any lapse.

The supreme leader, Victor Gerber, enacted a decree that any German serviceman who wanted to return to Germany could do so. About two-thirds of the three hundred thousand troops in the United Kingdom and another one hundred thousand in Ireland took up this offer. These consisted mainly of the older soldiers and senior ranks, who had wives and children back in Germany, or the younger ones with sweethearts there. One hundred and thirty-five thousand mainly young German soldiers were left in the United Kingdom and Ireland.

Lieutenant Schmitt from the village applied to return to Germany. He wanted to try and salvage his marriage and remove pressure on Sally. Captain Vloch in the village and Captain Gerard in Scotland decided to stay.

Victor Gerber, seeing there was a possible problem, contacted Andy through his interpreter. 'As you know, we have decreed that any German soldier stationed in Britain and Ireland can return home if they wish. We have found that two-thirds have taken up this offer. Many who have taken up this offer are the more senior in rank. So we are left with a large number of rank and file with no commanding officers. As you were an officer in the British army, what do you think about using well-educated British officers to take the place of these German officers? Of course, they must be willing to take a crash course in the German procedures and language. This would only be junior officers to begin with.'

'Well, Mr Gerber, this is an interesting proposition. I'm sure there would be many former British officers willing to give it a try. How do you propose we go ahead?'

'I hoped you would have some ideas on how we could achieve this.'

'Sir, I think we must put out some advertisements stating the officer positions required. All applying must be willing to take a crash course in German, as you say, be educated to degree level, and be robust enough mentally to handle the ribbing and other things they may have to put up with when it comes to controlling their men. As there was a lot of aristocratic privilege in the commissioned part of the British army, I suggest we also consider non-commissioned officers, like sergeants and warrant officers. I know a military psychologist who would be a great help.'

'If you are considering using non-commissioned officers, we will have to give the German rank and file the same opportunity. We need up to three thousand officers, so can you please go ahead? Ottomar knows. I've spoken to him, and he will speak to you.'

'I will get onto it straight away, sir.'

'Please keep me directly informed.'

'Yes, sir, I will do that. Just to let you know, I will start by discussing the proposition and then the strategy with good people I know in the army before it was disbanded.'

'Good. I want an update tomorrow.' Gerber hung up.

Andy thought this proposition was amazing and would cement the relationship between Britain and Germany. He contacted his psychologist friend in Scotland and they came up with a strategy. They placed a large advertisement in all local and national newspapers and put up notices in town

The First EU

halls to recruit men to join the German army as officers stationed in Britain. The leader and Ottomar were kept informed.

The response was overwhelming. One thousand applicants were accepted within a few days, through recruitment teams around the country. As time went by, more former British army servicemen were signed up. By April 1943, this number had reached well over two thousand. These individuals came from all three services, although the majority were from the air force and army. The Germans had many army and air force personnel in the occupying forces, so this worked out well.

With this latest innovation, which was fully reported in the German media, there was even more clamour by young Germans eager to emigrate to Britain. By the beginning of April, thousands were waiting.

Chapter 99

SALLY'S LAST FLING

With tears in her eyes, Sally met with Lieutenant Schmitt to bid him farewell. 'Toby, I'm really going to miss you.'

'It's for the best, Sally. Would you like to make love before I leave?'

Sally was quite taken aback by his directness. 'You have never suggested it so candidly before.'

'I know, but I couldn't leave here without asking. If you say no, I will fully understand.'

'How could we do it without being seen?'

That's a good sign, thought the lieutenant. *At least she is considering it.*

'It's getting warmer now,' he said aloud. 'I could take the patrol car and drive us into the country. I know some hidden places in woods where people never go. We would be quite safe. I could even take a mattress to make it more comfortable. We would be quite happy by ourselves, I'm sure.'

'It sounds like a plan,' she said in a rather high-pitched voice. 'When can we do it?'

'Whenever you have an hour or so free.'

'You have got me all in a fluster. I'm free now. It's a warm, sunny day for the time of year.'

'Let's do it then.'

'Have you got all the stuff?'

'You don't think I would ask you without getting all that first, do you, my darling?'

'Oh, I think we have started already. I'm feeling so sexy.'

'Me too, my darling.'

As they were walking out, the vicar was just returning from his rounds. He entered the garden from the back. 'Oh, hello, Ray,' Sally said. 'We are just going to Dale Farm to check on progress.'

'Good. See you later.' The vicar knew the lieutenant was leaving and didn't think there was any danger now.

Lieutenant Schmitt had been to Dale Farm so many times, he knew all the hidden places. In this case, he went up a lane and then off the road near an old church, into a cluster of trees. No one could see anything unless they drove into the same small wood.

As soon as they were parked in this hidden place, Sally couldn't control herself; she pulled him towards her, stroking his thigh.

'Hold on,' said Schmitt. 'Take it easy. Let's get the bedding out. It's a lovely day.'

She complied, but as soon as the groundsheet and blankets were down, it was a race to strip enough to be able to make love. She took his trousers off, proclaiming, 'Oh, you have a nice one there.'

He loved kissing her all over. Her passion was prolific. 'Take your bra off,' he insisted. 'I want to kiss you there.'

In no time they had most of their clothes off. Sally still had a cardigan on, but he was naked. His athletic build really turned her on. 'I'm coming. I can't help it. I've never felt like this before.' He kept working on her until she shuddered and pushed up. She was climaxing. 'Oh, what about you?'

'Don't worry about me. You are so sexy. In a minute, I'm going to take you hard. Then you can come again if you want, and I can have my pleasure.'

She wondered what he meant by taking her hard, and marvelled at his manhood.

'Now, my darling, are you ready?' He knew he was large, so he took it slowly. 'Is that nice?'

'Oh, my darling Toby, it is unbelievable.' She pushed back in time with him.

'Let's take it slow and make it last.'

'Whatever you say. I want it to last forever.'

'Oh, you are so sexy, Sally. Why haven't we done this before?'

'You are here for another three weeks.' Then her French kissing became desperate and her thrusting wild. 'Oh, Toby, I'm coming again!'

'So am I, my lover.'

They went mad in time, and then, with a shudder, they were done. She didn't care. Locked together, they fell into a comfortable position and closed their eyes, feeling the warm midday sun on their naked bodies and tasting the fresh spring air. They didn't want to go back to reality. They wanted to stay with one another.

The First EU

Reality could not be put off, though, and they finally got dressed. They drove to Dale Farm and quickly checked progress. Auntie Joyce was there with Uncle Albert. She was working hard, trying to help him.

The previous day, the German media head, Horst Geissler, had told Uncle Albert the authorities wanted to knock the farmhouse down and build a brand-new, state-of-the-art farmhouse for him. He was a bit hesitant, but Auntie Joyce soon pulled him around and he agreed.

Auntie Joyce, knowing about these things, couldn't help but notice Sally and the lieutenant looked like they had just made love.

Sally decided she had to somehow spend a weekend away with Toby. She knew a place they could go where no one would know them, about forty miles north. What to tell Ray though?

She booked a luxury room in a hotel in this country town. Schmitt made sure he had enough fuel. Sally decided to tell Ray she was going to see some old school friends in Stoke on Trent and would be back Monday.

Ray realised then what was going on, but didn't stop it. The lieutenant was leaving soon. Ray just hoped things would then return to normal. Sally arranged for their daughters to stay with the captain, who had plenty of accommodation and liked Sally's children.

Sally caught the Uttoxeter bus and got off just on the outskirts of the town. Toby, in civilian clothes, was following the bus at a distance and picked her up. They travelled on together to the hotel. It was an ideal place for a honeymoon, a time for them to cherish. Making love in a beautiful hotel was a luxury compared to the lanes and woods near Dale

Farm. They didn't need to go out, ordering in room service for the whole weekend.

By the time Lieutenant Tobias Schmitt left from Birmingham airport on one of the regular army transports back to Germany, Sally knew she was pregnant. Oh well …

CHAPTER 100

THE YOUNG GERMAN INFLUX

At the beginning of April, the first of the German immigrants arrived in the United Kingdom. Most were coming to work on the farms initially, to help with the efficiency programme, even if they were well qualified for other professions. Their pay was the same as that of the Brits doing the same jobs. There were an equal number of men and women. This was a deliberate ploy to get more young German women into Britain.

After a while, the well-educated among the immigrants found it easy to progress, as they had the German language advantage. Most of the young people from Germany were the better educated and skilled than the average Briton. By the end of April, the total number of applicants for emigration had gone up to one hundred and thirty thousand, with forty thousand in the United Kingdom already.

Victor Gerber was happy with the prospect of having thousands more young Germans who actually wanted to live in the United Kingdom. He embraced immigration and set up think tanks to discuss the best way to handle the influx. The main thing was to turn the situation to good advantage and make sure it went off as smoothly as possible.

Integrating these young Germans was an urgent priority. They had to be protected. There were still nearly one hundred and thirty thousand German troops left, and a third of these were commanded by British junior officers. Most of the young men immigrating were asked to do a three-month stint in the army. In this way, thirty-five thousand German soldiers were added to the existing number. Most were available to protect the immigrant Germans.

One thing the discussions highlighted was the fact that, because of the stipulation of German language proficiency for all new positions, immigrants had the advantage when applying for jobs. The requirement was put on hold for new hires, replaced with a time limit for attaining proficiency after hire.

The young British leaders were slightly alarmed at the numbers of Germans immigrating and asked Victor Gerber if these could be capped. Finally in April, a number of one hundred and sixty thousand was established. This number of applicants had already been reached before the first week in May. Women were 60 per cent of those applicants, so they didn't have to worry about getting the numbers of ladies, which had been a worry to begin with.

Britain was in a unique position. The young leaders were supported by an absolute force to implement their new civil administration. The older establishment had no choice but to fully comply. Some of the older political people had been liquidated in the bad days of Heydrich's reign. Now,

The First EU

although he was gone, there was still the fear that if they didn't cooperate, the same could start again.

Germany was stagnating and the United Kingdom was on course to be a great success. The influx of skilled immigrants helped projects like the jet propulsion project in Coventry, where the Germans gave the latest input from their own programme. This was the most advanced in the world. German prototype jet planes flew at phenomenal speeds.

Meantime, a nuclear explosion, thought possible in theory by splitting the atom, was considered and pursued on a low-key basis by a joint team from Germany and the United Kingdom. Intelligence was that no other country was spending much money on this quest, so as hostilities ceased and money ran short, it was not thought a priority. Even so, the team was kept busy investigating various possibilities.

Amazingly, there were friendships being formed between the young Germans and young Britons. Friendship functions, especially aimed at the young, continued at a pace. Many actual friendships were created between the workers. Victor Gerber was delighted at this. He started learning English himself, although it was quite slow going for him. The Prime Minister was learning German at the same speed. Of course, the media got wind of this, and the two men agreed to be filmed together at their lessons.

Chapter 101

POLITICS AND EMPIRES

The British regime in the United Kingdom, which now included the whole of Ireland, was set to become the lead after Germany in Europe. The far-flung British Empire, except for Canada, was brought under Anglo-German control by a young, efficient blended army and administration. This seemed to brush off onto the older people who were the leaders of the British colonial administrations throughout the empire.

All the armies of the British Empire were returning home from war fronts. Former officers in the United Kingdom, having been given the opportunity to re-join, were in some cases being sent straight back out to India, Burma, Borneo, Australia, and New Zealand, not to mention all the African countries.

Germany was determined to control the empires of the European countries it now occupied, the majority of that territory being British. Any freedom or self-rule aspirations in those countries were disregarded. The Germans would

The First EU

not tolerate any dissent. They were greatly supported by the British, Dutch, and French.

The Americans had sent warships from Hawaii to Australia. But early on, before the German invasion of Ireland and the United Kingdom, there was quite a large British naval presence in that region. Most of this was left in place because it could not have returned home soon enough to help the situation in the United Kingdom. Australia was vulnerable to Japan and the USA, both with massive navies in the area.

A large German-commanded fleet with four aircraft carriers and six battleships set out from Europe for India, and then on to join the vessels already in Australia. The smaller boats, including the submarines, could go through the Suez Canal, which was still not fully operational after the recent fighting. Three of the battleships and all the aircraft carriers had to travel around Africa, and of course destroyers and two long-range submarine escorts had to accompany them.

In all, there were forty-four vessels under German command when the two fleets joined up, not to mention quite a few U-boats. These vessels sailed for Sydney harbour post-haste, where the American contingent had been posturing in an intimidating way.

American intelligence informed their fleet that a massive joint task force was sailing towards them, to arrive in five days. After the debacle in the Atlantic, there was panic among the Americans at the prospect of confronting British naval power. Although they were encouraged to stand fast by their government, the admiral of the fleet decided to up anchor and return to Hawaii.

Now the vast island continent of Australia, with all its minerals, was under the rule of Germany. The same regime was implemented as in the United Kingdom. People thought it would be easier there, as there had been no fighting or bombing in Australia. Unfortunately, there were clashes with resistance fighter groups in the outback. In the end, there were 110 deaths, some among the young British officers commanding the German troops. But common sense eventually prevailed and a cease-fire took effect.

Once Australia and New Zealand were secured, the Anglo-German fleet set sail for Malaya, Borneo, The Dutch East Indies, Singapore, Vietnam and Hong Kong, where the Japanese Imperial Navy had been seen in force many times over the last months. The Japanese had not been as blatantly aggressive as the Americans. They hadn't entered harbours uninvited. Even so, when the European fleet entered these areas, it sent out a strong message. The outer edges of the German's newly acquired empire were secured.

There were now four superpowers: The Soviet Union The Japanese Empire, the United States of America, and the Europeans under Germany. Central and South America were still neutral, in those areas not under colonial control.

The USA was a bit jittery about Japan, but even more jittery about the new United Europe. The rival empires had fast navies large enough to isolate the USA and push it out of its traditional sphere of influence in Central and South America. The border between The Soviet Union and The United Europe was mainly peaceful, owing to the non-aggression pact between Germany and Russia signed in the days of Hitler.

The First EU

Stalin was the only important leader from the 1930s still alive. Mussolini, the Italian leader, had been assassinated recently. Franco, the Spanish leader, was ousted and imprisoned by the Germans, and a more moderate leader was installed. Sweden and Switzerland became associate members of The United Europe. Finland were more than happy to join as well; it wanted protection against Russia

Chapter 102

HEIDI RETURNS

Heidi, one of the young German ladies brought over for the friendship campaign, had hastily return to Germany because of the resistance attacks. But after breaking up with her boyfriend, she was missing the UK. In the end, she persuaded her sister to sign up with her for the immigration programme. They were in one of the last groups before the cap of one hundred and sixty thousand was reached. It was May by the time they arrived in England. For Heidi, it was different circumstances.

Initially, they were screened by a joint panel of assessors. Because of the influx, these panels had been set up all over the country. It was noted they were sisters, so they were kept together. Both were allocated to a large farm in southern England, near the seaside town of Brighton. They were more than happy. Their accommodation was an ex-army barracks. British and German men and women were housed there in separate accommodation. It was almost like a kibbutz.

The First EU

Heidi had hoped to go back to the village near Dale Farm, but she soon became happy on this large farm, as did her sister. There was much for the young people to do on the farm efficiency programme and infrastructure rebuilding programme. The people in these camps, especially the Germans, were encouraged to go out to visit young British people in the area. Heidi's sister met a young Englishman who was two years older.

After that, Heidi was set on returning to the Midlands again. She managed to get transport to Birmingham one Friday afternoon, and from there continued on by bus to the village. She managed to get booked into the smaller hotel where Uncle Albert was staying. She had a good bath to wash all the travel grime away, put on some nice scent and make-up and her most alluring clothes, and was ready for action.

Hearing Angela was at Irene and Dieter's language school, Heidi decided to visit there first. When she arrived, Terry Bassett was having a German lesson from Angela. Angela was surprised to see her. 'Heidi! I thought you were back in Germany.'

'Well, I was, but when things straightened out here, I persuaded my sister to immigrate. We are assigned to a farm in southern England. I want to move back to this area, however. Have you got any work for me?'

'Mm, yes, well, it just so happens I'm in a hurry today, as my boyfriend is waiting for me. You've taught English. If you want a job, you can start right now. Just work through this book with Terry, correcting him whenever he makes a wrong sound. That's where he's up to; you can take this book.'

'You mean you are going to just leave me here?'

'Oh, sorry. Terry, this is Heidi. Heidi, this is Terry. Look, Heidi, if you want to come back, we are short of German/English tutors. Take it or leave it.'

'It's all a bit sudden, but you are right. It looks like you really want to see your boyfriend.'

'Oh, I do. Can you find somewhere else to work with Terry? I have to lock up when I leave.'

'My hotel is that small one down the road and hasn't got much of a lounge.'

Terry chipped in, 'We can go to the Hollyhurst. I have a room there, and it has two bars, a lounge, and a dining room.'

'Thank you. Heidi, if you want a job here, I will speak with Miss Irene.'

'Yes, I would like that.'

'All right. I'm away for the weekend; leave your contact information with Terry.'

'Thanks, I will.'

At the Hollyhurst, after about an hour, Terry said, 'Heidi, are you hungry? I can get us a nice meal here in the hotel.'

Heidi thought she might have seen Terry in a movie clip with the new young leaders. Terry had seen Heidi with Angela. He was definitely taken with Heidi, and he wasn't a bad-looking man himself.

Heidi taught Terry more German and other things over this weekend. It was the start of her reintroduction to the village. Irene readily agreed to employ her as a German/English tutor. Her sister was quite happy to stay near Brighton with her English boyfriend.

Chapter 103

FLORENCE AND TIM'S BABY

Florence gave birth to a lovely baby girl on 17 April 1943, in the clinic near the Oat Farm. It was an uncomplicated birth and everything went off well. Florence named the baby Michelle.

Dave looked after Florence as he said he would, and by the time she came home from the clinic, everything was in place for her and the baby to have a comfortable life. She had given up the idea of being with Tim. Her mother had advised her to do this, so she could be calm before the birth.

Tim knew about the birth, but as long as there were no problems, he was content to be kept out of it all.

Florence wanted to get her body in shape after the birth. She exercised at home, following the latest books on the subject. There had been no proper workouts for her since she left London, although she had been exercising as allowed by her pregnancy while on the farm. She looked around the area; it seemed there wasn't much on offer as far as sport was concerned. She would have to go to Dumfries for anything meaningful.

Then she had a brainwave. What about joining Auntie Joyce for a month or so? Auntie Joyce was going to be moving back onto Dale Farm with Uncle Albert. The place had been completely rebuilt. Nothing of the old farmhouse remained. Florence had seen on the news clips that there was plenty of exercise to be had in the local village, what with dancing and unarmed combat practise most evenings of the week. Not only that, Florence had heard much about the village. Her previous visit had not allowed her time to look around. She was interested in finding out for herself what was going on.

Florence's mother wasn't too happy with the idea, but she could see how determined her daughter was. Unfortunately Dave didn't have a say, as he wasn't her husband. Obviously, he wasn't happy. The one person who was crucial was Auntie Joyce, and she was in favour.

So, a month after the birth, Florence was on her way south to stay on Dale Farm. The authorities permitted it as long as Auntie Joyce was there. The new farm building was much larger than before, with many more rooms especially made for the children and Irene and whoever else wanted to stay there.

One person frequenting the farm at this time was Roger Shawcroft. He had been a captain in the regular British army and had been glad to get an opportunity to work in the military again. At age twenty-eight, coming in as lieutenant, he was near the age limit set for the British officer recruitment. His platoon included Dieter Vollmar

The First EU

and sixteen others. Shawcroft was a big, muscular type whom no one would want to mess with.

When Florence arrived at Dale Farm, Shawcroft got to know about it through his men and offered her assistance with transportation and anything else she wanted. She had money, and when her room was allocated at Dale Farm, she purchased furniture: a double bed, a chest of drawers, a wardrobe, two bedside tables, and the like. She also put a nice carpet down. In the end, she didn't have to pay for these items—she was told it would all be coming out of the allocation from the German occupational administration, authorised and insisted upon by Victor Gerber himself.

Florence's German language knowledge was good and she had had nothing else to do when in confinement than to practise German. She could converse easily with everyone on Dale Farm. Florence became a sort of mascot for Shawcroft's platoon and spent a lot of time with them. As Shawcroft's German was still at the early stages, Florence was a great help in interpreting. Michelle was a good baby and didn't cry or play up much while her mother worked.

A week or so after arriving, Florence attended the hall for unarmed combat training. She had never done this before, but at least it gave her exercise.

Right at the beginning, when the money was authorised for her furniture, Victor Gerber insisted she be assigned a bodyguard, as she didn't have a man around. This man came from the Lieutenant Shawcroft's platoon. Initially, they took it in turns, but after a week Florence asked for one particular soldier she had been getting on well with to be stationed permanently. This soldier had been dating the choir girl who was killed in the resistance attack. This gave Florence more exposure to the German language in conversation. The soldier wasn't complaining. He was allocated a small car and became her driver.

After a few weeks, it seems Florence was becoming part of the furniture on Dale Farm and in the village. Dave wasn't happy, but what could he do? He was needed on the Oat Farm now that Andy was away most of the time.

The idea of another German language show with the women was mooted, but this time to be based out of the Midlands village. John's girlfriend, Susan, didn't want to leave Scotland, so Florence and Jean were one short. They asked Angela if she would be interested. She was a beauty, although a little young at just coming up to twenty. The media people decided to give it a try.

Captain Hans Gerard and the team from Edinburgh came down to run the shows, which encouraged Jean no end. The shows gave the girls a nice little income and other privileges.

Chapter 104

THE CHILDREN AFTER THE ATTACK

After Wendy was discharged from hospital, she had to be looked after and taken to the village clinic every day. So Captain Vloch decided he would keep all the farm children at his house for the time being, especially as the new farmhouse wasn't completed.

By the end of May, when Wendy had been out of hospital for a month and the new farmhouse was completed, it was finally time for the children and Irene, who was nearly recovered, to move back. They had been told Florence was already installed, but there was no problem with space. The farmhouse was three times as large now, with seven bedrooms downstairs. There were also two living rooms and a large double kitchen. They were still building outbuildings, which could also be used as accommodation if need be.

There was an intensive system of sheds for rearing pigs. The same was so for the chickens. These intensive areas were a few hundred yards downwind from the house, for obvious reasons.

The apple orchard had been extended at the back, with three thousand of the latest varieties. Tim supervised Lieutenant Shawcroft's platoon as they planted, showing them how the tractor worked. The rest of the farm was given over to growing crops for the pigs and chickens to eat. There were no cows and just two horses left. The horses had stables near the pigs and chickens.

So the farm looked much more organised and was easier to live on, with little smell.

Auntie Joyce and Uncle Albert shared the largest bedroom. The farmer was a bit embarrassed about it, but Auntie Joyce told him not to be so old-fashioned. Irene had her own room, as did Jamie. The little girls shared. Florence had the baby in with her. The bodyguard had a room, and there were still spare bedrooms.

There was a massive loft with a room at either end. The middle section was large enough for table tennis and a snooker table, and there were internal stairs.

For transport, Florence had her bodyguard-cum-driver. Irene had been given a small patrol car, and Uncle Albert had his lorry. The children normally got a lift to school with Irene in the morning. For the return journey, Gunter, Florence's bodyguard, would run them if he was free. Once the little girls had to walk the three miles, and there was much complaining.

Jamie was getting some money from the media people for filming. He purchased a nice bicycle with lights, a dynamo, and a carrier. Hanna purchased a similar lady's bike. Jamie's bike could often be seen at Hanna's house if he was in a hurry and could get a lift home.

Florence was going to the unarmed combat training and taking dancing as well, so she was getting into good shape just two months after the birth. The girls at the farm were so happy to have a baby there. Michelle was getting a lot of attention. Wendy still had a limp, but every day it was improving.

Now that summer was coming, the children started riding the massive plough horses. Gunter was quite alarmed, but the horses were docile and the children used a ladder to mount them—sometimes three at a time. The horses didn't always go where the children wanted, but somehow they all managed. Auntie Joyce, who had taken over supervision of the children from Irene, initially stopped Wendy going on the horses after she re-injured her leg. But that only seemed to last a week before she sneaked back on again.

Chapter 105

FLORENCE ON DALE FARM

Albert Black had a set procedure to follow for everything now, as per the efficiency programme. It was quite simple, but even so, Uncle Albert got flustered sometimes. This was where Auntie Joyce helped out.

Tim was also a regular visitor, just to see that all was going well. He took an interest in his daughter Michelle but was careful not to put out any wrong signals to Florence. The crew was out quite often for this or that, especially as Florence appeared to be living there permanently.

Irene was non-committal about Florence living there. She didn't say much. Irene was keeping herself to herself and working hard on her language school. With Dieter and the captain, she had set up a franchise, and schools were opening everywhere. As well as the occupational forces, there were another one hundred and sixty thousand young German immigrants who needed to learn English. They were very busy.

Florence didn't know how in love Irene had been with Tim nor he with her, so she didn't worry about them being together. She still wanted Tim back, but in the meantime she was having a great time flaunting her beauty and personality. Gunter, her bodyguard, was the most affected. It could be seen that he was falling for her.

Florence was looking quite stunning. The media team started working on a new German language show, and she was the star. With Angela, a native German speaker, on the team, the show took a slightly different format.

Victor Gerber asked if he could have a preview. After viewing it, he was so impressed that he invited the three girls to dinner at his home at St James's Palace to meet his wife. They were flown from Lichfield in his personal plane and were in London in no time. Florence had to take the baby, and Auntie Joyce also accompanied them.

The dinner was a grand affair. The leader's wife was interested in the baby, of course, and impressed with the British girls' German ability, especially Florence's. When she found Florence had studied the language from the age of fourteen, she was even more impressed. The leader's wife also had a chat with Auntie Joyce, using Florence as an interpreter. They all stayed in rooms at St James's Palace and were impressed. If their private thoughts took them back to the war and the now-departed king, they kept these to themselves.

Heydrich had stayed at Buckingham Palace during his short tenure as the United Kingdom's occupational leader. Victor Gerber did not want to live there, knowing it would cause more resentment among the population. Buckingham

Palace was used as an administrative centre now, with some of it being closed off.

The next morning the village contingent had a tour of London with the leader's wife before flying back in the evening. It was a thoroughly lovely present the leader had given them, and they sent their thanks to him through his wife.

One thing the girls noticed was the devastation wreaked in London by the recent fighting. The village had been shielded from this, as had the Oat Farm in Scotland, although Florence and Jean had seen some in Edinburgh. Florence said to the group, 'You can understand why there is still animosity between the people when you see all the devastation here. There must have been a lot of dying. Of course, I know there was a lot of dying in Germany near the end, when Churchill stepped up the heavy bombing of civilian areas in a desperate attempt to change the tide.'

'You are so right, Florence,' said the leader's wife. 'With people like you, Jean, and Angela, who suffered greatly by losing her family, we can get through this time of sadness. Your show promotes cooperation and friendship. I know there will be problems, but we must solve them with the help of people like you three.'

'Thank you, my lady.'

Florence interpreted their exchange for Auntie Joyce.

They were all a little subdued after seeing the devastation. The leader's wife bade them farewell and wished them good luck with their show. They boarded the leader's personal plane again and flew back to the Midlands.

Chapter 106

SOME COUPLES

It was decided by Captain Vloch to send Jamie to Germany for three months to improve his German and get him acclimatised to the German way. Jamie stayed with a family in Frankfurt who had a boy of his age. This boy had already spent two weeks with the captain and had met Jamie. They got on well. Jamie didn't have much say in the decision. He was going to miss Hanna, but could look forward to seeing her on his return. Hanna was upset that he was going to Frankfurt and was convinced her dad had instigated the trip to keep them apart.

Jamie had hardly returned to Dale Farm when he was off to Germany. His mother was just told he would be going. She was quite alarmed to begin with, but when told he would be in good hands and with a bodyguard, she sort of agreed.

Jamie attended a gymnasium, a senior grammar school, and he spent all his time there learning German. In the evenings and on weekends, he went out socialising with girls and boys of his age. He was quite a film hero, and it just so happened that three girls from this school had sent him fan mail. Of course, they made themselves known to him. One in particular was rather nice. Brigitte was her name.

Jamie was quite taken up with Brigitte, and they started going around together. But as young love goes, nothing blossomed. Jamie was waiting for the time he could be with Hanna. Brigitte had a sort-of German boyfriend who watched her when he could. It didn't worry Jamie. He was a strapping lad by now and had a bodyguard to boot. Brigitte helped with Jamie's German, as his long-haired dictionary.

Back in the village, Jamie's old nemesis Gordon now considered Hanna fair game, but she didn't like him right from the start. There were other boys who would have liked to be friends with her, but she was not interested. She just waited for Jamie. In fact, she was a bit lost without him, and her school marks started to suffer. Her mother wished the captain hadn't insisted on sending Jamie to Germany.

Jamie went on a youth camp there. The captain had been thinking of sending Hanna, but his wife wasn't sure. In the end, they sent her for half the three-week camp, and she was united with Jamie again. Being a bit of an oddity and petite, she was picked on by some of the other girls. Jamie couldn't always help her, as she was sleeping on the girl's side, but whenever he was with her, no one gave her any grief.

This put Brigitte in her place, and she drifted back to the boy who had been watching her.

After the camp, Hanna stayed with the same family Jamie was with. They couldn't believe how attached this young couple was. They didn't worry but made sure Hanna

The First EU

and Jamie were never together at night nor left on their own for too long.

It was a happy time for the young couple. They were allowed to stay another three weeks, finally returning to the village in the second week of September, when the new school term had just started. By now Jamie's German was really coming along. He was the son the captain never had.

***

Dave was upset about Florence returning to England and especially Dale Farm, but he knew he could never control her. John's girlfriend, in cahoots with Florence's mother—who had no reason to stay now that Florence had gone—got a nice-looking local girl to take over the housework and cooking at the Oat Farm. This released Florence's mother to return to London. She hoped this young lady might hit it off with Dave, thus solving his broken heart.

The new girl, Constance, was a bit of a flirt at age twenty-five. Her boyfriend had been killed in the Middle East two years before. Since then she had a succession of partners and was thought to be rather loose with her morals, although she didn't go with any Germans. She knew that she had been employed to look after Dave, although Dave didn't know.

As it became quite evident that Florence would not be returning to Scotland, Dave started to warm to Constance's blatant flirting. She was a pretty woman, whose build definitely showed she liked her food. She was a good cook and housekeeper, and soon started to get on well with Dave who became less obsessed about Florence and accepted the inevitable. He should have realised there was only one person who could control Florence, and that was the man she loved—her husband Tim.

Soon Constance moved into Dave's room. Auntie Joyce was never on the farm and Constance knew Susan, John's girlfriend, quite well, so there was a good atmosphere. Dave was learning a lot about farming and attended a course at Dumfries College for one day a week. He was knowledgeable about the German efficiency programme and became quite an asset to it, especially now that Andy was away most of the time.

After a few months, Constance slimmed down a bit. There was talk of marriage, which accelerated when she fell pregnant.

John and Dave were still helping the Germans in Scotland with the roll-out of the farm efficiency programme. The Germans realised they were a bit short-staffed without Andy so didn't put too much pressure on them. Their farm didn't get much media attention, as it had already been highlighted and was efficiently run before the Germans arrived. Moreover, two of the three women who had been in the German language show were now gone.

***

In the Midlands, Sally fell pregnant in April, and by August was beginning to show. It was highly likely that this baby was Lieutenant Schmitt's. She made sure she had unprotected intercourse with her vicar husband Ray straight after the lieutenant returned to Germany. At least then Ray could consider the baby as his.

Sally was rather mixed up emotionally and took time off from her teaching job. Her daughters didn't know anything about the affair, but were quite excited at the prospect of a baby. Ray just treated the situation as though nothing were wrong. He didn't want to know anything further. Unfortunately, a few people had seen Sally and Toby driving in the lanes, so maybe the truth would come out in the end.

The lieutenant was trying to save his marriage in Germany. At a distance, he'd had little success, but he had a few different strategies to exhaust before he would give up completely. By the end of July, he was at a dead end. He was thinking about Sally again. He had told her he would come back for her, but she was non-committal, knowing the implications for her children.

At the beginning of August, Toby sent Sally a letter, saying he would take care of her and her girls and he had a plan. The plan was to get a good job in England with his English language skills, knowledge, and experience of the farm efficiency campaign. His friendship with a number of the young people involved with Victor Gerber's new way was also key.

He went ahead, contacting Tim, who received him encouragingly. He was offered a senior position in the administration, working directly with Tim and Tim's team. Tim knew the lieutenant's long-time moderate stance, crucial to making the village so important in the cooperation campaign. Toby started his new job and initially took up residence in Lichfield.

He tried desperately to persuade Sally to leave Ray and start a new life with him, but Sally wasn't convinced. Ray was being very supportive in his way, and she was wavering. In the weeks when they were making love regularly, before Toby's departure, she had felt very differently. She had been caught up in the moment of passion and romance. Now reality had kicked in. She was thinking of the disgrace. To be labelled a German whore was not what she wanted, especially for her girls.

People had already been talking. One of her teaching colleagues had a heart-to-heart chat with her regarding the rumours. She then told Toby she was going to stay with Ray and raise the child with Ray. As she didn't want to lift Toby's hopes, she refused to see him altogether.

Toby was distraught at her decision and retired, concentrating on his new job. He knew Sally well enough to know her decision was final.

CHAPTER 107

GOODBYE TIM

Initially, Toby's office was a small room in the village centre, next to Irene and Dieter's language school. There he started to notice Irene in a different way. She was twenty-seven now. He was in his early thirties, with an athletic body and good looks. He reminded her of Klaus.

Irene and Toby started slowly, some days having a tea break together. Toby had heard of Irene's feelings for Klaus in general talk about the village. After a week of getting to know Irene's situation, Toby decided to make a play for her. At first, it didn't go well. Irene had no idea Toby had these thoughts about her. She spurned his initial direct request to become his girlfriend. To her, it had come out of the blue. He hadn't read the situation properly and his approach was too straightforward.

That evening, Tim was on one of his visits to Dale Farm, and as usual he spoke with Irene. She wanted to know how he was getting on with Molly and how he was thinking about his wife and baby daughter.

'Hey, Irene, what is this? Some type of inquisition?'

'You know I've always had the hope we could get back together again. Even now, being with you is wonderful for me. I still have strong feelings for you. What do you feel?'

'Well, you know, we had such a good time in those days. But I messed it all up. It would not be right for me to say we will ever get back together. Forget about me, Irene. I don't deserve you.'

'But Tim, you will always have me.'

'Don't say that. You are a fine-looking women and so intelligent and knowledgeable. You will be such a catch for somebody, but not me.'

'Oh well. Maybe this is the end then.' She expected him to say more, but he didn't want her to have even the slightest signal from him.

The silence stretched for several moments. Then Irene started to cry. 'We have been through so much together.' He held her as she sobbed, and became quite emotional himself. This was a big moment for him. He knew she was right—they had been through so much together—but he didn't waver.

'I'll see you around, Irene.'

He had to quickly compose himself before seeing his wife and daughter.

'Are you all right, Tim?' Auntie Joyce inquired as he exited Irene's room.

'I'm fine; it's just a touch of hay fever.' He disappeared into one of the bathrooms. After quite some time, which Auntie Joyce took note of, he emerged looking nearly normal.

Florence had been waiting for him and knew he had been talking to Irene. 'Hi, Tim. Are you all right?'

'Oh yes, just a touch of hay fever.' There was a lot of that about, especially around the farms, but Tim had never suffered from it before. Florence knew her husband well enough to know there was something else wrong, but she didn't ask more questions.

'How is my gorgeous daughter?' cooed Tim, sticking a cuddly soft toy into Michelle's hands.

'She's got a touch of colic. It's normal for a baby of her age, according to Auntie Joyce. We have just finished the second German language show made in the village. It will be on general release this week.'

'I know you will be the star. You are such a talent, with your looks and your bubbly personality.'

'Why don't we get back together, Tim?' she said in that familiar pleading tone.

'Oh, Florence, don't say that. My life is so complicated. I must go now.' Tim hurried out. One emotional encounter was all he could handle in one evening. He heard the baby crying as he put his car into gear and drove rapidly down the drive.

Chapter 108

IRENE SETTLES ON TOBY

Tim didn't visit the farm when Irene was there from then on if he could help it. Irene avoided Toby for a week, but then one evening when she knew he would still be in his little office, she visited. She had been back to Dale Farm that afternoon to doll herself up. Everyone said she had a nice pair of legs, and this dress showed them off well.

'Hi, Toby. I wondered if you wanted to go for a cup of tea.'

'Wow, you look fabulous. I just want to finish off. It will take me two minutes. You look so great. Why don't we go for a meal at the Hollyhurst Hotel?'

'I would rather go somewhere else. Do you know a nice place in Lichfield? That's quite a way, but I don't have to sleep at Dale Farm tonight.'

Immediately Toby knew Irene had considered his offer and decided to accept. This time he made sure he was more tactful.

The First EU

'That would be lovely. We can work something out. There are plenty of nice places to eat. It could be English or French, whichever you prefer.'

'I think I would prefer French tonight.' She gave him a knowing sideways look.

There was a little silence while he shuffled papers. 'Fine, I've finished now.' He had wanted to do a little more but thought better of it. 'Let's go. I need to get washed up; you can wait in the bar at my hotel.'

'We will see about that. May I use your phone? I must tell Auntie Joyce I may be out tonight.' Dale Farm had received a phone in the rebuilding. The line had to come all the way from the village.

'Of course.'

'Auntie Joyce, I may stay over in Lichfield tonight, so don't worry about me.'

Auntie Joyce was a bit inquisitive. 'Oh? What are you doing there?'

'Sorting out one of the franchises. See you later then.'

'Fine, see you tomorrow.' They hung up with Auntie Joyce not completely convinced.

As they drove to Lichfield, Toby could see Irene was glowing. It made him feel rather erotic, but he kept himself under control, not wanting to mess this fledgling relationship up again.

He didn't have to worry. Irene had been thinking about him for the whole week after he made his ill-fated approach. She had considered him from the amorous side. He was definitely a fine specimen. She was also happy with his intellect. She wasn't sure of his humorous side yet, but thought she shouldn't be too critical. It was early days.

As they pulled up at his hotel, she said, 'I would rather wait in your room. I'll close my eyes. I don't want to be in the bar by myself.'

'All right.'

Irene was feeling amorous but didn't push it. She thought an approach would be better after he had his shower; they would both feel absolutely ready then.

He could see she was feeling amorous. When he came out of the shower, he asked her if she wanted a kiss.

'I wondered when you were going to ask. I thought there may be something wrong with me.'

'Well, my darling, I didn't want to frighten you away for another week. There is definitely nothing wrong with you.'

'Oh, that will never happen again. It was just that I wasn't expecting your approach. You can take me whenever you want from now on.'

'Wow. I would love to take you now. I know you like … French things.'

'Oh, do whatever you want to me.'

'Let's take it slow. First, I will take your dress off.'

'And I will take your towel.' She ripped the towel away with a giggle, which turned to a look of surprise as she viewed him. 'Oh, Toby, I hope I can handle you.'

'Of course you will, my lovely. I will take it slow and get you in the mood first.'

'I'm feeling so sexy.'

Having taken her dress off, he was now removing her bra. Suspenders, stockings, and panties followed. The flesh wound she had received on her lower left leg had completely healed, showing only a small scar. Her legs were still a beautiful shape. The more serious wound to her right arm was a bit delicate, and it hurt her when pressure was applied, like lifting something heavy. He knew he must be careful.

'You have such a gorgeous pair of legs. I love them,' he said.

'You have a wonderful body.'

He caressed her breasts.

'Oh, that's so beautiful,' she breathed.

'You will like it even more when we discuss French things.'

They enjoyed one another. Both were experienced enough to know the different ways of lovemaking. As they disengaged and rolled over, Irene gave a little cry.

'Oh, sorry! I've hurt your arm.'

'Don't worry. I'm all right. Let's kiss, darling, Oh, Toby, that's lovely. I hope we are going to have a long relationship.'

'Yes. Let's get cleaned up and go for a meal. We can see what happens when we return here.'

'I look forward to that, my lieutenant.'

Irene really wanted to say, 'Well, Sally could handle you,' but she thought better of it. That sort of conversation could ruin their relationship at this early stage.

It all went off well after their French meal. She was a bit hesitant, but he prepared her well.

This was the beginning of a long and happy relationship.

They decided that Toby would move in with Irene at Dale Farm. As usual, Auntie Joyce persuaded Uncle Albert. There was plenty of space.

It was a full, happy household, flush with money. They decided to employ a cook/housekeeper, who lived in in one of the upstairs rooms. Jamie was in the other as he liked it up there.

CHAPTER 109

FLORENCE'S BODYGUARD

Florence was four months past the birth and had returned to perfect condition, doing all the exercises prescribed in the latest books. She was breastfeeding for the sake of the baby and herself. She was happy with the work she was doing, having made two language shows for general release and various short clips for advertising. She was dedicated to improving her German and didn't realise this was affecting Gunter, her bodyguard, who was falling for her. She insisted they only converse in German, and they talked all the time. She was a friendly, easy-going girl, similar in character to Tim. She was also stunning and with increased confidence now that she was a mother.

Gunter became so affected by her that he asked to be replaced. He wanted to find another girlfriend and couldn't possibly do that if Florence was with him.

'Where's Gunter?' exclaimed Florence one morning as she witnessed a different soldier exit from the bedroom where Gunter was normally accommodated.

The First EU

'He has asked to return to duty in the village,' said the replacement soldier.

'He didn't say anything to me. Please run me to the village. I want to see him right now.'

'I don't know if he will be there. I will have to ask my lieutenant.'

'If you won't run me, I will ask Irene.'

'All right, I will run you.'

When they got to the village, Gunter was out on a patrol at a farm having problems with the efficiency campaign. Florence insisted on being run to that farm. Everyone was surprised when she arrived. The farmer and his workers recognised her from the village and the language shows.

Florence went straight up to Lieutenant Roger Shawcroft. 'Could I please have Gunter back as my bodyguard?'

'Gunter asked to be moved.'

'Oh. I see. In that case, could I please have a private talk with him?'

She persuaded Gunter to return to her for a week. In that time, she intended to find out what the real problem was. The soldiers were swapped there and then, and Gunter drove Florence back to the farm. On the way through the village, he picked up his kit.

'Gunter, what is the problem? Why don't you want to be my bodyguard any more?'

'Miss Florence …'

'Gunter, how many times have I told you to call me Florence?'

'I don't want to sound too familiar. I've told you before, miss.'

'Well, I don't want you to go.'

'Look then, Florence, I'm in love with you. Didn't you know that?'

Florence was astonished and fell silent. Finally she said in a tearful voice, 'Gunter, I should have known that my happiness about you was because I have feelings for you. I don't know what I can do now. I'm a free woman, as my husband is with his girlfriend. I think I could be happy with another man. You've had a sad time after the killing of your girlfriend, and because of that, I wanted to be kind to you. Now I have feelings for you, and you are in love with me.'

'I want to be your boyfriend. I can't be only your bodyguard.'

'What can we do? If we make love, we will never be able to go back to how we were. I feel like making love right now.'

At that statement, Michelle woke up, which stopped the headlong advance to the bedroom only temporarily. There was no one else in the Dale Farm house, it being mid-morning. But people could turn up at any time. They were both feeling amorous but had to hold on for a while.

Auntie Joyce returned with Uncle Albert. Florence seized the opportunity. 'Auntie Joyce, could you please look after Michelle? I just want Gunter to run me into Lichfield to buy some clothes.'

'All right. That's no problem. Have you fed her?'

'She has just woken up. I will feed her right now. She should be fine for a couple of hours after that, and I will make a bottle just in case.'

Auntie Joyce didn't say anything. Florence wasn't sure if she suspected any amorous intent—one couldn't normally get anything by Auntie Joyce. She didn't care, actually.

The First EU

'Don't worry about the bottle,' Auntie Joyce said as Michelle was handed over. 'I'll make one.'

'Thank you, Auntie Joyce. We will try to be back in two hours.'

'You don't have to rush back. I think I should be able to handle Michelle,' said Auntie Joyce with a knowing look. Then Florence knew Auntie Joyce was aware.

'Thanks, Auntie Joyce.' And they were gone.

Florence had this thing about wanting to be compatible with a man before she committed herself. She knew the problems with Dave at the beginning of their relationship had probably contributed to their break-up later on. 'So what are we going to do now, Gunter?'

'It's a lovely, sunny day, and I have a groundsheet and blanket. I know the lanes at the back of Dale Farm; we searched them for the resistance fighters.'

'Can we drive there without people seeing?'

'If I drive around from the back, it should be all right. It's about a two kilometres from anywhere.'

'Oh, Gunter, I can't wait.'

She massaged his thigh as they drove through the lanes. It was a supreme moment for them when they consummated their relationship. Florence didn't have any doubt afterwards—that side would be fine.

'We must still go to Lichfield,' she said when they had caught their breaths.

'Yes. I must drive straight away, in that case.'

They got to Lichfield in no time with some fast driving by Gunter. Both were still feeling very together after their lovemaking.

'I want you to choose my underwear,' said Florence.

'You embarrass me. Even if you wore a sack, you would turn me on.'

'I'll wear black. How about these sexy underclothes with all the tassels? What do you think?'

'I think they're great. You buy them, and I'll look forward to seeing you in them.'

'Have we got time to have a good look around? There are a number of things I want, and this store looks like it could cover all my needs. As well as you, of course, my lover.'

'It's up to you and Michelle. Perhaps we can spare another thirty minutes?'

Florence purchased the underwear and some knick-knacks. She was recognised with some jollity, especially regarding the underwear. One or two people hinted that she seemed to be very familiar with her German bodyguard. The attention caused delay as she made her tour of the store with an ever-growing crowd in tow. Gunter became rather agitated about her security, but she didn't want to be rude. Besides, she enjoyed the banter, especially with the men.

Florence held court for well over an hour as she purchased more items. The store manager took photos and didn't want to charge her for the purchases, but she refused his offer, saying she hoped he could make good use of the photos.

She and Gunter got back to the farm over three hours later. By that time, Auntie Joyce had given Michelle a bottle, but Michelle wanted the real thing and wasn't too happy. That was soon rectified.

There was no point in keeping things secret, so that evening, Florence announced, 'Auntie Joyce, I'm going to be with Gunter from now. I hope you will be fine with Gunter sleeping in my room. I must get on with my life. Gunter loves me and I'm feeling for him. I'm going to make him happy.'

'Yes, Florence, I'm all right with that. I'll speak with Uncle Albert, but he will go along with me. Is this it, do you think?'

'It's early days, but I think we are going to be all right.'

Chapter 110

MOLLY DECIDES ON DIETER

Molly wasn't happy about Florence being on the farm, but she couldn't do much about it. She was feeling very uncertain again because Tim was spending a lot of time at Dale Farm. For Molly, there were three problems: Irene, Florence, and now Michelle. She was beginning to wonder why she should always have this worry as Tim's girlfriend. She knew he was weak when it came to women. How could this be handled? She couldn't ask Tim not to see his own daughter. As things stood, there would always be that worry.

Dieter was looking very sad nowadays. Irene was once again not responding to his obvious attention, which had briefly been much needed at the time of her injury. Instead, Irene was having tea with Toby.

Molly's office was close to the language school. She dropped by one day. 'Hi, Dieter! Do you want to come for a cup of tea? If you are busy, you can call me when you're finished.'

'Oh, that would be lovely. Let me just finish this file. I'll be there in ten minutes.'

The First EU

As he didn't want to keep her waiting, he left his work in five. They both liked coffee and had some nice cakes. Rationing didn't seem to apply to the village.

'Dieter, what can you tell me?'

'Well, Miss Molly …'

'Please call me Molly. I insist. We are equal, you know.'

'All right, Molly. I'm working very hard in the language school. We are franchising our methods all over the country.'

'That sounds wonderful, I would like to help you promote it. I think I'm good at that sort of thing. You must show me how I could do it.'

'I'll ask the others; I know they will be very interested.'

'Could we go for a meal one evening? Maybe tomorrow in Lichfield?'

'What about Tim?'

'Oh, Tim is always at Dale Farm. He has three women there.'

'*Three*?'

'Yes, three: Irene, Florence, and now Michelle the baby.'

'Oh, I see.'

'Irene and Florence are still in love with him, you know. I just don't know where I stand, and it is making me unhappy. I need someone to talk to, Dieter, and we go back a long way, don't we? To the first dance, when I was listening for your voice.'

'Tomorrow then. I'll have to get transport.'

'If you have a problem, I can get a patrol car for you. When Tim's not around and I'm out and about, I have to have a bodyguard. You will be my bodyguard.'

'Good, I'd like that.'

Later, Dieter asked Toby about Lichfield. 'I can tell you about a nice French restaurant. You must pop in to my hotel if you are with Molly.'

Molly left a note for Tim that she had gone to Lichfield. Dieter was in smart civilian clothes but had his Luger with him in a shoulder holster.

'Oh, Dieter, I feel so special tonight going to dinner with you. I feel I should have done this when we first met, but maybe it wouldn't have worked out then. I feel so excited.'

'I don't understand why you feel like that, but it's nice that you do. Let's have a lovely evening together and talk about anything and everything. I feel special tonight also.'

'Yes, let's, without a care in the world.'

They arrived at Toby's hotel feeling happy. They had talked in the car and continued non-stop into the hotel. Dieter was a good storyteller when happy. He was certainly happy now.

It was the best hotel in Lichfield, and the doorman recognised Molly. 'Miss Molly and your gentleman, welcome to our hotel.'

'Thank you, kind sir. We would love to have a quiet drink in the bar, and then we will be going over the road to the French restaurant. We may call back later.'

'Certainly, Miss Molly.'

'Are there any rooms here tonight?'

'I'll check at the counter for you.'

They ordered their drinks, a good red wine. The doorman returned. 'Yes, there are two rooms, Miss Molly—a luxury double and a standard double.'

'Can you please reserve the luxury double, just in case we don't feel like driving back tonight?'

'Certainly.'

When he had gone, Dieter said anxiously, 'I should be all right to drive back, Molly.'

'We'll see. This is just in case.'

Toby entered the bar. 'Hi, Toby,' they both said.

'Hi, you two. You look happy.'

In fact, Toby couldn't believe how happy Dieter looked. He didn't seem like his slightly awkward self with Molly. After all, they had been the original mixed couple in the village. It was nice to see them so happy now. He felt out of place with this love-struck couple and made an excuse that he had work in his room. 'Probably see you in the village tomorrow.'

'See you, Toby.'

Molly and Dieter talked as though the floodgates had opened. It was mostly about recent things, but also about their families. After a couple of drinks, they went for a meal. After another drink or two with the meal, they were both feeling rather amorous.

'Well,' said Molly boldly, 'do you feel like having me tonight, or do you want to drive back to the village?'

'That's not a choice, but maybe I won't be very good. I haven't been with any women for such a long time.'

'Oh, I'll help you.'

'I can't believe this is happening.'

They didn't have a change of clothing, but they collected toothbrushes and washing stuff from the front desk. It was about ten o'clock when they entered the room—and two minutes past ten when Dieter entered Molly.

'Can you make it last, Dieter?'

'I'll try.'

'You are very good. It's in deep.'

'If you start moving, I won't be able to last long.'

'Kiss me. Put your tongue in my mouth like this. Oh, take me, I'm coming!'

Dieter did what he was told. He was still trying to control himself. Molly was going wild. After another minute, she gasped, 'Oh, I'm coming again. Come if you want. You are so good.'

'Do it. Kiss me again.' He intensified his rhythmic movement, and Molly was pushing in time. Then Dieter came, and Molly came for the third time. Dieter withdrew. There was quite a lot.

'You didn't have to pull out. I just finished my period. You won't have to worry.'

'What will everyone say when we arrive back late?'

'I don't care. I've had such a lovely evening and night.'

They cleaned their teeth and had a shower, then slept naked in a comfortable embrace. The following morning Dieter did discharge in her as instructed and she came twice. Molly hadn't been having much sex with Tim lately; he seemed preoccupied. After her night with Dieter, she was very satisfied. To think in the first place he had never turned her on, when all those high-ranking Germans wanted them to get together!

Now she was happy. He had a slim body and could perform. She would teach him more. He was also kind, and she thought he would be very loyal. She would tell Tim tomorrow and leave him straight away. Dieter wasn't as good looking as Tim or as proficient in manly things, but she was happy with him. They had been destined to be together from the start. A girl didn't have to worry about Dieter. He didn't have a wandering eye. She would be true to him.

Florence had seen Tim the night before she got together with Gunter. Then Tim didn't come around again for nearly a week. When he finally did appear to see his daughter, he already knew Florence was with Gunter. Almost at the same time, Molly had gone with Dieter and Irene had joined Toby. So now suddenly Tim was on his own.

He said as much to Vloch. 'Well, Captain, it seems I'm on my own now. I expected this might happen, especially with Molly, but for Irene and Florence to find people almost at the same time surprised me. It doesn't matter. I feel happy for them. I just want to make sure my main purpose in life is not diverted from the new way programme.'

'Yes, you're on your own now, but let's face it: you don't have to be for long if you choose not to be.'

'Maybe, but I don't want anything or anyone to interfere at the moment.'

Chapter 111

CHILDREN OF THE NATIONS

The German leader in Britain knew that it was important to integrate the German immigrants with the local population as soon as possible. Young Germans were attached to all schools in the country, including night schools for adults. This employed tens of thousands of young Germans, and many friendships were built up in this way. Many immigrants were too old for regular schools, but they joined Irene's franchised language schools in droves.

Jamie and Hanna were very advanced with their language proficiency, probably more so than any other teenagers. Of course, they had an unfair advantage which had been thrust upon them through circumstances.

As it was coming up to summer, an exchange programme was devised whereby all children over twelve were encouraged to holiday in Germany, and all German children of the same age would have the same opportunity to holiday in Britain. For the month of July, the British children would be in Germany, and for the month of August, the German

The First EU

children would be in Britain. In both countries, homes with children of this age were preferred. If there weren't enough of these, childless families and other places like hostels and former army barracks would be used.

The French had had a similar programme with the Germans in the summer of 1941, with limited success. The summer of 1942 had been all war.

Captain Vloch made sure all six girls in his extended brood went to families near one another, and those families sent their girls to homes in the village. The extra accommodation built on Dale Farm became really useful. All the girls had fun on the farm and elsewhere in the village, and of course there were many other German children there too.

Everyone was given the opportunity; this was decreed by Victor Gerber. But not all parents wanted their children to go to Germany. In the end, more than half a million British children took up the offer, probably less than 50 per cent of the eligible total. Even so, it was quite a logistical challenge. Heavy transport planes were used that could take nearly one hundred and fifty at a time, and the two navies were also used.

As this exchange was the brainchild of the leader, Victor Gerber, he took a personal interest and actually visited the village. He was happy and impressed with the results of this initiative.

One of the good sides for the German schoolchildren was seeing the free and easy atmosphere in the United Kingdom, especially towards the Jews. Jewish communities were not evenly distributed countrywide, but where the Jews lived, the youngsters could see they were completely integrated into schools and public life.

Many in Germany and even more people in the occupied countries were uneasy about the anti-Semitism the Nazis had preached and practised. This had been reversed to a certain degree, and people were encouraged to give back property and goods that had been stolen from the Jews. Obviously, this wasn't always popular, especially among the ones who had benefited from the theft. There were still many Germans who had been brought up with anti-Semitic teachings and were inclined that way.

Although Britons had some anti-Jewish sentiments, these were negligible compared to the state-instigated anti-Semitism preached and legislated in Germany. When the British schoolchildren visited Germany, they witnessed this racist mindset. It was confusing to them, and some expressed their opposition, which didn't always go down well. No one had said this school exchange would be without problems.

The Germans tended to be rather hard on their children when it came to schooling and summer camps. Jamie took it in his stride. He could have been hardened by violence he'd experienced in his young life, but he was more matter-of-fact.

At the end of the summer, when the children had all returned home, Victor Gerber could say his initiative had been a success. There had been a few unpleasant cases of violence, and some children on both sides had injuries, but there were no deaths and the perpetrators were stamped on hard in both countries.

The most unfortunate occurrence was when one of the first transport planes returning children to Germany crashed just after take-off. This took 150 lives, including 142 children. The plane involved was a Messerschmitt, which was thought to be the better of the two makes of heavy transports. Yet it had had a complete control malfunction.

A day of mourning was held in both countries, and all transport planes both Messerschmitt and Heinkel were grounded until the root cause of the failure was fully understood and rectified. The unfortunate incident pulled the British and German people together even more.

Chapter 112

SNAGS FOR THE YOUNG LEADERS

The original list of requests from the young leaders was coming up against some resistance, especially when it came to ownership. The solution was to allocate shares to workers of up to half a company or property's value, with certain conditions such as allocations for time served and restrictions on selling shares. Even Andy and John had to give up one-half of the value their farm. As their only worker was Dave, they came to a compromise with him by giving him a third of the value and retaining a third each. In the end, this programme of allocation to the workers was successful, and it still left the owners with majority control of their companies.

Unions were not needed now. All workers were owners and therefore interested in the success of their company. Works councils were set up in large companies, and all could attend. There were many things that still had to be sorted out for casual workers. A minimum wage was brought in. If

The First EU

a worker was employed for more than six months then the shared ownership rule kicked in.

As Andy had the ear of Victor Gerber regarding the army, he became the young leader for the armed forces. Because of its size, the Germans kept the Royal Navy intact and used it as the lead surface force with its own and other navies.

After Victor Gerber's various initiatives, the integration of Britain into the German system was going well. There were still many Germans on the waiting list to immigrate, and with the agreement of the young leaders, he allowed another ninety thousand in.

So by the close of 1943, Britain and Germany had become much closer—more so than the French and Germans had achieved over the previous three years. Britain was the number-two country in Europe and had the lead when it came to things like the empires and the navies. Tim and his associates, who had the trust of Victor Gerber, were the British leaders now, although the protests of the establishment were numerous.

The United Kingdom and Ireland would never rival Germany in Europe with only half the population, at about fifty million. Greater Germany including Austria and Switzerland had well over one hundred million. On the other hand, worldwide there were many more people who spoke English.

Britain was being run on a much more efficient basis now, as laid out by the farm efficiency campaign and the new way. A national bank for infrastructure development was set up and the population was encouraged to save. The money was used for rebuilding programmes and new infrastructure projects. This gave a lot of work to the young, and they were happy to do it with their German friends.

Chapter 113

CURRENT ROMANCES

The three new romances seemed to be going well. Florence was happy with Gunter, who was much more assertive than Dave. She liked it that way. It gave her a feeling of security that she needed in an uncertain world. Gunter had always been more assertive than any of the other bodyguards; maybe this is why she had preferred him right from the beginning.

Dieter had become more confident since taking up with Molly. He looked more relaxed and happy, which improved his appearance no end. Molly was looking more relaxed and happy also, not having the constant worry of wondering what Tim was up to at Dale Farm. Dieter served Molly well, which added to their relationship.

Irene was happy with Toby. He had caught her eye right from the very beginning, when he had first visited Dale Farm, although her attention had been on Tim then. Any woman would recognise he was a fine specimen of a man. She soon found that he was kind, intelligent, and

The First EU

gentle. What more could she ask for? She realised that he was still getting over Sally, and after some tactful inquiries found that there was a high possibility Sally's pregnancy had something to do with him. He never said anything about it directly.

As these three heroines in the German charm offensive were now all attached to German men, they were big news in Germany. A visit to Berlin for Florence and Molly with their partners was arranged for October. As Irene's German wasn't so good, she declined. Florence and Molly were both fluent and conversed all the time in German with their partners. Of course, Auntie Joyce was asked to go to care for Michelle. This was accepted. She wanted Uncle Albert to attend, but he refused. She was excited to be going to Germany.

The girls were well received in Berlin and did a lot of promotional shows, sometimes with Dieter and Gunter, and sometimes on their own, mostly talking in German. Because Gunter was a salt of the earth type from Kassel, he and Florence and Auntie Joyce were very popular there and in other working-class places around the country. Dieter, from Cologne, was also popular, but as he was more academic, he and Molly appealed to a different following. After their visit, even more young Germans wanted to immigrate to the United Kingdom.

Irene's English language schools were progressing well, and Toby helped wherever he could in Dieter's absence. But Toby also had his own position, working with Tim on the new way programme.

Molly was working on promotion all the time for the German charm offensive, and making short fictional movies also. Dieter was fine with Irene being with Toby, as he had Molly. But he still had feelings for Irene and enjoyed working with her.

Florence was happy to be a mother and to work on her language shows and promotional affairs with Gunter as her bodyguard and lover. She visited her mother and father. They weren't initially happy with her new choice of partner, but her father warmed to him after sharing a couple of beers.

So all seemed to have worked out fine. Even Tim was happy, as he wanted so much to make his perfect society project a success. He had the ear of Victor Gerber, who often contacted him on all sorts of issues.

There were some German families in the village now. The immigration programme had been pulling in families since the security situation had improved, and German children were being integrated into the local schools. In some cases, it took private tuition to get the children up to speed, but there would be no German-only schools opening.

The Oat Farm in Scotland was progressing well. Dave and Constance were married and waiting for the birth of their first child. John was planning his marriage to Susan. Auntie Joyce was permanently settled on Dale Farm, so Constance and Susan managed the farmhouse. Andy still owned his share, but Dave and John were running the Oat Farm now.

Chapter 114

THE ACCIDENTAL DEATH

It was Guy Fawkes Night, 5 November 1943. Bonfires blazed in many backyards and fields around the village, with a massive one behind the vicarage. All the children were excited. It was the same all over the United Kingdom.

Tim and Andy were late in the office. 'Well, Andy, what do you think? Are we going to make it all work our new way?'

'You know, Tim, I wasn't too keen on you to begin with. I thought you were a womaniser who hadn't taken an active role in the fighting.'

'You were right on both counts. I feel like getting drunk tonight, and yes, I could do with a woman.'

'Neither of your wishes should be a problem. I'm sure Angela is besotted with you. You can tell by the way she looks at you.'

'I don't believe you. She's got a long-time boyfriend, Brian. But I must say we've been working well together lately.'

'Let's have a chat over a beer. I'm so impressed with what you have done because of your friendship with the Germans.

You are the one in the group, more than anyone, who has made things happen. I think we are in a good position to succeed with our objectives. What do you say?'

'It's not only me. Everyone had their input, especially you, of course. Come on. I don't want to talk shop. Let's go to Lichfield. I know there's a dance there tonight. It's not only Guy Fawkes Night, it's Friday night. We can have some fun.'

'You are fine, Tim, but I've got Sarah.'

'Yes, but she's been in Scotland for two weeks.'

'To see her mum. We haven't broken up.'

'Yer yer, are you coming?'

'You'll get me into trouble, Tim Handle.'

'When it comes to women, trouble is my middle name. Come on, let's go. I'll take the patrol car.'

Driving the short distance to the hotel, the air was heavy with the smell of gunpowder. A cacophony of sound came from the fireworks that seemed to be going off all over the place. Excited little feet ran here and there, with cries of happiness everywhere.

They both stayed in the Hollyhurst Hotel and were ready in their best dude clothes in half an hour. Tim made himself a bit of a disguise. He had already grown long hair, and was wearing glasses for tonight. He didn't want to be recognised. Andy wasn't such a public figure, so he didn't bother.

'Hey, you'd better take it easy around the lanes tonight, Tim. There's not much in the way of lights, and there'll be plenty of people out and about, especially kids. Not only that, the German army is on high alert. Something could start, disguised by all the noise.'

The First EU

'Don't worry, Andy. I know these roads well.'

They arrived at the regular Friday dance near the main square at nine thirty, when the fireworks were dying down a bit. Paying their money, they entered. A live jazz band was playing the latest numbers. Because of Guy Fawkes Night, the crowd was thin, but it was expected to get busy later.

They sat at the back bar where they could talk. After a couple of drinks, they had a good conversation going, discussing everything that hadn't been spoken about since the German invasion. Still, Andy didn't feel he could mention his part in the assassinations. Why put Tim in that position?

'Hi, you guys. Are you so involved in your chat that you don't want to dance?' said one of two athletic-looking women.

'Let's give these ladies a workout,' said Tim. 'This is a dance after all.'

'I'm not as good as you, Tim.'

'Ladies, I'm Tom!' Tim lied. 'I can dance a bit. Who wants to take me on?'

'I'll try you out, Tom. My name is Tina.'

'Fine, Tina, let's go.'

Tim propelled her around the floor to a few fast numbers and insisted on sitting down when a slow number came on. 'Hey, don't you want to get close to me, Tom?' Tina insisted.

'Come on, I'll buy you a drink.'

'You know, Tom, you look familiar. I'm sure I've seen you somewhere.'

'Not me! I never come to Lichfield.'

'I know! It was in one of those German media films. You're the famous Tim Handle!'

'Am I now?'

'Yes, you are.'

'Well, if you keep it quiet, we can have a nice evening together. But if you blab it about, I'll have to leave.

'All right, let's have a nice evening then.'

'Fine. What would you like to drink?'

'A gin and tonic, please,' she said, in awe at how important he was. She'd seen him talking with Victor Gerber and the Prime Minister—and he always seemed to be with a very pretty woman.

'Let's dance to this slow number,' Tim said. 'I'll keep my glasses on.'

'I wondered when we were going to get up close and personal,' she said, pushing herself against him.

'That feels nice. What can you tell me about yourself? You already know about me.'

'Well, I'm a local girl and work in the council offices.'

Just then there was some shouting. A number of men rushed in, demanding to know who the German patrol car belonged to.

Andy heard this. He had been sitting with the other member of the female twosome, but got up and came over to Tim straight away, sensing some danger. Tim's patrol car was parked in the middle of town, which had caused the interest. It was soon established as the one he normally drove, and that he was attending the dance. A member of the local aristocracy found out and gathered some burly men. He wanted to give Tim a thrashing. He had lost an uncle in the Heydrich purges.

'It belongs to me,' Tim finally admitted. 'Is it illegally parked?'

The First EU

'Don't be smart with me, boy,' said the aristocrat. 'Look who we have here. I would say it's Tim Handle, the ultimate collaborator.'

'I'm enjoying a pleasant evening with friends. Unless you want to join us, I suggest you mind your own business.'

'Well, listen to him, ha ha. I think we should teach you a lesson, Mr Handle. You're too full of yourself with your German protectors. Let's see what happens when you're on your own.'

'Look, I don't want any problems. You know if you do anything to me or my good friend here, you will be in terrible trouble.'

'There's no one here to help you right now, is there, Tim?'

There were five of them, and they'd all had a drink or two. The posh speaker took a lunge. Tim stepped aside and the guy went sprawling. The others waded in. They were rougher-looking types. Tim had to draw on his street-fighting skills. Andy had also been trained to fight, but with guns rather.

Tim didn't pull any punches, as he could see these men really meant business. One mighty upward chop under the nose, driving it into the brain, dispatched the second man to attack. The posh one came again. Tim broke some ribs with a vicious set punch to his body, finishing him off with a kick in the groin and then the head as he went down.

Now Andy started to get involved. There were three thugs left, and when their leader and friend didn't get up, they asked to stop.

The only problem was that the man who had been chopped under the nose was in a bad way. The police and ambulance were called. Tim was taken back to the police station to make a statement. It was established by witnesses, including Tina, that the five men had started the fight. The posh one who had thrown the first punches was now in hospital. The second attacker died soon after.

Tim knew he had made a mistake. He shouldn't have used his full capability as a street fighter. But, being confronted with five burly men who looked intent on harming him, he had panicked—or maybe he'd had no choice.

There wasn't much the police could do to Tim, but as there had been a death, there had to be an investigation. Tim was put on notice that he would have to attend an inquest. The Gestapo man at the Lichfield police station couldn't understand what all the fuss was about and didn't get involved.

Tim didn't get into too much trouble, as there were plenty of witnesses to back him up. The police commissioner commented that Tim's unarmed combat training had contributed to his violent and disproportionate response, but acknowledged that there had been five men who'd wanted to do him harm.

This death affected Tim for a long time. He apologised to the dead man's family. They were not happy, but luckily this man wasn't married and didn't have any children.

The German media people played the story down. They wished it had never happened. Obviously, the normal press found out about it and ran stories. The Germans controlling the papers just made sure nothing too adverse came out.

The incident was a wake-up call. Tim couldn't go out in public without worrying about being recognised. There were plenty of others in the country who didn't like what he was doing. Tim and the others had a lot of work to do to win over all these people in the time running up to the elections in two years.

Tim went out with Tina a couple of times. He appreciated the support she'd given him that night. She was a normal, well-presented young lady who could dance. Tim didn't do anything more with her for fear of disappointment from her side, but he did open up to her regarding the way he felt about the death. She was a shoulder to cry on, which he appreciated. The press contacted her but didn't get anything. Tim put in a word with his powerful friends to make sure the press didn't bother her too much, which seemed to work. They parted on amicable terms; he bought her a nice coat she particularly wanted. Tim knew she wouldn't be without a boyfriend for long.

The young aristocrat who'd made the first move was not pursued, on instructions from Tim. He was asked to visit Tim to see if he could help in the new way programme, but he declined.

Andy had some explaining to do when the news broke, but Sarah seemed to accept his explanation that Tim had asked him to go. After that, she never left Andy alone for more than a week. Andy also went with her to Scotland more often. After all, he still had a third share in the Oat Farm.

Chapter 115

TIM AND ANGELA

Tim stayed by himself for a while. There were a few ladies chasing him. When he started working with Angela, as usual, he didn't realise his normal persona was influencing her.

But she came under his spell. It affected her existing relationship with Brian, which ended soon enough. Neither Tim nor Angela ever knew that Captain Vloch and Horst Geissler had colluded in getting Angela to work with Tim, knowing the probable outcome. Horst Geissler was from Frankfurt and knew Angela's family. Her father had been a senior banker, and, with one of her uncles, Horst had instigated her move to England in the first place. He promised himself to keep an eye on her after the terrible loss of her whole family. This was why she was working in his media department.

It came out of the blue when Angela said one evening a week after the accidental death, 'Tim, I love you. I can't be with you or work near you unless we become a couple. If you say no, I will have to leave and work somewhere else.'

The First EU

'I had no idea, Angela. I do like you. You are beautiful. If we become a couple, what then? Don't let's rush things. You've got me in a fluster; I don't know what to say.'

Angela knew she was good-looking and wondered why Tim hadn't made a pass at her already. Maybe she should have told him more forcefully that she had left her boyfriend, or maybe he was too involved in his new way project to notice. She'd had three boyfriends before and enjoyed the passionate side. Tim, until this night, hadn't realised how feisty she was.

'Oh, Tim, I want to be with you. Let's stop work tonight. It's late now. Come here and kiss me.'

Tim could see she was very enthusiastic and couldn't help himself. She kissed him passionately, pulling him to the couch. He returned her kisses. They were all over one another.

'Angela, stop. We can't do anything here. Someone may come in. Let's go to my hotel room.'

'Oh, yes, quickly, we must go.'

'I must lock up.'

'Oh, darling Tim.'

They were still kissing passionately as they left the building. Fortunately, it was quite late, and not many people were about.

By the time they got to the hotel room, Angela was so amorous that Tim didn't quite know how to handle her. He decided not to think. He had never been with such a lively woman, and it was great—not only that she wanted him but that she was such a beauty.

He hardly had time to lock the door before she was naked and pulling at his clothes. He helped and then they leaped onto the bed.

'Darling, you can do whatever you like to me,' she promised.

'I'm going to give you such a good time tonight, you will never forget it.'

'Oh, my darling, this is beautiful.' Her body was writhing, and it seemed like she was having multiple orgasms. 'What about you?'

'It will be very beautiful and slow, and we must look at one another while we are doing it and talk. I want to practise my German, ha ha.'

'Oh, darling, let's do it then. Please fix me. you can even f— me if you want, ha ha ha.'

They started slowly, and he thought maybe she hadn't been serviced like this before. 'I want to be with you forever,' she moaned.

'Angela, you are wonderful. How can I say no? I think we must be a couple. I should have realised before. I've been working too hard.'

After they'd taken some time to wind down, she said, 'We haven't had anything to eat tonight.'

'What do you want?'

'Anything, but especially you,'

'Let's get dressed and go to the fish and chip shop. It's late for hotel food. I'll walk you home.'

'I don't want to sleep at the vicarage anymore.'

'Just tonight, Angela. It's late and all your stuff is there. I must see if I can move back into the honeymoon suite. I hope it's free.'

'Oh, I'm so happy!'

'My darling, this has been fantastic. We will be a happy couple, I know.'

The First EU

Tim just hoped he could keep up with her. He'd had no idea this slightly sad beauty was so sexy. As usual, he thought things would sort themselves out—and this time they did.

In her own way, Angela was better for him and different from all his other girlfriends. He had been warned about Angela being besotted with him by Andy. Others had also made comments jokingly that he'd taken no heed of. After their night of passion, he had to make a quick decision. He decided he would love to have Angela for his girlfriend. She was a beautiful young woman with blonde hair and a shapely body.

Having been without a regular girlfriend for a while, he didn't have much thinking to do. She was lovely and loved him, and he got on well with her. He would love her in time. Angela was a gift from heaven. They started living together after two days. She was insatiable in bed, and they were a perfect match.

The biggest problem was all Tim's exes. They were always around, albeit settled with partners. To get over any uncertainty, Tim asked Angela to marry him after a few weeks. He had to divorce Florence first, of course. Florence was in agreement, as she wanted to be free so she could wed Gunter.

Angela was looking radiant. Tim was good for her and her for him.

Chapter 116

VICTOR GERBER AND UNCLE ALBERT

Victor Gerber was a regular visitor to the village in the Midlands. Often he had a sudden urge to attend, and then hasty arrangements had to be made, normally using the honeymoon suite where Molly and Tim had previously stayed. After he and his wife lodged once at Dale Farm, however, his wife always wanted to stay there. Auntie Joyce and she could just about hold a conversation in German, and Florence was always around should they need help. If Gerber wanted to check the progress of the young people's new way project, he would stay in the village and his wife on Dale Farm.

Uncle Albert wasn't happy about having Victor Gerber at the farm, but as Auntie Joyce got on so well with the leader's wife, he was happy for her. There were many young happy people around him, but his own sons were gone forever.

Gerber knew there was this sadness. He tried to help Albert and prayed for them at the church. The leader gave an instruction in October that the bodies of Black's missing sons be found, using information from British army records that were still available.

Soon enough, they found one son, the eldest, buried in a mass grave just outside Dunkirk. After a further week, they found information that the other son could possibly be alive in Persia. Two years before, he had been stranded with a scouting party when they were fighting Rommel near the Persian Gulf. There was an outside chance he could be alive.

Uncle Albert was overjoyed. He thanked Victor Gerber ecstatically when he saw him. Victor Gerber hoped it was true and made hasty arrangements for the young man to be sought.

Chapter 117

THE CARING PERSIANS

Going back to the summer of 1941 when Rommel's army entered northern Persia from Turkey. The German plan was to secure the oil refineries in the Persian Gulf vicinity. The largest in the world was there owned by British Petroleum.

So fast was Rommel's advance that the British had little time to get defences around the oil fields and refineries. Just one hundred thousand troops were in place, drawn from the Far East, India, the Suez Canal, and Australia, to meet the three hundred thousand of the German force.

When this army approached the oil fields there was fierce fighting. A further one hundred thousand British troops were shipped in over the first three weeks. At first, the RAF had air superiority, but the Germans soon made landing strips in the desert. Air battles were fought as well as attacks on the British ground forces. Equipment, supplies, and further German troops flooded in along the line of communication set up by Rommel's initial assault. The tide turned, and, after six weeks of fighting, it was becoming very one-sided.

Albert Black's son Malcolm had been sent into the desert in a mechanised brigade of two thousand men. They were to disable and destroy aircraft and airfields behind enemy lines. They hoped for help from local tribesmen.

Malcolm was a sergeant. His platoon had been scouting far away from the rest, out in the desert. In two armoured cars carrying extra fuel, they could travel for days.

The rest of his brigade, after attacking an airstrip, had been surrounded and destroyed. There was tremendous loss of life. Hearing the news, Malcolm's scouting party pushed further into the desert. They were finally found by enemy aircraft and attacked, but with the latest experimental anti-aircraft guns mounted, they brought down four German planes and weren't bothered again. In these exchanges, they lost one patrol car, with four killed and five injured.

At this point, their young lieutenant decided to look for help. They stripped the bombed-out vehicle of all intact essentials, including food, water, and fuel. Malcolm was one of the walking wounded. He had a deep flesh wound in his right calf. This wouldn't have been a serious injury in normal circumstances, but with only a limited medical kit and in the desert heat, it was another story.

They picked up one of the shot-down German pilots, who was concussed but otherwise all right. The other pilots and crew didn't survive. After travelling for a further day over very difficult terrain, they came across an oasis settlement in the desert.

There were three wounded now. Two had died on the rough journey. In addition to the German pilot, who could speak a bit of English, they had another seven able-bodied men.

Tribesmen rode out to meet them—inquisitive more than anything, but with their rifles at the ready. There were about twenty tents and makeshift houses neatly placed around the oasis, with goats and camels in attendance. It was a picture-book desert scene.

'We come in peace,' the lieutenant proclaimed with both hands in the air.

Luckily, one of the tribesmen could speak a bit of English and nodded.

'We need help for our injured,' went on the officer, pointing to his wounded.

The ten tribesmen went into a huddle. The English speaker then said, 'You follow.'

They were taken around the settlement to a firm piece of ground fifty yards from the nearest dwelling. Soon, it seemed the whole community was there, wide-eyed children and inquisitive adults. The injured were taken by the tribesmen to a tent, where women tended to their wounds. Here they could rest and get sustenance. The able-bodied soldiers talked to the tribesmen. A few knew some English, and one was quite proficient.

First the lieutenant asked if they could cover the patrol car to make it look like another dwelling. This needed to be done straight away, so they wouldn't be spotted. Then he asked where they were in relation to the nearest large town.

After two days, the British patrol departed—without Malcolm. He had developed a severe fever and couldn't be moved. His lieutenant promised to return for him, but when the patrol reached the town, they were arrested and handed

The First EU

over to the Germans. They managed to destroy the patrol car first. The Germans were not happy about this, but they noted the good treatment given to their pilot, and so they treated the Britons well as prisoners of war.

Malcolm, unaware of all that, only gradually realised he was stranded with the tribesmen. It took him a month to get better and start walking. After two months, he was walking without a limp.

The fifteen-year-old daughter of the tribal leader was a girl named Fatima. Her mother had been tending Malcolm. Fatima took a shine to him—he was barely twenty himself. She took it upon herself to teach him their language.

Word eventually trickled back that his buddies from the platoon had been arrested and turned over to the Germans, and that the British had lost the war. Malcolm waited for the time when he would be found and taken prisoner. In the meantime, with a number of rifles and handguns available to him, he started teaching the tribesman how to clean and handle these high-powered weapons. Up until then, they had preferred their own archaic rifles. In this way, he made himself very valuable.

The inevitable happened with Fatima: she fell in love, and then she fell pregnant by Malcolm. He was happy to marry her, as was their law.

The tribespeople didn't worry too much about Malcolm and Fatima. Malcolm was useful to them. Now, being able to speak Arabic and ride a horse, he had become part of the furniture. His skill with the new weapons meant the tribe had increased influence regarding local rivalries.

The chief wanted Malcolm to change his name and become his son. Not to be disrespectful, he agreed, as long as he could keep answering to the name Malcolm. He and Fatima were given their own tent near the oasis.

More than two years passed. Their firstborn boy was a toddler and Fatima was pregnant with her second child when news came that the Germans were searching for Malcolm.

Malcolm's old platoon lieutenant, safely returned to England and now one of the young British officers in charge of a German squad, had been approached by Gerber's men. He had no qualms about giving the details of where he had left Malcolm in those dark days over two years before. He only knew the approximate coordinates, but he had a good memory of the beautiful oasis. To speed things up, they sent him with his German platoon to locate the site. After they flew in to Basra, it only took a further day to locate the oasis by spotter plane.

Chapter 118

FATIMA AT DALE FARM

As the German patrol car came over the brow of a dune, labouring through the soft sand, all the tribesmen were on edge. The lieutenant took the German platoon straight to the firm piece of ground on the other side, where his British patrol had been taken the first time.

This time, it was different. No one came out to greet them. The lieutenant got out of the vehicle and walked towards the tents, telling his soldiers to cover him. As he got halfway. a shot rang out. He dived to the ground, calling to his men that he was all right and not to fire.

This initial German instruction wasn't picked up. He got up and called out, 'Malcom! Are you here? It's Jack, your old lieutenant! I've got some good news for you and want to talk.'

There was silence for a few seconds.

'I'm here, Jack.'

Then Malcolm called out something in another language, and Jack heard the kerfuffle of the settlement starting up.

Malcolm came out to meet his old officer. Jack could hardly recognise his young sergeant, so tanned and bearded. 'Malcolm, it's so good to see you,' Jack said, shaking his hand vigorously and hugging him. 'When I left, I didn't think you would make it.'

'I made it, thanks to these fantastic friends of mine here. But what are you doing? We lost the war, didn't we? And you have a German vehicle.'

'I will explain. Can my men stand down and enter your village?'

'How many?'

'Twelve. We would normally be in two patrol cars.'

Malcolm spoke in Persian with the two men behind him. 'Fine, Jack. Six at a time, as long as they leave their weapons behind.'

Jack shouted to his platoon in German.

'What on earth did you just say?' Malcolm asked.

'Oh, it's a long story, Sergeant, but my men are all German.'

'Wow. This is astonishing. I'll introduce you to my father-in-law and godfather and a couple of the other elders. Then we can go to my tent and you can meet my son and wife.'

'Well, Malcolm, this is a bit of a surprise from my side.'

After the introductions and niceties, Jack told Malcolm the whole story, culminating with Jack being sent to find Malcolm and take him back, if possible, to his father at Dale Farm.

The First EU

'I will only come if I can bring my wife and boy with me. Even so, I may not stay. My home is here now. What you have told me is terrible. I must see my father.'

'This is coming from the very top. There should be no problem with you bringing your family. Your wife is pregnant, I think?'

'Yes, five months.'

'She should be all right to fly still. I promise you if you say yes, you will be in the United Kingdom within a few days.'

It happened that a large oil well had been found near the oasis settlement, and the tribespeople were about to become very wealthy. The Germans, as the British had done before them, were paying good money to the locals, not wanting anything to disrupt the supply of oil.

They flew into London Heathrow and then changed to a smaller plane on to Lichfield. Jack's platoon was on the same plane to Heathrow, and then went to their normal location in southern England. They had been quite fussed over in the oasis settlement and were sad that their visit to Persia had been so short.

Malcolm and his wife were given a conventional change of Western clothes before flying out of Basra. The clothing fitted reasonably well but not perfectly, and Fatima was five months pregnant, which didn't help. Fatima could speak enough English to hold a conversation, which helped no end once they arrived at Dale Farm.

Uncle Albert was over the moon to see his son, and of course the media people could see a fantastic story. Needless to say, Angela and Molly undertook to advise Fatima about Western clothing and make-up, which she had no knowledge of. By the time they had completed their makeover, Fatima was conventionally presentable.

Irene and Toby had been thinking of moving from Dale Farm and had lined up a bungalow in the village. They wanted more privacy, as it was a bit hectic on Dale Farm sometimes. This made it quite convenient for Malcolm to stay on with his young wife and son.

Auntie Joyce was her normal take-charge practical self and sorted their room out. They were used to a Persian tent and it was a bit of a shock for them, especially Fatima. The toddler just took it in his stride. He liked to play with the two cats and two dogs around the house.

The story of Victor Gerber and Uncle Albert praying together and then the miracle of finding Malcolm in the desert was a fantastic media coup. They just couldn't keep away from Dale Farm now.

'You wanted to see me, Auntie Joyce?' said Roger Shawcroft.

'Yes. Good afternoon, Lieutenant. There is a problem here with the media people bothering Fatima. She needs rest and peace as she is nearly six months pregnant. Can you please sort it out?'

'I will do my best, but the media people need their story and have powerful backers.'

'I also know powerful people, Lieutenant.'

'Yes, ma'am, I know that.'

'I'm glad you know, Lieutenant. I expect things to change. Good day to you.'

'Ma'am.' Doffing his hat, the lieutenant departed.

As it happened, the media people had already got all the footage they needed. Word was put around, and Fatima was hardly bothered again.

Malcolm had gone native in the desert and wanted to get back there with his family. Unfortunately, at that point the doctors recommended that Fatima not fly. This meant spending another few months at Dale Farm until the baby was at least two months old.

Uncle Albert was delighted. It gave him more time to get to know his younger son again. Malcolm felt sorry for his dad and didn't tell him he was yearning to get back to the desert.

It was coming up to Christmas again. News came that Florence and Gunter would be moving into their own newly built house in the village early in the new year, after spending the holidays with Gunter's family in Kassel, Germany. Auntie Joyce wasn't needed by Florence anymore as Michelle was eight months old.

Chapter 119

LOOKING FORWARD TO CHRISTMAS

Auntie Joyce's two sons, Andy and John, with their partners came to stay on Dale Farm for Christmas and New Year's Day. It was a happy time in the large house. Jamie and his two sisters were constantly visited by or visiting their friends, and all the family members were together.

The children's mother from Birmingham visited over Christmas, staying in with her daughters. A special fuss was made of her. She brought some nice presents for everyone and offered money for the children's keep, which was refused.

Fatima's English was improving no end with help from Irene's language school, and she was becoming more relaxed. This was as well, with the birth approaching. Coincidently the birth of Sally's third baby and Fatima's second were expected at the same time.

Tim didn't see his parents over the festive season. He didn't want to expose Angela to any unpleasantness, especially from his mother. He had received some adverse

The First EU

correspondence from her. But his sister Ann visited by herself and started a good friendship with Angela, who was just a year older.

Tim and Angela were staying in the honeymoon suite of the Hollyhurst Hotel, and Tim put Ann up in the hotel as well. She soon decided to stay on until the new year. She was pleasantly surprised by the friendly atmosphere between the Germans and locals in the village. She had heard about it, but it was another thing to experience. Her mother and father were pretty anti when it came to the Germans. Unfortunately, the East End of London had been hit badly by the bombing, especially towards the end, and they had lost a number of friends.

Tim was sad about not being able to see his parents over the Christmas, but his father phoned on Christmas Day to wish him well. Tim told him he was getting married and hoped his parents would attend the wedding.

'Son, I wish you both well, and I'm so proud of what you are trying to do, seeing you on the news with all these top people. Regarding your mother, you just have to realise she lost her best friend in the bombing, as well as other people she knew. I also lost a friend. It will take time. Goodbye, my son, and have a lovely Christmas. May I speak to Ann?'

'She is out with some German friends. I will get her to call you.'

'My word, both my children are collaborators. I better not tell your mother.'

'Don't speak like that, Dad. Ann is young, alive, and enjoying herself. What more does she need at her age?'

'You are right. I'm being too negative.'

'When you speak with her, please don't put a damper on things. She is really having a great time here and making good friends with Angela as well.'

'All right. I promise, Tim.'

Tim knew he would have an uphill battle with the majority of his countrymen when it came to getting people to cooperate with the Germans. But he was determined to endure all the adversities and see the new way programme through to the end. He had Angela now to stand beside him, and hopefully his sister. She was meeting German men of her age to talk to. This was almost impossible in her home at West Ham, East London.

Florence visited her parents for one night in Dagenham on the way to Germany. After some misgivings to begin with, her father got on with Gunter and they had a pleasant day. Her father said he would have taken Gunter to his local pub, but was worried about how he would be received. It was the East End of London, after all. Maybe next time.

Molly visited her parents for a few days over Christmas with Dieter, who initially was a bit worried about her father. In the end, her mother talked him round. They soon found that Dieter was a rather shy, kind, caring young man. He adored their daughter, who was looking happy and radiant. With this scenario, how could they be harsh on Dieter? Molly was doing well under the Germans, and the war was over. So a happy Christmas was experienced in this household in Coventry, and Molly and Dieter met some of her old friends.

Irene and Toby visited her mother just outside Birmingham, having been in regular postal and phone contact with her since the resistance attacks. 'Hi, Mum. This is Toby. We have been together for a few months now.'

'Pleased to meet you, Mrs Butcher. I wish you a merry Christmas.'

'Likewise. What do you do, Toby?'

'I used to be a lieutenant in the German army. Now I have a senior position working with Tim Handle on the new way programme.'

'Oh, my word, your English is so good! I didn't even know you were German. Irene never told me.'

'Does it matter then?'

'No, of course not, but it's nice to know. I can see my daughter is very happy with you, so nothing could be better. She has been through some bad times, as I'm sure you know.'

'Well, the whole country found out after the resistance attacks.'

'Yes, of course.'

'Mum, let's discuss happy things. How are you? Do you need any help?'

'You know me, Irene. I'm a survivor. But I can't deny I struggle sometimes without a husband.'

'Well, Mum, I can help you. I'm doing well with franchising my language school. How do you get by?'

'I still have Uncle Ted, you remember him. He pops round every so often. And then I have a cleaning job and do typing for a few people.'

'Why don't you move to the village? I could find you work there, and you wouldn't have to worry too much about money.'

'All my friends are here, and I can get by.'

'All right, but I'm going to put some money aside for you just in case. If you are ever in difficulties, you must let me know.'

'Let's leave it like that. I've made a nice room for you and Toby, and I hope you will spend Christmas and New Year here.'

'That's a long time, Mum. Have you got your Christmas shopping done yet?'

'Well, I have a large chicken and some Brussels sprouts and potatoes. I've still got to make the stuffing and need this and that.'

'Let's make a list. We can spoil you this Christmas, but we only have a day to do all the shopping.'

They had a nice Christmas. Irene took Toby, who one would hardly think was German, to see most of her friends. They hadn't seen her for three years except in the newsreels. She told some of them Toby's true identity, thinking it would be best to tell others next time she visited.

Chapter 120

AN IMPORTANT VISIT

Victor Gerber and his wife no longer had children; their only son had been killed in the invasion of France. Christmas was a sad time for them, although they had many high-ranking friends around London. Tim knew the situation and mentioned it to Auntie Joyce.

'You know, Tim, I was wondering about asking Victor Gerber and his wife here for Christmas. I was embarrassed to do it, as he is such an important man, although he enjoys his visits here.'

'I think you should. Your house is rather full, but his room is still free, isn't it? I'm staying in his usual suite at the hotel. Angela and I would be more than happy to move out for him and his wife if they prefer. He knows so many of the people here. He may just be waiting for the invitation and, like you, feel embarrassed to ask.'

'All right. I will phone his wife and see what she says.'

Auntie Joyce's German had been coming along well. She had been practising with Mrs Gerber and whoever else she could. She phoned and Mrs Gerber accepted the invitation straight away. The Gerbers couldn't come until Boxing Day because of official duties in London. She said he would then be able to stay until just before New Year's Day, when he had further official engagements. She said they would stay in the Hollyhurst Hotel to begin with, and then see if there was room for them at Dale Farm.

There was great excitement in the village when word got round that the German leader of the United Kingdom was attending for the festive season. Although he had visited before, this seemed a bit special. The Dale Farm contingent were thrilled.

Tim phoned. 'Hello, Auntie Joyce. I just wanted to mention that I'm going to ask Horst Geissler if he can arrange some special German Christmas food, and if he knows what the leader likes. Horst will be in the village for Christmas.'

'Yes. It's going to be so good, Tim. It's only three days to Boxing Day. I'm so excited!'

The Dale Farm finances were in good shape, owing to the various payments the people there received and Auntie Joyce's good governance. Although the Oat Farm had been left to her two sons, her husband's will had given her a generous monthly payment from the farm finances. She knew the farm was doing well, so she didn't worry about taking this money. Although the other good money earners, Irene and Florence, had left or were just about to leave, the children got a generous allowance from the German administration, and the media people paid for making their films and stories of the farm. Auntie Joyce made sure of that. The farm itself wouldn't be making much money for a year

The First EU

or so, but at least all the young farmhands were financed by the German administration, as was the building of the new farmhouse and all the new pig and chicken sheds.

The cook/housekeeper was kept on after Irene and Florence left, and the house continued to be a happy, well-run family home. The housekeeper had Christmas Eve and Christmas Day off, but promised to come back for Boxing Day, just in case the leader decided to stay.

In the end, the leader and his guards decided it would not be a good idea to stay on the farm with so many people. The hotel was quiet, which made it easy for Victor Gerber, his wife, and a small entourage to stay there. Needless to say, however, he did visit Dale Farm at the insistence of his wife.

Tim ate with him on a number of occasions at the hotel. Ann, Tim's sister, had a twenty-two-year-old German in tow by Boxing Day. He was one of the new immigrants. As a trained accountant, he was working on the new way programme and improving his English as fast as he could. At the moment it was good enough to allow him to converse with Ann. Michael was his name. He was overawed at being introduced to Victor Gerber and dining with him, although Ann just took it in her stride.

A number of senior members of the Nazi party accompanied Victor Gerber this time. They were people Tim had not seen before. The day after Boxing Day, the most senior and aggressive of these party members caught Tim in the hotel lobby and asked to speak with him privately. Tim took him to a room he knew wasn't being used.

Chapter 121

THE GESTAPO OVERLOOKED

'I want all the details of progress made so far on your new way programme,' the Nazi demanded.

'Look, sir, I don't know who you are, but I work for Ottomar Weiss, and I would have to get his permission before sharing these details. He didn't tell me I would be so interrogated. I must contact him before proceeding.'

'That won't be required. I'm his senior.'

'You haven't even introduced yourself. I'm not doing anything until I speak with Ottomar.'

'Don't get smart with me. I can make life difficult for you. I can even make you disappear.'

Tim was getting a bit worried with the way the conversation was going. 'Well, sir, who are you then?'

'I'm Volker Klass, head of the Gestapo in the United Kingdom.'

'All right, Mr Klass. As head of the Gestapo, I understand you have great power. But why do you need this type of information?'

The First EU

'In my position, I need to know everything.'

'To go through everything would take weeks. What I can do is put together a synopsis and go through it with you tomorrow.'

'I want the synopsis in two hours, and I want to go through it with you today.'

'I will do my best, Mr Klass.'

All their conversation had been in German. Tim decided to give Klass information that was already public knowledge, so he would not be putting anyone or any decision at risk. He would definitely inform Ottomar of the encounter on his return from Berlin.

Tim went through as much as he could with Klass in the time allotted. Klass took the synopsis and seemed reasonably happy with what he had been given. 'I want to keep this between us. I need to know everything, but not everyone needs to know everything about me. Do you understand?'

'Mr Klass, I will have to think about that. I was trained as an engineer to get things done and solve problems in a logical manner, using procedures. I deal with facts. I don't get involved in intrigues.'

'Be careful, Tim. Goodbye for now.'

All of a sudden, Tim realised how vulnerable he was. It was a wake-up call. Things weren't always going to run smoothly.

Although Victor Gerber knew Tim had been with the head of the Gestapo, he didn't say anything, and Tim didn't say anything to him.

Over the days after seeing Tim, Volker Klass and his associates started getting rather obnoxious: drinking, embarrassing women, and interrogating in a menacing way a number of the people in the new way programme, including Andy and one or two of the young women. They were really making nuisances of themselves.

When the identity of Volker Klass got out, the locals became very nervous. They approached Tim, who in turn approached Horst Weiss, the most senior German around bar Gerber. Horst was at a loss about what to do but spoke to the Gestapo men unofficially, and things quieted down a bit. Even the leader seemed unable to entirely control them. Tim just hoped this was not a sign of things to come.

Because of these uninvited guests, things weren't as good as people expected in the village over the festive season at the end of 1943. That was a bit sad, but at least Ann seemed to have found a German friend.

Tim suspected that the Gestapo and the army did not always see eye to eye. The army had supported the charm offensive in the first place, which seemed to have had a good effect from soon after the invasion. But the Gestapo, the ultimate police force, had never been integrated and operated independently most of the time.

Tim had a discussion about the problem with Andy. Before the leader returned to London, they asked to have a private meeting with him. They could both speak enough German now to converse without an interpreter.

Gerber said, 'Look you, young men, I understand your concerns. I know there are problems in the regime with rivalries between the sectors, and the biggest is the Gestapo. On the other hand, they are above everyone in keeping the regime safe from insurrection and terrorists.'

'Yes, sir. But the way they have been acting over the last few days is not good for relations between the countries.'

The First EU

'I know. I'm going to bring this up, and I hope I can improve the situation. But they are very powerful men, with connections in Germany right to the top. Andy, you deal with the army. The army is the only force that can discipline these people. Still, as I said, the Gestapo have to do their surveillance work to keep us all safe. There was great consternation, after the resistance attacks, that they hadn't been picked up.'

Tim knew Andy was a bit embarrassed about his German proficiency. Because of the importance of what Gerber had just said, Tim interpreted for him. Andy came back in broken German, 'Sir, things seem to be going very well from my side, but we haven't got anyone representing the Gestapo. People are scared of them—with good reason, as you will appreciate. I think it would be a good idea if we had a young member of the Gestapo, one who has some authority, with us. I must apologise that we haven't thought about this before.'

Victor Kerber nodded his understanding and said, 'Gentlemen, I will see what I can do. Now let's try and enjoy the rest of the festive season.'

'Thank you, sir,' they replied in unison.

The following day, Volker Klass spoke to Tim in his usual menacing way. 'I thought I told you to say nothing of our little chat.'

'You did, but I didn't say I agreed.'

'You are a brave man, Tim. I tell you what I'm going to do. I'm going to hold you directly responsible for reporting progress to me. You will not get rid of me that easily. As the leader has asked, I will allocate a member of the Gestapo to be on your team. He will also report to me and will be my eyes and ears. Like you, he is an expert in unarmed combat. He is here now and has been involved in meeting the people, as you might say, already. You will meet him this afternoon. I believe you are unbeaten in unarmed combat. You actually killed someone a couple of months ago?'

'Yes. I'm not proud of that. It was an accident, and I'm very sad it happened. Look, I'm out of practise. I haven't been doing much training since that death, so don't expect me to fight your man just yet. He is welcome to join our training, and then we will fight in the normal course of events.

'We realise your job is to keep the country safe. I apologise that we did not include the Gestapo in our team. It was a grave omission on our part. And I hope this man is familiar with the etiquette involved in unarmed combat—I don't want myself or anyone else to end up with their nose pushed into their brain like that poor man in Lichfield.'

'I can see you are not afraid of much. I respect that. We can go far together. I know you have the ear of Victor Gerber, but remember that will not always help if you don't have my cooperation also.'

Klass turned around. 'Wolfgang!' he shouted. A burly-looking man appeared from the other room. 'Tim, this is Wolfgang, who I have decided will represent us in your group.'

'Pleased to meet you, Wolfgang. My name is Tim Handle. You may have seen me in the news. Welcome to our team.'

After this meeting, issues with the Gestapo calmed further. Victor Gerber had breakfast with Tim and Angela before they all went to Dale Farm. Angela was sometimes

The First EU

needed as an interpreter, although Auntie Joyce's German was improving. Fatima's little boy received much attention, which he took in his stride. The leader was interested in the story of Malcolm and the Persian tribe. Of course, Malcolm thanked Gerber for his part in locating him. Uncle Albert was very happy nowadays.

Ottomar Weiss wasn't happy with the Gestapo turn of events on his return from seeing his family in Berlin, but Tim was happy enough. He thought it was better to have people like Volker Klass on his side.

The new man Wolfgang wasn't all that good at unarmed combat after all. Tim and one or two of the others prevailed over him, and then he didn't continue to attend the training much. Wolfgang wasn't that bright either. It was difficult to explain things to him.

In the end, Tim had to dedicate one of his bright young Germans to the task of coordinating with the Gestapo. Tim too had regular meetings with Volker Klass, which reduced the initial anxieties considerably. Both men got the measure of the other. Wolfgang was replaced with a brighter specimen whose English was better.

Late in January 1944, within a week of one another, Sally and Fatima had their babies in the local clinic. The babies were two healthy boys.

Chapter 122

MARRIAGE AND HONEYMOON

Tim and Angela were married at the end of January as well, just two and a half months after getting together. Angela's eldest uncle from Germany gave her away. The wedding, conducted in English and German at Lichfield Cathedral, was attended by some very important people: Victor Gerber and his wife, the Prime Minister and his wife, plus many in the new leadership. Angela didn't have any close family, but her two uncles from Germany attended with their children.

There had to be authority given by the church for the wedding, as Tim was divorced, but pressure was brought to bear and permission was granted in these special circumstances. Not surprisingly, Florence didn't attend, but Irene and Molly with their new partners did.

Tim's parents were not impressed with his fraternisation and only showed up because of representations by Auntie Joyce. The village captain, Martin Vloch, was best man. Tim's sister Ann was maid of honour with the six girls as

The First EU

bridesmaids. Jamie and Hanna were there as a smart young couple. Arthur and his family also attended.

Tim was fond of his young, quirky, vibrant partner with her animated ways. At the time of their marriage he was returning her love in almost equal amounts. Needless to say, Horst Geissler and the captain were well pleased with the outcome of their little scheme. Making Angela Tim's personal assistant had definitely achieved the desired result.

Their honeymoon was in a small seaside town on the south coast which hadn't been affected by the invasion and had already been cleared of its beach defences. Tim arranged this five-day break, but when Victor Gerber found out, he covertly arranged for the whole area to be given a security check. The hotel was surprised when two senior German officers with a platoon arrived a week beforehand. They checked people residing and booked to reside in all accommodation in this seaside town.

Tim drove himself and Angela there in his patrol car, taking extra fuel with them for the return journey. They even spoke German on their honeymoon. Why not? It didn't matter what the language of love was for them.

Their hotel was the best in town. Tim had made sure of that. Once the hotel staff realised who this young couple were, they reserved the best room for them, one overlooking the sea. Being winter, it was quiet, although there were guests there—probably for the peace of the place.

'Oh, Tim, I'm so happy, happier than I've ever been. But I'm also sad that my family can't share in my happiness.'

'Don't worry. We will make our own family, Angela.'

'Yes, I know, darling.'

'We are just going to be together with no one to disturb us for the next five days.' There was a four-poster bed they could see the sea from.

Later they got freshened up and went downstairs to the dining room, where there were two German officers seated. Tim nodded to them; they returned his gesture. Before any conversation could ensue, Tim pulled Angela to the door. 'Let's go for a walk to see if there are other places we can eat.'

It was a brisk evening, so they went up to their room to collect their winter coats. As they walked, it was evident that the same German officers were also strolling around the picturesque village. They covered the whole place, but there didn't seem to be any other restaurant open, apart from a fish and chip shop. They decided to have some fish and chips to take away.

Tim asked for some rock eel. Angela, having never heard of rock eel, decided on cod and chips with peas. Tim also took peas. At least fish wasn't being rationed anymore, especially in coastal places.

They took their food back to the hotel, which was only a hundred yards away. The hotel people would have preferred them to eat in the hotel restaurant, but by then their celebrity status had been completely uncovered, so there was no objection when they took the food to their room. They did order a bottle of red wine to be sent up.

'You know, those German officers, they seemed to be everywhere. I wonder if they are checking up on us? I'm going to confront them tomorrow.'

'Oh, Tim, don't cause any trouble.'

'I won't, but it would be nice to know.'

The First EU

Tim had been taking precautions, but for the last month they hadn't been bothering, knowing the wedding was imminent. They enjoyed making love more than usual. Angela had a suspicion she was pregnant, although at this stage her period was only a week late. Maybe that was why she wasn't as animated as usual, Tim thought. Or maybe it was the stress of getting married without any close family, although Auntie Joyce had done her best.

In the morning after breakfast, they saw the same two German officers walking— coincidentally, no doubt—a hundred yards behind them. Tim turned to them and said in German, 'Hello, gentlemen. Every time we go out, you seem to be there. Have you been sent to check up on us?'

The Germans looked rather embarrassed. They were not used to this direct approach from a young Englishman; they were used to being regarded with fear by the locals. But they knew who Tim was because indeed they had been sent to keep an eye on him.

'Well, sir, let us first introduce ourselves. This is Captain Hess, and I'm Captain Speer.'

'Good morning, captains. We are Tim and Angela Handle. We have just been married and would appreciate a bit of privacy.'

Angela was looking worried. She remembered what it was like back in Germany when dealing with the military. They had supreme power. Tim had no such memories and knew he was well connected.

'All right, Tim,' said Captain Speer in English. 'Let us buy you and your pretty new wife a drink, and we can have a little chat.'

'Fine then, but my original request still stands.'

They were becoming a bit friendlier, so Angela was beginning to relax. In the local public house saloon bar, they sat down.

'We are under instructions to look after you,' said Speer, 'and see that nothing bad happens. We have been tailing you all the way from the Midlands, which obviously you didn't pick up. We will keep ourselves out of your sight as much as possible, but we have been instructed by our high command and we believe the original request came from Victor Gerber, so we have no way of leaving you. If anything happened to you or Angela, we would be in big trouble.'

'All right, Captain Speer. I understand. I have great respect for Victor Gerber and can imagine this instruction came from him. But try and leave us alone as much as possible. We are on our honeymoon, after all. Tomorrow we will probably drive into Lyme Regis. Please give us a bit of space. We want to enjoy some time on our own. We will also be going walking along the coast later today, and I hope the same can apply.

'Are there any decent places to eat around here? Besides the hotel, I mean. If you find somewhere, maybe we can have a meal together tonight and get to know one another a bit. If possible, bring some young ladies for Angela to talk to.'

'We will let you know at noon. There is a platoon of fifteen billeted here. We have just arrived, so we will ask them about eating out.'

'What, a platoon? Is that just for us?'

The Germans said nothing.

Tim sighed. 'We will hopefully see you tonight, then, captains.'

The First EU

With that, Tim and Angela struck out for the coastal path. Tim had brought the latest German Leica camera and binoculars with him. 'Oh Captain Speer, before we leave, can you please take our photograph together with the sea in the background?'

'Certainly.'

That evening, the captains arranged a meal in a private house. There were two sisters of eighteen and twenty for Angela to talk to. Angela had a good chat with them and Tim had a good chat with the captains, discovering that they had been landed in Scotland with light infantry equipment and patrol cars and then been involved in fierce fighting.

The lady of this cosy house overlooking the sea was the mother of the young ladies and renowned for her cooking. Being told about the dinner date by mid-morning gave her time to put on a real feast using the best of her recipes. Beer and wine were supplied from the hotel, and a good time was had by all.

The following day, Tim and Angela visited Lyme Regis. Their protectors kept well out of sight initially. Walking along the front by themselves, the honeymooners were not recognised as there weren't many people about. But as soon as they went into the town, Tim and Angela were approached everywhere they went. What could they do? At least there was no animosity; people just wanted to say hello. This is when the captains had to get involved, especially when people wanted to take photos.

'Captains, Angela and I want to talk to these people. They are friendly. Please don't make things too difficult for them.'

'We won't,' said Speer, 'but we must be vigilant, especially when cameras are involved.'

'Yes, I understand.'

The last two days were peaceful, spent mainly walking along the coast. There was another meal at the house of the renowned seafood lady. This time the young ladies brought their boyfriends to dinner instead of the captains. This was relaxing, especially for Angela.

The honeymoon was a great success. They wanted it to go on much longer, but they both knew there was important work waiting for them.

Angela wasn't as outgoing and bubbly as Molly, but Tim thought this was at least partly due to the loss of her family. On the other hand, people did warm to her, especially when they found she had lost her whole family in the war.

The drive back was with the captains in attendance, since they didn't have to keep in the background anymore. Tim came to accept the fact that this was going to be his measure from now.

Tim and Angela were close, and he was happy she might be pregnant. They had spent a magic time together, which would set them up for life. Tim's German was coming along well, to the extent that he was comfortable phoning Victor Gerber to thank him for thinking about them and providing security for their honeymoon. Angela also spoke to Gerber to fill him in on more of the details. She also spoke to Mrs Gerber.

Soon after their marriage, Tim had to visit Germany with the other young leaders. Since Angela was with him, there was great interest, and they were paraded before one

The First EU

and all, which they enjoyed. Angela was gaining confidence all the time, and couldn't help but look beautiful.

Angela was found to be pregnant soon after her marriage and got a bit of motherly help from Sally, who was nearly twelve years older. A new four-bedroom house was built for Tim and Angela, a hundred yards from the vicarage.

In the end, Auntie Joyce was a great help too. At the time of the birth, Angela and Tim moved to Dale Farm for a few months. Malcolm's family had by then returned to the desert with Fatima's people. Auntie Joyce took control, which was much appreciated by Tim. She was kindly in a firm way with Angela, and the delivery of a baby boy in the local clinic went off without a hitch.

They stayed on Dale Farm until the baby was three months old. On many occasions, Victor Gerber's wife found some excuse to attend. It seemed she almost considered Angela as her daughter and the Dale Farm people as her extended family.

There wasn't much love from Tim's mother regarding Angela, although his sister Ann visited. Maybe Tim's parents would warm to her as time went by. There were enough people around the village to help out with the baby.

Chapter 123

AS THE YEARS ROLL BY

The United Kingdom and Ireland became prolific in food production as a result of the German farm efficiency campaign. As the years passed and orchards and other crops came on stream, this would only improve. With enough to eat, people were becoming happier.

The Germanification of Britain was progressing well, although not for those who found it difficult to learn German. Unfortunately, this was mainly the older generation. Even so, Britain was becoming almost as important as their German conquerors. By mid-1944, four hundred thousand German immigrants were in the United Kingdom. This number was much more than the original number agreed. Each increase had to be approved by the young leaders. As an incentive, assistance was offered in a range of other areas by Victor Gerber.

The children continued to get on well. Three were now teenagers. Dale Farm was exhibited as a model farm brought into the German way of efficiency. It was filmed regularly.

The First EU

As Toby and Gunter had left, there were no armed men living there, so Victor Gerber arranged for three soldiers to be permanently stationed there. In the end, these soldiers were integrated into the young workforce running the farm. An extra driver/bodyguard always accompanied Victor Gerber's wife on her visits.

Uncle Albert still owned the farm but was taking a backseat. He handled the work involving the apple trees and the crops grown for the pigs and chickens as much as he could, and enjoyed being with Auntie Joyce, who ran the house. They had a few mixed young people in the outbuildings, who handled the intensive farming of the chickens and pigs.

Captain Vloch kept horses there for his girls. They could often be seen with their friends, who also had two horses on a nearby farm, riding in the meadows and lanes. The ages of the girls encouraged boys, of course, and there were a few from nearby farms who rode their horses with the girls. Two brothers had ex-racehorses, which made things quite interesting. The two large farm horses couldn't always keep up.

The farm children visited Germany every year, and their German friends reciprocated on the school exchange initiated by Victor Gerber. But Jamie and Hanna broke up after Jamie started seeing another girl in the year below. Their young love had run its course.

Hanna drifted into another relationship with a eighteen-year-old German immigrant. Jamie was covered by the money paid by the state for his education. After getting good marks in his subjects, he was accepted into university to do a degree in aeronautical engineering. He was sponsored by the research centre where Tim had worked. Hanna was accepted to a university in Germany to study languages.

As the girls started having boyfriends, Auntie Joyce kept an eye on the ones living at the farm. Of course, there were the normal adolescent tantrums involved. The captain and Tim kept a fatherly eye on Jamie, whose paternal father was nowhere to be seen.

Hanna and Jamie got back together in their early twenties and were married soon enough. They moved to be near the centre where Jamie worked, and he got his pilot's licence.

Sally and Ray, her vicar husband, managed to weather the storm of her affair with Toby. No one was nasty enough to openly doubt the parentage of her young son. Her girls were completely unaware of any suspicions.

Jean, Andy's ex-girlfriend, finally broke up with Captain Gerard and then took up with a senior German army officer. She was still in the team of young people, her job being to promote the German language, and she still did media work for this cause. As she already had a law degree and her father had a law practise in Edinburgh, she also had an input on that side in the young leader's group, working with Andy and Tim.

There was talk of the young leaders moving out of the village, but they didn't want to leave this lovely, peaceful, secure place. So instead of moving out, a new structure was built which would house all involved. Basically, this was where the country was run from until the first elections.

All the fundamental aspirations and conditions laid down at the beginning of the new way project were still being met, but the details were more complex than most had realised. In this, the Germans always had the last say. Experts of all ages were brought in from the United

The First EU

Kingdom and Germany. Lichfield also received some new buildings, where a lot of these experts worked.

Regarding the resistance fighters, the ones who had killed British people were put on trial. Where proof was agreed and a guilty verdict decided, they were sentenced to death. The executions were held over until after the elections.

Unfortunately, this procedure didn't apply to anyone who had killed a German. Nothing would budge the Germans on this, although the young leaders pleaded for clemency. After a short stay of execution, these people were put in front of firing squads—twenty men and two women. The Germans made absolutely sure of the evidence for every one of them and showed this to the young leaders.

The decrees and laws restricting the Jews were completely rescinded by the spring of 1943. This was part of the moderate priorities of the new regime in Germany.

There was still passive resistance in the United Kingdom, especially to the introduction of the German language. Schools that dropped behind were penalised, their benefits and allowances reduced. Tim and the new leaders had to go to rallies, make Radio broadcasts, and film presentations to encourage people. Even Jamie and Hanna got involved. The German language show was reintroduced from time to time over the years. But people remained unhappy with this Germanisation policy. In the end, the regime pulled back a bit, owing to pressure from the USA and the English language still kept its dominance. Even so, the ones who wanted to get on knew they needed to be proficient in German.

After a while, people became complacent and pulled back from the policies being put forward by Tim and his young team. In 1944, amid much general dissatisfaction, an attempt on Tim's life was triggered. People didn't want to live under the Germans. But whatever people may have wanted, there were so many Germans living in the United Kingdom and so much integration by this time that the Germanisation couldn't be reversed.

This minor glitch caused the elections to be postponed for another three years until a more balanced outlook came to pass. That suited the Germans.

Tim, much to the annoyance of Ottomar Weiss but with the approval of Victor Gerber, still met Volker Klass of the Gestapo on a regular basis. What Tim gave out was already public knowledge, but some of what he got back was very much classified. This included suspected plots and resistance activity. Also, to the annoyance of Volker Klass, Tim always related everything he learned back to Ottomar Weiss.

The attempt on Tim's life was not picked up because it came from a lone person with a grudge and no previous record. It did reflect the mood of some in the country at the time. It was a knife attack. If the attacker had done his homework, he would have known he probably couldn't succeed. Tim had fighting skills and quick reactions.

The attempt occurred when Tim was walking on his own in the village. He always had a Luger pistol on him, but in this case, it wouldn't have helped. The man ran up behind him, coming out from the back of a hedgerow. Sensing something, Tim turned and disarmed the attacker, flooring him and applying an armlock.

Unfortunately for this individual, there were witnesses. Tim didn't want to make a fuss; he felt a bit sorry for this sad soul. But as soon as the Gestapo got involved, it was out

The First EU

of Tim's hands. He tried to get some leniency for the man and did not press any charges.

In the end, because they couldn't find any conspiracy and concluded the man had acted alone, they relented and turned him over to the local police, where Tim had access. It turned out that the attacker had lost his mother, father, and brother in the war. Now on his own, he could not handle life in general. Tim talked to him and even brought Angela along. Eventually, the man calmed down and was given two years' hard labour, reduced to six months for good behaviour. Tim put in a word and helped the man get a job after he served his sentence.

Although people were doing well, with work for all on the many building and manufacturing programmes, they were still not completely happy. This was reflected in the opinion polls. So the elections were put back again.

In the event, no elections took place until 1955, when most people were well integrated and things progressing well. The Germans did not want an election until they were confident the outcome would reflect what they sought, and that was what happened.

As the wartime damage to infrastructure was repaired and further new infrastructure put in place, hundreds of new factories were built to manufacture consumer goods—everything from automobiles to electric toasters. With all the new homes being built, times were becoming good for the average person. Britons didn't want to go back to confrontation and were coming to terms with the wartime defeat.

The number of Germans living in Britain helped the situation. They had been encouraged to integrate, and most people had one or two German friends or colleagues. Many in society were not happy. These were mostly previous establishment figures who had lost their power. Of course these were in the minority, the more so as time passed.

People had to accept they were doing well materially under the stewardship of the Germans and the aspirations of the young leaders the Germans were supporting. They knew about the alternative, which had happened in Eastern Europe and in France. It was catastrophic. These countries rebelled against the conquerors and suffered for it.

Victor Gerber was an outstanding leader who could see the potential of fully assisting and cooperating with the people who had been beaten. Along with Tim and the other young people in the German media campaign, Gerber made it happen, although it took much longer than expected.

In 1955, Ottomar Weiss was still responsible for the young leadership team. He had been given the assignment from the highest level in Germany and Victor Gerber in the United Kingdom. This was straight after the resistance attacks when the country could have deteriorated into lawlessness and revolution. As far as Ottomar Weiss was concerned, the longer the elections took to be called, the better. Delay gave time for the young leaders to gain much-needed experience and maturity. This was one thing the German high command had worried about initially: although young people like Tim and Andy were competent, they were green for such leadership roles. The high command didn't want to rush these young people towards democracy too fast. By 1955, the cohort was in their mid-thirties and had seasoned with twelve years of experience.

CHAPTER 124

A SORT OF DEMOCRACY

There was a rule in the UK that if young German workers had been in employment continuously for three years, they could bring their parents over to live in England. Not surprisingly, by the time of the elections, there were four million Germans living in the United Kingdom. These people were mostly well-educated and young. Some with their parents, many with families. Some were mixed couples, Tim, Florence, and Irene being in the forefront of this trend.

Immigration had become a two-way exchange: there were one and a half million Britons in Germany. After two years, these people had full citizenship and voting rights.

There were a hundred thousand German army personnel stationed in Britain and Ireland still. It was a favourite posting for the German rank and file, with 75 per cent of the officers being British. As time passed, many of these officers had progressed well beyond the original criteria for captains and lieutenants, but the top ranks were still filled by Germans. The British Empire was run in vast majority by British personnel, while the navy was run more as a joint affair. The top ranks in that case had many more Britons.

Tim, after virtually running the country for twelve years with German backing, was elected leader of the winning party at age thirty-six, the youngest Prime Minister in a long time. His good friend Andy was the minister of defence. There were inevitably some German ministers. All candidates for election had to have certain qualifications before they could be put forward and had to have reached a minimum age of twenty-one.

There were three parties. Tim's party was the Social Democrats, with a big emphasis on equal opportunities and equality in life, following the original principles laid out in the new way programme. There was the Conservative party, based on the old, elitist system in place before the invasion. And there was the Nationalist party. Their support came from the older population. Neither Conservative nor Nationalists had much support at this stage. They were definitely not favoured by the regime. They complained about the fact that the Social Democrats were getting unfair coverage. As far as possible, Tim insisted the regime give the other parties equal air time on the new television, the radio and the cinema. But with him often on the news for other reasons than political, their coverage would never be completely equal.

What helped Tim's party very much was Tim himself, with his beautiful German wife Angela and their three children. They were often seen on television broadcasts and news clips at cinemas. This was just a continuation of the original charm offensive by the German media people. Molly, Florence, Andy, Irene, and the others all supported

The First EU

the Social Democrats, and through this they gained almost 100 per cent of the German immigrant vote, plus a large percentage of the young vote.

In his dealings with Volker Klass, Tim was told about many coups and plots. Some of these people just quietly disappeared. Some, when there was conclusive evidence, were put on trial to show the country the stick part of the German carrot-and-stick approach. If there had been no deaths involved, no death sentences were handed out, but this was not always the case.

Tim did not get involved with these trials if he could avoid them, but sometimes they were unavoidable. He often complained to Volker Klass about people disappearing; sometimes he would get a result and sometimes he wouldn't. The Gestapo man was adamant that he was not going to allow another resistance attack, and Tim could understand this. As time went by, fewer disappearances took place.

Although the press, with great penalties involved, were barred from reporting on a whole range of things, including police and Gestapo activities, news often got out when known dissidents mysteriously disappeared. There was a high-profile case of someone vanishing running up to the elections. This cut the Social Democrats to 67 per cent of the vote when they should have had a landslide.

Needless to say, virtually the first thing debated in the new parliamentary sessions was enforcing laws to control police and Gestapo activity, and introducing laws concerning imprisonment without firm evidence. The introduction of a new security force that would eventually replace the Gestapo—encompassing the police plus internal and external security, the old MI5 and MI6 respectively—was the other urgent thing debated. Before the election, this system was already being put in place and was finally introduced fully a year after.

Victor Gerber had a veto on all new laws going through parliament, but with great courage and powers of persuasion vis-à-vis his fellow countrymen, he hardly stopped anything. He was the constitutional head of state.

When the elections took place in the autumn of 1955, most of the young leaders had children. Molly and Dieter had only stayed together for eighteen months and then broken up by mutual consent, as Molly was having an affair with her leading man in a new movie she was making. This was not a German promotional movie, but a commercial production of love and romance for the cinema box office. With the original drama tuition given her by her German employers, she was well prepared for a career as a film star and progressing well along those lines. She had also learned to sing.

After marrying her latest film producer, Molly declared she was going to settle down and start a family at thirty years old. Dieter had still not found a lifetime partner. Some said he was too nice and too soft.

Tim and Andy came out as the outstanding young leaders, and their friendship stayed firm. This helped the new way mission. Gunter was not involved so much. He trained to be a special police leader, in the more moderate force coming in to replace the Gestapo. He eventually ended up in a high position.

Dave and John on the Oat Farm in Scotland were also both married with children. Dave's mother resided on the farm to help out after the birth of his first child.

The First EU

Auntie Joyce was permanently at Dale Farm, enjoying being with Uncle Albert. In the early days, she saw much of her son Andy, who was working in the village. After their marriage, Sarah and Andy lived for a time on Dale Farm. Auntie Joyce was happy about this, especially as within a year Sarah had a baby. Andy, like Tim, had to move to London after the elections.

Over the years, Malcolm and Fatima visited on a number of occasions to see his father. Malcolm got involved with the young leaders. As he spoke Farsi, he became quite important in dealings between the Germans, British, and Persians concerning the oil wells. Fatima's father had a leading role as a tribal chief.

Victor Gerber's wife still visited the farm to see Auntie Joyce, but the leader only accompanied her about every third time for pleasure and relaxation. The business of running the country had fully moved to London after the elections.

Chapter 125

THE POLITICAL OUTCOME

France and the occupied Eastern European countries were less inclined to be friendly with the Germans, as they had suffered greatly, so these countries were not as far along in democracy as the United Kingdom. Where possible, the Germans were guiding them in this direction though. Because of advances in technology from the USA and Britain, English was still an important world language, but the German language was encouraged.

The killing of thousands of Polish army officers had been proven against Russia, causing a lot of resistance and unrest in their occupied part of Poland. Similar things had happened under the Nazis, but with the removal of the old leadership, things in the areas the Germans controlled were improving.

Germany and United Europe put economic pressure on Russia by purchasing grain from the USA, transported in bulk carrying ships. The ultimatum was that United Europe would purchase grain only if the Russian-occupied

The First EU

part of Poland could be reunited with the rest of Poland and consequentially become part of United Europe. It wasn't a difficult choice for Russia to get rid of this troublesome occupied territory for the goodwill and business of their major trading partner.

The repatriated land was a substantial area with Polish speakers. This gave a boost to the Polish stance towards United Europe. A self-governing democracy was approaching there, which materialised a few years after the United Kingdom's democracy.

No one trusted Stalin. He was doing terrible things to his own people. But Germany definitely didn't want to mess with Russia. It became apparent that the people of the Ukraine, part of the Soviet Union, wanted nothing to do with Stalin and Russia and were longing to be in United Europe. In the 1930s, millions had died through a famine induced by Stalin. Another ultimatum was given to Russia, this time just that they treat the people of the Ukraine fairly. This was an ongoing story in 1955.

After the war, Hitler was still revered by most Germans, who were happy that he had come along and pulled the country from the brink of bankruptcy caused by the First World War and the heavy reparations inflicted by the Allies, especially by the French. For the brilliantly implemented invasions that gained Germany control of Europe, he was loved in his lifetime. Many memorials were erected in his honour all over Germany.

But bad things were surfacing as time rolled by. Mass killings, especially in Eastern Europe, and concentration camps for political opponents, Jews, and the mentally handicapped were difficult for people to comprehend and

Hitler's aura started to slip. Investigations were launched against people involved in these crimes. At one time, this nearly caused a civil war in Germany. The United Kingdom, having become quite stable leading up to the democratic vote, might have taken over as the lead nation in Europe.

This didn't happen. There were enough sensible, moderate people in Germany to stop the country slipping back into Nazi doctrines, and they successfully pulled through these difficult times. Clemency was shown to the culprits of the war crimes, although most of Hitler's memorials were dismantled. The swastika was gradually phased out, apart from being kept as the political emblem of the Nazi party. Among the armed forces and on national flags, the swastika was replaced by the German iron cross.

Needless to say, it took the German military quite a few years to get things sorted out politically and return the country to democracy. The regime leaders left the elections until it was clear the Nazi party would not gain power again. The election was a resounding victory for the Christian Democrats, with 63 per cent of the votes. The Nazi party only gained 17 per cent. As in the United Kingdom, the political system was completely shaken up, being made simpler and fairer. Once democratic rule returned to Germany, the exodus of the young dropped off.

So this is how we end the story: a peaceful, prosperous United Kingdom, administered together with the whole of Ireland, working with and loosely controlled by Germany. These are the two lead nations in Europe. The English language is retained, but everyone under thirty and most over thirty are now conversant in German, which is used for more and more official business. As there are so many

Germans in the United Kingdom, many of the programmes on the new television service are in German. There is one channel solely for the German language and one solely for English. Other channels are a mix of the two.

Britain lost the war but won the peace. With the help of the young collaborators, the old establishment was neutralised and a completely new structure put in its place. This was only possible through the supreme power of the German occupiers being put behind their appointed young leaders. It wasn't a kingdom; the Germans wouldn't allow the king to return. The leader was Victor Gerber, exercising the ultimate power the king would have had.

The British parliament was limited to two hundred members. Self-ruling assemblies were set up with limited powers in each of the four countries: England, Ireland, Scotland, and Wales. No upper house replaced the disbanded House of Lords.

Three years before the elections, the parliament buildings, including Big Ben, were completely refurbished and modernised. Some buildings were demolished—probably more than the British would have liked. Buckingham Palace was renovated and used as a government administration building. It also hosted state occasions and banquets, but was not lived in apart from caretakers. With only three hundred MPs and no lords, things were not too crowded. There were seats for all in the new parliament building. The new system of proportional representation meant there were eighty-odd opposition MPs.

If we compare the true state of affairs in 2018, the United Kingdom is regulated by the European Union, which in turn is controlled by its most economically powerful member—Germany. Not much different to the outcome in my story. Although we supposedly won the Second World War, we have nevertheless ended up in a position of compliance to the EU and Germany. At least in my story, we would have had a more equal relationship, although obviously a more Germanised one. This is as opposed to being Americanised, as we are now.

In general, it was the young in the United Kingdom who voted to stay in the European Union recently. In my book, it was the young who joined with the German occupiers to make Britain a democratic member of the German United Europe.

When you think about it, the Second World War made the United Kingdom absolutely bust. We were a superpower before, with the largest navy in the world. The USA would have let us carry on fighting by ourselves, happily selling us whatever they could, including thousands of World War One rifles, for instance. Japan changed things by dragging the USA into the war. I'm sure something terrible would have happened to Britain if Hitler had not attacked Russia.

In my story, there is a better outcome for the United Kingdom. The English language and the British Empire made us more of a partner to Germany in Europe over time. The USA is still a major power, but just one of four.

In 1955, United Europe was the greatest superpower, its vast combined navy exercising influence on uncommitted countries around the world as well as maintaining their empires. China was still in disarray at that time, with Japan and Russia trying to exert control over vast areas adjacent to their territories.

Chapter 126

EXPLANATION

Just to clarify, as many people, especially the old who remember the war, have said they are not interested in a book that portrays the Germans in a good light: I remind readers that this story is fiction that begins in September 1940, the Battle of Britain. Anything in actual history that occurred after this date never occurred in the fictional world I have created. For instance, my grandparents may not have been bombed, because they were killed in November 1940. In my version of history, the German bombers weren't targeting civilians then, only strategic installations.

Some might say that I have glossed over the Jewish problem, yes there was definitely much killing up to September 1940, but then it all changed as explained in my story.

As the actual war progressed, the Germans undertook some shocking and horrendous actions. We hear almost on a daily basis about these, and they obviously influence people's opinion of that generation of Germans and Germans in general. These things never happened in my story, and my fictional Germans were not that bad. I hope readers can bear this in mind.

I have a friend who was a young child in the Channel Islands at the time of occupation during the war. She told me how well some German and English people got on there, where love and friendship flourished. Remember, I said some, not all. It is this friendly and moderate "some" from both sides who are prevalent in my story.

Chapter 127

AN ACTUAL ACCOUNT

The following poem, given to me by my good friend Charlie Allen, covers his time in the Second World War. It is what happened to him. I feel honoured to be allowed to use it as part of my book.

The TV Crews won't come to say,
Charles, this is your life.
This little poem is my way,
To tell of war and strife.

Charlie Allen is my name,
A bit of history I will tell,
Mum and Dad from London Came,
Sister Margaret, 4, as well.

When I'm 6 the King is Dead,
So then we have another,
Before the Crown is on his head,
It's changed, to George, his Brother.

Edward decides to abdicate,
Mrs Simpson is the reason,
The nation won't accept his mate,
Some even talk of treason.

Few memories of my early years,
Just one date comes to mine,
A siren wailing in my ears,
3rd September '39.

On the Friday, just before,
We're told, 'Evacuate',
The adults only talk of war,
Of Hitler and of hate.

Alan J Caulfield

With gas mask in a cardboard box,
Around my neck a label,
My name on shirt and pants and socks,
I'm taken to a stable.

To keep us out of Hitler's harm,
T'was on a train we went,
Sis and I were on a farm,
For fruit, in Swanley, Kent.

Damsons, Apples, Plums as well,
Pears shaped just like Figs,
But also a peculiar smell,
Around the corner, pigs.

Our billet though was very good,
Seven weeks we stayed,
The war for us was understood,
For now had been delayed.

Meanwhile in Europe, Germans spread,
Throughout the land reaches,
Close enough to see ahead,
Our troops on Dunkirk's beaches.

The little boats went through the foam,
To save the lines of men,
A quarter million were brought home,
Most to fight again.

For quite some time my lessons nil,
With spitfires overhead,
Battle of Britain visions fill,
Nightmares in my head.

September 7th evening fires,
The Jerries start the blitz,
On London houses, pubs and spires,
All night the gunfire spits.

My Dad, a first war veteran.
Has come through lots of trouble,
Is now a London Fireman,
Face black with soot and stubble.

For days we rarely see him now,
His strong steel helmet bent,
Near deafened by constant row,
We, North to Shropshire sent.

Mum's Sister, in a cottage small,
Took Margaret, Mum and me,
With lessons in a village hall,
Country life we see.

Our sailors on the Ocean,
Some no more than boys,
Hunting 'U' Boats all is motion,
Protecting our convoys.

With Warships chasing 'Bismark',
Things are looking good,
Then a shell from the dark,
Goodbye, 'H.M.S. Hood'.

Three more days the search is on,
In North Atlantic waves,
Another battle, 'Bismark's' gone,
To join the watery graves.

In the desert things are bad,
Tanks stuck in the sand,
But at the siege of Stalingrad,
Winter lends a hand.

The Germans are defeated,
Their morale starts to crack,
Supplies are all depleted,
Start a turning back.

The First EU

The bombers of the R.A.F,
More than just, 'The Few'.
Make noises that could turn you deaf,
As to Germany they flew.

The 'Dambusters', trained for low level flight,
To test their Bouncing bomb,
When their target came into sight,
It splashed, & skipped along.

Two Dams destroyed, in their attack,
The cost was high, we were told,
Nineteen planes started eleven came back,
Fifty-three crew, no chance for them to get old.

8th army at El Alamein,
A barrage has begun,
The Tanks are on the move again,
Rommel's on the run.

Our most valuable possession,
Is called a ration book,
With the wars progression,
There's little food to cook.

Margaret met a soldier, Don,
He came from Winnipeg,
On Sunday leave he'd come along,
For tea, we'd have dried egg.

Mum and Dad are worried,
Adult talk is hushed,
My Sister is getting married,
It all seems rather rushed.

I don't know why, but something is wrong,
Margaret's sick each dawn,
But then I know when April's gone,
My nephew, Ken is born.

The baby is just one month old,
The soldier gone so soon,
The wireless on, this we're told,
Is 'D' Day, 6th of June.

Our troops invade, being bold,
Taking quite a chance,
They fight their way to get a hold,
Right there, in Northern France.

For months the Russians took the brunt,
Of Germany's full might,
But now there is a second front,
It would be a different fight.

A funny sort of airplane,
With spluttering sort of sound,
At the back a 6 foot flame,
Then silence, 'ere it hit the ground.

Hour after hour the Buzz Bomb Flight,
Throughout the night and morning,
Gives us all more weeks of fright,
But a Rocket gives no warning.

We plan to go away again,
As soon as we are able,
This time to Yorkshire, take the train,
And leave our big steel table.

Alan J Caulfield

Marion and her husband Jack,
Live on the edge of the moors,
Look after me, won't let me back,
To sleep on London Floors.

Those happy, lovely Yorkshire folk,
Say my London voice is funny,
But to me theirs is a joke,
'Bah't at', 'Ee by Gummee'.

Things quieter now, we came back home.
Dad needs looking after,
We thought no more need to roam,
On wireless there was laughter.

Tommy Hanley, 'ITMA 's' bunch,
Glen Miller is the choice,
Worker's Playtime with your lunch,
Europe waits for London's voice.

Its 45, the War goes on,
Until one day in May,
Germans beaten, Battles Won,
The 8th is V.E. Day.

But in the Far East War-Zone,
There are thousands of our chaps,
The 'Forgotten Army', far from home,
Fighting Jungles, Disease, and Japs.

They fought their way through Burma,
It could go on, and on,
But then at Hiroshima,
Explodes, an Atom Bomb.

A second at Nagasaki,
The Japanese surrender, fast,
Everyone is happy,
The world sees peace at last.

Lightning Source UK Ltd.
Milton Keynes UK
UKHW04f0106170718
325817UK00001B/1/P